MICHAEL WARD
Chief Pilot
Pilot's Pad

THE BLACK TIDE

Also by Hammond Innes

FICTION

TRAVEL

HISTORY

Hammond Innes

THE BLACK TIDE

DOUBLEDAY & COMPANY, INC.
GARDEN CITY, NEW YORK
1983

Library of Congress Cataloging in Publication Data

Innes, Hammond, 1913–
The black tide.

I. Title.
PR6017.N79B54   1983   823'.912
ISBN 0-385-18331-3
Library of Congress Catalog Card Number 82-45498

To
Marjory and Ian

In admiration, for reasons that
will be apparent to all their
many friends

CONTENTS

THE BLACK TIDE

PART I

Prelude to Pollution

CHAPTER ONE

IT WAS NEW YEAR'S EVE. The last weather forecast had given wind southwesterly force 5 increasing to 6 with poor visibility in sleet or snow showers. Between Land's End and the Scillies, and already into the northbound traffic lane, the tanker *Petros Jupiter*, with 57,000 tons of crude for the Llandarcy refinery in South Wales, made a long slow turn to starb'd, finally settling onto a course of 095°.

Her cargo had been resold late that afternoon, but delay in obtaining signature on certain documents had meant that it was not until 2254 that her master was informed of the transaction and instructed to alter course for Rotterdam. Less than an hour later, at 2347, the alarm bells sounded on the bridge.

Like many of the early VLCCs, the *Petros Jupiter* was just about worn out. She had been built for the Gulf Oil Development Company in the sixties, at the height of the Japanese expansion in shipbuilding. Her design life at maximum efficiency was about eight years and GODCO had sold her to a Greek company in 1975. She was now in her seventeenth year, and since rounding the Cape steam leaks had been creating an almost permanent fog in the engine room with the evaporator barely able to produce sufficient distilled water to replace the loss. The log would show that on two previous occasions loss of distilled water had been so great that the automatic cut-out on the single boiler had been tripped.

For ships taking the inside route between Land's End and

the Scilly Islands, the northbound traffic lane is the one nearest to the mainland. But the *Petros Jupiter* had been on the outer edge of the lane when she had made the turn to starb'd, and being on a slow-steam voyage she was moving at barely eleven and a half knots through the water, so that when the alarm bells sounded and the single high-pressure boiler cut out, bringing both the steam turbines to a halt, she was still not clear of Land's End.

Engine-room staff immediately switched to auxiliary power to keep the alternators going and to provide electricity, but power to drive the ship could not be restored until the accumulation of leaks in the steam pipework had been repaired and the loss of distilled water for the boiler reduced. The ship gradually lost way until finally she lay broadside to the waves, rolling sluggishly.

There she remained for over two hours, during which time she drifted about three miles in the general direction of Land's End. By then emergency repairs had been completed and at 0204 she was under way again. At 0213 the unbelievable happened: the secondary reduction gear—the gear that drove the single propeller shaft—was stripped of its teeth. A journalist would write later that it had made a very expensive sound, which was the phrase used by Aristides Speridion, the Greek second engineer, who had been at that end of the engine room when it happened.

With the secondary reduction gear useless, there was no way the *Petros Jupiter* could proceed and at 0219 the master contacted Land's End coastguard station on VHF to inform the watch officer of the situation and inquire about the availability of a tug.

The tanker was now lying helpless, wind-rode and wallowing heavily, her hull broadside to the seas, which were big and breaking. If she had been fully loaded she might still have survived, but half her cargo had been off-loaded at Corunna and she was riding high out of the water, her huge slab-sided hull acting as a giant sail.

Her position at this time was eight and a half miles from Land's End with the Longships light bearing 058°. The wind was still southwesterly, still increasing, and the barometer was falling. The latest forecast was for SW7 increasing to gale 8, veering later with a possible temporary increase to strong gale 9.

The coastguard officer on watch at Land's End told a reporter later that at this point, in the early hours of the morning with the threat of another *Torrey Canyon* on his hands, he very much wished he still had his SAR radar capability so that he could have monitored the tanker's drift. Unfortunately, the radar had been dismantled when the new coastguard station for the South West on Pendennis Point at the entrance to Falmouth had been completed. Even so, it did not take him long to figure out that the *Petros Jupiter* would need to have a towline on board within the next four to five hours if she was not to be driven onto the rocks at Land's End. He informed the master accordingly, warning him not to place too much reliance on his anchors and only to use them when the depth of water was shallow enough to give him a good scope of chain. At 0223 he alerted the Falmouth station officer of the tanker's situation, inquiring, on behalf of the master, whether there was a tug stationed in the vicinity. Fortunately, the Dutch tug based on Falmouth was in port.

Nevertheless, almost another hour went by before the master finally requested the coastguards to inform Lloyd's that tug assistance was required. This delay may have been due to the *Petros Jupiter* contacting other ships in the vicinity. It would certainly explain why she did not speak direct on W/T with Telecom International at the Land's End radio station, all messages being routed through Land's End coastguard station on VHF.

The tug left immediately, steaming out past Pendennis Point at 0327 with an ETA at the probable position of the drifting tanker of about 0630. By then Falmouth coastguards had alerted the Naval Flag Officer, the Sennen lifeboat had been put on standby, and the duty officer at the Department of Trade's Marine Division, Sunley House, High Holborn, had been informed and had immediately called the retired admiral who headed the Marine Pollution Control Unit.

As anticipated, the weather was now worsening rapidly so that by 0400 the wind was force 8, gusting 9, and the tug, out from under the lee of the Lizard and punching westward into heavily breaking seas, was forced to reduce speed. Shortly before 0500, the tug master contacted the *Petros Jupiter* and informed her master that owing to heavy seas his ETA would now be 0730 or even later.

By then the tide had turned, wind and tide pushing the ship in a northeasterly direction. Falmouth coastguards, plotting the shifting direction of the tidal stream between Land's End and the Scillies, calculated that with a wind drift of approximately one knot the ship would go aground in the vicinity of the Longships about an hour before the tug could reach her. This warning was passed to the master and the advice repeated to let go his anchors when he was in a depth that would give him sufficient scope of chain. In the weight of wind and with the seas now big, the chain would almost certainly snap, but there was just a chance that the anchors might hold long enough for the northgoing tide to take the tanker clear of the Longships, and with the extra fetch provided by Whitesand Bay the tug might still get a line on board before she struck.

Meanwhile, the secretary of the Sennen lifeboat, in consultation with his cox'n, had decided to launch. The time of launch was 0448 and the lifeboat reached the casualty at 0607. By then the *Petros Jupiter*, with two anchors down and her bows pointed in the general direction of the Wolf Rock, was barely a mile from the Longships. An hour later, as dawn began to break, first one anchor chain, then the other parted, and the lifeboat, which was lying in the lee of the tanker's stern, reported the grey granite tower of the lighthouse just visible through mists of wind-blown spray and driving snow. It was very close, the cox'n radioed.

It was a dark, cold dawn, full of scudding clouds. A Sea King helicopter from RNAS Culdrose, hovering overhead, taking photographs and checking for pollution, gave the distance between the tanker's stern and the lighthouse as barely five hundred meters. The pilot also reported that he could see no sign of the tug. This information was passed to the MPCU at Sunley House, which was now fully manned and already operating on the assumption of a major disaster, alerting tugs and aircraft fitted with spraying equipment and arranging for the transportation of stockpiled dispersants to Land's End.

The *Petros Jupiter* struck at 0723, but not on the Longships. By then she had drifted clear of the lighthouse and the sunken ledges on which it was built, and with the wind veering, and the direction of the tidal stream already changing, she went onto the shallow reef southwest of the Shark's Fin, swung round, and finished up with her stern almost touching the flat of the rock known as Kettle's Bottom.

The tug did not reach the casualty until almost an hour later, and though the wind had eased by then, the seas were still very confused and it was another hour and a half before a line was got across to the tanker's bows. The first attempt to tow her off was made shortly after ten.

Meanwhile, on the other side of England, at Colchester, where the Casualty Room at Lloyd's Intelligence Services kept a twenty-four-hour watch, the Casualty Reporting officer, informed by Land's End coastguards that the *Petros Jupiter* was on the rocks with two ruptured tanks spilling oil, began notifying all those organizations which took the service. This included, of course, the media, so that it was on the BBC eight o'clock news and all subsequent broadcasts. Information about the casualty was also transmitted by telex from the Communications Room on the same floor direct to the Lloyd's of London building in the City for posting on the Board, so that underwriters entering the Room for the start of business after the New Year's Day holiday would see it there.

The lead underwriter for the *Petros Jupiter* cover was Michael Stewart. He headed three of the top marine insurance syndicates, a position he had inherited on the death of his father just over a year ago. He was still relatively young, only just turned fifty, but he had a good track record and was generally regarded as having his father's underwriting flair. He heard the news on the radio and immediately phoned his Claims Manager. Holiday or no holiday, he was urgent to get things moving—the Salvage Association in particular.

Michael Stewart's syndicates were not deeply involved in the *Petros Jupiter*, for though he had agreed to continue the cover following the change of ownership in 1975, he had increased the extent of the reinsurance. But it was still his responsibility as the lead underwriter and it looked as though this was going to be the second casualty in two months with which his name would be associated.

The first had been the *Aurora B*, a 120,000-ton tanker belonging to GODCO. She had simply disappeared somewhere off Sri Lanka. Gulf Oil Development Company vessels had always been operated at such a high standard, and had always had such an outstanding record, that his father had allocated to his most favored syndicate a greater proportion of the total premium, and consequently a greater proportion of the liability, than was normal. His son had seen no reason to change the practice. The GODCO policies had an excess of £500,000 to be met by the Company, and as a result, Syndicate OX71 had done very well out of this line of underwriting over the years.

In the case of the *Aurora B*, it wasn't just one syndicate that was heavily involved. In dealing with the reinsurance that spread OX71's liability round the market, he had allocated a larger than normal percentage to his two other syndicates. The *Petros Jupiter,* on the other hand, was no longer a GODCO vessel. But though he could comfort himself that at least he had had the sense to reduce his syndicates' involvement, it was still basically a GODCO policy and he was still the lead underwriter.

The loss was thus a blow to his pride, as well as to his pocket, for there was nothing to indicate on that bank holiday morning that the stranding was anything other than an accident. It was just another disastrous tanker casualty that Lloyd's, and his own syndicates in particular, could have done without.

PART II

Aftermath of a Wreck

CHAPTER ONE

Twelfth Night and it was after lunch, after the fog had lifted, that the first oil-sodden bodies began to come ashore. I had just left the rough board table where I did my writing and was out with spade and pick breaking up a little patch of new ground above the cottage. The air was cold and very still, a high hanging over us with the pressure close on 1040 and the sea lying like pewter against a white opaque sky, no horizon and the remains of a westerly swell barely creaming the base of the Brisons.

From the new ground, where I was planning to grow sorrel and lamb's lettuce, possibly some bush tomatoes close under the rocks that sheltered it, I looked straight down onto the sloping roof of our cottage, and beyond it, beyond the rock outcrop that looked like the head of an elephant, the grey granite tower of the Longships lighthouse was just beginning to emerge, a dim, blurred finger still wreathed in mist. And almost alongside it, that bloody tanker looking like a ghost ship, the fog still swirling about it.

I stopped digging and lit my pipe, thinking once again about how it must have been up on the tanker's bridge that night almost a week ago when the gale had stranded her on Kettle's Bottom. A faint breeze stirred the peat smoke of our cottage chimney and the fog rolled back from the Longships so that the wreck, the rocks that held her pinned at the stern, and all the attendant ships were suddenly revealed in startling clarity against the white miasma glimmering now in pale sun-light. The *Petros Jupiter* was all of three miles away, but in that strange watery brightness every detail of her seemed magnified, so that even at that distance I could identify the salvage equipment littering her deck—the pumps, compressors, hoses, and coils of rope and wire.

Incredibly, because of the unseasonable quietness of the weather during the days following the gale, she was still intact and, except that she was down by the stern and her afterdeck almost awash, she might have been anchored there. All this side of the wreck the sea was a flat oily brown. I left my spade and went up to the knoll above the elephant head rock. When I had been out to the wreck on the Friday, the spillage had all been to seaward and I was hoping it would prove to be some trick of the iridescent light. But it wasn't. It was oil all right. Two antipollution vessels were spraying close inshore along Whitesand Bay and the slick ran in a long dirty line from the tanker right across the bay until it disappeared from sight below the cliffs on which I was standing.

Karen must have been looking at it, too. From the door of the cottage you could see straight down the rocky pathway to the little patch of sand wedged into the rocks of the gully where we kept our inflatable. The anguish of her cry cut the stillness. She was out of the door, searching wildly and calling to me, "Trevor! Trevor!" She looked up to where I stood. "D'you see it?"

"See what?" I called down to her, though I knew damn well what she'd seen.

She turned. "There! On the sand." Her voice was high like the screech of a gull. We had been expecting this for almost a week now. "By that rock." She was standing in the cold, wa-tery sunlight, her left hand shading her eyes, her right stretched out, pointing down into the cove.

From where I stood I couldn't see it; the little cove was blocked from my view by the top of the elephant rock.

"I can see it moving." She had turned, looking up at me again, the smooth rounded beauty of her face shattered by the violence of her emotions—a fishergirl's face, I had described it in a magazine piece, with the high-necked fisherman's jersey she wore in winter and the blue scarf tied in a bandeau round her head. And then she was running, her feet flying on the grass slope to the path.

"Careful!" I shouted. She was a big girl and running like that, at such a crazy pace, I was afraid she'd go flying headfirst down among the rocks.

But it was no good. She took no notice. She never did. Once her emotions took charge, nothing stopped her. The cottage, the birds, everything—our whole way of life—it was all hers. She was so impossibly lovable, so damnably difficult, and now I was running after her, and it seemed to me, in exasperation, I'd always been adapting myself, excusing myself, ever since she'd faced me, holding onto the handlebars of her bike, eyes wide and spitting like a cat. That had been at the back end of Swansea docks, our first meeting, and a gang of teenagers using a puppy for a football. They'd broken its back and, instead of going after them, I'd got hold of the jerking little rag of a body and put it out of its misery with a hand chop to the back of its neck. The teenagers were Arabs, and she had thought I was one of them.

Now, as I joined her on the little V-shaped patch of sand, she was in the same sort of mood. "Look at it!" She thrust the feebly flapping bird at me. Her hands were wet and covered with oil, her brown eyes almost black with anger.

The bird lifted its head, squirming and opening its beak. It was a razorbill, but only recognizable by the strangely bulbous shape of its beak. The beautiful black and white plumage was coated with a thick film of heavy black oil. No sound came and its movements were so weak that it was almost certainly near the point of death.

"How many *more?*" Her voice trembled on the edge of hysteria. "Last time—remember? November, it was. The night we had that bonfire on the beach. Mrs. Treherne's little boy found it flapping in the shallows, and the very next day they began coming ashore." Her breath smoked in the cold air, her eyes wide and very bright. "Dead birds, dead fish—I can't take it." Her lips were trembling, tears of anger and frustration starting. "Spilling their filthy oil, ruining our lives, everything . . . I can't take it. I won't take it." And then, gripping hold of me, holding my arm so tight I could feel her fingernails through the thick sweater, "We've got to do something, fight back . . ."

"I'm doing what I can, Karen." I said it gently, keeping a tight hold on myself, but she thought I was on the defensive.

"Talk, talk, talk, nothing but talk. That silly little committee of yours—"

"There's an Under-Secretary coming with our MP this evening. I told you, be patient. It's a big meeting. The press and the media, too. We're trying for the same rules and sea routes that the French established after the *Amoco Cadiz*, and tonight . . ."

"Tonight he'll say yes; tomorrow, at Westminster, he'll have forgotten all about it." She said it bitingly, her eyes contemptuous. She looked down at the razorbill. "Remember that first time? And last March, how many was it we took into the cleansing station—twenty-seven? All those people working for hours. Three hours to clean each bird. And they all died, every one of them." The bird lay passive now, no longer struggling. "We've got to stop them—do something—make them realize."

"Do what?" I asked. "What can we do that we're not doing?"

"Bomb that bloody ship, set the oil ablaze. Destroy it. That's what. Make the government act. And if the government won't do it, then do it our bloody selves."

"But I've told you . . ." It was ridiculous, arguing there in that tiny cove with the waves lapping at our feet and Karen still clutching that limp bundle of oil-soaked feathers. I had told her before that it wouldn't work. The experts had said it wouldn't, that the effect would be to produce an even worse mousse, a thick mess of black long-lasting globules of tar big as cow pats. But she wouldn't listen.

"Just do something," she screamed at me. "Or are you afraid?"

"Of what?" My voice had risen, the lilt that was always there increasing—I could hear it. "Why should I be afraid?"

But she backed away from that, her eyes wide, sensing the violence of my reaction if she put it into words. Only I knew— we both knew—what had been on the tip of her tongue. Once the blood's mixed, it can always be thrown in your face. And the sensitivity—the stupid, bloody, helpless sensitivity . . .

"You want me to do something . . ." I said it slowly, keeping a tight hold on myself. "But what? I'm not Cornish, you know. Indeed, to the local people we're both of us foreigners. So what is it you want? What do you expect me to do?"

She shook her head quickly. "No good asking me. Work it out for yourself." She was staring at me then as though she hated me. I could see it in her eyes. They were blazing as she said, "This is a man's job." And then, standing there, the bird held in her two hands, and spitting the words out—"But I'll tell you this, Trev. If I were a man . . ."

"Go on," I said, for she had suddenly stopped. "If you were a man you'd do what?"

"Set fire to it myself." Her teeth were gritted. "I'd do something . . ."

"And how do you set fire to an oil slick? Use a box of matches like you'd light a fire, or a torch of newspapers? Oil doesn't burn that easily, not crude mixed with seawater."

"Of course it doesn't. I'm not that stupid. But there are other things, that old paraffin flamethrower thing Jimmy Kerrison was using a few years back to burn the weeds off his drive. Don't tell me that wouldn't set the stuff alight. Or a bomb, like that man Hals in Africa—that got results."

"It got him the sack."

"But he forced them to act, didn't he? And that American, flying his own slick patrol. All over the world there are people fighting back. If you won't do anything . . ."

"Oh, for God's sake." I didn't take her seriously and suddenly she seemed to give up, standing there very still with a frozen look on her face. "Perhaps it's my fault," she breathed. "I shouldn't have persuaded you—" She was gazing seaward. "Tourists seemed the only pollution we had to fear. I never thought of oil. Oh yes, I know you warned me. But it was all so clean, so perfect—so very, very beautiful. Something I'd always dreamed of, brought up in Swansea, among all the squalor—" She was staring down at the bird. "Here, you take it." She thrust it into my hands so violently that its muscles contracted in an effort to beat its wings and it turned its head and stabbed at my hand with its powerful beak. "I'm going up to the cottage. I'm going to bed. And I'm going to stay in bed until that slick's dispersed. I don't want to see it. I don't want to know about it. This time, I'm going to pretend it isn't there. And when it's gone, when you've stirred yourself out of your lethargy and done something about it—"

"I've told you, I'm doing what I can. All of us, we're all doing everything—"

"Balls! You're in love with the sound of your own voices, you and Jimmy and that fellow Wilkins. A visit from a junior minister and you're over the moon, so full of your own importance you forget—"

"Shut up!"

"I won't shut up. I'm telling you the truth for once."

We were shouting at each other and I was so angry I could have hit her. The bird was struggling and I took hold of its neck and wrung it. Anything to stop her yelling and put the wretched thing out of its misery, but my hands slipped on the oil and I botched it, so that I had to finish it off by slamming its head against a rock.

She flew at me then, shouting at me to stop, and I had to hold her off. I held her off until the bird was dead and then I flung the mangled corpse of it back into the sea. "Now, go to bed," I told her. "Bury your head in the sand and don't come out until it's all over and the slick's gone."

She didn't move for a moment, standing there, staring at me as though seeing me for the first time. "You bastard!" she said quietly. "I'll show you." And she turned and walked slowly off up the path, back to the cottage.

I stayed there for a moment, thinking back over all that had been said, wishing I could have handled it differently. But it had been building for several days now, ever since the *Petros Jupiter* had stranded within sight of our home. I was out of understanding, totally exhausted by her emotional behavior and her refusal to accept that everything was being done that could be done. She was so impractical. She knew about ships. She'd been brought up with them—her father a crane driver in the docks. But she'd never understood the sea, how cruel it could be—not until she had come to live here.

My gaze lifted from the lifeless razorbill—sloshing back and forth like an oily rag in the suck and thrust of the wavelets—to the edge of the slick pushing a dirty brown tongue round the rocks that hid the tanker from view. Something moved in the film of oil, a wing flapping. I turned away in disgust, climbing the path slowly, but not to the cottage. I struck away to the right, across the knoll above the elephant rock, striding out furiously as I reached the top.

I was cursing under my breath—not at Karen, not entirely, but at the whole sodding bloody mess, the way our idyll of a simple life was breaking up under the pressure of outside events. I could remember so clearly the day we had first seen Balkaer snugged into the grass and wild flowers and rocks above the cove, so remote, so peaceful on that still, sunny day in early spring two years ago. Doubtless that was why it was being offered at such a reasonable price. For a quick sale, they had said, but it was really the lack of any amenities. Who wants a cottage perched on an exposed coast with no services and the nearest track for vehicles over five hundred meters away? Only people like ourselves. Karen from the dust and polyglot overcrowding of a Welsh port, and me with my earliest memories of a tiny hospital on the edge of the desert. For us that Atlantic coast, its soft salt air, the solitude of the cottage perched above the cove, it was all irresistible. We had put our deposit down that afternoon, moved in a week later, and for almost a year we had been sublimely happy. The tourists hadn't bothered us as much as we had feared, I had sold several magazine pieces and had started on a book, *Mate of the Balkaer*. And then, at the tail end of a March gale, the first oil had come ashore and we had spent hours clearing up the beach.

That was when I discovered how unreasonable Karen could be, how taut her nerves were under that beautiful, smooth, rain-soft skin. The birds that came ashore the first time were all dead and whenever she found one she'd hold it out to me in mute accusation. Perhaps she didn't mean it that way, but that's how it had seemed to me. And though she said she remembered my warning, I doubt if she really remembered what I had told her that day when we stood in the cottage doorway and decided Balkaer was what we wanted. Three years tramping round the world, then two on the Gulf-Karachi-Bombay run; I knew the sort of men who manned the smaller, older vessels. "There'll be engineers," I had told her, "who'll pump the bilges out whatever the regulations, tanker skippers who'll turn a blind eye to tank cleansing at sea, even order it—and sooner or later Cornwall will have another oil spillage disaster like the *Torrey Canyon*." But she was happy, dreaming dreams. She hadn't been listening, she hadn't really taken it in. And then, when it happened . . .

I had slowed my pace, staring ahead beyond the white sand sweep of the bay, beyond the road slanting down to Sennen and its cluster of houses, to Land's End and the rocks off, and that tanker sitting there, stern-on to the rocks and leaking oil. The slick now stretched in a great, smooth, brown, greasy layer right across the bay, the spraying vessels moving through it with scarcely a ripple like two water beetles. I was thinking back to the other spillages then. The first one hadn't been too bad, a minor slick that had stayed offshore. But the second, which had happened sometime in the early hours of the morning, had been different—bigger, longer-lasting, heavy, black, glutinous oil that stuck to the rocks like glue—and because it was spring and the start of the breeding season many more birds had been involved. A shift of wind had brought them ashore, some of them still very much alive, so that we had spent time and money getting them to the cleansing center.

Now, here, staring me in the face, was the thing I had dreaded. I wondered how much of her cargo they had managed to pump out. Three small tankers festooned with fenders had been working in relays to lighten her all through the quiet weather period. Doubtless, they'd tell us at the meeting to-night. But the glass had started to fall and now that the sky was visible I could see mares' tails showing high up to the southwest. If it started to blow . . . I stopped and stared back along the coast to Cape Cornwall and beyond. In the stillness and the cold, slanting sunlight it all looked green and fresh, everything washed clean as though waiting for the spring. But for us it wouldn't be a spring like our first spring. If it were going to blow and she broke up, if the *Petros Jupiter* split open, spilling the rest of her oil, all that lovely shoreline would be polluted, the marine life killed off and birds that should be nesting coming ashore again as oil-sodden bundles. It would drive Karen out of her mind.

Bloody, stupid, incompetent bastard! I was thinking of the master, risking a ship like that so close to Land's End just for

the sake of a few miles and a tiny saving in bunker fuel. Or
. . . had it been deliberate? First the boiler out of action, then
the secondary reduction gear stripped. If it wasn't an accident,
then the chief engineer would have to be in on it—one of the
engineers, anyway. Would any man in his senses deliberately
cause a tanker breakdown close off such a notorious headland?
But then, if the money was right . . .

I shrugged. No doubt the inquiry would produce the answer
and we'd probably be told tonight when it would be held.

I walked as far as Sennen, where I had a word with Andy
Trevose, the lifeboat's relief cox'n. One of the salvage boys had
told him in the pub that if the weather held there was a
chance they'd float the *Petros Jupiter* off on Monday's tide.
Apparently she'd been given enough buoyancy for'ard to lift
most of her hull clear of the rocks. Only her stern remained
fast on Kettle's Bottom. He also told me there was a rumor the
second engineer had jumped a foreign trawler off Porthcurnow
and disappeared.

The sun had set by the time I got back to Balkaer, night
closing in and the mares' tails gone, the sky clear again and
beginning to turn that translucent green that indicates cold.
The door was on the latch, but Karen wasn't there. I thought
at first she had gone up to see old Mrs. Peever. She did that
sometimes when she was upset about something. Or Jean Kerrison perhaps. Jean was more her own age and they got on well
enough. It would have been natural, considering what had
happened and the mood she was in.

It wasn't until I went out to the stone cleit I'd built above
the path to get peat to bank up the fire that I thought of looking down into the cove. I saw her then, out in the rubber
dinghy. She was paddling it along the edge of the slick, not
using the outboard, though she had it mounted. I called to her
and she looked up, but she didn't wave. I thought she was out
there to pick up any live birds caught in the slick and I went
back into the cottage, banked up the fire, and got my things.

The meeting was at six in Penzance and Jimmy had said he would pick me up at the bottom of the lane at five-fifteen.

I called to her again as I left, but she didn't answer. The light was fading as I went off up the path to the lane, but I wasn't worried about her. She knew how to handle the inflatable and, like me, she enjoyed being on her own sometimes. It's not easy when people are cooped up in a lonely little Cornish tin-miner's cottage in winter. You tend to get on each other's nerves, however much you're in love. Even so, if it hadn't been for that bloody tanker . . . But Karen would get over it. They'd get the tanker off and then, when the spring came—everything would look different in the spring.

So I comforted myself. I was really quite cheerful as I approached the lane, the black mood dissipated by the walk to Sennen. It would be the same for Karen, I thought. I didn't re-alize how her emotions had been working on her imagination this past week, what depths of passion and desperation had been building up inside her.

Jimmy was already waiting for me in his battered blue van and I didn't think any more about her as we drove across the moor to Penzance. He farmed a few acres, pigs and chickens mainly, but mostly he made his living out of the tourists, rent-ing two cottages he owned in Sennen, so that he had a vested interest in the coastal environment.

The meeting, which was in the Town Hall, proved to be a much bigger affair than anything Wilkins, the secretary of our Preservation Society, had so far been able to organize locally. Just about every organization involved was represented, and since it was open to the public the place was packed. The local MP was in the chair and the chief speaker was the Under-Secretary for the Marine Division of the Department of Trade whose theme, of course, was that everything was being done that could be done. He pointed out that his own emergency information room—his Ops Room, which was on the top floor of the Marine Division's HQ in Holborn—had been activated and continuously manned since January 1, the day the *Petros Jupiter* had been stranded. The local antipollution plan had been put into operation immediately, including the setting up of a pollution operation control room at Land's End. The oil company involved had had tankers and pumps available for transferring cargo within fourteen hours, and the owners and Lloyd's had had salvage teams, ships, and equipment on the spot the following day. Of the 57,000 tons of crude oil carried in the ship's tanks, 39,000 had already been pumped out. It was estimated that no more than 9,000 tons had leaked into the sea and this was being dissipated by spraying from the ships everyone could see from Land's End. "With luck the salvage operators hope to have the *Petros Jupiter* off the rocks tomorrow or the day after."

Andy Trevose, a few feet in front of me and talking to another Sennen Cove fisherman, suddenly got to his feet. "Tedn't laikly th'all get 'er off'n tamorrer."

"The salvage operators assure me—"

"Then th'are kidding themsel', an' thee—t'll be blawing tamorrer, d'you see."

"Have it your own way," the Under-Secretary said mildly. "I'm not an authority on local weather and I can only repeat what the salvage operators have told me. They are optimistic—very optimistic—of getting the ship off on tomorrow's tide." And on that he sat down.

His speech, which had lasted almost half an hour, was followed by a question-and-answer session. Here he was at his best, combining an air of authority with a touch of humor that had the effect of softening his slightly offhand manner and making him more human. Yes, he thought the Minister would be giving close consideration to the setting up of some sort of committee to reconsider the question of tanker routes in the sea area between the Scillies and Land's End. This in answer to a question by the representative of the International Tanker Owners' Pollution Federation. Both Nature Conservancy and the local representatives of the inshore fishermen pressed him hard on this point, but all he would say was, "I will convey your observations to the Minister."

Nobody seemed to think this was good enough. The demand was for a tightening of regulations in the waters between Land's End and the Scillies and regular patrols to insure that tankers and other bulk carriers of dangerous cargoes reported in as they had to on the French side off Ushant. And, similarly, they wanted them routed outside the Scillies. The Under-Secretary said, of course, it would take time, that there were a great number of interests to be considered, as well as the whole legal question of the freedom of the seas. At this point he was shouted down, first by local fishermen and their wives, then by some of the coastal farmers; finally a group of boardinghouse operators led by Jimmy joined in. There was so much noise for a time that even the local MP couldn't get a hearing.

In the end the Under-Secretary departed with nothing settled, only his promise that he would convey the feelings of the meeting most forcibly. It was by then almost eight-thirty. Jimmy and I, and several others from the Whitesand area, talked it over in the bar of a nearby pub. Most of us felt nothing had been achieved. Andy Trevose said he reckoned nothing would be done until we got a disaster as big as the *Amoco Cadiz.* "An' tedn't no use pretending—tha'll put paid to the inshaaw fishing for a generation." And he went off to phone his wife.

When he returned we had another round, and then Jimmy and I left. It was very still by then with wisps of sea fog trailing up from the direction of the harbor. "Looks like the man from London could be right." Jimmy was crouched over the wheel, straining to see the road. "If this weather holds they've a good chance of getting her off." The mist was thick on the moor, but when we reached his house the barometer was already falling. It was as we were standing there, staring at it, that Jean handed me a printed card. "Give that to Karen, will you? I said I'd try and find it for her, but it's so long since we used it . . ."

"Used what?" I asked.

"That flamethrower. But it's very simple and I told her how it worked."

"You told her—" I was staring down at the instructions card, my mind suddenly alerted, seeing Karen out in the cove and remembering there had been something beside her in the dinghy, something with a bell-shaped end like a blunderbuss resting on the bows. It must have been the flamethrower, but the light was so dim by then I hadn't been able to see it clearly. "When was this? When did she borrow it from you?"

"This afternoon. She was up here . . . oh, it would have been about three—well before tea anyway."

"God Almighty!" I breathed. "You gave her that thing?"

"It's all right," she added quietly. "I explained it all to her—how to pressurize the tank and get the flame ignited. I even lent her a pump and some meths."

"She didn't say why she wanted it?"

"No."

"You didn't ask her?"

"Why should I? It's for burning off weeds."

I turned to Jimmy then and asked him to drive me down to the end of the lane, and when we got there he insisted on coming down the path with me to the cottage. The mist had thickened, a blank wall of vapor blocking the beam of my torch. "What are you worried about?" he asked. "She wouldn't be fooling about with it at this time of night."

"She didn't want it for weeds," I said.

"What, then?"

"That oil slick."

"Oh, I see." He laughed. "Well, you can relax. Even if she did get it going, it wouldn't do much good. That's pretty heavy stuff, that slick."

The cottage loomed, a darker grey in the fog. No sign of a light. The door was locked and I was shouting for Karen before I had even got it open. But there was no answer. The cottage was still and dead, wrapped in the fog, and only the faintest glow from the peat fire in the big fireplace. "Karen! Karen!" I searched quickly. There was nobody there. Then I was running, stumbling through the fog, down into the cove. The little stone boathouse was empty, the door hanging open and no sign of the inflatable anywhere on the sands, only the marks where she had dragged it into the water.

I stood stock-still for a moment, my heart hammering and trying to think, trying to prove to myself that what I feared couldn't be, that she couldn't be such a fool. But I knew she could. The fog swirled to a breath of wind and I turned, the path and the cottage suddenly clear in the long-throwing beam of my torch. Andy Trevose! That would be the quickest. Drive to Sennen and get Andy to take me out in his boat. I called to Jimmy, climbing the path in long strides, not bothering to lock the cottage, heading for the van, and behind me Jimmy said, "You think she's going to use that flamethrower on the slick?"

"Yes," I panted.

"But I told you, that stuff's too heavy—"

"The ship then—something. She wanted to make a gesture. I'm afraid she'll hurt herself."

We reached the van. "Sennen?" he asked as he started the engine.

"Yes. Andy Trevose. He should be back by the time we get there."

"She's probably stranded on the sand somewhere. If the outboard broke down . . . Shall I stop for Jean?"

"No. Hurry."

But he stopped all the same, to tell her where we were going, and then we were feeling our way up onto the Sennen road, with the mist closed down and getting thicker. It seemed an age, both of us peering into the murk and the refracted beam of the headlights, but at last we were down by the hard and pulling up at the Trevose cottage near the lifeboat station. Andy was back and he had his oilskins on. "Seen your wife?" he asked. "Is Karen home?"

"No."

"She was here," he said. And his wife, behind him, added, "Karen came up from the quay abaht eight-thirty, asked me what Andy thawt would be the result of the meeting, and when ah told her he'd promised to phone she asked to stay. She was that urgent to knaw what happened."

"And when you told her, what did she say?"

"Nothing much. She'd been very withdrawn, all the taime we were waiting. Very edgy-laike, knaw what ah mean? And then, when ah tauld her nothing had been decaided, she laughed. 'I knew it,' she says, the laugh a little wild and her voice a bit high-laike. Very white, she was. Very tuned-up—laike she wanted to scream but was managing to throttle it back." She gave a big, full-breasted shrug. "Tha's all. She went out then."

"She didn't say where she was going?"

"No. The only thing she said was 'I'll show 'em.' At least, ah think that was it. She was muttering to herself as she flung out of the door. Ah ran after her, but the mist had thickened and she was already gawn."

"Rose thinks she'd be off to the ship," Andy said, and his wife nodded. "Tha's right. Ah don't know why, but tha's what ah think."

And Andy Trevose in oilskins and seaboots. "You were going to take your boat out," I said. "You were going to look for her?"

"Aye, but not my boat. The ILB, I think."

I thanked him, glad I didn't have to waste time trying to convince him of the urgency of it. "You'll need oilskins," he said as we started down toward the lifeboat station, a single streetlight shining dimly and a cold breeze swirling the mist over the roofs of the cottages. Away to the southwest the Longships' explosive fog signal banged twice, and far away I could just hear the moaning of the Seven Stones' diaphone. "Rack'n we'll take the inshore boat," he said. "Tha'll be quicker." He had the key to the lifeboat house and—after issuing Jimmy and myself with lifejackets, oilskins, and seaboots—he motioned us to take the stern of the high-speed rubber boat and the three of us dragged it out and ran it down into the water.

Visibility was virtually nil as we went out from under the stone breakwater on a compass bearing, Andy crouched in the stern over the big outboard, Jimmy and I in the bows. I have only a vague recollection of the passage out, my mind concentrated on Karen, trying to visualize what she was doing, where she would have got to by now. Maybe Jimmy was right. Maybe she was just lost in the fog. But the double bang from the Longships light made it seem unlikely. Andy hadn't thought she was lost. He'd put on his oilskins as soon as Rose had told him, prepared to go out after her alone. I could just see him, a dark shadow in the stern leaning forward away from the engine, a VHF handset to his ear.

Through The Tribbens it was only about a mile and a half from Sennen to Kettle's Bottom, and before we had gone half that distance the five-minute fog signal from the Longships was audible even above the roar of the outboard. Another ten minutes and Andy was throttling back, listening out on his walkie-talkie. "Tha's one of the tugs. Rack'ns he's seen a laight by the starn o' that tanker. 'Farg cawms an' goes,' he says. He's got a searchlight trained on 'er an' he'll keep it so till we get thar."

He opened up the throttle again and we bounced across what appeared to be a small tide rip. The tide would be ebbing now, pulling us down toward the rocks. There was movement in the fog, an iridescent glimmer of light. The light was there for a moment, then it was gone, the fog closed up again.

"Getting close now," Andy shouted, leaning forward and passing me the big torch. "As soon as 'ee see the wrack—" He shouted a warning and swung the boat over in a hard turn. The slop of wavelets running over rocks awash slid by to port, just visible in the beam of the torch. The fog signal on the Longships cracked out, sharp and very clear, and in the same instant the landward-facing fixed red peered at us through thinning mist like some demented one-eyed Cyclops, and to the right of it the shadowy shape of the stranded tanker showed black in silhouette against the brightening beam of a searchlight.

I don't know how far away the wreck was—four, five hundred yards, three cables perhaps. But it was near enough for me to see that all the huge length of her was clear of the water, save for the stern, which was right against the rocks and sunk so low that the deck was awash. It was only a few seconds that we saw her clearly, then the fog closed in again. But it was still long enough for me to see a rubber boat snugged against the after rail and a figure moving along the sloping deck pinpointed by a flickering light.

I shouted. But at that distance and with the engine running . . . What the hell did she think she was doing? It had to be her. Nobody else would be out to the wreck in a fog like this. I turned to Andy. "Did you get a bearing?" I screamed at him.

He nodded. "'Bout three-one-oh. We're in among the rocks." He had cut the engine right down, maneuvering slowly. "Gi' us some laight." I switched on the torch again, swinging the beam of it in a wide arc. Ripples everywhere, the white of little waves breaking as the tide ripped the shallows.

"Was that a torch she had?" Jimmy asked. But he knew it wasn't. There had been no beam, and a faint, flickering light like that, it could only be that damned flamethrower. The beam from the tug's searchlight was growing, the fog like a luminous curtain getting brighter all the time. Then suddenly it was swept away completely and we had a clear view of the tanker again, a little nearer now, her decks deserted, no sign of anyone. Had I dreamed it, that figure with the ghostly flame? But then I saw her, coming out from the shadow of the super-structure, a small shape high up the sloping deck and holding out ahead of her that tiny flame of light.

There was an open hatch and my eyes, staring through the cold humidity of the atmosphere, were beginning to water. It had to be a hatch, the entry hatch to one of the fuel tanks, and a void opened up inside me, my breath held and my body trembling. Oh God, no! And nothing I could do, no way I could stop her. I saw her reach it and she paused, crouched down on the deck. "She's pumping," Jimmy breathed. "She's pumping up the pressure, building up the flame."

She stood up, the flame much brighter as she pushed it for-ward. That's what I shall never forget, that I could see her pushing that flame toward the hatch and nothing I could do to stop her. I may have screamed. I don't know. We were too far away, the engine roaring, and nothing I could do—nothing. I could see her, but I couldn't stop her. The mist closed in and I sat there—my mouth open—dumb and appalled, waiting.

And then, as the silhouette of the tanker faded to a shadow, it came—a lurid whoosh of flame burning the fog to a blazing incandescent fire that shot upward with a terrible roaring sound.

The engine was idling again and we sat there, stunned and in a state of shock as the heat hit us through the fog glare. And the noise—it was a roar like a thousand trains going through a tunnel, a great eruption of sound.

I remember Jimmy suddenly yelling, "It's gone. The whole bloody ship's gone! My God!" And Andy muttering close behind me, "Tha'll show 'em, arl raight, poor gal." His hand gripped my arm, a touch of sympathy. "She'll be remembered —a long taime for this."

I didn't move. I didn't say anything. I was thinking of Karen, wondering if she'd really known—what she was doing, what the result would be. But she must have. She must have known. Oil and air, the fumes an explosive mixture. She wasn't a fool. She'd known. Christ! And I'd let her go. I'd seen her, down there in the cove in the dim evening light, the flame-thrower there, in the bows, and I'd waved to her, and gone off up the path to that useless meeting.

The heat was burning up the fog now. I could see the bright white heart of the fire and the billowing cloud of smoke rising like a volcanic eruption. I couldn't see the wreck, only the rocks of the Kettle's Bottom all red with the glare. Either it was sunk or else the smoke and flames had engulfed it completely. The effect was terrifying—the thunderous roar, the whole appalling conflagration seeming to burst up from the surface of the sea as though fueled by some underwater vent. Lightning flashed in the smoke and I sat there, thinking of Karen, trying to imagine . . . I must have been crying, for my eyes became crusted with salt and I could feel my mouth trembling. But the intensity of the heat burned up my tears, so that I stared, dry-eyed, at the pyre she had made for herself.

I should have known. After three years—God! I should have known. And we'd been here almost two—two years living in expectation, waiting for just such a catastrophe.

The heat was scorching my face and there was wind. Jimmy's hand gripped my arm. "Hold it!" he said urgently. "Nothing you can do." I realized then that I had been struggling to my feet. "Nothing at all." His face was close to mine. "Not now. Just sit there . . ."

Just sit, do nothing. The tanker blazing and Karen's body—her lovely, soft body—burned to nothing. Had it been quick? An explosion like that, such a holocaust of flame—she wouldn't have known? Surely to God, it wouldn't have hurt? I tried to imagine myself there beside her when it happened, but it was no use—my mind couldn't grasp what it would have been like, what the impact of it would have been on flesh and bone. The nerves . . . it would have been her nerves that took the full shock of it, reacting like a seismograph, shrieking information to the brain in that split second of exploding flames.

My head was turned, still facing the lurid glow. But it was over the stern now. Andy had swung the inflatable away from it. The wind was growing, whipping the surface of the water to spray, and it was cold—cold air being sucked in by the rising heat of the flames.

I don't know what happened after that. My mind seemed to blank out, so that I wasn't conscious of anything until we were inside the Sennen breakwater and carrying the ILB up to the boathouse. The sea mist was almost gone, torn to shreds, and out where the ship had been there was nothing but billowing smoke lit by a red internal glow. The fog signal on the Longships banged again, the red light glaring fixedly. Somebody was talking to me, asking questions, and I became aware of a small crowd gathering. There was a police car there and a young helicopter pilot I knew.

"It was your wife, was it, sir—the young woman they say went out to blow up the ship? Can you give me her name please, her full name . . ." And another voice—a camera reporter from one of the TV companies that had been waiting to film the ship being hauled off the rocks—said, "What the hell did she do it for, going out to a wrecked oil tanker with a thing like a miniature flamethrower? Did she want to kill herself?"

His eager, hungry little eyes stared up at me, the camera cradled on his arm. I could sense his excitement. "Did you see her? Was she really out there?" And then, as I told him to go to hell, he stepped back, the camera raised, and his mate switched a spotlight on, suddenly blinding me. "Just tell it to us in your own words, Mr. Rodin. Why did she do it?"

I started toward him, but Andy stopped me. I thought better of it then. At least it was a chance to tell people . . . "Are you recording this?" I asked him.

"Yes. You tell us. Now." And I heard the whir of the camera. So I told them—I told them what the quiet and beauty of Balkaer had meant to Karen, to us both—and how cheap flag-of-convenience ships, badly officered, badly equipped, were destroying the coastline, ruining everybody's lives. "And that tanker spilling oil. Nothing came of the meeting tonight, only an assurance they'd get her off tomorrow. But Karen knew . . . she knew the pressure was falling and a storm due. She knew they'd do nothing, so she . . ." I heard the hesitation in my voice—"so she must have made up her mind—" I couldn't go on. My voice caught on a sob, my words unintelligible. "She just—decided—she'd do it herself. Set the slick alight. Nobody was going to do anything, so she'd—" I was conscious of the silence around me, everybody hanging on my words, the camera whirring. "That's all," I muttered. "She didn't realize—she didn't mean to kill herself—only to save the coast and the seabirds." I heard him say, "Cut," and the camera stopped.

"Thanks," he said. "You'll wring a lot of hearts with that stuff. Pity your wife isn't here too." He gave my arm a quick pat. "Sorry. Terrible shock for you. But thanks. Thanks a lot."

I shook my head, feeling dazed, the world going on around me and myself not part of it. The camera crew were packing up. The police officer was at my elbow again, asking more questions, writing it down. "You say she didn't mean to blow the ship up and herself with it?"

I turned my head, seeing his eyes blue like gemstones in the beam of a car's headlights. "She was killed," I said dully. "It was accidental."

It didn't mean anything to me now. It was as though talking to the camera had got the shock of it out of my system for the moment.

"She loved life," I told him. "Why should she want to kill

herself? She went out there with only one thought—to burn up that oil slick."

He took it all down, then he read the statement back to me and I signed it, resting the paper on the warm hood of the police car. After that, I was able to get away, back to the Trevose cottage. I didn't go in, I just stood outside by the parked van. I wanted to get away, to be with Karen—back to the cottage, to the memories . . . all I had left.

Jimmy says I didn't utter a word all the way back, except to ask him to drive me straight down to the bottom of the lane. He wanted me to stay the night with them, of course, but I wouldn't. "I'll be all right." I thanked him and got my torch out of the back. Then I was going down the path to Balkaer, alone now and on my own for the first time since it had happened.

The chickens stirred in their shed at my approach and in the cleft of the cove the suck and gurgle of waves lapping against the rocks came to me on an updraft of wind. There were no stars, the night dark and the sky overcast. It would be blowing from the sou'west by morning. The cottage door was unlocked, the peat fire glowing now in the wide fireplace, the place warm and snug, but terribly empty, as though it knew she wouldn't be back.

I remember thinking—*It will always be empty like this now.* But there was movement on the far side, under the table. I lit the lamp and in its bright flame I saw five of the cardboard boxes they'd given us to carry the oil-soaked birds when driving them to the cleansing center. It hit me then. It hit me so hard that I just sat down, a sort of strangled cry coming from inside me, tears falling. I was remembering that scene down in the cove with her holding the wretched bird out to me. If only her tongue could be scolding at me again. Anything rather than this deadly quiet.

And that night, lying alone in the big untidy bed, the loneliness of it was unbearable. Without Karen what was there to life? She was all I had, all I'd ever had. She was this cottage, Balkaer, the life we'd been leading. It was her idea—the way we lived, everything. Without her it had no meaning. I was back to the nothingness of my existence before we met. Ever since I'd stowed away on that dhow in Dubai, got myself across to Gwadar and up to Peshawar by way of Quetta, ever since then I'd been tramping the world, living out of suitcases, owning nothing, belonging nowhere—no one belonging to me. Only Karen had ever belonged . . .

The wind was rising. In the end I couldn't stand it, lying there staring into the dark, listening to the wind and seeing her figure moving along the sloping deck of that tanker, the flickering flame held out in front of her, and then the flash of the explosion, the roaring holocaust that had followed. Poor darling! Poor wonderful, adorable, emotional darling! If only I'd gone down into the cove, instead of waving and climbing the path and leaving her there. She must have tried to ignite the slick with that garden flamethrower right after I had left. And when she'd failed, she'd motored across the bay to Sennen to wait with Rose to hear the result of the meeting.

I should have known. If I hadn't been so angry . . . God! If —if—if . . . I flung off the bedclothes and got the bottle of Armagnac I kept for emergenices at the back of the kitchen cupboard. It was the last of the bottles I had brought with me when I had finally come ashore to become self-employed instead of a salaried ship's officer. There wasn't much of it left, but it was over the remains of that bottle, sitting in the rocking chair with two oiled-up cormorants and three razorbills in boxes under the table beside me, listening to the roar of the wind outside, the crash of the rollers in the cove below, sensing the movement of the stone walls round me in the gusts, that I began to come to terms with what had happened. Times like this we'd have had each other—talking together, working together, going to bed together, making love; one way and another we'd always kept the gales at bay, locking ourselves into our own little world and shutting out the wind.

But now there was only myself. And with Karen gone I was intensely conscious of every battering blast of wind, so that the cottage seemed no longer a protection, the wind entering it and the waves beating at its foundations. And my love out there by the Kettle's Bottom. Tomorrow or the next day, a week, two weeks maybe, somewhere along the coast they'd find the charred remains of her floating in the sea, or smashed up on the rocks—and I'd be expected to identify her. Or would that rounded, full-breasted form have been reduced to ashes? If it had been cremated beyond recognition . . . I could see her still, sitting in the wing chair on the opposite side of the fireplace. We had bought that chair in a gale, junk from a nearby homestead that had gone for nothing, no dealers there, and she had laboriously re-covered it with material from an old Welsh *cardden* that had belonged to her mother.

I could see her now, sitting there like a ghost with one hand propping her chin, the other holding a book, or sitting staring intently at the fire as I read aloud to her what I had written during the day. She was doing the typing for me, of course— she was a trained typist—but I think it was my reading to her that developed her interest in books. She had never been much of a reader before, but then she started borrowing from the traveling library, always wildlife books or stories about animals. Sometimes she would borrow a book about Wales, but mostly it was wildlife, and because much of what I was writing was about the birds and seals that visited our coast, she became in a sense my sounding box, our relationship deeper, more intimate, so that now, for the moment, I could still see her, sitting there in that empty chair.

That was really the start of it, that was when I saw the pattern of my life, how it all added up—so that what had been without purpose before suddenly became purposeful.

It's hard to explain, for in the hours I sat there, sleepless, with the noise of the front coming in out of the Atlantic steadily increasing, I went through several stages. I had already passed through shock and had reached the point of feeling sorry for myself when I came down seeking the comfort of the Armagnac. But then, as the fire of it gave me courage to face my loss and the loneliness that would follow, I came to feel that Karen wasn't dead, that she still existed, not in her own body but in mine—that she had become part of me.

It was a strange feeling, for my thinking immediately became different. It was as though death had opened the door for me so that life had a new meaning, a new dimension—all life, not just human life. I was beginning to think like her. I suddenly felt at one with the Green Peace movement and all those people who had tried to stop the harp seal killers of Canada or to prevent the slaughter of the dolphins by the fishermen off Iki.

The world as I drank seemed to be shrieking aloud the cruelty of humans—not just to themselves, but to all living things. Greed, and a rage against nature. Karen was right. A rogue species. She'd read that somewhere. And about vested interests, too. There'd always be vested interests, always be reasons for not interfering, for allowing another species to be wiped out, for letting them cut down another rain forest, pollute another stretch of coast, another sea, an ocean even, with oil or nuclear waste. She'd seen it. Now I was seeing it. And I hadn't reasoned it out—it was just suddenly there in my mind, as though she had put it there.

A gust shook the walls, the wind tugging at the door and a sheet of spray lashing at the windows. The peat fire glowed and I saw her face in it, the long black hair let down and burning like a torch. Slumped in the old rocker, I relived the moment, the holocaust, confusing the peat glow and seeing her body shrivel in the heat of it, and with that hallucinatory sight the anger that was there, deep inside me, boiled over, vengeance then my only thought. An eye for an eye, a life for a life. Somebody had put that bloody ship on the rocks, somebody had been responsible—for the pollution, for Karen's death.

Speridion? Another gust, the cottage trembling, and I spoke the name aloud. Aristides Speridion. And he'd got away in a boat. That's what the marine consultant, an oil pollution specialist from Cardiff, had said at the meeting: that the second engineer of the *Petros Jupiter* was missing and they'd traced him through a Penzance fisherman to a stolen dinghy and a Breton fishing boat.

I'd hunt him down. I'd kill the bastard. The wind howled and I emptied my glass, hugging that thought to me.

A bloody little Greek—they were always Greek. I'd find him and I'd get the truth out of him, and if he was responsible, if he'd deliberately caused that damned tanker to go on the rocks . . .

Dawn was breaking as I finished the last of the bottle and began to dress. The razorbills were dead by then, only the cormorants still alive, and the room was very dark, a lot of noise. There always was a lot of noise with a gale blowing out of the west and a big sea running. Lloyd's! That was what was in my mind now as I shaved and dressed. With an insurance claim in, Lloyd's would know where the man had gone to earth if anybody did. Lloyd's of London—I'd phone them as soon as I had banked up the fire and got myself some breakfast.

CHAPTER TWO

I DIDN'T BOTHER TO CLEAR UP. I just got my anorak, picked up the containers holding the two live cormorants, and shouldered my way out into the gale. One night. One single night. A split moment of time, and now everything changed, my whole life. Clear of the cottage the wind took hold, thrusting me up the path. It was blowing a good force 9 and I could hardly breathe, the collar of my anorak whipping against my chin with a harsh whirring sound, and the waves thundering below me, the cove a white maelstrom of broken water thrown back by the rocks.

It was quieter when I reached the lane, a grey miserable morning with ragged wisps of cloud flying in the wind, the moors all hidden. A herring gull sailed past my head, a scrap of paper blown by the gale. She would have liked that—one bird at least without oil on its feathers.

The blue van was parked in the yard of the Kerrisons' place and I found Jimmy cleaning out the chicken roost at the back of the outbuildings. I handed him the cardboard containers holding the cormorants. "The last thing she did," I said.

"Okay, I'll see they get to the cleansing center."

"Can I use your phone?"

He nodded and took me through into the house. Jean called down to see if I was all right. The phone was at the foot of the stairs and she leaned over the bannister to ask if I could use a cup of coffee. I answered her automatically, trying to remember the departmental details given in *Lloyd's Nautical Year Book*. I didn't want underwriters or salvage experts; I wanted the people who dealt with fraudulent claims. But I couldn't remember what the section was called, only that it was located outside London.

By the time I had been through Directory Inquiries and Lloyd's of London switchboard I was sweating, my nerves on edge, tiredness coming in waves. Colchester, the girl said—Intelligence Services. And she gave me the number.

"You all right, Trevor?" It was Jean, looking anxious and holding a cup of coffee out to me.

"Yes, I'm all right." There were beads of sweat on my forehead. "It's very warm in here, nice and warm after being outside."

"Come and sit down, then. You can phone after you've had your coffee."

"No. No thanks. I'll get this over, then I'll sit down for a moment." I dialed the Colchester number, mopping the sweat from my forehead, and when I told the girl I was inquiring about the engineer of the *Petros Jupiter* she put me through to a quiet, friendly-sounding voice: "Ferrers, Special Inquiries Branch. Can I help you?" But as soon as I asked him whether it was negligence, or if the tanker had been put ashore deliberately, his manner changed. "Have you any reason to suppose it was deliberate?"

"The engineer," I said. "A Greek named Speridion. He took a dinghy from Porthcurnow. They say he was picked up by a Breton fishing boat."

"It doesn't prove anything," the voice said. "A man who's been shipwrecked . . ." There was a pause, and then the inevitable question. "May I know your interest in the matter? Are you representing anyone in particular?"

"No. Only myself." I told him my name then and where I was speaking from, and he said "Trevor Rodin," repeating it slowly. "It was your wife . . ." The voice trailed away, embarrassed, and I heard him say, "I'm sorry." After that there was a long silence. And when I asked him for information about the engineer—where he lived, or where the fishing boat had taken him—he said, "I can't answer that. There's nothing through yet. Why not try the police, or maybe the solicitors . . . ?" He hesitated, "May I have your address, please?"

I gave it to him, also the Kerrisons' telephone number. "Could you ring me here if it turns out to be a scuttling job?"

"What makes you think it might be?"

"He's fled the country, hasn't he?" And when he didn't answer, I said, "Well, hasn't he? Somebody put that bloody tanker on the rocks."

"That's a matter for the courts." His voice sounded suddenly a little distant. Silence then. I thought he'd cut me off, but when I said, "Hullo," he answered at once. "Just a moment." A long pause. Then he went on, "Sorry—I've got a telex here, and I was just looking at a newspaper report of what happened last night . . . you've been a ship's officer, I see. Gulf, and Indian Ocean. You know Mina Zayed?"

"The Abu Dhabi port?"

"Yes."

"Is that where he's headed?"

"It's where the tanker was loaded. Do you know it?" And when I told him I'd been into it only once since it was built, he said, "Well, that's more than most ships' officers have." And he asked me whether I was ever in London.

"No," I said. "Not for a long time." But then I remembered about the book and the publishers I had sent it to. I'd have to sort that out, think about what I was going to do. "Maybe now . . ." I murmured.

"You'll be coming to London, then?"

"I expect so."

"When?"

"I don't know—soon. It depends."

"Well, let me know." He repeated the number I had given

him, promised to phone me if they heard anything definite, then hung up.

I drank the rest of my coffee there by the phone, wondering why he wanted to know if I'd be in London. There was nothing I could tell him. I took the empty cup through into the kitchen. Jean was there, looking a little tearful as she insisted I lunch with them. "You're going to leave Balkaer now, aren't you?"

I nodded. There was a sort of extramarital closeness between us. Perhaps it was her mixed Romany blood, but she always seemed to know what was in my mind. "Yes, time to leave now." Time to go back to the superficial companionship of officers' quarters on some tramp.

"Back to sea?"

I nodded, not relishing the thought.

"What about the book?"

I shook my head. It was over a month since I had sent it to the publishers and not a word. "It'll be back to the Gulf again, I suppose. But first—" I stopped there, my hands trembling, my mind on that engineer. I couldn't tell her what I planned to do. I couldn't tell anybody. "I'll take a break first." My voice sounded faint, little more than a mumble. "Try and sort things out."

She put the saucepan down carefully and caught me by the arm. "Two wrongs don't make a right, Trevor. They never did." And she added, "I know how you feel, but . . . just leave it be, love. The thing's done. Leave it be." And then, without waiting for an answer, she said, "Now go on down to the cottage, clean things up, and come back here for lunch just after twelve. Cold ham and salad. And I'll do you some meringues." She knew I liked meringues.

"All right," I said.

But instead of going back to Balkaer, I went with Jimmy in his van to the cleansing station. We helped there for a while, getting back just in time for lunch. And afterward I stayed on, enjoying the warmth of their company, the cozy heat of the coal fire. The wind had dropped, but there were still clouds over the moors and it got dark early. I didn't think about it when they switched the television on for the news, but then, suddenly, I was sitting up, electrified, seeing it all over again through the eyes of the camera—the red glow of the blazing tanker and the ILB coming into the slipway, the three of us caught against the furnace glare of the burning oil with ragged wisps of fog in the background, and myself, dazed and speaking slowly, as though in a trance, trying to answer their questions, telling them what had happened. The wind was blowing in my hair, and my face had the pallor of death in the hard glare of the spotlight.

Back at the cottage, with the aftermath of the gale beating into the cove, it was my own TV shadow, my wild, ghostly appearance that stayed in my mind, not the words I had spoken. I was tired by then, so emotionally exhausted that I fell asleep by the fire. I spent most of the night there and in the morning, when I went up to the top, above the elephant rock, and looked across to the Longships, all that remained of the *Petros Jupiter* was the blackened bridge housing, half sunk and leaning drunkenly against the Kettle's Bottom.

It was a bright, sparkling morning, the sort of morning that would have had Karen bubbling with that almost childishly excited Welsh enthusiasm of hers. I walked on, across the fields and down the road into Sennen, and there I found the story of what she had done plastered all over the papers with eyewitness accounts and statements from the salvage boss and pollution experts, also from several politicians.

Reading about it, I found it all strangely remote, as though it hadn't been Karen out there, but somebody else. Reporters came and a girl from the local radio station with a portable tape recorder. But by then I was in a daze, answering their questions automatically. It didn't seem real, any of it, the seas now rolling in unobstructed to break on the Shark's Fin, only the top of the hull's twisted wreck just showing at low water and no slick, the oil all burned up or driven ashore. It only seemed real when I was back at Balkaer. Then the emptiness of the cottage was like a constant nagging ache. Or when I was down in the cove. Wreckers from far and wide were prowling the shores of Whitesand Bay, searching all the headlands. They were picking up bits and pieces of the *Petros Jupiter* as far north as Cape Cornwall.

I began to get a stack of mail, letters from all sorts of people, conservationists chiefly, though some of them attacked me for encouraging Karen to sacrifice herself unnecessarily or accused me of standing by while she committed suicide. They were from women mainly, the bulk of them praising what she had done. Saturday the mail included several invitations to speak at conservationist meetings and a letter from the publishers. This I saved until after my return from Penzance, where I saw the agents and put Balkaer up for sale. The letter was signed "Ken Jordan, Senior Editor." He wanted me to go up to London and see him, but with Karen gone, the cottage for sale, that part of my life was ended. It didn't seem important anymore, the book no longer meaning very much to me. And on the Sunday, which was sunny with an easterly breeze, families wandered down the path from the lane to stand and point, and giggle in embarrassment when I told them to bugger off. There was even a man who pushed open the cottage door to take pictures of the interior. He was quite upset when I slammed it in his face. Because he had seen Balkaer on TV in his own home he seemed to think in some curious way that he owned the place.

And then, about dusk, when all the gawpers and souvenir hunters had gone, there was a knock at the door and I opened it to find a man dressed in a sheepskin jacket and a polo-necked sweater standing there. He had a fur cap rammed tightly down on his bullet head.

I recognized him at once, though it must have been three

years or more since I had last seen him; those broad powerful shoulders, the beer-barrel belly, the little pig eyes, and the round heavy face. He was of that breed of Englishman that has made Brits a word of contempt.

I didn't ask him in. I just stood there, waiting. The last time I'd seen him was at a shipboard party on a Liberian tanker waiting to load at Bahrain. "Remember me?"

I nodded. I had met him several times—on different ships, in different ports, and in hotel bars where he was always flush with money, always buying rounds of drinks. The word was that he was front man for a drug-smuggling ring.

"Len Baldwick," he said, holding out a big paw. "Can I have a word with you?"

"What about?"

"You. The future." The small grey eyes were watching me, the whites as clear as if he'd never touched a drop of alcohol in his life. "You'll be thinking of a ship now?"

"Will I?"

He ducked his head, pushing his way in. "Saw you on the telly." He unzipped the sheepskin jacket, pushing the fur cap to the back of his head. "Peat fire, eh? You always were a bit simple-like. I told you, way back, didn't I—being honest and licking the arses of the owners don't pay. Now look where it's got you. You lost your wife. She's gone and you're on your own. You got nothing, laddie, nothing at all."

"What the hell do you want?" Any ordinary man I'd have thrown out. But he was well over six foot, massive as a rock. "Why are you here?"

"To offer you a job." And he went on to explain that he was headhunting for a consortium going into the tanker business. "Oil money," he explained, drooping an eyelid. "You know how it is. Bubbles out of the arse of any Muslim in the Gulf. These people are starting their own fleet, see, an' while crew's no problem, it's not so easy to find officers. The right sort, that is." He was watching me out of the corner of his eyes. "The money's good. Double British rates." He hesitated. "And a bonus at the end."

"End of what?" I asked. "What's the bonus for?"

He shrugged. "For getting the ship there. End of voyage bonus." He was standing with his legs apart, staring at me. "Air passage out, of course. Everything provided."

The two years since I'd come to England fell away. I was back in the Gulf, back in a world where promises are seldom met, nothing is what it seems, and men like Baldwick scavenge the hotels and clubs fomenting bar talk that is the never-never land of salesmen's dreams. Nothing would have induced me to accept an offer from him, but I didn't tell him that. I excused myself on the grounds that I had written a book and would be seeing the publishers shortly.

"Jesus!" he exclaimed and burst out laughing. "I come here offering you the job of first officer on a hundred-thousand tonner, and you talk about a bloody book. You out of your mind?"

"No," I said. "Just a question of values. I know what I want to do with my life."

"Pollution. On the telly you was talking about pollution and crooked tanker owners, the need for government to introduce new laws." He hesitated, eyeing me speculatively. "Maybe these people can help." He said it tentatively and I nearly burst out laughing it was so damned silly. Baldwick, of all people, on the side of the angels! Quick as a flash, he sensed my reaction. "So you won't even discuss it?"

I shook my head.

"I come all the way from Bristol to make you an offer most men would jump at—"

"Then why haven't they? Why come to me?"

"I told you. I saw you on the telly." And he added, "These people, they understand about pollution. They can afford to run their ships so there won't be any. The idea is to improve the tanker image, and they'll put pressure on any government that doesn't behave sensibly."

"What pressure?" I asked.

"How the hell do I know? Political pressure, I imagine. Anyway, Pieter Hals is one of the skippers. He wouldn't have signed on if he hadn't believed they were serious about it."

Hals was the man who had stood on the deck of a flag-of-convenience tanker in the Niger River with a bomb in his hand threatening to blow it up, and himself with it, if the effects of a collision weren't remedied before he sailed. She was scored along one side and leaking oil. The account I had read had commented that he was wilder than the Green Peace movement or the Union leader in Brest who'd called his men out to stop a Greek cargo vessel sailing with an oil leak in the stern gland. "Who are these people?" I asked.

He shook his head, laughing and telling me he wasn't here to gossip about the consortium, just to offer me a job, and if I didn't want it what the hell did it matter to me who the owners were. "They operate in the Gulf, of course, and they want ships' officers, deck as well as engineers." He stood there for a moment, feet apart, with his back to the fire, watching me out of his bright little button eyes. "Tonight I'll be in Falmouth," he said. "I'll be talking to the captain of the *Petros Jupiter*. He'll be looking for another job I wouldn't wonder." He waited, and when I didn't say anything, he nodded. "Okay, suit yourself." He pulled a business card from his wallet, took out what looked like a real gold pen, and after copying some entries from a leather diary onto the back of the card, he handed it to me. "If you change your mind, those are my immediate movements." The card described him as "Consultant." On the back he had written down dates and telephone numbers for Liverpool, Nantes, Marseilles, Dubai.

He stood there a moment longer, pointedly surveying the stone-walled room and the junk furniture. Then he turned and zipped up his fleece-lined jacket. I opened the door for him and as he was going out he paused, looking down at me. "You're not a company man any longer. You want a berth, you got to go out into the market and face all the other ships' officers that's out of a job." His little eyes were cold, his lips a hard line. "I'm warning you, Rodin, you'll find the going rough. A VLCC—you never had anything like that. It's the chance of a lifetime for a man like you." He stood there a moment longer, staring down at me as though to check that his words had sunk in. Then he nodded. "Okay. It's your loss. But if you change your mind, ring me before I leave for France."

He left then and I stood there, watching him as he climbed the path, leaning his body into it, and thinking how odd it was, the power of the media. First the publishers, conjured out of the blue because of the publicity, and now Baldwick, appearing like some evil genie and talking of pollution as though oil slicks could be eliminated by rubbing a few gold coins together.

I went back into the cottage, to another night of loneliness with only the memory of Karen for company. And next day I had a service for her in the local church.

There was still nothing to bury. Nothing had been found of her, nothing at all, so it was just a sort of memorial service to a girl who had immolated herself in protest against oil pollution. Most people seemed to regard it as a futile gesture, but they were kind and they turned up in force. The environmentalists made a bit of a demo out of it, the local press were there and two BBC men from Bristol. The little church was packed and it was raining.

The service was very moving, I think because of all the people and the strength of feeling that reached out to me. And afterward, when one of the reporters started questioning me about her motives, I was in such an emotional state that I just let my feelings rip, telling him I'd get the bastard who put the *Petros Jupiter* on the rocks, killing Karen, killing the birds, ruining our bit of Cornwall. "If the government won't stop it, I will." There was a camera running, everybody staring, and when somebody asked me if I meant to take on the oil companies, I answered him, "No, the shipowners—the tanker owners—the bastards that switch names, companies, ownership —the whole stinking, sodding mess of corrupt tanker dealing . . ." Somebody pulled me away then, Andy I think. I was in tears, coming out of the church, straight from that service. And that night they had a brief flash of that interview on nationwide. I watched it in the lounge of a Penzance hotel over a farewell drink with the Kerrisons, shocked as much by the haggard look of my face, and the tears streaming down it, as by the violence of my words. Then they drove me to the station and I caught the night train to London.

It was five days since it had happened, five miserable days alone at the cottage. On the Saturday, when I had seen the estate agents in Penzance, I had told them they could deal with the contents when they liked, but to leave the cottage until the spring, when the evenings would be drawing out and the daffodils in bloom in the sheltered patch behind the elephant rock. It would sell better then. But though it wouldn't be on the market immediately, the mere fact of having arranged to sell it had had the effect of making me feel an interloper, the place we had striven for and loved so much suddenly no longer part of my life. It added to the bitterness of my departure as the wheels rattled me eastward through the night.

I hadn't bothered about a sleeper. I sat up all the way, dozing fitfully, thinking about the *Petros Jupiter* and what I'd do to that dirty little Greek when I caught up with him. It was either that or start thinking about Karen, and I couldn't face that, not anymore. Not after that service. I felt drained, too nervously exhausted to plan ahead. I didn't even think about the letter from the publishers. That meant thinking constructively—about my writing, about the future. I didn't want to think about the future. I didn't want to face up to a future alone. And so I sat there, my mind drifting on the edge of con-

sciousness, nerves taut and the wheels hammering the name
Speridion into my tired brain. *Aristides Speridion. Aristides
Speridion.*

Dawn broke, cold and grey, the wind blowing out of the
north, a curtain of sleet beginning to whiten the roofs of the
buildings backed on to the railway. It was much too early to
ring the solicitors when we pulled into Paddington, so I took
the Inner Circle to Liverpool Street, checked my two cases
into a locker, and just had time to buy some papers before
catching the next train for Colchester.

Except for a brief paragraph in the *Telegraph* headed "OIL
SLICK DEMO AT CORNISH CHURCH," the *Petros Jupiter* seemed to
have dropped right out of the news. The lead story in all the
papers was the arrest of four more terrorists at the GB Shahpur
Petro-Chemical Company's offices in the City. They were
charged with being implicated in the Piccadilly Underground
explosion that had killed eleven people just before Christmas.

Feeling drowsy as the train ran into the flat Essex country-
side, I went into the snack bar for some coffee. There was a
line and while I was waiting the guard came through, checking tickets. The dining car was full, every seat occupied, and
when I finally got my coffee I took it through into the next
coach and sat down in an almost empty first-class compartment. There was only one occupant, a neat elderly man with
rimless half-glasses who sat hunched in an overcoat in the far
window seat reading the *Economist.* He was making notes and
on the seat beside him several articles on insurance lay on top
of a slim black leather briefcase. Outside the windows, the drizzle had turned to snow, a thick driving veil of white. I held
the paper cup in both hands, sipping the hot coffee and wondering whether I was wasting my time traveling all the way
down to see Ferrers when it would have been so much sim-
pler to phone. Quite probably, Lloyd's Intelligence Services

wouldn't know anything more than had already been released to the press. And if they did, would he tell me?

One thing I was sure about, however . . . if they did know anything more, then I had a far better chance of getting it out of him if I saw him personally. Also, by going to their offices I could see the setup, form some idea of what their sources of information were. I knew they had agents all over the world, but though I had been conscious of the extraordinary global network controlled by Lloyd's of London ever since I had become a ship's officer, I had no real idea how the organization worked, least of all how its Intelligence Services operated. And from Colchester of all places! Why not London?

The answer to that was supplied by the man opposite me. As we neared Colchester, he put his *Economist* carefully away in his briefcase and began gathering his things together. I asked him if he could direct me to Sheepen Place and he looked at me quickly with a little smile. "Lloyd's Shipping Press?"

"No, Intelligence Services," I said.

He nodded. "Same thing. You're a ship captain, are you?"

I shook my head. "Mate only, though I've got my master's certificate. I left the sea a few years back."

"Ah, you work for marine solicitors, eh?" He glanced out of the window. "Snowing quite hard now. My wife's meeting me with the car. We can give you a lift." And when I said I could get a taxi, that I didn't want to take them out of their way, he said, "No trouble. It's quite close. Within walking distance." He gave a little laugh. "Except that it's not a good day for walking, eh?"

The train was slowing now, and as we took our place in the corridor, I asked him why such a vital part of Lloyd's should be tucked away in an East Anglian coastal town. He looked at me, frowning. "I suppose because members of Lloyd's traditionally live in East Anglia. The best of 'em, anyway," he added, smiling. "In the great days of the railways, Liverpool

Street was a handy way of getting out into the country. Now a lot of the big insurance companies—some of the largest of the Lloyd's brokers—have moved their administrative organizations out of the City, to Colchester, Ipswich, even as far north as Norwich. Costs are a lot less than in the City and staff don't have to commute so far." The train jerked to a stop and we got out into a bitter wind.

It was much colder than it had been in London, the snow small-flaked and hard like ice. The car his wife was driving was a brand-new Mercedes, their background a whole world away from mine. We drove down under the railway bridge, the road curving away to the right. The snow was heavier now, the Town Hall tower, which marked the center of Colchester, only just visible on its hill. The insurance man turned from answering his wife's queries about a frozen tap and said, "You know, I envy you ships' officers who handle marine solicitors' inquiries. Not only does it take you all over the world, but you're dealing all the time with case histories, all the exciting side of insurance. Whereas people like me, we make money, of course, but broking, looking after Names, dealing with accounts, finances, that sort of thing—it's all very humdrum, you know. Down here I've got an office employs between two and three hundred, and all the time flogging back and forth to London." We were on a new road, crossing a big double culvert where the Colne ran between banks of snow. "Across the A12 traffic circle, then left and left again at the next," he said to his wife, and she answered sharply, "I know where it is, Alfred."

He waved a hand to the ruins of a colossal flint and tile wall that climbed away from us as the car swung. "That's the outer remains of Camulodunum, the Roman center of East Anglia." SHEEPEN PLACE appeared on a nameplate edged with snow, an industrial estate doubling back toward the A12 traffic circle and the meadowland beyond. The car slowed, turned right into the entrance of a printing works. "Don't forget the ramps," he said. "Two of them."

"I haven't forgotten." She almost stalled the car as we bumped over the first, which showed only as the slightest hump in the wind-drifted snow. A board announced LLOYD's SHIPPING PRESS and I saw there was a three-story brick building beyond the printing works. No mention of Intelligence Services.

"You've not been here before?" He was watching for the next ramp, not looking at me, and I guessed it was just an idle question.

"No," I said.

"Anybody in particular?"

"A Mr. Ferrers."

We bumped over the second ramp. The Shipping Press building was stretched over the parking lot on steel pillars. "What department?"

"Special Inquiries."

He nodded. "Ah yes, of course, Marine Frauds." He turned in his seat, eyeing me curiously as the car slid to a stop outside the plate-glass entrance doors. "Which particular marine casualty are you investigating—or aren't you at liberty to say?"

I hesitated. "I've come to see him about the *Petros Jupiter*."

He nodded. "That was an odd one, eh?" He turned to his wife. "Remember, Margaret? A young woman—she blew it up and herself with it."

"Yes, I remember, Alfred."

"An odd way to end your life."

"She didn't—" I began, but then I stopped myself. Better leave it at that. No good trying to explain about oil slicks and pollution and seabirds dying. I began to get out and he said, "Intelligence Services is on the second floor."

I thanked him. I thanked them both and stood there in the bitter wind until their car was out of sight round the other side of the building. Now that I was here I wasn't quite certain how to proceed. A muddy Triumph pulled into a parking place and a big, fair man in a rumpled suit and no topcoat got out. I pushed open the plate-glass door. There was an elevator and some stairs and it was warm. I took the stairs. The swinging doors facing the elevator on the first floor were clearly marked SHIPPING PRESS. Through glass panels I could see men working at their desks, some in their shirtsleeves. It was an open-plan office covering virtually the whole floor, and there were visual-display units scattered about so that I knew the operation was computerized.

The swinging doors on the second floor were completely anonymous, no mention of Intelligence Services. As on the floor below, the offices were open-plan with a lot of electrical equipment—VDUs and telex machines—particularly on the far side where the wind, blowing straight in off the North Sea, drove the snow in near horizontal white lines across the large, clear, sheet-glass windows. The elevator doors opened behind me. It was the fair man in the rumpled suit, and as he was pushing past me, he paused briefly, holding the swinging doors open with his shoulder. "Looking for somebody?"

"Ferrers," I said.

"Barty Ferrers." He nodded and I stepped inside. "Expecting you?" He was already slipping his jacket off.

"Yes," I said and gave him my name.

The large open-plan floor was very warm. A lot of men there, most of them in their shirtsleeves, the desks flat tables littered with books and papers. A few women on the far side, and one girl sitting with seven or eight men at a big table with a card on it marked CASUALTY ROOM.

I could see he was a bit doubtful and I said quickly, "It's about the *Petros Jupiter*."

His eyes widened then, a sudden glint of recognition. "Yes, of course. The *Petros Jupiter*." He gave me a sympathetic pat on the shoulder. "I'm Ted Fairley. I run *Lloyd's Confidential Index*." He gave me a big jovial smile. "That's the prudent in-

surers' index to vessels of doubtful virtue." He turned and sur-
veyed the room. "Can't see Barty at the moment. But Tim
Spurling, the other half of the Marine Fraud twins, he's there."
He had his jacket off now and I followed him between the
crowded tables. "Barty contacted you, did he?"

"No. Was he going to?"

"Yes, I think the legal boys want to talk to you." He stopped
at a desk with a typewriter and a litter of books and tossed his
jacket onto the empty chair. "That's my square foot or so of
lebensraum. Casualty History on one side, Casualty Reporting
on the other. Very convenient and never a dull moment. Ah,
there's Barty." He veered toward an area of the floor jutting
out to the north and full of the clatter of telexes and operators
keying information into visual-display units. "Information
Room," he said over his shoulder. "This is where our two thousand agents all over the world report in by telex. Barty!" He
had to raise his voice against the clatter.

Barty Ferrers wasn't in the least what I had expected. He
was a plump, jolly-looking man with a round, babyish face and
thick horn-rimmed glasses that were bifocal. He looked up
from the telex he was reading, and when he realized who I
was, his eyes seemed to freeze behind the thick glasses. They
were pale blue, the sort of cold blue eyes that Swedes often
have. "What the hell are you doing here?" I started to explain,
but he cut me short. "Never mind. I've been trying to get you
at that Sennen number."

"The ship was wrecked deliberately, then?"

"We don't know that."

"Why were you phoning me, then?"

"Marine solicitors. They want to see you."

"Why?"

He shook his head. "Can't talk here. First—read that." He
handed me a telex slip one of the operators had passed across
to him. "Came in last night."

It was from Lloyd's agent at La Rochelle and dated the pre-

vious day, January 11: VAGUE D'OR LOCKED INTO TRAWLER BASIN
HERE TWO DAYS AGO. CAPTAIN HAS NO INFORMATION ARISTIDES
SPERIDION. MAN TAKEN ON BOARD OFF PORTHCURNOW IS SHIP'S
ENGINEER HENRI CHOFFEL. THIS MAN LEAVES IMMEDIATELY FOR
PARIS EN ROUTE BY AIR TO BAHRAIN. THIS IS CERTAIN, AS ALL NEC-
ESSARY BOOKINGS MADE LOCALLY. The telex then went on to
describe Choffel as short with dark hair—POSSIBLY PIED NOIR,
SPEAKS FRENCH WITH AN ACCENT, AQUILINE FEATURES, AGE 46,
WIFE DEAD. DAUGHTER ONLY. ADDRESS 5042 LES TUFFEAUX,
PARNAY, NEAR SAUMUR-ON-LOIRE. HOLDS FRENCH PASSPORT.

Time and occupation right, the Breton fishing boat, too. I
was remembering a list I had read in one of the papers giving
the names of French boats operating off the Cornish coast. I
was almost certain one of them had been the *Vague d'Or*.
Only the man's name was different. "He must have had two
passports," I said.

Ferrers nodded, handing me another telex. "This just came
in."

It was from Bahrain: SUBJECT OF QUERY ARRIVED BAHRAIN
Y-DAY MORNING. WENT STRAIGHT ABOARD FREIGHTER CORSAIRE,
BUT NOT AS ENGINEER, AS PASSENGER. CORSAIRE NOW TAKING ON
FUEL PREPARATORY TO SAILING.

So by now he would have gone. Ferrers took the telexes
from me and passed them to one of the operators with instructions to transmit the information to Forthright & Co. "They're
the solicitors." He gave me a quick, searching glance, then
jerked his head toward the far corner of the floor. "We don't
encourage visitors," he said as we got away from the clatter of
the telexes. "So I'd be glad if you'd keep it to yourself that
you've been here."

"It doesn't give the ship's destination," I said.

"No, but I can soon find that out." He pushed past a man
with an armful of the *Lloyd's List* and then we were in his little corner and he had plunked himself down at a table with a
VDU on it. "Let's see what the computer says." While his

fingers were busy on the keyboard, he introduced me to Spurling, a sharp-featured, sandy-haired man with a long freckled face and bushy sideburns. What the computer said was INSTRUCTION INCORRECT. "Hell!" He tried it again with the same result. "Looks as though our fellow in Bahrain got the name of the ship wrong."

Spurling leaned over his shoulder. "Try the French spelling —with an 'e' at the end, same as in his telex."

He tried it and immediately line after line of print began coming up on the VDU screen, everything about the ship, the fact that it was French and due to sail today, also its destination, which was Karachi. He glanced up at me and I could see the wheels turning. "That ship you were mate on, plying between Bombay and the Gulf—based on Karachi, wasn't she?"

I nodded.

"And the crew—Pakistani?"

"Some of them."

"So you speak the language?"

"I speak a little Urdu, yes."

He nodded, turning his head to stare at the windows and the driving lines of snow. "Choffel," he murmured. "That name rings a bell." He turned to Spurling. "Remember that little Lebanese freighter they found waterlogged but still afloat off Pantelleria? I suddenly thought of her in my bath this morning. Not in connection with Choffel, of course. But Speridion. Wasn't Speridion the name of the ship's engineer?"

Spurling thought for a moment, then shook his head. "Speridion, Choffel—not sure." He was frowning in concentration as he lit a cigarette from the butt of his last and stubbed out the remains in the tobacco tin beside his IN-tray. "It's quite a time back. Seventy-six, maybe seventy-seven." He hesitated, drawing on the cigarette. "The crew abandoned her. Skipper's name, I remember—"

"Never mind the skipper. It's the engineer we want."

"It'll be on the file. I'm certain I put it on the file." He reached over to a small steel cabinet, but then he checked. "I need the ship's name. You know that. Just give me the name . . ."

But Ferrers couldn't remember the name, only that there had been a Greek engineer involved. From what they said I gathered the cabinet contained confidential casualty information that included the background of ships' officers and crew members known to have been involved in fraud. Then Spurling was muttering to himself, still frowning in concentration: "A crook Lebanese company owned her. Can't recall the company's name, but Beirut—that's where the ship was registered. A small tanker. I'm sure it was a tanker." And he added, "Pity you can't remember the name. Everything in that file is listed under the name of a ship."

"I know that."

"Then you'd better start searching again."

"I've been through two years of casualty records already this morning. That's seventy microfiches."

"You love it." Spurling grinned at me, nodding to a shelf full of thick loose-leaf volumes on the wall behind us. "All our casualty records are microfilmed and filed in those binders. The VDU there acts as a viewing box and you can get a printout at the touch of a button. It's Barty's own personal toy. Try the winter of seventy-five–seventy-six."

"Back to where we first started keeping records?" Ferrers got slowly to his feet. "It'll take me an hour to go through that lot."

Spurling smiled at him wickedly. "It's what you're paid for, isn't it?"

Ferrers gave a snort. "May I remind you we're supposed to be keeping tabs on over six hundred vessels for various clients?"

"They'll never know, and if you pull the information Forthright wants out of the box, who's to say you're wasting your time?" Spurling looked at me and dropped an eyelid, his face deadpan. "Come to think of it, I doubt if it was winter. They were several days in an open boat. Try March or April, seventy-seven. She had her tanks full of arms—that's why you remember her."

Ferrers nodded, reaching down the second volume from the far end of the shelf. I watched him as he searched quickly through the fiche pockets, extracted one, and slipped it into the scanning slot. Immediately the VDU screen came alive with information which changed quickly as he shifted from microfilm to microfilm. And when he had finished with that fiche, I put it back in its pocket for him, while he began searching the next. Each fiche, measuring about six by four inches, was imprinted with rows of tiny little microfilms hardly bigger than pinheads.

He was over half an hour, working first forward through 1977, then backward into '76. He worked in the silence of total concentration, and with Spurling's attention divided between his typewriter and the telephone, they seemed to have forgotten all about me. At one point Spurling passed me a telex giving the latest report on the *Petros Jupiter* salvage situation. Smit International—the Dutch salvage people—had announced their intention of withdrawing from any further attempt to salvage the wreck. Their divers had only been able to operate for two days since the explosion, a total of eight and a half hours. But apparently this had been sufficient to establish the general condition of the wreck, which was now lying in three sections to the north of Kettle's Bottom, with only the skeletal remains of the superstructure awash at low tide. The effect of the explosion—followed by the intense heat generated by the ignition of the five tanks containing oil—had been such that they regarded any attempt to salvage the remains of the vessel as quite profitless. And they added that, in its present position, they did not consider it a danger to shipping. Further, all tanks were now completely ruptured and empty of oil.

There were three sheets of the telexed report and I had just come to the end of it when Ferrers suddenly exclaimed, "Got it! The *Stella Rosa*. March 20, 1976." Spurling looked up and nodded, smiling. "Of course. The *Stella Rosa*."

"Outward bound from Tripoli to Algiers." Ferrers was reading from the scanner, his face close to the screen. "Arms for the Polisario—Sam-7s and Kalashnikovs." He straightened up, pressing the button that gave him the printout, and when he had it, he passed it to Spurling. But by then Spurling had the *Stella Rosa* file out and was running quickly through it; "Skipper Italian, Mario Pavesi from Palermo. Ah, here we are. Second engineer: Aristides Speridion. No address given. Not among the survivors. First engineer—now we have something— guess who? None other than Henri Choffel, French. He was picked up and is described here as suspect on his past record. He was chief engineer of the *Olympic Ore* and is thought to have been implicated in her sinking in 1972. At the inquiry into the sinking of the *Stella Rosa*, he claimed it was Speridion who opened the sea cocks." He passed the file to Ferrers. "Good hunch of yours."

Ferrers gave a little shrug. "No indication then that Speridion got away in a boat?"

Spurling shook his head. "No. And no record that he managed to land on Pantelleria. All it says is—'no indication that he is still alive.'"

"So Choffel knew he was dead. He must have known, otherwise he wouldn't have used the man's name. And to use Speridion's name he'd need his papers." Ferrers was staring down at the file. "I wonder what really happened to Speridion? It says here—'At the inquiry held at Palermo, Chief Engineer Henri Choffel stated that he and two of his men tried to stop the flow of water into the engine room, but the cocks on the seawater inlet to the cooling systems had been opened and then damaged. Speridion had been on duty. Choffel thought he had probably been paid to sink the ship by agents of the Moroccan government.'" Ferrers shook his head, sucking in air through his teeth. "And on the *Petros Jupiter* he was using the name Speridion. That means it's almost certainly sabotage."

"And if he did have the Greek's papers and the police start looking into the *Stella Rosa* sinking—" Spurling hesitated. "It could be murder, couldn't it?"

I thought he was jumping to conclusions. But perhaps that was because I had been thinking all the time in terms of Speridion. Choffel was something different, something new. It took time for my mind to switch. But murder as well as sabotage . . . "God Almighty!" I said. "Nobody who'd killed his second engineer, and then accused him of sabotaging the ship, would dream of using the man's name."

"Wouldn't he?" Spurling had turned to his typewriter, the file beside him. "If I let you loose on that filing cabinet, you'd be surprised at the stupidity of some of the marine frauds and the damn fool things men do. They're amateurs, most of them, not professionals. Remember the *Salem,* sunk off the West African coast right within sight of a BP tanker? They never seem to realize it takes time to sink a really big ship. I tell you, they do the craziest things."

"If they didn't," Ferrers said, "there isn't a member of any marine syndicate at Lloyd's who'd be making money. They'd be losing their shirts instead." He turned as Fairley appeared at his elbows, a telex in his hand.

"Just come in," he said. "Michael Stewart's box. Anything we can tell him about the *Howdo Stranger.* It's gone missing." He placed the telex on Spurling's typewriter. "I've checked the *Confidential Index.* Nothing. Hardly surprising. It's owned and run by Gulf Oil Development."

"A tanker, then?" Spurling picked up the telex and began reading it.

Fairley nodded. "About the same size as the *Aurora B,* the GODCO ship that went missing two months ago." He leaned over Spurling's shoulder, checking the telex. "This one's 116,000 tons. She had a full cargo for Japan. Same destination, you see. And loaded out of the same port, Mina Zayed." He straightened up with a shrug. "She's ten years old, but she'd just passed survey A1, yet now, suddenly, she fails to report on schedule."

"Where?" Ferrers asked.

"Estimated probable position somewhere southwest of Sri Lanka."

"And the radio schedule?"

"Twice weekly. Same as *Aurora B*."

"Okay," he said. "I'll look up the *Aurora B* details, let them have a printout of that. Then we'll see what else we can cobble together."

Standing there, totally ignored now, I was surprised at the speed with which their attention had switched—Spurling already hunched over the VDU, checking with the computer, Ferrers reaching for the nearest binder, searching for the fiche on which the microfilmed details of the *Aurora B* casualty has been stored. "Two of them can't have blown up." Fairley pushed a hand up through his fair hair, which was now as rumpled as the rest of him. "Two GODCO tankers in two months—it's not possible."

"What about the *Berge Istra* and the *Berge Vanga*?" Ferrers said without looking round. "Norwegian, and just as good a stable as GODCO."

Spurling looked up from the telex he had been reading and said, "She left the Abu Dhabi port of Zayed at 1800 hours, January 5." He turned to Fairley. "When did she miss her radio schedule?"

"Yesterday afternoon. It's in the telex."

"Yes, but it doesn't give the time."

"I checked the *Aurora B* schedule," Fairley told him. "She was reporting in at 1400 hours, Tuesdays and Fridays."

"So this one could be the same time, but Mondays and Thursdays." Spurling had the *Lloyd's Maritime Atlas* open at the Indian Ocean page and was penciling figures on a slip of paper. "That's it, then. West or southwest of Sri Lanka. Just about where the *Aurora B* missed her schedule. Previous schedule would have been roughly between Muscat and Karachi, so if she really is a casualty, then it could have happened anywhere between there and Sri Lanka."

Fairley nodded. "You're thinking it could be fraud."

"We've had radio frauds before. It became quite fashionable a couple of years back."

"That was cargo," Ferrers said over his shoulder. "Cargo that didn't exist, shipped in vessels that didn't exist or else had their names borrowed for the occasion. And all of them owned by companies Lloyd's wouldn't consider insuring. But GODCO. That's something entirely different." His machine suddenly rolled out a sheet of paper, which he tore off and handed to Spurling. "That's the *Aurora B* casualty information. Not very much to go on." He suddenly seemed conscious of the fact that I was still standing there. "I'd better run you up to the station. You're not supposed to be here, and this doesn't concern you."

"You've nothing more you can tell me about the *Petros Jupiter?*" I asked.

"No, nothing."

"Except," Spurling said, "that the lead underwriter for the *Petros Jupiter* is the same as for these two tankers. Same solicitors, too."

"That's confidential," Ferrers cut in sharply.

No question now of getting anything more out of them. Ferrers hustled me out of the building and into his car, driving fast, in a hurry to get back. I envied him his total involvement. He really seemed to enjoy it. "We're just backroom boys really, but when it's a case of fraud—well, it gets quite exciting at times." We were crossing the Colne, now a black gut between the white of snow-plastered buildings. "Our job is to feed information to the marine solicitors; in extreme cases, to the police." He grinned at me as we skidded on the traffic circle.

"When Lloyd's is faced with marine crooks, then it's our wits against theirs and every case is different. It's teamwork mainly—and sharp memories, a bloody good filing system, and a computer."

He skidded the car to a standstill outside Colchester station ticket office, then scribbled a name and a telephone number on one of his cards and handed it to me. "Forthright & Co.— they're the marine solicitors for the three syndicates run by Michael Stewart." He pushed open the door for me. "A Mr. Saltley. Give him a ring while you're in London. He wants to speak to you."

"About the *Petros Jupiter?*"

He hesitated. But all he said was, "Just give him a ring— that's all." And he added, leaning across to talk to me as I pocketed his card and stepped onto the hard-packed snow, "He's a nice guy is Michael Stewart. Lives only a few miles away, and if this tanker really has gone missing, then he's in trouble. That's what I hear anyway. So go and see Saltley, will you?" He drove off then, slamming the door shut as the Cortina's wheels churned the snow, and I went into the station wondering why he thought I could help when all I was interested in was the *Petros Jupiter*.

CHAPTER THREE

IT WAS JUST AFTER TWELVE-THIRTY when I got back to London. It had been a slow journey with several stops and as I made my way to a telephone booth I was feeling tired and cold, my mind still on the *Petros Jupiter,* knowing I would have to move fast if I was to catch up with Choffel in Karachi. I hadn't much money, and an advance on the book was the only chance I had of raising the air fare.

But when I phoned the publishers, the man who had written to me had already left for lunch. I made an appointment for three that afternoon, and then, because it was still snowing and I didn't imagine the sort of lodging I could afford would have a phone, I rang Forthright & Co. Again I was out of luck, Saltley's secretary informing me he was out and she didn't know when he would be back. She tried to discourage me from ringing later, but when I told her my name, she seemed to brighten up. Mr. Saltley, she said, would definitely like to see me, and as soon as possible. He was attending a twenty-first birthday luncheon party at the Savoy and would be back by four at the latest. Could I ring again then?

I had some food at the station snack bar, then got my suitcase out of the locker and took the tube to Stepney Green. Outside the station the Mile End Road seemed strangely quiet, the sound of the traffic muffled by a dirty carpet of salted slush. I crossed the road and headed south for a boardinghouse I had used before. It was in a long street of terraced houses down toward the river, and when I knocked at the door, it was opened by the same big-bosomed, bold-eyed landlady. I had forgotten her name until she reminded me. It was Mrs. Steinway. She put me in the basement, which was the only room she had vacant, and after settling in and having a quick cup of tea with her, I walked back through the snow to Stepney Green station and took a train to South Kensington.

Jordan's, the publishers to whom I had sent my book, was a small firm specializing in wildlife and natural history. It was just after three when I reached their office in Queen's Gate, one of those white porticoed buildings almost opposite the Natural History Museum. A pretty little girl with a streaming cold took me up to Ken Jordan's office on the first floor, which was little bigger than a partitioned cubicle, the ceiling showing part of the ornate plaster design of a larger room. There was a window looking across to the Museum and the walls were lined with bookshelves that overflowed into stacked heaps on the floor.

Jordan proved to be a rather intense individual with sandy hair and eyes too close together, his face long and the lips turned up at the corners in what appeared to be a perpetual smile. He had my typescript on the desk in front of him, on top of an untidy litter of books, letters, and galleys, and as soon as I was seated, instead of talking about my book he went into a long monologue about the one I ought to write. "You owe it to your wife." He said that several times. He wanted me to start again, writing the whole story of Balkaer from Karen's point of view . . .

"Write it in the first person. Imagine you're really your wife, everything from her angle, right?" His pale, rather protuberant eyes stared at me urgently. "I'm sure you can do it. Her feelings as she's cleaning up those half-dead birds, what she thinks about the government, the oil companies, the men who run the tankers, how the idea gradually forms in her mind—immolation, a spectacular, suicidal gesture—"

"It wasn't suicide," I said quickly.

"No no, of course not." He gave a high little laugh, almost a giggle. "But that's how the public sees it now. And it's the public that buys books. So you give them what they want, use your imagination. A little invention. Dramatize it. Build it up." And then he had the nerve to ask me whether she had tried it before.

"How do you mean?" I could hear the hostility in my voice, feel anger building up inside me.

"Just that. Had she tried it before—" He stopped there and opened the folder, leafing through the pages Karen had typed so carefully. "That oil slick you described. Not the first one." He found the page he was looking for. It was near the end. "The one in November. Now, if she tried to set fire to it and failed . . . You see what I'm getting at? It would make it so much more dramatic—her feelings when it didn't work, the sense of anticlimax." He paused, staring at me. "A nice buildup, you see, to the end of the book—very exciting, very moving . . . the reader having been through it all before when it didn't work, and then, the next time, knowing it's for real, that she's going to kill herself."

"She didn't mean to," I said again. "She wasn't thinking of suicide, only of setting light—"

"No, but you see what I'm getting at. So dramatic, eh? And that's what you want, isn't it, to make the point she was trying to make? The news story—that's over, finished now. What we want is something much more personal, something deeply moving." He was leaning forward, his voice quiet and persuasive. "I'm sure you can do it, Mr. Rodin. It's just a question of putting yourself in your wife's—er, seaboots"—he smiled, trying to lighten his words—"seeing it as she might have seen it, and building the whole thing up, dramatizing it, making it exciting, sensational even—it needs fictionalizing, you see."

"You aren't interested then in what I've already written?"

"No." He shook his head. "No, not really." And he added

quickly as I began to get to my feet, "It's nicely written. Don't misunderstand me. You can write. But these are difficult times. I don't think we could sell it, not now. But the book I've just outlined . . . I'm sure we could sell that. It has excitement, emotional involvement, action—it could be a very moving book. We could try one of the Sundays too. It could make a good two- or three-part serial."

"But not if I wrote it the way I saw it, the way it really happened?"

He shook his head. "No." He banged the typescript shut. "What we're talking about is a first book. Trevor Rodin. Nobody's heard of you, you see. You're new, unknown. So we've got to give it depth, excite people, give the reader something to get his teeth into—'Husband writes the full intimate story of his wife's final, terrible decision.' See what I mean? It's moving. It would tear at their hearts—"

"No." I was on my feet now, staring down at him, hating him for his callous rejection of all those months of work, for the way he was trying to get me to twist the truth to fit his own idea of what was marketable.

"Please," he said, leaning forward again and gazing urgently up at me. "Don't misunderstand me—I'm only trying to help. Our job as publishers is to produce books that authors like you write, and then to market them. Each book is a joint venture as it were, the author investing his time and his expertise, the publisher his money. It costs money to launch a book and my job is to see that the final product in each case is something people will want to buy." And he added, "Take my advice, Mr. Rodin—I have some experience—write it the way I have suggested, from your wife's point of view, building it up to the point where she is so emotionally desperate she goes out to blow the ship up, and herself—"

"It was an accident," I said angrily. I could see so clearly what he was driving at, and there was a part of me that was prepared to accept that he was right, that this was the way to handle it if it was to capture the imagination of the public. But it wasn't the truth; it wasn't the way it had happened. "She didn't mean to kill herself."

"How do you know? You can't be sure what was in her mind." And he added, "A little author's license . . . what difference does it make? Or can't you do it? Is that the trouble, that you don't feel you're a good enough writer—"

"I could do it," I said angrily. "But I won't." I reached across his desk and picked up the typescript. If I stayed in that untidy office any longer I knew I'd be tempted. Everything seen through her eyes, using my imagination—I'd always wanted to be a writer and I needed the money. Of course I could do it, the scenes already flashing through my mind. But in the end my memory of Karen would be blurred, the reality of her and what she had tried to do lost in a ghost creature of my own imagination.

"You won't do it, then?"

"No."

"I'm sorry." He pushed his chair back and stood facing me. "If you change your mind—"

"I shan't."

"But if you do, don't leave it too long. A few months and there'll be another tanker on the rocks spilling oil somewhere else." He held out his hand, limp and cold, and I left him, hurrying down the stairs and out into the street, clutching the typescript. The pavements were tight-packed ice and the ornate Victorian edifice of the Museum facing the Cromwell Road was picked out in thick white snow lines.

I was so angry I felt like flinging the typescript into the gutter. I had been sure they would take it, ever since I had received Jordan's letter. I had been so certain I would come out of that meeting with a contract and a check for the advance that I hadn't even checked the tramp rates or looked at the *Shipping Index;* I hadn't the slightest idea what the chances of a berth were for anyone who had been ashore as long as I had.

My breath smoked in the cold air and I became conscious of the traffic building up, moving sluggishly through the snow as London headed for home early. It seemed to be getting colder by the minute, the wind northwesterly now, the snowflakes like glass flying in horizontal lines past my face. How disappointed Karen would have been, all those evenings spent listening to me as I had read passages aloud in the lamplight—all the typing! She had felt at times almost as involved with it as I was. And now . . . How long would it be before the *Corsaire* reached Karachi? Or had the ship already arrived? Perhaps she would be anchored outside with all the other freighters waiting for a berth . . . But then I remembered the new harbor. It would be finished now and once the *Corsaire* docked Choffel could disappear into the labyrinth of the bazaars. Or maybe he'd find a berth on some vessel headed for Japan, Australia—some distant part of the world beyond my reach.

The man's escape and the book's rejection became fused in my mind, the anger of despair gripping me as I tramped through the snow, the cold eating into me. And then suddenly there was a new thought in my head. Dramatize it, the man had said, so that's what I'd do. I'd rewrite it—the whole story, her death, everything. And the end of it would be my search for Aristides Speridion or Henri Choffel, or whatever he might be calling himself when I caught up with him. I'd find him somehow. I'd find the bastard, and when I'd done with him, then I'd write it all down, just as it happened—for Karen's sake, for the sake of all those birds, for my own peace of mind. And reaching that decision, the emptiness, the hopeless feeling of depression was gone, determination taking hold.

I don't know why, but I was suddenly remembering my mother, conscious of the same obstinate streak that had made her go it alone, bring up a child on a nurse's pay in post-Mau Mau Nairobi, and later in the Gulf, in Dubai, where she had died of pulmonary pneumonia from overwork. I could hardly remember what she looked like, only that she was small and neat, and that she'd a lot of guts, a lot of nervous energy that had burned her up before she was forty. That and the climate, and the men she couldn't resist.

Back at South Kensington station, I went straight to a phone booth and rang Forthright. Saltley was back from his luncheon at the Savoy, but he was on the phone. I hadn't enough change to hang on, so I rang off and stood there, feeling very alone as I watched the milling crowd of office workers hurrying to get home before railway lines froze and roads became impassable. They were all so busy, so engrossed in their own worlds. I tried again a few minutes later and the girl said he was still talking. I had to ring twice more before she was finally able to put me through and a quiet, rather abrupt voice said, "Saltley here."

Ferrers had clearly briefed him about me, and of course he had read the papers. He said he'd like to see me as soon as possible, but he had a rather urgent case on and would be tied up for a couple of hours at least. I suggested that perhaps I could see him at his office the following morning, but he said he would be preparing a brief and in court most of the day. He hesitated, then told me that, because of the weather, he had arranged to stay the night at his club. "You a sailing man, by any chance?"

"I had the loan of a boat once in Karachi," I told him. "A dinghy really."

He seemed relieved. "Then at least you won't be entirely out of your depth." And he suggested I had supper with him at the Royal Ocean Racing Club in St. James's Place. "Seven-thirty suit you? And if the bar's crowded, then we'll go into the Fastnet Room and talk there."

I had two and a half hours to kill. I went into the Science Museum, which being a government building was pleasantly warm, and stayed there until it closed, idling the time away activating all the working models, the steam engines and looms and laser beams. There was hardly anybody left when they pushed us out into the night. The wind had dropped, the air still and deathly cold. I took the Underground to St. James's Park, bought an evening paper, and read it over a cup of coffee in a cafeteria off Victoria Street. The City page carried the year's results of the Norwegian subsidiary of a large British shipping company. They had half their ships laid up and had been operating at a loss throughout the second half of the year.

I wished to God I hadn't seen it, for it did nothing to lift my morale as I went out into the frozen streets of London again. They had a dead look now, hardly any traffic. I walked up to St. James's Park. There wasn't a soul there. It was as though I were the ghost of somebody who had returned after some terrible science fiction disaster. The water was a black pit under the bridge. The ducks and wild geese stood motionless on the ice, the flat white covering of snow scuffed with the imprint of their feet. The scene matched my mood. I could no longer conjure the soft Welsh lilt of Karen's voice, or see her standing there beside me. I was alone now—intensely, intolerably alone —with only anger and hatred for company.

I stayed there, keeping a frozen vigil with the birds, until Big Ben boomed out the quarter after seven. Then I walked slowly across the Mall and up past the Palace to St. James's Street. I seemed to be the only human being left alive. A taxi crept past me as I turned into St. James's Place. The Royal Ocean Racing Club was right at the end, past the Stafford Hotel where the taxi was now trying to turn. Somebody entered the Club ahead of me; the portholes of the inner doors momentarily revealed two brass-rimmed eyes staring out at a dirty heap of snow piled against the railings.

Saltley was waiting for me in the bar, which was up the stairs past a nasty-looking picture of the Fastnet Rock in a gale. It was a bright, cheerful place full of members locked into London by the state of the roads. He came forward to greet me, small, almost gnomelike, with straw-colored hair and thick glasses through which a pair of sharp, intensely blue eyes peered owlishly. He was younger than I had expected, mid-thirties, perhaps a little more, and as though to put me at my ease he said his odd appearance—those were the words he used, giving me a lopsided grin—was due to Swedish fore-bears, the name, too, originally Swedish, but bastardized to Saltley by dumb Anglo-Saxons who couldn't get their tongues round it. The way he put it, I thought he probably knew my father had been a Scot.

Even now I don't know Saltley's Christian name. Everybody seemed to call him by his surname, his friends shortening it to Salt or Salty, even Old Salt, but what his initials, C.R., stood for I still don't know. It didn't take me long in the atmosphere of that club to realize why he had asked me if I were a sailing man. The conversation as we stood drinking at the bar was general, the talk all about sailing, ocean races mainly—last sea-son's and the Southern Cross series in Australia which had just finished with the Sydney-Hobart.

It was only when we went into the dining room that his at-tention focused on me personally. Those blue eyes, that crooked, very sensitive mouth, the soft, quiet voice—instead of finding out what it was he wanted to see me about, I found myself telling him about my life with Karen and the strange urge that had taken hold of me very early in life, trying to ex-plain why I had wanted to become a writer. I told him some-thing of my background, too, the way I had been brought up. "So you never knew your father?" He said it very quickly, reaching for the wine bottle.

"No." Fortunately, we had a table to ourselves, the back-ground noise of conversation drowning my words as I added with that mixture of belligerence and frankness that I could never quite conceal, "And my mother never married."

He filled my glass, smiling lopsidedly at me. "That worry you?" He drank slowly, watching me and letting the silence run on. Oddly enough I felt no hostility to him, no anger at the expert way in which he had maneuvered me into blurting out more than I had intended. "It shouldn't," he said. "Not now. But, of course, things were different in the fifties. Something we're apt to forget. We live in the present and our memories are short. But scars—deep, emotional scars—they remain in all of us, rooted there and producing gut reactions." He cut into his steak, concentrating on his food for a moment. "So you ran pretty wild as a kid?"

I nodded.

"Where?"

"I told you, Nairobi, Dubai . . ." I stopped there, remembering a scene on the waterfront, a little Baluch boy they'd drowned.

"And Karachi?" he asked. "Ferrers said something about Karachi."

I nodded.

"That was after your mother died."

"Yes."

"You were fourteen then. Was it to contact your father's old regiment that you jumped a dhow headed for Karachi?" He was suddenly looking straight at me.

"I went to Gwadar," I said.

"Ah yes." He nodded. "Dubai-Baluchistan—the old pearls-and-slaves route. Quite a journey for a kid of fourteen on his own, down the Gulf, out through the Straits of Hormuz to Gwadar, then to Karachi and almost the length of West Pakistan to Peshawar."

I stopped eating then, wondering how the hell he knew all that. "It was a long time ago," I said.

He gave me a little apologetic smile. "I've had somebody checking up on you."

"Why?"

He didn't answer that. And when I asked him what else he had found out about me, he said, "Your father was a lieutenant in the Khyber Rifles. After Partition he joined the Trucial

Oman Scouts. He was stationed near Sharjah. That's how he met your mother. She was a nurse, an Anglo-Indian, I think."

"If you know all that," I said angrily, "then you'll know that he was killed in the Muscat war. You'll also no doubt know that my mother's mother, my grandmother, was from the North West Frontier, an Afridi." And I added, the tone of belligerence back in my voice, "My mother was hot-blooded, very beautiful, a wonderfully exciting person—but it's nothing to do with you what she was. Nothing to do with the *Petros Jupiter* either."

"I'm sorry." He gave a shrug and the same little apologetic smile. "Force of habit. I make my living asking awkward questions." The strange, bony features were touched suddenly with humor, the eyes smiling at me. "Please—don't let your food get cold." He waved his hand at my plate and switched the conversation to dinghy sailing. He navigated now for a man with a Class I ocean racer, but he'd started in dinghies.

It was after we had finished eating, sitting over our coffee, that he finally came to the point. "I think you know roughly what my job is, but probably not much about the way marine solicitors operate." And he went on to explain that there were only about a dozen firms in the City specializing in the legal side of marine insurance. At Forthright they concentrated on hull insurance. There were other firms that concentrated on cargoes. "But as I say, there are only a handful of us trying to sort out all the legal problems that occur when there is an incident—fire, collision, fraud, anything concerning ships or their cargoes that results in an insurance claim. It's very specialized and often there is a great deal of money involved. We're so specialized, in fact, that we're involved worldwide, not just the London market." He suddenly got to his feet. "Sorry, you haven't got a drink. Brandy or port?"

"Rum, if I could," I said, and he nodded.

"Good idea. Help keep the cold out."

The bar was crowded and while he was getting the drink, I

was wondering why he was taking all this trouble, what possible use I could be to such a specialized firm of solicitors operating in the City. I said as much when he handed me my drink and sat down again. He smiled. "Yes, well, let me explain. We have forty or so partners. I'm never certain what the exact number is. They're solicitors, all of them. They each have their own clients, their own reputations. Then there are a number of trainees, a mass of articled clerks, lots of secretaries. In addition, we employ over a dozen ship captains, men who can go off to any port in the world where we have a problem and by their training and long experience can ask the right questions of the right people and assess what the answers are worth. Some of them develop a remarkable nose for ferreting out the truth. And, of course, each claim being different, and therefore requiring an individual approach, we use any method we feel may be necessary to protect our clients' interests. And that," he added with a slight emphasis in his voice, "sometimes includes the employment of people whom we consider have special qualifications for getting at the truth of a particular case."

He sipped his port, the blue eyes watching me behind the thick-lensed glasses. "You know Karachi. You speak Urdu. And you've been a ship's officer. I think you're the man I need."

"For what?" I asked.

He laughed. "If I knew I wouldn't need you, would I?"

"But it's not the *Petros Jupiter*."

"No, it's not the *Petros Jupiter*. It's another ship. In fact, it's two now." And when I told him I was only interested in the *Petros Jupiter*, he said, "Yes, of course. I understand that." He was leaning forward, still watching me. "That's why I wanted to meet you. Ninety percent of the time I'm just a hardworking solicitor slogging through the paperwork. But there's ten percent of the time I'm operating by the seat of my pants, sleuthing out the truth like some amateur detective. That's the fun side—or it can be when you get it right and a hunch pays off." He stopped there. "It's not the ship you're interested in. It's the engineer, isn't it?" He said it tentatively, not looking at me now. "Did Ferrers tell you he's changed his name, flown to Bahrain, and is now on board a small freighter bound for Karachi?"

"Yes, he showed me the telex. It was from the Lloyd's agent in La Rochelle where the fishing boat landed him."

"Suppose we were to send you to Karachi, everything paid, and a fee . . . You fly out, you'd be there about the time the *Corsaire* arrives." He looked at me then. "That's what you want, isn't it? You want to talk to Aristides Speridion, who now calls himself Henri Choffel." I nodded and he smiled. "One of our partners would be interested in that, too. He's handling the *Petros Jupiter* case." He paused then, watching me. "Well, what do you say?"

I didn't answer immediately. In fact, I was thinking of Baldwick and his proposition. This, in a way, was even odder. Saltley misinterpreted my silence. "Sorry," he said. "Afraid I've put it to you very abruptly. Let me fill you in a bit. First, the seat-of-the-pants side of it. Back in November the *Aurora B* disappeared. We don't know where. All we know is she missed her radio schedule when she should have been west of Sri Lanka and hasn't been heard of since. Now, just a few days ago, another VLCC, the *Howdo Stranger*, misses her schedule."

"I was with Ferrers when the news came through," I said. "They both missed their schedules in the same area."

He nodded. "With a twice-weekly radio schedule it's just guesswork where they disappeared. But yes, the same area roughly. Both insured at Lloyd's, and the lead underwriter in each case Michael Stewart. He's a member here and a friend of mine. In fact, I was at his daughter's twenty-first today. We both started our racing together, you see, in the Lloyd's yacht *Lutine*." He shook his head sadly. "Not the best day to pick for a party. And the poor fellow wrote the slip for the *Petros Jupiter* as well, all three of them for the same syndicate, including the Sinister Syndicate, which is hard luck on the girls. He took quite a slice of it for them."

I suppose he sensed I didn't really understand what he was talking about, for he said, "You know how Lloyd's works, do you? The Members—Names, we call them—operate in syndicates. There are around twenty thousand Names and their personal financial commitment is total. Each is limited in the extent of the premium income he, or she, can underwrite, but if things go wrong, then there's no limit at all to the amount they may be called upon to pay out, even to the point of complete bankruptcy." And he added, "One of the syndicates involved here is a rather special one. It's a marine syndicate composed entirely of Members' wives and daughters. My wife's a member of it, so is Mike's, and now his daughter Pamela. She's one of his regular racing crew, and her birthday being on New Year's Eve, the party today was really more to celebrate the start of her underwriting." He smiled wryly. "Virgins Unlimited, or the Sinister Syndicate, those are the tags the syndicate has got stuck with and I'm afraid they may prove more apt than intended. They could be facing a very big loss on these three vessels if all the claims are substantiated. And that won't do Mike's reputation any good. He might not even survive it."

And then abruptly he switched back to the missing ships. "GODCO—that's the company that owns the two missing VLCCs—operates right through the Gulf. They have offices not far from here, in Curzon Street of all places. But the center of their operation is Dubai. If you went out, I'd see you had letters of introduction to Gulf Oil executives, the Lloyd's agents of course, also some very useful contacts I've built up over the years. But," he added, "that's on the official level. Much more important, I feel, is what you, with your knowledge of Urdu, might pick up unofficially, in the docks, or the bazaars, also in hotel bars. I'm thinking of Karachi, you see. I don't know why, but ever since this second GODCO tanker went missing I've had a feeling . . ." He hesitated, staring at me, then gave a little shrug and picked up his drink.

"You think it's sabotage?" I asked.

"It has to be, doesn't it? Two GODCO ships in two months. They haven't lost a VLCC in eight years. But even if I'm right, I've still got to prove it."

"And the *Petros Jupiter?*" I asked. "Who owned her?"

"A Dutch company."

"I thought it was Greek."

"It was, but they sold her a few months back. We'll be checking on the Dutch company, of course, but I'm told it's a perfectly reputable outfit." He didn't know its name or anything about it. Another partner—a man named Pritchard—was handling the *Petros Jupiter*. And he explained that he'd been fully occupied recently, preparing a briefing for arbitration in the matter of a £30-million claim where it was suspected that navigational negligence was a contributing factor in the loss of a giant tanker. But now, with the *Howdo Stranger* failing to keep its radio schedule, Stewart was pressing him to begin a full-scale investigation of the *Aurora B* claim. That meant, not one, but two new casualties added to his work load. "Look," he said, "I've made you a proposition. You go away and think about it. Tomorrow come along to our offices and have a look through the files." And he added, with a quick little smile, so that I knew he was baiting the hook for me, "The *Petros Jupiter*'s cargo was resold on the spot market the day before she was wrecked, and the skipper's statement makes it clear that his instructions to alter course for Rotterdam reached him when he was midway between Land's End and the Scillies." And he added, "I can arrange for you to see that statement. In fact, the whole file, if you like."

That was how, on the following morning, with the snow still falling and half of England a "no-go" area because of blocked roads, I came to be sitting in the offices of Forthright & Co., marine solicitors, at Saltley's desk, with the *Petros Jupiter* file in front of me. All I had been given on arrival were the papers relating to the *Aurora B* claim. There was nothing on the *Howdo Stranger*. At least, that was what I was told by the only girl I could find who knew her way around the files. Saltley's secretary hadn't made it to the office, nor had half the Forthright staff, so that the whole place had a slightly deserted air, particularly the reception area, which must have cost a fortune in rental it was so vast. A matronly, grey-haired woman in tweeds, standing in as receptionist because neither of the girls at the two big desks had arrived, took me down a long corridor through fire doors to Saltley's empty office. "Phone me if you want anything." She gave me the number to dial on the interoffice phone, then shut the door on me so that I felt like a prisoner being locked into his cell.

It didn't take me long to go through the *Aurora B* file—the failure to meet her radio schedule on November 7, details of loading at Mina Zayed, condition and rating of vessel, information about the recent installation of antiexplosion precautions, all the basic, humdrum details on which any assessment of what might have caused the vessel's mysterious disappearance would depend. There was nothing about crew—no photograph, nothing—which was odd as GODCO always photographed and dossiered crew personnel before every voyage. I knew that because I had shipped a man once who had refused to sail on a GODCO tanker at the last moment because he wouldn't be photographed. In the end, he told me the reason he was camera-shy was that he was bigamously married and afraid that his first wife, whom he described as a right bitch, might see it and come after him. Why we all leap so readily to fanciful conclusions I am not sure, but until then I was convinced that he was either one of the train robbers still on the run, or else a murderer.

There was an interoffice and an outside telephone on the desk. I lifted the outside receiver and asked the switchboard operator for a line. She didn't ask who I was or who I was going to ring at the office's expense, she just gave me the line. But when I got through to the GODCO offices in Curzon Street and asked for the current voyage *Aurora B* crew details and pictures, they said all crew information was held at their Dubai offices. They gave me the number and the man to contact.

I might not have followed it up, except that I had asked for the *Petros Jupiter* file and the girl had come back to say that it was with Mr. Pritchard and he was asking who I was and why I wanted it. While I waited, hoping he'd let me see it, I asked the switchboard if it was possible to get me the Dubai number, and in a matter of minutes I was through to the GODCO Marine Superintendent's office. The man in charge of crew dossiers said that copies of all information concerning the *Aurora B* and the *Howdo Stranger* crews, including copies of the crew pictures, had been dispatched airmail to London two days ago. But when I rang the London office again the man I had spoken to before finally admitted their staff was so depleted that morning that he couldn't tell me whether the crew details had arrived or not.

After that there was nothing for me to do but sit there waiting in that empty office. It was an odd feeling, as though I was suspended in limbo—the frozen world outside, and here, encased in concrete and glass, an organization that fed upon disaster, encapsulating the realities of existence—the gales, the sandstorms, the oiled-up beaches, the furnace heat of raging fires—into typed reports and telex messages compressed and neatly filed between plastic covers. Cargoes, ships, dockside greed and boardroom chicanery, the remote cold-bloodedness of owners whose decisions were based on money, not humanity, it was all there, neatly filed and docketed—remote, unreal. Legal cases, nothing more.

The previous night, just as I was leaving, Michael Stewart had come into the Club with his wife and daughter. They had been to the theater, but when Saltley introduced me to him I could see the evening had not been a success. The man was under intense strain. And that morning I had spent the first hour or so visiting two shipping offices close to the Baltic Exchange in St. Mary Axe. Rates were low, a lot of vessels still laid up, and the chances of employment very slight unless you happened to be in a place where the need of a ship's officer was urgent.

Humans, not files—that was the real world. In the circumstances I could count myself lucky I'd had two offers of a job and hadn't had to go looking for either of them. There was a tap at the door and a sharp-faced man with a little brushed-up mustache sidled in, a file under his arm. "Rodin?" He had a tired voice that matched the weary look on his face. He gave the impression of having seen too much of the wrong side of life.

I nodded and he said his name was Pritchard. His eyes, which were dark, had a nervous, sort of clockwork tic, shifting back and forth, left and right, avoiding contact, but at the same time examining me closely. "Salt told me you'd be asking for the *Petros Jupiter* file. Any particular reason, apart from your wife's involvement?"

"Isn't that sufficient?" I disliked the darting eyes, his lack of sensitivity, the coldness of his manner.

He put the file down on the desk in front of me, flipped open the plastic cover and pointed to the most recent item, a telex. "That arrived this morning." And he stood over me while I read it, watching me closely all the time, waiting no doubt to see how I would react to the news.

The telex was from the Lloyd's agent at Karachi. The *Corsaire* had docked that morning at first light. PASSENGER CHOFFEL NOT ON BOARD. TRANSSHIPPED TO DHOW HORMUZ STRAITS 1100 GMT YESTERDAY. CORSAIRE'S CAPTAIN UNABLE TO IDENTIFY DHOW'S NATIONALITY. NO NAME. NO FLAG. SKIPPER SPOKE SOME ENGLISH, NO FRENCH. ALL ON BOARD PROBABLY ARAB. ADVISE CONTACT AGENTS UAE PORTS.

So he'd gone, got clean away. The chances of finding him now . . . I closed the file and sat staring at the phone. I could do as the Karachi agent advised, start ringing round the ports of the United Arab Emirates. But how would the Lloyd's agent in Abu Dhabi, Dubai, Doha, Bahrain, or Kuwait know which dhow it was? There were so many in the Gulf.

"You've seen all you want?"

I nodded.

"Your only interest, then, was Choffel?" He was leaning over me, his eyes darting.

"Yes."

"Pity!" He hesitated. "I never had a case like this before. Stranding is one thing. We might have been able to claim negligence in their employment of a man like Choffel, particularly as he had assumed a different name. In any case, both the ship and its cargo could have been salvaged. That was what the Dutch said. But then your wife's action . . . quite unprecedented. It introduced a new dimension altogether."

"She's dead," I said.

The words meant nothing to him. "There's no policy I've ever seen covers that sort of thing. You couldn't call it sabotage, could you?"

I stared at him, disliking him intensely. No use telling him I'd seen her die, watched the ship go up, and the man who'd caused her death running free somewhere in the Gulf. I opened the file again, leafing through the thick wad of papers. It was similar to the *Aurora B* file, but much fuller, of course, since the vessel had been there on the rocks for all to see. Salvage reports were interspersed with newspaper cuttings and both shore and marine pollution assessments . . .

"Salt said you might be going out there for us."

"Yes. I might." But where? Where would that dhow have taken him? Where the hell would he have gone? Dubai? Dubai was at least one hundred miles from the Straits. Ras al Khaimah perhaps, or Khor al Fakkan, which was outside the

Gulf on the shores of the Arabian Sea, or Muscat even. There were so many places and all of Arabia for him to get lost in. Iran and Pakistan, too. The dhow might have headed north to the coasts of either of those countries, or to one of the islands in the Gulf.

"If you do go out there for Saltley—" I was searching back through the file as he went on, picking his words carefully: "He'll be employing you on behalf of his own clients, to try and discover what happened to the *Aurora B* and this new one that's disappeared." Another, longer pause. I wasn't really listening. I had reached a wadge of newspaper clippings and was living again that night when I'd gone out with Andy in the ILB. "But you'll keep me informed, won't you? If you do find Choffel, I mean. That's why you're going, isn't it? And if you find him, then try and get a written statement out of him."

He was leaning right over me, his voice insistent, and I felt like throwing the file at him. Couldn't he understand what I was feeling, reading through those cuttings? And his voice going on again, cold, incise: "It could be worth quite a lot to you. I'm sure my clients would not be ungrateful. There's usually a reward, something quite substantial, when an insurance claim is refuted. And the claim here is in the order of eleven million, so we're not talking about—"

I looked up at him then, hating him for his stupidity. "What the hell are you talking about?" My voice sounded high and uncontrolled. "Money! I'm not going after him for money."

He had the grace then to say he was sorry, a muttered apology as he turned away and opened the door. I think he was suddenly a little scared of me. "I'll leave the file—you might like to look through it . . ." The clockwork eyes darted back and forth. "I'm sorry," he said again. "I didn't quite realize . . ." The door closed, and he was gone, leaving me alone with those macabre cuttings.

A lot of the newspaper reports I hadn't seen before. They were spread over several days, and there were pictures. For

factual details the *Telegraph* coverage seemed the best, and
both the *Telegraph* and *The Times* had run long articles on
the problems of pollution. And then I came upon this, from a
weekly magazine: "Was she a nut case, or just a totally impractical young woman determined to set fire to the slick? Or
was it done in full command of her senses, an act of great
courage undertaken with one aim in mind—to shock the country into taking action to deal with the terrible and growing
menace that successive governments have swept under the
carpet?" And there was a headline I thought Karen would have
appreciated—"GIRL'S TANKER PYRE SAVES SEABIRDS." The pictures, too—the whole front page of the *Sun*, a night shot with
the mist lit by flames, a photograph of Karen inset on one side
and one of myself on the other, a clip probably from the TV
interview after I'd come back with Andy, my hair plastered
over my face, my mouth open and shouting, my eyes wild.

I glanced at them all, pausing here and there to read. And
then I had passed beyond that terrible Twelfth Night, back to
cuttings, that reported the effects of the stranding, the damage
to the environment, the probable cost of pollution control, the
proportion of the insurance claim to be borne by the London
market, Lloyd's in particular. There were pictures from two of
the Sunday papers of the wreck and the salvage ships taken
from the air. And then I was looking at a picture of the crew
being landed at Sennen Cove. They looked Chinese, all except
the officers whose names were given in the caption below.
"Aristides Speridion, Second Engineer." It was the first time I
had seen a picture of the man. He had a lined, rather sad face,
squarish with a mustache and dark hair, and a hooked nose so
that he might have passed as a member of almost any of the
Mediterranean races. He was wearing a sweater under his uniform reefer and his ears stuck out prominently on either side
of the peaked cap, which he wore pushed up onto the back of
his head and at a jaunty angle as though he was pleased with
himself and to hell with everybody else. The picture also

revealed that, if this were the full complement, officers and crew numbered only fifteen.

I was sitting with my chin in my hands, my elbows on the desk, concentrating all my mind on absorbing and retaining the image of the man I now knew to be Choffel, and then suddenly my attention was caught by the face of a bystander right on the edge of the crowd to the left of the picture—a big man, half a head taller than any of the others, broad-shouldered, thick-set. He was in profile, but even so I could see the heavy set of the jaw, the big jowls, and the round bullet head. The size of the man alone, the way he stood, the arms slack but the body balanced and alert—I didn't need a caption to tell me who it was. Baldwick! And the date of that cutting was January 3, which meant he had come from Bristol immediately the news of the stranding broke. Why! That Sunday when he had come to Balkaer . . . he hadn't said anything about having been in Sennen over a week before.

I leaned back, staring out of the window with its rime of snow, wondering why he had been there. Was it Choffel he had been after? At Balkaer all he had said was that he'd be in Falmouth that evening, to see the captain of the *Petros Jupiter*. No mention of the second engineer, no reference to the fact that he had been there, in Sennen, when the whole crew were brought ashore. In any case, it wasn't the captain who'd put the engines out of action. No, it had to be Choffel, and if I was right, then the one man who knew where the little bastard would be now was Baldwick. The card he had given me was in my pocket.

When I rang the Liverpool number he had scribbled on the back of it he had already left—for France, the hotel said, but they had no forwarding address.

His next destination was Nantes, a river port on the Loire, so probably Choffel had given him the names of possible ships' officers he knew who needed money and were not too particular how they came by it. I phoned the Nantes number. It was the Hotel du Commerce. Yes, Monsieur Baldwick had a reservation, but he do not arrive yet. His room there was booked for two nights.

I leaned back again, staring out at the darkening sky, thinking about Len Baldwick and a story I had once heard of his early life in Sheffield, from a little rat-faced Sparks I'd met at an oilman's flat in Basra. He'd been a shop floor convener in a privately owned steelworks then, a paid-up card-holding Communist, the man had said, and to his certain knowledge Baldwick had set fire to the home of a well-known Labour supporter who had accused him of intimidation. Was that what he'd done to Choffel, intimidated him? Had he fixed it all—the *Vague d'Or*, the *Corsaire*, the dhow in the Hormuz Straits? Was he the link by which I could catch up with the man?

My hand reached slowly out to the interoffice phone, trembling slightly as I lifted the receiver and dialed the grey-haired woman's extension. Phone me, she had said, if you want anything . . . and Saltley the night before trying to insist that I go out to Karachi for him. The woman answered. I took a deep breath and asked her to contact their usual travel agents and have them book me on the next flight to Nantes. She didn't argue. She just took it in her stride as though a sudden request like that from a total stranger was the most natural thing in the world. All she said was, "Return or single, Mr. Rodin?"

"Single," I said. I thanked her and put down the receiver, and after that I just sat there, not caring what Saltley would say, only wondering what the hell I was letting myself in for.

It must have been about ten minutes later that the door was pushed open and he came bustling in, a briefcase in one hand, a file of papers in the other, his face still pink with the cold outside and his overcoat glistening with melted snow. A bright red woolen cap was perched incongruously on his head. "So you're going to Nantes." He dumped his papers and briefcase on the desk. "Mrs. Shipton asked me to tell you they've booked you on tomorrow's flight." He glanced at his watch, then passed me my anorak from the chair where I had thrown it. "We'll be late, I'm afraid. I said one o'clock and it's that already." He hurried me out, along a corridor that led to another set of elevators, explaining as we went that after I had left his Club the previous night Michael Stewart had suggested we had lunch with him in the Captain's Room at Lloyd's. "That's if you were going to work for us. I take it you are?"

"So long as I have a free hand," I said.

He gave me a quick hard look. "The *Petros Jupiter?*"

I nodded.

The elevator came. "I don't think we'll object to your running the inquiries in tandem. I know Mike won't. He knows now he slipped up on the *Petros Jupiter.* He should never have written the slips. As good as told me so last night. But it's the other two claims . . . if he has to meet those—" He gave a little shrug. We were out into Lime Street, picking our way diagonally across the dirty, churned-up slush of the roadway and into the great arched portals of Lloyd's itself.

I couldn't help it. I suddenly felt overwhelmed, a sense of excitement, of awe almost. All my life, ever since I had gone to sea, I'd always heard of Lloyd's. It had always been there in the background, to initiate inquiries into any misadventure, any slipup in navigation, to survey the ship, check seaworthiness, pay for damage, arrange salvage, the cargo too— and here I was entering the building, being taken to lunch in the Captain's Room. A waiter took our coats, a magnificent figure in long scarlet greatcoat, black-collared and -cuffed, the whole elaborate archaic paraphernalia topped off with a gold-banded tall black hat. The grandeur and opulence of that entrance; it was more like a museum, except the undercover roadway went through to the offices of the Baltic Exchange. "I said I'd pick him up at his box," Saltley said. "Give you an opportunity to see the Room."

We went through swinging doors into a high room floored in

black, white, and grey marble, half a dozen flags flanking a
stained-glass window at one end, and at the other a scarlet-
coated waiter sitting at a desk. Saltley said good morning to
him, produced a plastic pass card, and went on through revolving doors that were posted as PRIVATE—FOR THE USE OF
MEMBERS AND THEIR ASSOCIATES, through into a lofty, galleried
room the size of a football field, filled with dark-suited men
armed with papers, books, and files. They stood about, talking
softly or hurrying between the ranks of "boxes" that were the
underwriters' pitches and looked like old-fashioned, high-
backed pews, except that the men sitting in them were writing
busily or looking up information in the books and ledgers that
were stacked on the shelves.

"It goes on like this all day," Saltley said over his shoulder
as he pushed his way to the far end of the Room. "Most of the
fellows you see rushing about are brokers and their clerks,
busy getting underwriters to sign the slips that give insurance
cover to whatever the business is they're handling. Looks a
madhouse, but the box arrangement is the most space-saving
way of handling such a huge volume of business."

The wall to the left was papered with telex sheets and typed
information, the Stock Exchange news running into weather
forecasts and sports results. There were three elevators, but
Saltley turned away from them, threading his way quickly between ledger-piled boxes, heading out from under the balcony
into the center of the Room. Michael Stewart's box was in the
far corner. There were three men in it and a line of three or
four clerks waiting upon him with papers ready in their hands.
He handed over to one of the others and came hurrying across.
I saw him glance at Saltley, who gave a little nod, then he was
greeting me. "We'll have a quick drink first. I've sent my
daughter up to grab a table. She insisted on lunching with us."
His hand was on my arm, steering me to the elevators near the
Lime Street entrance, and I was remembering my meeting
with the girl the previous night. She had been quite plain-

looking, with a squarish face, very little makeup, and no jewelry—a big, sensible girl with strong hands and a nice smile. "You've seen the files, have you? Got all the information you need?" His voice sounded tense. "That's the Casualty Board, incidentally." He nodded to two short display panels opposite the elevators peppered with yellow pages of typescript secured with bulldog clips. "That's where all the bad news is posted. The 'Ulcer Board,' a friend of mine calls it. Every year, it seems, the casualties get worse. When are you leaving?"

"Tomorrow morning," Saltley answered for me. "He's flying to Nantes."

"Nantes! Why Nantes?"

"A contact," I told him. I turned to Saltley. "A hunch really." I knew he'd understand that.

"And after Nantes?" Stewart asked.

"One of the Gulf ports. Dubai most probably, since that seems to be my man's present base. But from my knowledge of him I'd say he operates in any port of the Gulf where there's drugs or arms or something equally nasty to be shipped. At the moment he's headhunting officers for a consortium starting up in the tanker business. I think he's recruited Choffel."

"And you're going to let yourself be recruited, that it?" His assumption came as a shock, though I suppose the thought had been there at the back of my mind. We were in the elevator then and he was smiling, his manner suddenly easier and more relaxed. He turned to Saltley. "Looks like you've picked a flier." And then to me: "You don't waste time. How did you hear this man was recruiting ships' officers?"

I explained briefly and by then we had reached the second floor and were out into a big room with high narrow windows. It was very crowded, the waitresses bustling from table to table with trays of drinks. "Ah! There's Pam, and she's got a table." His face had brightened, his manner suddenly almost boyish. "Best of running a boat—even daughters do as they're told."

Pamela Stewart was holding the fort at a table in a large annex guarded by white pillars. There was an oil painting above her head of the Room cleared of boxes with a diamond-spangled ball in formal swing. She jumped to her feet, her eyes lighting, and in that instant she looked quite lovely, brimming over with youth and vitality. Perhaps it was her presence, the way she leaned forward, her eyes on me all the time, but before I had even finished my bloody mary I had filled them in on Baldwick and how he and Choffel were a possible lead. And over lunch, in one of the wooden cubicles of the solid, rather old-fashioned restaurant they called the Captain's Room after the room in the old Lloyd's Coffee House where the insurance business had all started, I even talked about my book. And all the time I was conscious of Pamela's brownish-green eyes watching me intently. She was dressed in a close-knit woolen dress—very plain with a high neck. It was the color of autumn gold and there was a golden eagle clutching a round globe of some deep-red stone at her throat.

And afterward, when we had finished our coffee, she insisted on taking me down to the Nelson Exhibition on the Gallery floor. It was a beautiful room, all rich woodwork and flanked by glass display cabinets full of Nelson letters and a lot of silver. There was an alcove to the left with a big oil canvas of Nelson by a painter named Abbott, and at the far end Hardy's golden Trafalgar sword was displayed in a separate case below some more Nelson letters and a Hopner print of him. And then I was leaning on the only other glass table case in the room, staring at the log of H.M.S. *Euryalus* covering the period May 23, 1805 to March 11, 1806. It was open at the page recording Nelson's "England expects" signal.

"Something I want you to understand . . ." She wasn't looking at the logbook. She hadn't commented on it, or on anything else in the room. The visit to the exhibition was just an excuse, and now, with her back to the priceless relic, leaning her handsomely shaped body against the case containing

Hardy's sword, she went on in a quiet, throaty voice, "We're in trouble, and after listening to you today, over drinks and during lunch, I've got a sort of feeling . . . I don't know how to put this. But it's as if you are our only hope, if you see what I mean."

She checked there, swallowing hard as though she was struggling to suppress some deep emotion. Then she continued, her voice more controlled. "If these claims stick, particularly the *Aurora B* and the *Howdo Stranger* claims, then I think Daddy's finished. He's underwriting the premium maximum and the family has always taken a lot of the GODCO insurance. I'm not affected, of course. I didn't start underwriting till this month. But Mother's been one of his Virgins for years, so both of them are in very deep." She put her hand out and gripped hold of my arm. "This is what I want you to understand. It's not the money. The money doesn't matter so much. We'll survive, somehow. But I don't think you quite understand what this means to my father. He's the third generation. His father, and his father's father, they were both underwriters here at Lloyd's. In marine insurance they were the tops. It was their life, their raison d'être. They lived and breathed Lloyd's, totally dedicated to the Society." And she added, "You might even say obsessed. That's how Daddy is. It's his life, his whole world." She smiled. "That and sailing," she said, endeavoring to lighten the emotional intensity with which she had been speaking. "I didn't want you to feel . . ." She paused, shaking her head. "I don't know how to put this. Our backgrounds must seem very different."

"You know nothing about my background."

"Oh yes, I do." And when I laughed and told her not to make erroneous comparisons, she said quickly, "Last night, after you'd gone, Salty showed us a dossier on you somebody had got out for him—where you'd been, what you'd done. Daddy was impressed. So was I. Especially what you did after your mother died. Did you really go right through Baluchistan and the North West Frontier—to the Khyber and up into the Murree Hills—on your own, when you were only fourteen?"

"Yes. But it wasn't like it is today."

She didn't seem to hear. "And then—this morning—I went to the Overseas League and looked through the newspaper files. I'm only just back from Gib—we've got our boat down there, you see—so I didn't know the details, about the *Petros Jupiter*, I mean. I'm sorry. It must have been quite terrible for you—seeing it."

"Yes, but I'll get him." I said it without thinking, but all she did was nod her head, accepting it as though that were the inevitable sequel to what had happened. There was a long silence. Finally she said, "What I wanted to explain . . ." She shook her head. "No, it's too difficult." A moment's pause and then she went on, "We're just people, you see. Like anyone else really. I know we've got money, a big house, cars, a yacht —but it doesn't mean anything. Not really. What I mean is . . . well, when you're racing, in a force 8 gale with a big sea running, you don't worry then about whether you've got more money than the next guy—you're too tired, too battered, too bloody scared sometimes." She gave me that warm smile, the eyes large and fixed on mine, her hand touching my arm. "I just wanted you to understand. I'm afraid Salty may have got you into something . . ."

"I got myself into it," I said. I could feel her fingers through my jacket. "So no need for you to worry."

"Yes, of course." She took her hand away, shifting her position, her mood suddenly changing. "Daddy will be back at his box now. And I have a boy I promised to see who's desperate to crew with us in the Med this year." She gave a quick little laugh. "I'm not sure yet whether it's me or the boat he's interested in. Can you find your way back to Forthright's?"

She left me almost immediately, and I didn't think about her again until that night. I was all set then—tickets, traveler's checks, contacts, everything the marine solicitors could provide me with—a contractual letter, too. And then, alone on the hard iron bedstead in that dingy basement, unable to get to sleep, I found myself thinking about her. God knows, there'd been nothing sexy about her. Quite the reverse, in fact. Just a nice, plain English girl, hooked on sailing and probably half in love with her father. And yet . . .

There wasn't a sound to disturb my thoughts. A little room in the East End of London, and I might as well have been in space. Everything deathly still, frozen into silence. No sound of the sea now, no gulls screaming, no rollers thundering. The stillness of death, and my thoughts not on Karen, but on a lump of a girl propped against a case with a gold sword in it belonging to Captain Hardy of the *Victory* and talking endlessly about how they were just ordinary folk, while I stared at her tits and wondered what she'd do if I grabbed hold of them, in Lloyd's of all places!

The next thing I knew it was daylight and the sun was streaming in out of a hard clear sky. It was still shining three and a half hours later when I took off from Heathrow in a half-empty Fokker Fellowship, flying over an England that was mantled deep in snow and brilliantly white. It was only when we were over the Channel and approaching the coast of France that we ran into cloud.

PART III

The Road to Dubai

CHAPTER ONE

THE CLOUDS WERE THINNING when we landed at Nantes, fitful gleams of sunlight flickering on wet Tarmac, and in the city itself the French moved quickly, huddled in topcoats, for it was cold, with an east wind blowing down the river. Baldwick was out when I reached the Hotel du Commerce, and not expected back until evening. I scribbled him a note, and after checking into a room, took a taxi to the address of the Lloyd's agent. His name was Louis Barre and he had a small, untidy office looking out over the quay to a glimpse of the river through the superstructure of a cargo vessel.

"Mistair Rodin?" He was on his feet, waving a telex at me as I entered. "Zis arrive thees morning to say you are coming to me. Sit down, sit down, please." He waved me to a chair. "You want to know about Choffel, eh? The *Petros Jupiter*. I have made inquiries." He was large and energetic, bouncing up and down on the balls of his feet, jiggling a bunch of keys in the pocket of his jacket. "He is what I think you call my patch." His English was quick, almost staccato, the words ejected like grape pips through half-closed teeth. "It is a big river, the Loire, but Nantes is not like a seaport. It is more . . . what is the word? More a port of the region. Along the quay here we know many people, and Choffel, he has a house at Parnay, a few kilometers beyond Saumur, so it is not difficult for me to find out about him."

He bounced across to the door of the outer office, rattled

some French at the girl who had shown me in, then turned back to me: "She has now finished typing the report. You like coffee while you read it? Milk, sugar?" I said I'd like it black and he nodded. "*Deux noirs,*" he said and handed me a single sheet of typescript. "It gives the background, all I can discover about him. If you want more, then we drive to Parnay and talk to his daughter. She is secretary at a clinic in Saumur. But today she is at home because she has a bad cold."

The report was in the form of notes and typed in English:

Dossier of Henri Alexandre Choffel, ship's engineer: Age 46. Medium height, appearance swarthy, black wavy hair, large ears, nose like hawk. Address: 5042 Les Tuffeaux, Parnay. Place of birth—no information.

First employed in the locality by Réaux et Cie as replacement for engineer who is sick on board the coaster *Tarzan* in 1959. Married Jeanne Louise Gaston from Vertou in 1961. One child, a daughter, Guinevere. Continued in employment with Réaux until 1968 when he became chief engineer of the bulk carrier *Olympic Ore.* This vessel is Greek-owned at that time and sailing on Panamanian flag-of-convenience. She is sunk in 1972.

After that there is no information about Choffel until 1976, except that he buys the house at Parnay and his wife dies in February 1973, after a transplant of the kidney operation. It is her husband who gives the kidney.

In 1976 Choffel's name occurs in connection with the *Stella Rosa.* This is a small Lebanese vessel sunk off Pantelleria and Choffel is chief engineer. The inquiry, which was in Palermo, exonerated Choffel from any involvement in the sabotage of the sea cocks. But the ship is gunrunning for the Polisario and on his return to Nantes in March 1977 his connection with these two ships, the *Olympic Ore* and the *Stella Rosa,* makes it difficult for him to gain employment as chief engineer. He is, in any case, not a Frenchman, though he has been naturalized for over twenty years. This is evident from his papers, which are already French when he is first employed by Réaux in 1959. This leads me to believe he may have been from North Africa originally. I can inquire of the relevant department of government if this information is required.

In 1978 I understand he tried to establish a small mushroom business at his home in Parnay, but this does not seem to have success, as he is back in Nantes looking for employment on a ship early in 1979. I can discover no information concerning this man in Nantes between June 1979, when he shipped out as third engineer on the Colombian-registered cargo ship *Amistad* and this year when he is second engineer on the *Petros Jupiter*. I have not so far made inquiries of his daughter, but will do so if it is thought necessary.

(SIGNED) LOUIS BARRE

The coffee arrived and I read the report through again, conscious all the time of the Frenchman's impatience. It told me very little I didn't already know, except about Choffel's personal life, but that was no concern of mine. The *Stella Rosa*—nothing new there. And no information about the sinking of the *Olympic Ore*. I wished I had asked about that at Colchester, but there had been so much information to absorb. All the report amounted to was confirmation of a doubtful record. I finished the Nescafé, concentrating on the last part of the report. Why mushrooms? Why spend a year or more a long way up the river at Parnay? And the daughter—would she know where he had gone? If they were close, which was possible with his wife dead, then she might have had a letter.

"What is it?" Barre suddenly exploded. "You are not satisfied? There is something more you think your people require?"

I hesitated. The man had done his best. But it was disappointing. "Choffel left the *Corsaire* in the Straits of Hormuz, did you know that?"

"Yes. I have a telex from Pritch-ard two days ago to that effect. He is trans-shipped to a dhow."

"But you don't know where he is now."

He stared at me as though I had said something outrageous. "Pritch-ard ask only for background information. He does not ask me where he is gone, what his plans are. How could I possibly tell him that? A man like Choffel, on the run as you say, does not shout his destination from the rooftops."

"His daughter might know. It's almost a week now. He could have written."

"You want to question her, she is at her house today. Or I take you to Réaux." He produced the names of several individuals who had given him background information. "You wish to question them yourself?"

I shook my head. I didn't see how that would help.

"So why do you come?" he demanded angrily. "Why don't you stay in London till you receive my report?"

I hesitated. "Did any of them mention a man named Baldwick in connection with Choffel? Len Baldwick. He's at the Hotel du Commerce."

He shook his head. "What is he? What is he doing here?" And when I told him, he said, "But if he is recruiting these types, why Nantes? Why not Brest or Marseilles, some big seaport where he has more chance of finding what he want?"

"That's something I hope to discover this evening."

"So that is why you come here, to see this Englishman who is staying at your hotel?"

"Partly." I was looking down at the sheet of typing again. "How do you know Choffel's daughter is at home today?"

"I phone the clinic in Saumur this morning."

"But not her home."

"No."

"Can we phone her now?"

"She is not on the phone."

"You think she knows where her father is?"

He didn't answer that, his sharp eyes staring and a frown on his face. "So! That is why you are here." He leaned forward, his elbows on the desk, the knuckles of his hands pressed into his cheeks, looking straight at me. "It is not the man's background that interests you, it is where you can find him. Why? You are not the police. You cannot arrest him. Even if you discover where he is—" He stopped there, silent for a moment, his eyes still fixed on me. "All right, then. Okay." He suddenly bounced to his feet. "I take you to see her. It is only two hours, a bit more per'aps, according to the traffic. And there is a little restaurant I know, just beyond Angers, where we can eat."

He had a Renault 20 and he drove fast, the radio on all the time so that conversation was almost impossible. I leaned back and closed my eyes, lulled by the husky voice of a singer crooning a French love song, wondering about the girl, what she would be able to tell me. And in the evening I would be meeting Baldwick. The thought depressed me—that and Barre's hostility. I could feel it in the silent intensity of his driving. He didn't understand, of course. He hadn't connected me with the woman who had blown the ship up. And it had been tactless of me not to conceal my disappointment at his report. Two years living an isolated existence with just one other human being—I had forgotten the pressures of everyday life, the sensitivity of men whose pride was part of their individual armor against the world. Rationalization, self-justification . . . God. How tired I was! How very, very tired.

The drone of the engine, the voice singing, the sky overcast and the wind battering at the car in gusts . . . I had a feeling of remoteness, my mind transported, drifting in a daze. Emotional exhaustion perhaps, or just the loneliness. Sitting there, my eyes closed, my cap pushed back, my body enveloped in the heat from the engine—heavy trucks thundering by, the flash of headlights in the murk . . . Christ! What a filthy, lousy day! And here I was being driven by a stranger, a Frenchman, through a land gripped in winter, to meet the daughter of a man I'd sworn to kill . . . Guinevere—a name from Arthurian legend—was that important? Would she have heard from him? He could be in the desert now, or at sea, or buried in the teeming masses of some Arab town. Dubai, Sharjah, Ras al Khaimah, Khor al Fakkan—the Emirate names passing through my mind like a refrain—and Muscat, too, El Ain . . . all the names of all the places I had ever visited in the Gulf. Where would it be—where would I catch up with him? And when I did, would I really kill him? Would I have the guts?

And then, after a long time, I saw his newspaper-picture face twisted in pain—the wide stare, the shocked surprise, and the blood spurting. What had I used? In God's name, was it a knife, or was it my bare hands? My teeth were bared and gritted, my fingers wet and feeling flesh, squeezing, squeezing, and I was cursing as the tongue came out and his eyes glazed . . .

"Angers," Barre said and I blinked my eyes and sat up. We were off the dual highway, driving into the center of a city. "I'm sorry," I murmured. "I must have fallen asleep."

"You're tired, I think. You were talking to yourself." He switched off the radio. "We are coming now to one of the great châteaux of France." He turned off to the right, away from the river which he said was the Maine, and above us I saw a line of great black-banded towers. "A pity you don't have time to view the tapestries of the Apocalypse—this city has some of the most remarkable tapestries in the world." He talked then about the Angevin kings and the Plantagenet connection until we stopped at a little hotel in Bohalle for lunch.

What I had said while I was asleep in the car I don't know, but all through the meal, it seemed, he avoided the purpose of our journey, putting himself out to be entertaining as though I were somebody to be treated with care. It was only at the end, over the last of the wine and some excellent local cheese, that he suddenly said, "That girl, what are you going to say to her, have you thought?"

I gave a little shrug. What the hell was I going to say to her? "Does she know her father wrecked a tanker?"

"It's not certain. There's no proof yet. But of course she knows he's under suspicion. It is in all the papers. And yesterday the local press print a statement from the skipper of the *Vague d'Or.*" And he added, "Is better you leave it to me, eh? She may not have any English and if I talk to her—"

"Ask her if she's heard from her father; if possible, get his address."

"And how do we explain ourselves? She might talk to me, but with two of us there—I don't know." He was frowning. "I think if I were her I would be asking some questions before giving any answers."

We were still discussing it as we drove out of Bohalle, the road now hugging the bank of the Loire, through Les Rosiers, St. Clément-de-Lévees, and St. Martin-de-la-Place. At Saumur, with its fairy château perched above the river, we crossed over to the south bank and almost immediately the road was bounded by shallow limestone cliffs along which conventional house fronts had been built as façades to what were apparently troglodyte dwellings. "Les Tuffeaux," Barre said, and talked for a moment about the mushroom industry that had grown side by side with the wine business in caves carved out of the limestone to provide the building material for medieval churches.

He stopped at a riverside café to inquire the way and afterward we turned right at Souzay to join a narrow road close under the cliffs. Mushrooms, he said, were a by-product of the Cavalry School at Saumur. "What you call horse shit," he added, laughing. It was a long, very narrow road and the Choffel house was at the end, in a little cul-de-sac where there was a cave half-hidden by a drooping mass of vegetation, the entrance sealed off by an iron door with a dilapidated notice announcing VIN À VENDRE. We parked there and walked back. The figures 5042 were painted black above the rough plaster porch and from a rusty iron gate opposite that led into a small rose garden there was a fine view over tiled rooftops to the broad waters of the Loire glinting in a cold shaft of sunlight. Clouds hung over the northern bank where the vineyards gave way to forest.

I had no preconceived mental picture of Choffel's daughter. I expected her to be dark, of course, but I hadn't really thought about it, my mind on how I could persuade her to give us the information I needed. It came as a shock, when she opened the door, to find there was something vaguely familiar about her. She was about twenty, well-rounded with black hair cut in a fringe that framed a squarish face, and I had the feeling I had seen her before.

Barre introduced us and at my name she turned her head, staring at me with a puzzled frown. Her eyes were large and almost purplish like sloes, very bright, but that may have been because of her cold. She looked as though she was running a temperature. Barre was still talking, and after a moment's hesitation, during which her eyes remained fixed on my face, she let us into the house. "I have told her we are here about the *Petros Jupiter* insurance, nothing else," Barre whispered as she ushered us into what I suppose would be called the parlor in that sort of house. It was a comfortably furnished room and almost the first thing I noticed was a photograph of her father, the same prominent nose I had seen in the newspaper pictures, but clean-shaven and bareheaded, the crinkly black hair carefully smoothed down, and he was smiling self-consciously, dressed in his engineer's uniform. Standing beside it, in an identical silvered frame, was the photograph of a young woman with the most enormous eyes staring out of a long, gaunt face. She had a broad brow and a mass of curly brown hair. "My family," the girl said to me in English, and then she had turned back to Barre, speaking in French again, the tone of her voice sharp and questioning.

It was a strange room, more than half of it natural rock that had been plastered over and then decorated. This and the color of the walls, which was a pale green, gave it a certain coldness, and with just the one window it had an almost claustrophobic feel. I heard my name mentioned and Guinevere Choffel was repeating it, staring at me again, her eyes wide, a shocked look that was mixed with doubt and confusion. "Why are you here? What do you want?" Her English was perfect, but with something of a lilt to it, and she said again, "Why are you here?" her voice dropping away to a note of despair. "It was an accident," she breathed. "An accident, do you hear?"

She knew! That was my first reaction. She knew about Karen, what had happened. And the reason I was here, she must have guessed that, for she didn't believe me when I said I represented Forthright & Co., the marine solicitors dealing with the case, and needed her father's address so that we could arrange for him to make a statement. "No. It's something else, isn't it?" And in the flash of her eyes, the sound of her voice, I had that sense of familiarity again, but stronger now. And then it dawned on me. She was like Karen in a way, the same sort of build, the same high coloring against the raven black hair, that lilt in the voice; that emotional quality, too, the voice rising and those wide eyes bright with the flash of her anger: "You don't understand. You don't know my father or you wouldn't think such a thing." She pulled a handkerchief from the pocket of her skirt and turned away to blow her nose. "He's had a hard life," she mumbled. "So many things gone wrong, and not his fault—except that once." This last was swallowed so that I almost lost it. And then she had turned and was facing me again, her voice rising: "Now you're here, blaming him. It's been the same, always, you understand. Always. Do you know what it's like, to be accused of things you don't do? Well, do you?" She didn't wait for an answer. "No," she said, her voice higher still and trembling. "Of course you don't. It's never happened to you. And now you come here, asking me, his daughter, to tell you where he's gone. You think I would do that when you have already passed judgment on him?" She seemed to get a grip on herself then, speaking slowly and with emphasis, "It's not his fault the ship is wrecked. You must believe that. Please."

"You saw him in La Rochelle, did you?" Or perhaps he had only had time to contact her by phone.

"In La Rochelle?" She stared at me.

"In the trawler basin there, when he arrived in the *Vague d'Or.*"

"No, I don't go to La Rochelle. Is he in La Rochelle?" She sounded surprised.

"He didn't contact you?"

"No, how could he? I didn't know." She was still staring at me, breathing heavily. "La Rochelle, you say?" And when I explained, she shook her head. "No, I don't see him there, or anywhere. I didn't know he was in France."

"But you've had a letter from him?"

"No, not since—" she checked herself. "No. No letter."

"But you've heard from him. You know where he is."

She didn't answer that, her lips tightly shut now.

"Do you know a man named Baldwick?" I thought there was a flicker of recognition in her eyes. "He's in Nantes. Has he phoned you, or sent you a message?"

She lifted her head, the dark eyes staring into mine. "You don't believe me, do you? You've made up your—" She shook her head. "You had better go, please. I have nothing to tell you, nothing at all, do you hear?" Her voice, quieter now, the lilt stronger, had an undercurrent of tension in it. "She was your wife, I suppose. I read about it in an English paper." And when I didn't answer, she suddenly cried out, "She did it—herself. You cannot blame somebody who wasn't there." I could smell her fear of me then as she went on, "I'm sorry. But it's her fault. Nothing to do with my father."

"Then why didn't he stay in England? If he'd waited for the inquiry—"

"It's nothing to do with him, I tell you." And then, vehemently, almost wildly—"It's the chief engineer. He's the man you should ask questions about, not my father."

"Is that what he's told you?"

She nodded.

"You have heard from him, then," I said.

"Of course. He wrote me as soon as he landed in Cornwall."

"Did he tell you he was planning to get away in a Breton fishing boat, that he didn't dare face the inquiry?"

"No, he didn't say that. But I was glad—glad when I knew. For his sake." She must have been very conscious of my hostility, for she suddenly shouted at me, "What do you expect him to do? Wait to be accused by a chief engineer who isn't sick, but drunk and incompetent? It's happened before, you know. Why should he wait, an innocent man, to be accused again?" She was standing quite close to me, looking up into my face, her eyes wide and desperate. "You don't believe me?"

"No," I said.

And then she did something so unexpected it shocked me deeply. She spat in my face. She jerked her head and ejected her germ-laden spittle straight into my face. "*Maquereau!* You're like all the rest. When you've got a man down, you kick his teeth in. My father is the finest, most generous, kindly man I know, and you use him, all of you, as though he is nothing but a turd under your feet. I hate you. I hate the whole world." Tears were streaming down her face and she rushed to the door, pulling it open and screaming, "Get out! D'you hear? *Allez!* And tell your friends—everybody—that he is clear of you all now. He's free, and you'll never find him. Never."

The door banged behind us.

"Is not a very rewarding visit, eh?" Barre said with a

chuckle as we walked back to the car. He seemed to enjoy my discomfort, and as we drove back down to the main road he said, "Nothing is what it seems to be, isn't it so? The man you regard as a terrorist, others think of in ideological terms. So what about Choffel, eh? You see him as a wrecker, a man who has deliberately caused a tanker to go onto the rocks, but to his daughter he is a kindly, generous man who would not hurt a soul and you are the enemy." He glanced at me quickly. "How do you think he sees himself?"

I hadn't considered that. "I've had other things to think about," I told him.

"That is not an answer." He waited a moment, then said, "But why does he do it?"

"Money," I said. "What else?"

"There are other reasons—anger, frustration, politics. Have you thought about those?"

"No."

He gave a little shrug and after that he didn't ask any more questions. It was a filthy drive, night falling and the traffic heavy after we had passed through Saumur. He seemed withdrawn then. A dusting of sleet gradually laid a white coating over everything. He had the radio on, the windshield wipers clicking back and forth—my eyes closed, my mind drifting into reverie, no longer thinking about the girl, but about my meeting with Baldwick. It loomed closer every minute and I had no idea where it would take me, what I was letting myself in for. Suppose I was wrong? Suppose he hadn't recruited Choffel? Then it would be to no purpose and I could find myself involved in something so crooked that not even my letter of agreement with Forthright's would protect me.

It was just about six when we pulled up at the entrance to my hotel. "I'm sorry you don't get what you want," he said. "But the girl was frightened. You realize that." And he sat there, staring at me, waiting for me to say something. "You frightened her," he said again.

I started to open the door, thanking him for the trouble he had taken and for the lunch he had insisted on buying me, but his hand gripped my arm, holding me. "So! She is right. It was your wife. I had forgotten the name. I did not connect." He was leaning toward me, his face close, his eyes staring into mine. "*Mon Dieu!*" he breathed. "And you have no proof, none at all."

"No?" I laughed. The man was being stupid. "For God's sake! The chief was sick, or so he says. Choffel was in charge, and for the secondary reduction gear to go right after an engine failure . . . that . . . that's too much of a coincidence. He was quite close to it when it happened. He admitted that." And then I was reminding him that, at the first opportunity, the man had stolen a dinghy, got aboard a Breton fishing boat, then flown out to Bahrain to board a freighter bound for Karachi, and had finally been picked up by a dhow in the Hormuz Straits. "His escape, everything, organized, even his name changed from Speridion back to Choffel. What more do you want?"

He sat back with a little sigh, both hands on the wheel. "Maybe," he murmured. "But she's a nice girl and she was scared."

"She knew I was right. She knew he was caught up in some crooked scheme—"

"No, I don't think so." But then he shrugged and left it at that. "*Alors!* If there is anything more I can do for you—" He barely waited for me to get out before pulling away into the traffic.

There was a note for me at the desk. Baldwick was back and waiting for me in the hotel's bar-restaurant. I went up to my room, had a wash in lukewarm water, then stood at the window for a moment staring down at the shop-lit street below where cars moved sluggishly in a glitter of tiny snowflakes. Now that the moment of my meeting with Baldwick had come, I was unsure of myself, disliking the man and the whole

stinking mess of Arab corruption on which he battened. A gust
of wind drove snowflakes hard like sugar against the window
and I laughed, remembering the girl. If it were true what
Barre had said, that she'd been frightened of me . . . well,
now I knew what it felt like. I was scared of Baldwick, of
thrusting my neck into his world, not knowing where it would
lead. And the girl reminding me of Karen. God damn it! If I
was scared now, how would it be when I was face to face with
her father?

I turned abruptly from the window. It wasn't murder. To
kill a rat like that . . . Why else was I here, anyway? In
Nantes. At the same hotel as Baldwick. And she'd known
about Baldwick. I was certain of it, that gleam of recognition
when I mentioned his name. She'd associated him with her father's escape. And Baldwick in Sennen when that picture had
been taken of the *Petros Jupiter*'s crew coming ashore. To
recruit a man like Choffel meant he'd been told to find an
engineer who was an experienced wrecker.

I shivered, the room cold, the future looming uncertain. Another gust rattled the window. I made an effort, pulled myself
together, and started down the stairs.

The bar-restaurant looked out onto the street, the windows
edged with a dusting of ice crystals, the snow driving horizon-
tally. The place was cold and almost empty. Baldwick was sitting at a table pulled as close as possible to a movable gas fire.
He had another man with him, a thin-faced man with a blue
scarf wrapped round a scrawny neck and a few strands of hair
slicked so carefully over the high bald dome of his head that
they looked as though they were glued there. "Albert Varsac,"
Baldwick said.

The man rose, tall and gaunt. "Capitaine Varsac." He held out
a bony hand.

"First mate on a coaster's as far as you ever got." Baldwick
laughed, prodding him with a thick finger. "That's raight,
ain't it? You never bin an effing captain in yer life." He

waved me to a seat opposite. "Got your message," he said. His eyes were glassy, his mood truculent. He shouted for a glass, and when it came, he sloshed red wine into it and pushed it across to me. "So you changed your mind, eh?"

I nodded, wondering how far I would have to commit myself in order to catch up with Choffel.

"Why?" He leaned forward, his big bullet head thrust toward me, the hard bright eyes staring me in the face. "You good as told me ter bugger off when I saw you down at that little rat hole of a cottage of yours. 'Get a't,' you said. 'I don't want anything to do wi' yer bloody proper-propositions.' Raight?" He wasn't drunk, but he'd obviously had a skinful, the north country accent more pronounced, his voice a little slurred. "So why're you here, eh? Why've you changed yer mind?" His tone was hostile.

I hesitated, glancing at the Frenchman who was gazing at me with drunken concentration. "The reason doesn't matter." My voice sounded nervous, fear of the man taking hold of me again.

"I got ter be sure . . ." He said it slowly, to himself, and I suddenly sensed a mood of uncertainty in him. In that moment, as he picked up the bottle and thrust it into Varsac's hands, I glimpsed it from his point of view, engaging men he didn't know for some crooked scheme he didn't dare tell them about or perhaps didn't even know himself. "You piss off," he told the Frenchman. "I wan' ter talk to Rodin 'ere alone." He waved the man away, an impatient flick of a great paw, and when he'd gone, he called for another bottle. "Now," he said. "Let's 'ave it. Why're you here?" He was leaning forward again, the hard little eyes boring into me, and I sat there for what seemed an age, staring at him speechless, not knowing what to say, conscious only that it wasn't going to be easy. The bastard was suspicious.

"The book," I said finally, my voice no more than a whisper. "The publishers turned it down."

"The publishers?" He stared at me blankly. Then, suddenly remembering, he opened his mouth and let out a great gust of laughter. "Turned it da'n, did they? That bleedin' book of yours. An' now you come runnin' ter me." He sat back, belching and patting his stomach, a smug, self-satisfied gleam in his eye. "Wot makes yer think I still got a job for yer, eh?"

There was a sort of cunning in the way he said it, but his acceptance of my explanation gave me confidence. "The desk said you were booked out to Marseilles in the morning," I said. "If you'd got all the officers you needed, you'd be headed for Dubai, not Marseilles. And you didn't get the master of the *Petros Jupiter*, only the engineer."

I was taking a chance in saying that, but he only grinned at me. "Been makin' inquiries, have yer?"

"Where's the ship?" I asked. I thought he might be drunk enough to tell me. "Abu Dhabi, Dubai—"

The grin faded. "Yer don't ask questions, mate. Not if yer wantin' a job a't o' me. Got it?" He leaned forward, the glassy eyes staring. "You've no idea, have you—no idea at all what a man like me 'as ter do ter turn an honest silver thaler." There was sweat on his forehead, his eyes glazing, and he was breathing deeply so that I thought for a moment he was going to pass out on me. "But this is different." He seemed to pull himself together. "The men I need—they got ter be . . ." His voice trailed away and he was silent for a while, staring down at his glass as though thinking something out. Finally he lifted his head, looking straight at me as he said, "I got ter be careful, see." His eyes held mine for a long moment, then he refilled our glasses. "You sold that cottage of yours?"

"Not yet," I said. "I've told them not to put it on the market till the spring."

He lifted his glass, swallowing half of it at a gulp as though it were beer. "Won't fetch much, will it?" He wiped his mouth with the back of his hand, smiling. "Yer wife dead and yer book in the dustbin—in a bit of a mess, ain't yer?" His eyes creased, smiling at me as though somebody in a bit of a mess was what life was all about. "Got anything tucked away?"

He said it casually, but I sensed that the question was important. "How do you mean?"

"You got enough to get here . . ." He sat there, waiting.

"Just enough," I said. "That's all."

"No return ticket?"

I shook my head.

"Christ, man! You took a chance." He nodded. "So you're out o' bread an' no way of getting back to the U.K., no prospect of finding work there anyway?"

I didn't say anything and he grinned at me. "Orl raight, so I still got a berth for a second mate." He leaned forward, peering into my face. "But wot makes you think you're the man for the job?"

"Depends what it is," I said. But he wouldn't tell me that, or who the owners were, not even the name of the ship. It was double rates and an end of voyage bonus, so what was I worrying about? "You want the job or don't you?"

I knew then that I had no alternative. To find Choffel I would have to commit myself. "Yes," I said.

"You got any money at all, apart from what you'll get from that cottage?"

"Enough to pay the hotel bill, that's all." I didn't know whether he was fishing for a bribe or not.

"No dole money, no redundancy?"

"I don't qualify."

"So you got nothing. An' now yer wife's gone . . ." He thumped the table, gloating at me. "You got nothing at all, have you?" He sat back, smiling and lifting his glass in his big fist. "Orl raight, Trevor—yer on. Nantes-Paris, then Paris-Dubai, an' after that you wait until we're ready for you, everything laid on—hotel, swimming pool, booze, girls, anything you want. Just one thing though—" He reached out a big hand and gripped my arm. "No tricks. An' remember—it's 'cos of me you're getting the job. Understand?"

I nodded. I hadn't been in the Gulf all those years not to recognize the glint in his eyes. "How much?" I asked.

"Voyage money will be paid in advance. You hand me half of it, okay?" And he added, "You'll still be getting full second mate's pay. And you keep the bonus." The bonus would be five hundred quid, he said—"So you don't ask questions, see."

And so it was agreed. For half my pay I put myself in his hands, committed to an unknown ship and an unknown desti-nation. "I booked your flight, by the way." He grinned at me slyly. "Did that soon as I heard you'd checked into the hotel." He emptied the bottle into our glasses and when we had finished it, he got hold of Varsac and we had a meal together. There was more wine and cognac with the coffee. The talk turned to sex, interminable sordid stories of the Gulf. Varsac had been in Jibuti. He was very funny about the madame of a brothel who changed into a man. And Baldwick became mo-rose. I mentioned the *Petros Jupiter* again, asking him whether he knew anything about the engineer he'd recruited, but he stared at me with such drunken hostility that I didn't persist. He knew I had been getting at something, but he was con-fused and he wasn't sure what. In the end I went to bed.

My room was close under the eaves. It was cold, the bed not aired and I couldn't sleep. The window rattled in the gusts and I kept thinking of that girl, the horror in her eyes, the way she'd spat in my face. I lay there, listening to the gusts, remembering that night off Sennen, the fog exploding into flame. And the Lloyd's agent trying to tell me I'd no proof. The girl, too. "It's not his fault," she had said—"she did it her-self." But they hadn't been there. They hadn't seen it. And Choffel. What would he say when I finally caught up with him, when I got hold of the murderous little bastard, my hands at his throat, the flesh yielding . . . ? The wind beat against the window, a cold draft on my face. God damn it! What sort of a monster had I become?

I was shivering then, my eyes wet with tears. God in Heaven! Why should I start on self-recrimination when I'd right on my side? It wasn't vengeance. It was justice. Somebody had to see to it that he never wrecked another vessel. And then I was thinking about why he'd done it. Greed! Stupid, senseless greed! But that wasn't peculiar to him. It was a curse affecting us all, the whole human race, harvesting the sea till there was nothing left but oceans and oceans of dead water, drilling for energy, tanking it round the world, feeding factories that poured toxic waste into the rivers, supplying farms with pesticides that poisoned the land, pumping heat and fumes into the life-giving atmosphere until it was a lethal hothouse. What was Choffel by comparison? A nothing—just a symbol, a symptom of human rapacity—and myself a Quixote tilting at the windmill of man's self-destructive urge.

It was an argument and a view of life that went round and round in my head as gusts rattled the door and the rafters crackled in the frost. And then I woke to complete stillness in a grey dawn that held everything in a grip of silence, the windowpanes frosted over and the rooftops opposite a glazed white. It was no longer freezing and by the time I was dressed there was a gleam of watery sunshine, the world outside beginning to thaw.

Baldwick was already there when I went into the bar-restaurant for breakfast, sitting at a table with a pot of coffee and a basketful of rolls in front of him. "Take a seat." He pulled out a chair for me, indicating the coffee. "Help yourself." He had his mouth full, chewing voraciously at a roll, his heavy cheeks glowing pink as though he had been for a brisk walk in the cold morning air, his big frame full of vigor. "Paris is no go, thick as a pig's snout. If the fog don't lift, you could be here another night."

He had settled with the desk and had given Varsac the air

tickets. All the time he was talking those little eyes of his were fixed on me intently. Something was worrying him, some sixth sense perhaps—"Keep yer mouth shut." He was suddenly leaning forward, his face close to mine and nothing in his eyes or his voice, nothing at all to indicate he had been drinking heavily the night before. "Understand? Anyone starts talking they could find themselves in trouble. I'm telling you that 'cos I reck'n you're far too intelligent not to know you don't get double rates and a bonus for a run-of-the-bloody-mill voyage. Okay?"

I nodded, finding it difficult to meet the bright beady eyes barely a foot from mine.

"You still thinking about the *Petros Jupiter*? 'Cos if you are . . ."

I shook my head, reaching for the coffee and pouring myself a cup as I inquired why he had asked.

"Last night. You were asking questions about the engineer."

"Was I?"

"You know bloody well you were. Did you think I was too drunk or something not to remember? How did you know I'd anything to do with the man?"

"You were in Sennen when the crew came ashore." But the instant I'd said it I knew it was a mistake. He pounced on it immediately.

"Sennen? Who said I went to Sennen? Falmouth, I told you."

I nodded, buttering myself a roll and not looking at him. "I heard you'd been at Sennen earlier, that's all."

"Who told you?"

"I don't know." I gulped down some coffee. "Everything was a bit mixed up at the time. A press photographer, I think."

"I never was at Sennen. Understand?" His fist slammed down on the table, rattling the crockery. "Forget it. Forget everything—okay? Just do the job you're paid for . . ." He looked up as Varsac joined us. The Frenchman's face was more cadaverous than ever, heavy pouches below the bloodshot eyes. "Mornin', Albert," Baldwick said brightly. "You look as though you've been tangling with Madame all night." He picked up the pot and poured him a coffee. "You'll take it black, eh?" And as Varsac sat down heavily and buried his long nose in the coffee, he added, "Bet yer if a nice plump Baluchi girl walked in now you couldn't do a thing aba't it." And he let out a great guffaw as he slapped the wretched Varsac on the back.

His taxi arrived a few minutes later and as he got up from the table, he paused for a moment, staring at me. "Meet you in Dubai," he said, "and no tricks, see?" He was smiling at me, but not with his eyes. For a moment he stood there, looking down at me. Finally he nodded as though satisfied, turning abruptly and going out to the waiting taxi.

Flights south were leaving on schedule, but Paris and all the north of France was fogged in. It looked as though we'd be kicking our heels in Nantes for some hours yet and I went in search of the papers. The only English ones I could find were the *Telegraph* and the *Financial Times* and I looked through them over a *fine à l'eau* in the bar. There was no news of the missing tankers in either of them, the front page of the *Telegraph* full of the trial of terrorists charged with the Piccadilly bomb outrage, and there had been a demonstration outside the Old Bailey in which shots had been fired at the police. It was in the *Financial Times* that I found a small paragraph tucked away on an inside page headed "TANKER CLAIM REJECTED: Solicitors for a Lloyd's syndicate operated by Mr. Michael Stewart have rejected a claim by the NSO Harben company of Schidam in respect of the loss of the tanker *Petros Jupiter*. No reason has been given, but it is presumably based on their assessment of the evidence that will be given at the inquiry due to begin on January 27. The amount of the claim is put at over £9 million for the hull alone. This is the largest marine insurance claim so far this year."

Just before midday we were informed that it was unlikely
we should get away until the following morning. A definite decision would be made after lunch. I got hold of a city plan and
walked down to the riverside quays where the cargo ships lay.
The sun was quite warm, the streets all dripping with melted
snow. At the offices of the Réaux shipping company, my
request to speak to somebody who had actually known Choffel
resulted in my being shown into a tiny waiting room and left
there for a long time. The walls were hung with the framed
photographs of ships, most of them old and faded, and there
was a table with copies of French shipping magazines. Finally
a youngster, who spoke good schoolboy English, took me
along the quay to a small grain carrier that had only just come
in. There I was introduced to an elderly chief engineer who
had been on the *Tarzan* in 1959.

He described Choffel as a quiet man who didn't say much,
just got on with the job. He had had very little French at that
time, but was eager to learn because he wanted to live in
France. I asked him why, but he just shrugged.

"Was he a good engineer?"

"*Mais oui—excellent.*" And then he said something that
came as a complete surprise to me. He said, "*Henri Choffel,
vous savez, il était anglais.*" English! That was something that
hadn't occurred to me. But then suddenly things began to fall
into place. The girl—it explained the lilt, that sense of familiarity, that vague likeness to Karen, the name even. Of course,
Welsh! How would a French engineer know the difference—
Welsh, English, it was all one to him.

But it didn't help me to an understanding of the man, and
he couldn't tell me what ships he'd been on or where he came
from. I asked him what sort of company Choffel had kept
when they were in port, but apparently he had usually stayed
on board, studying French and talking to the French members
of the crew. He was on the *Tarzan* almost a year, and by the
time he was promoted to another of the Réaux ships he was

quite fluent. There was only one other worthwhile thing he told me. Choffel had had the word FORMIDABLE and the date 1952 tattooed across his chest. The old man pronounced it, of course, in the French way, but it could just as easily have been English and the name of a ship.

Barre was out to lunch by the time I reached his office, but I arranged with his secretary for a telex to be sent to Pritchard advising that a search be made for the name of any Welshman serving as a conscript in the engine room of H.M.S. *Formidable* in 1952. It was a chance. Once Pritchard had the man's original name, he'd be able to find out what merchant ships he'd served in later and whether any of them had been wrecked shortly before he had joined the *Tarzan* under the name of Henri Choffel.

Back at the hotel, after a meal and a bottle of wine at a little restaurant by the river, I found Varsac waiting anxiously for me in reception with his bags packed. Paris was now clear and our flight would be leaving Nantes at 1610. I got my key and was told there was a Mademoiselle Choffel wishing to speak with me. She was having a coffee in the bar.

I left Varsac to order a taxi, got the bags from my room, and then went through into the bar-restaurant. She was sitting in a corner facing the door into the hotel and she got up with a nervous little smile as I went toward her. There were shadows under her eyes and her face was flushed. She held out her hand. "I had to come. I want to apologize. I was upset. Terribly upset. I didn't know what I was saying, or doing. It was such a shock." The words poured out of her as we shook hands, her clasp hot and moist.

"You should be in bed," I said. "You look as though you're running a temperature."

"It doesn't matter." She sat down abruptly, waving me to the seat on the opposite side of the table. "I couldn't let you—leave, like that. As if I had no understanding, no sympathy."

"You're Welsh, aren't you?" I asked.

"Half Welsh, yes. My mother was French."

"From Vertou."

Her eyes widened. "So you've been making inquiries?"

"Of course." And I added, "My wife was Welsh. But not her name. Her name was Karen."

"Yes, I know. I read about it. When I heard the news, I read all the English papers I could get . . ." Her voice faded, floundering over the macabre memory of what had been printed in the English press.

"Karen was from Swansea. That's where we met. In the docks there."

"It was nothing to do with my father," she whispered urgently. "Please. You've got to believe that. You must believe it, because it's true. It was an accident."

"And he's a Welshman, you say?"

"He was born there, yes."

"Where?"

"In the middle somewhere. I'm not sure."

"What was his name then?"

It was on the tip of her tongue, but then she hesitated. "Why do you ask?"

"A fellow Welshman . . ." I murmured, not looking at her now, knowing I had tried to trap her.

"You're not Welsh." Her voice was suddenly harder, an undercurrent of impatience. "The way you talk sounds like it sometimes, but if you were Welsh now—"

"It would make no difference."

"If you were, you would have the imagination to see—"

"I have plenty of imagination," I cut in angrily. "Too much perhaps."

She was staring at me now, her eyes wide and the same look of horror dawning. "Please. Won't you try to understand? He's never had a chance. Ever since the *Stella Rosa*. You know about the *Stella Rosa*, I suppose?"

"Yes."

"He was exonerated, you know."

"The *Stella Rosa* was gunrunning."

"There was no other ship available. My mother was sick and he needed the money."

"Honest engineers don't go gunrunning," I told her. "Then, when the ship was wrecked, he blamed one of his engineer officers, a man named Aristides Speridion."

She nodded slowly, her eyes dropping to her hands.

"What happened to Speridion? Has he told you?"

She didn't answer.

Varsac poked his head round the door to say the taxi had arrived. I waved him away. "Tell it to wait," I said. And then to the girl, "You realize that when the *Petros Jupiter* went onto the rocks by Land's End he was in charge of the engine room? And masquerading under the name of Aristides Speridion. He even had Speridion's passport."

"I know." The admission seemed dragged out of her, the words a whisper. She suddenly reached out, touched my hand. "There's some explanation. I know there is. There must be. Can't you wait—until after the inquiry? It's like a court of law, isn't it? The truth—the real truth—it'll all come out." Her voice was urgent, desperate to believe that he would be vindicated, his innocence proved. "He's such a kind man. You should have seen him when my mother was dying—"

"If there were a chance that the inquiry would vindicate him, he'd surely have stayed. Instead—" But I left it at that. His action in fleeing the country made it all so obvious and I'd no quarrel with her. I began to get to my feet. She should have had the sense to face up to the situation. The man was guilty as hell and no good her pleading his innocence when the facts were all against it. "I'm sorry," I said. "I've got to go now. The flight to Paris—"

"It's Dubai, isn't it? You're going to Dubai."

I nodded.

"When you see my father . . ." She got slowly to her feet,

tears in her eyes as she stood facing me. "Give him my love, will you? Tell him I did my best. I tried to stop you." She stood quite still, facing me, with her hands to her sides, as though she were facing a firing squad. "Please remember that when you find him." And then, in a sudden violent outburst, "I don't understand you. Will nothing satisfy the bitterness that's eating you up? Isn't there anything—" But then she stopped, her body stiffening as she turned away, gathering up her handbag and walking blindly out by the street door.

She left me with the bill for her coffee and a feeling of sadness that such a nice girl, so absolutely loyal, should have such a man for a father. Nothing she had said had made the slightest difference, his guilt so obvious that I thought she was probably convinced of it, too, as I went out to the waiting taxi. Varsac was already there, with the door open. I handed my bags to the driver, saw to it that he put them both in the boot, and then, as I was bending down to get in, the girl's voice behind me called out, "*Monsieur. Un moment.*" I turned to find her standing by the hood of the taxi with one of those flat little miniature cameras to her eye, and at that moment the shutter blinked. It blinked again before I had time to move. "Why did you do that?" I was reaching out for the camera, but she put it behind her, standing stiff and defiant. "You touch me and I'll scream," she said. "You can't take my camera."

"But why?" I said again.

She laughed, a snorting sound. "So that my children will know what the murderer of their grandfather looked like. The police, too. Anything happens to my father and I'll give these pictures to the police." She took a step back, the camera to her eye again as she took another snap. Then she turned, darting across the pavement into the hotel.

"*Dépêchez-vous. Dépêchez-vous. Nous allons louper l'avion.*" Varsac's voice sounded agitated.

I hesitated, but there was nothing I could do, so I got into the taxi and we drove out of Nantes across the Loire to the airport. And all the way there I was thinking about the photographs, her reason for taking them—"When you meet my father—" Those were her words. "Dubai," she had said. "You're going to Dubai." So now I knew, Choffel was in Dubai. He would be waiting for me there, an engineer in the same ship.

Two hours later we were in Paris, at the Charles de Gaulle Airport, waiting for the flight to Dubai. In the end we didn't board until 2030, and even then we were lucky in that there had been several cancellations, for this was the Thursday morning flight, delayed now by over thirty hours, and every seat was taken.

PART IV

The Dhow

CHAPTER ONE

IT WAS A SIX-AND-A-HALF-HOUR FLIGHT from Paris to Dubai and
nothing to do but sit there, thinking about my meeting with
Choffel, what I was going to do. Up till then I hadn't given
much thought to the practicalities. I had never owned a gun,
never even fired one. I had no weapon with me of any sort,
and though I had seen death out in the Hindu Kush when I
was a kid, it was death through cold or disease or lack of food.
Once, in Basra, I had watched from a hotel balcony as an ar-
mored car and some riot police gunned down a handful of
youths. That was before the Iraqi-Iranian war, a protest by
Shi'ah sect students and again I was only a spectator. I'd never
killed anyone myself. Even the little Baluchi boy, whose doll-
like features haunted me, had been thrown into the Creek by
the others. I had taken no part in it.

Now, as the big jet whispered through the sky at 37,000
feet, my mind was on Dubai, and the thought that tomorrow,
or the next day, or when we boarded the tanker, I could be
confronted with Choffel caused my skin to prickle and perspiration to break out all over my body. I pictured his face when
we met, how he would react, and the excitement of it shook
me. So vivid was the picture my imagination produced that,
sitting there, with the seat at full recline and a blanket round
my waist, the lights dimmed and all the rest of the passengers
fast asleep, the blood drummed in my ears, fantasies of killing
flickering through my brain so that suddenly I had an over-

whelming orgasmic sense of power. A knife. It would have to
be a knife. One of those big silver-hilted, curved-bladed *kanjar*
knives the Bedu wore tucked into the belts of their flowing
robes. Getting hold of a knife like that wouldn't be difficult,
not in Dubai, where Arab merchants along the waterfront sold
anything from gold and opium to slave girls, and a pistol
would be equally available. Still, a knife would be better. But
then what did I do? And where would I find him? At one of
the hotels in Dubai or holed up in some desert hideout? He
could be in one of the neighboring sheikhdoms—Abu Dhabi or
Sharjah, or at some Bedu house in the El Ain oasis.

And the tanker, where would that be berthed? The only
place Baldwick had mentioned was Dubai. If it was in Port
Rashid at the entrance to the Creek, then Choffel could already be on board. I pictured myself going up the gangway,
being taken to my cabin, then joining the other officers in the
mess room, and Henri Choffel standing there, his hand held
out in greeting, not knowing who I was. What did I do then—
wait until the end of the voyage? A full shipload of Gulf
crude, that would mean Europe, most likely—down Africa,
round the Cape, and up almost the full length of the Atlantic.
Five weeks at least, presuming the evaporators were in good
condition and the boiler didn't start cutting out—five weeks
during which I would be meeting Choffel daily, in the mess
room at the evening pour-out, at mealtimes in the saloon.

The thought appalled me, remembering what had happened, thinking of Karen. Even now, with Balkaer and the
Cornish cliffs far behind, I could still feel the soft smoothness
of her skin, the touch of her as she lay in my arms—and just
remembering the feel of her I was aroused. She had always
had that ability, to rouse me instantly, by a touch, often just
by a look, or the way she laughed. And then, just when we
had come to Balkaer and she was doing a lot of heavy carrying, discovering she was pregnant. I could see her face. It was
so clear in my mind it seemed framed in the Perspex window

against the star-bright night, her eyes alight with happiness and that big mouth of hers bubbling with excitement as she came out of the back room the doctor used as a surgery on his weekly visits to Sennen. "I'm going to have a baby," she'd cried and flung her arms round my neck, right there in front of the doctor's patients.

And then six months later she'd lost it. The pains had started at dusk, quite suddenly. One moment she was sitting in that junk chair of hers, the next she was writhing on the floor, screaming. It had been a black, windy night, rain driving in off the sea in sheets. The Kerrisons' telephone line was down and I had had to run all the way to the Cunnacks' farm, which was over the hill. God, what a night that had been! So much of it waiting, helpless, first for the doctor, then for the ambulance, with Karen clutching at us, her face screwed up in agony, her hair dank with sweat. And in the dawn, a wild wet dawn, carrying her up the hill to the ambulance.

By then she had miscarried and was quiet, sunk in a coma of exhaustion. She never told me what exactly went wrong, or what they did to her in the hospital in Penzance, only that she would never be able to have another child. It was then that she began to develop that deep emotional feeling for the wild-life around us, the birds in particular, and also for the book I was struggling to write.

I was thinking of her off and on all through that long night, and of Choffel—excitement, love, and hatred all mixed up—until at last, exhausted and so utterly drained I could have slept for a week, the engine note changed and we began the long run down the diamond-studded sky to our destination. Soon there was movement in the body of the aircraft, then the lights were turned on full and the DÉFENSE DE FUMER sign lit up. Blinds were raised and through the porthand windows the first pale orange glow of dawn showed the Gulf horizon in sil-houette, and beyond it, just visible, the snowy tops of the Iranian mountains. To starboard there was nothing, only the shadowy brown darkness of the desert stretching away in limitless monotony to the great wastes of the Rub al Khali—the Empty Quarter.

It was full daylight by the time we landed, but the sun not yet risen and the air still pleasantly cool as we crossed the Tarmac to the terminal building. The Arabs, who had looked so incongruous at Charles de Gaulle Airport in their flowing robes, with the black *agal* of the Bedu encircling their white *kayffiah* headgear, now blended into the desert sandscape and it was the Europeans in their crumpled suits who looked out of place. Varsac, who had hardly spoken during the flight, became suddenly talkative as we approached the Immigration desk, and when he handed over his passport, I noticed his hand was trembling. The Immigration officer glanced up from the passport, staring at him curiously. "*Vous êtes français.*" It was a statement, the dark eyes in the dark face lighting up. He turned to me. "*Et vous, monsieur?*"

"English," I said.

He took my passport and stamped it almost perfunctorily, talking all the time to Varsac in French. He was a Pakistani, proud of speaking French as well as English, and it seemed an age before he let us through with a flash of white teeth and a murmured "Have a good time."

"What were you worried about?" I asked.

Varsac shook his head, still nervous, his face longer and sadder-looking than ever. "*Rien.* I am afraid they might have some records, that is all." He shrugged. "You can nevair be sure, eh?"

"Records of what?" I asked him.

He hesitated, then said, "It is in the Gulf, an old cargo sheep from Bombay to Khorramshahr. It is August and we are lying with no engines, the sheep so hot the metal is blistering our hands. No morphia. Nothing." There was a long pause. "He is broken—crushed in the main drive. An engineer. Finally —I shoot him."

I stared at him. "You mean a man, you killed him?"

"He was my friend." He gave a half shrug. "What else? And such a nice boy, from Indo-Chine." He wouldn't say anything more, only that it was a long time ago and he had had to jump a big dhow bound for Muscat. The baggage appeared, and when we were through Customs we were met by a pock-marked Libyan in a smart new suit who drove us into town through dusty, crowded streets, to a hotel just back of the Creek.

It was five years since I'd been in Dubai, yet now it seemed but a few weeks, the smell of the place just the same, a compound of spices, charcoal fires, sweat, putrefaction, and desert —the dust of ages everywhere, the dust of old mud stucco crumbling into decay, of desert sands swirling against the concrete breakwaters of high-rise blocks, the scuff of countless human feet. I removed my tie and put it in my pocket. The sun was already throwing deep shadows, and it was getting hot.

Deeper into the town I saw how quickly oil had made its mark; the skyline altered and new buildings everywhere. The Persian wind towers, those dainty filigree turrets that were the earliest form of air conditioning, tunneling the sea breezes down into the rooms below—they were all gone now. They had been such a feature of the place when I had first come there with my mother, and the business section of the Creek had been crowded then with great merchant houses, ornate stucco walls that kept the world at bay, the secret inner courtyards inviolate. Now banking houses and company offices paraded their wealth in a façade of marble and glass.

So much changed since those faraway days before the oil tide reached Dubai. But not the crowd. The crowd was still as thick, still as cosmopolitan, a constant flow of movement, with only the Bedu Arabs motionless in the cafés waiting for the metallic Tannoy voice on the minaret of the nearby mosque to call them to prayer. And the Creek itself, that was still the

same, except that even more of the dhows had converted entirely to power, hardly a mast to be seen. But there were just
as many of them rafted against the wharves, a jumble of *sam-
buks, booms,* and *jalibuts* loading tramp ship goods from all
over the world for distribution through the Gulf, most of them
still with the traditional thunderbox built out over the side like
a small pulpit.

When we reached the hotel, the Libyan, whose name was
Mustafa, gave us his card, which was gold-embossed with an
address in one of the back alleys near the *Suk,* also the name
of a nearby store where we would be provided with lightweight trousers and sleeveless shirts. We would be at the hotel
for at least two days, he said—until L.B. arrived. No, he didn't
know the name of the tanker, or where it was berthed. He was
a travel agent. He knew nothing about ships. Anything we
spent in the hotel would be paid for—food, drinks, everything
—but if there was something special required we could contact
him. The dark eyes stared at us coldly and I wondered what a
Libyan was doing running a travel agency in Dubai. He left us
with the information that two of our ship's officers were already billeted in the hotel and another would arrive tomorrow.
Choffel was not among the names he mentioned.

After checking in, I went straight to the store. It was a
cheap place, if anything could be called cheap in Dubai, the
trousers and shirts poor-quality cotton and not very well cut.
But at least they were cool, for by the time I had had a shower
the sun, beating onto the balcony of my room, was very hot. I
went down to the desk again and had them check through
the names of all the guests in their hotel. The place was a
microcosm of modern Dubai, businessmen from Japan, Ger-
many, France, Holland, Britain, anywhere that produced the
machines and infrastructure the Gulf exchanged for its oil.
There were even two Chinese and a little group from Bye-
lorussia, all of them with briefcases brimful of specifications
and optimism. There were oilmen, too, and air crews staying

the night, as well as men like ourselves, officers from coasters in the Creek and ships in Port Rashid, all vocal testimony to the fact that Dubai remained the mercantile center of the Gulf, the entrepôt for the United Arab Emirates.

But there was no Choffel, no Speridion, not even anyone with a name that looked as though it might be Welsh. Something I did discover, however—there had been half a dozen guests booked in by Mustafa's agency the previous week and they had left three days ago, not in taxis, but in Land Rovers. Again, Choffel had not been one of them. Prior to that there was no record of any of Mustafa's clients having stayed at the hotel, though back in October he had booked accommodations and then canceled them. The receptionist remembered that because the hotel had been fully booked and the last-minute cancellation of four rooms had upset the management.

I walked down to the Creek then, turning left toward the bridge, and found a place where I could sit in the sun with a coffee and a glass of water and watch the world go by. There was a coaster coming in from the Gulf flying the Iranian flag, lighters and launches and small boats bobbing in its wake, the whole waterborne concourse a pageant of movement with a big oceangoing dhow, a *boom* by the look of it, though it was hard to tell, as it lay like a barge right in front of the coaster's bows, its engine presumably broken down. Noise and movement and color, every type of dress, every color suit, the smell of dust and spices, and the bloated carcass of a goat floating slowly past with its legs stiff in the air like the legs of a chair. I finished my coffee and closed my eyes, dozing in the warmth of the sun. The unhurried tempo of the desert was all about me, men walking hand-in-hand or squatting motionless, the leisurely, endless haggling over price at every shop and stall in sight. Time stood still, the Muslim world of Arabia flowing round me, familiar and relaxing. It is an atmosphere in which fatalism thrives, so that, dozing in the sun, I was able to forget my worries about the future. I was tired of course. But it was more than that. It was in my blood, the feeling that I was just a straw in the stream of life and everything the will of God. *Insh' Allah!* And so I didn't concern myself very much about the reaction of Baldwick and his friends if they were to discover I was visiting the Lloyd's agent and GODCO. My only problem, it seemed to me at the time, was which of them I should visit first, or whether to go at all. It was so much easier to sit there in the sun, but I did need to check those crew details with the oil company's Marine Superintendent.

In the end, after cashing a traveler's check at one of the banks, I went to the GODCO building first, largely because it was there in front of me, a towering new block dominating the downstream bend of the Creek. After the noisy, saffron-scented heat of the waterfront, the cloistered air conditioning of the interior hit me like a refrigerator. The Marine Superintendent's offices were on the fifth floor with a view seaward to a litter of cranes, masts, and funnels that was the Port Rashid skyline. Captain Roger Perrin, the name Saltley had given me, was the man in charge of the whole of the Company's fleet, and when I was finally shown into his office, he said curtly, "Why didn't you phone? I'd have had everything ready for you then." He was bearded, with pale cold eyes and a presence that I suspected had been carefully cultivated in the years he had been moving up the Company's marine ladder. He waved me to the chair opposite him where the hard light pouring through the plastic louvers of the venetian blinds shone straight on my face. "Well, why are you here? What do the solicitor people want to know that I haven't already told them?" And he added, "I'm responsible for Casualty Co-ordination, but I tell you now, in this Company we don't expect casualties. And in the case of these two tankers there's nothing to co-ordinate. They've just disappeared and your people know as much about it as I do. So why are you here?"

The only reason I could give him was the crew pictures, but when I asked to see them, he said, "I sent a full set of the pictures to our London office. That was three days ago. You could have seen them there."

"I had to go to France."

"France?" The fact that I hadn't come straight out from London seemed to make a difference. He gave a little shrug. "Well, I've no doubt you have your own lines of inquiry to follow." He reached behind him to a bookcase where a potted plant stood like a rubbery green sentinel, picked up two files, and passed them across the desk to me. I opened the one labeled AURORA B. There were copies of design drawings for the ship's hull and engines, detailed specifications, and, in an envelope marked PERSONNEL, a crew list, together with a full-face closeup of each individual. This was the only item of real interest, and while he was telling me how the Indian Air Force had mounted a search in the sea area west of Sri Lanka and the oil company's representatives had appealed through the local press and media for anybody who might have picked up a radio signal or voice message, I went slowly through the pictures. I had met so many odd characters in cargo runs around the Gulf that there was always a chance.

"Also we have checked the background of every officer—wives, girl friends, sexual eccentricities, everything." He had a flat, rather monotonous voice and my mind kept drifting away, wondering vaguely whether the Lloyd's agent would have heard from Pritchard yet. My contact was Adrian Gault. I had met him once, a little shriveled man who was said to have his ear to the ground and spies in every merchant house on the waterfront. An old Gulf hand like that, surely to God he would know by now what dhow had picked Choffel up, where it had taken him. It was four or five days since the man had left the *Corsaire*, time enough for news to filter through, for rumor to get its tongue round the story and spread it through the cafés and among the Gulf Arabs cooking over fires on the decks of dhows.

". . . no wreckage, only the dumped remains of ships' gar-

bage and one oil slick that was traced to a Liberian cargo vessel." He said it in an aggrieved tone, resentful of the trick Fate
had played on him. "I always run a tight ship here at GODCO
—maintenance, damage control, everything A1. Our record
speaks for itself. Since I took over this office, we've had a long
run . . ."

"Of course. I understand." I found myself embarrassed at his
need of self-justification, concentrating on the pictures then,
while he began talking about the absence of any radio signal.
Not a single ham operator had responded to their appeal, and
in the case of the *Howdo Stranger,* with the very latest in
tank-cleansing equipment . . .

I wasn't listening. There, suddenly, staring up at me, was a
dark Semitic face I had seen before—in Khorramshahr, on a
stretcher. The same birthmark like a burn blurring the full
lips, the same look of intense hostility in the dark eyes, the
womanish mouth set in a nervous smile. But it was the birthmark—not even the dark little beard he had grown could hide
that. "Abol Hassan Sadeq, born Teheran, age 31, electrical engineer."

I turned the picture round so that Captain Perrin could see
it. "Know anything about him?"

He stared at it a moment, then shook his head. "You recognize him, do you?"

"Yes, but not the name. It wasn't Sadeq." I couldn't recall
the name they had given us. It had been six years ago. Sum-
mer, and so hot you couldn't touch the metal anywhere on the
ship, the Shatt al Arab flat as a shield, the air like a steam
bath. Students had rioted in Teheran, and in Abadan there
had been an attempt to blow up two of the oil storage tanks.
We should have sailed at dawn, but we were ordered to wait.
And then the Shah's police had brought him on board, shortly
after noon. We sent him straight down to the sick bay and
sailed for Kuwait, where we handed him over to the authori-

ties. His kidneys had been damaged, he had three ribs broken, multiple internal bruising, and his front teeth badly broken.

"Interrogation?" Perrin asked.

"I suppose so."

"He wasn't one of the students, then."

I shrugged. "They said he was a terrorist."

"A terrorist." He said the word slowly as though testing out the sound of it. "And that's the same man, on the *Aurora B*. Does that make any sense to you?"

"Only that a bomb would account for her total disappearance. But there'd still have to be a motive." I searched through the file, found the man's dossier, and flipped it across the desk to him. It simply listed the ships he had served on.

"We'll check them all, of course," Perrin said. "And the security people in Abu Dhabi, they may know something." But he sounded doubtful. "To blow up a tanker the size of the *Aurora B* . . ." He shook his head. "It's got to be a hell of a big explosion to leave nothing behind, and no time for the radio operator to get off a Mayday—a suicidal explosion, in fact, for he'd have to be resigned to his own death. And it doesn't explain the loss of the other tanker."

I was working through the pictures again, particularly those of the *Howdo Stranger* crew. There was nobody else I recognized. I hadn't expected there would be. It was only the purest chance that I had ever set eyes on Sadeq before. And if it hadn't been for the GODCO practice of taking crew pictures for each voyage . . . I was still trying to remember the name the Shah's police had given us when they had rolled him screaming off the stretcher onto the hot deck plates. It certainly hadn't been Sadeq.

We discussed it for a while, then I left, promising to look in the following day. After the cool interior of the oil building, it seemed much hotter outside on the crowded waterfront. Noisier, too, and smellier. I crossed the Creek in a crowded launch to one of the older buildings just upstream of the warehouses. Gault's office was on the first floor. There was no air conditioning and the windows were wide open to the sounds and smells of the wharves with a view over the rafted dhows to the mosque behind the financial buildings on the other side. Gault was at the door to greet me, a thin, stooped man in khaki slacks and a short-sleeved shirt of virulent color. He had a wide smile in a freckled, sun-wrinkled face, and his arms were freckled, too. "Heard you'd arrived safely."

"Did you think I wouldn't?" I asked him.

"Well, you never know, do you?" He stared at me, still smiling. "Salt telexed yesterday. Last time we met, you were mate of the old *Dragonera.* Then you left the Gulf." He took me over to the window. "There you are, nothing changed. The Gulf still the navel of the world and Dubai the little wrinkled belly button that handles all the traffic. Well, why is he employing you?"

"He seems to think my knowledge of the Gulf—"

"There are at least two ships' captains on Forthright's staff who have a bloody sight more experience of the Gulf than you, so that's the first thing I want to know. Two tankers go missing down by Sri Lanka and you come out here, to Dubai— why?"

I began talking about Karachi then, but he cut me short. "I read the papers. You're after Choffel and you're onto something. Something I don't know about." He was staring at me, his eyes no longer smiling and his hand gripping my arm. "Those tankers sailed from Mina Zayed loaded with Abu Dhabi crude. But still you come to Dubai. Why?"

"Baldwick," I said.

"Ah!" He let go my arm and waved me to a leather pouf with an old mat thrown over it. "Coffee or tea?"

"Tea," I said and he clapped his hands. A small boy with a rag of a turban appeared at the door. He told him to bring tea for both of us and squatted cross-legged on the Persian carpet.

"That boy's the son of one of our best *naukhadas*. He's here to learn the business. His father doesn't want him to grow up to be nothing but the skipper of a dhow. He thinks the dhows will all be gone by then. You agree?" I said I thought it likely, but I don't think he heard me. "What's Baldwick got to do with those missing tankers?"

"Nothing, as far as I know."

"But he knows where Choffel is hiding out, is that it?"

I nodded.

"You'd better tell me about it, then."

By the time I had given him an account of my dealings with Baldwick, the tea had arrived—hot, sweet, and very refreshing in that noisy, shadowy room.

"Where's the tanker you're supposed to join?" he asked.

"I thought you might know."

He laughed and shook his head. "No idea." And he had no information to give me on Baldwick's present activities. "There's rumors of Russian ships skulking in the Straits of Hormuz. But it's just bazaar talk." As a youngster he had served in India and he still referred to the *Suk* as a bazaar. "You know how it is. Since the Red Army moved into Afghanistan the dhow Arabs see Russian ships in every hidey-hole in the Gulf. And the *khawrs* to the south of the Straits are a natural. You could lose a whole fleet in some of those inlets, except that it would be like putting them in a furnace. Hot as hell." He laughed. "But even if the Russians are playing hide-and-seek, that's not Len Baldwick's scene at all. Too risky. I've known the bastard on and off now for more than a dozen years—slave girls, boys, drugs, gold, bogus oil bonds, anything where he takes the rake-off and others the rap. Who owns this tanker of yours, do you know?"

I shook my head.

"So you're going into it blind." He finished his tea and sat there for a moment thinking about it. "Tell me, would you be taking that sort of a chance if it wasn't for the thought that Choffel might be on the same ship with you?"

"No."

He nodded and got to his feet. "Well, that's your business. Meanwhile, this came for you this morning." He reached across his desk and handed me a telex. "Pritchard."

It was the answer to my request for background information on Welsh national servicemen in the engine room of H.M.S. *Formidable* in 1952. There had been two of them. Forthright's had then checked four sinkings in suspicious circumstances in 1959, also two in late '58. There followed details of the sinking in October 1958 of the French cargo vessel *Lavandou,* an ex-liberty ship, off the Caribbean island of Martinique. She had been abandoned in deep water, but the edge of a hurricane had drifted her into the shallows northeast of the island so that divers had been able to get down to her. They had found extensive damage to the seawater inlets to the condensers. Second Engineer David Price, accused of sabotage by both captain and chief engineer, had by then disappeared, having taken passage on a vessel sailing for Dutch Guiana, which is now Surinam. The inquiry into the loss of the *Lavandou* found Price to blame. FINAL CLINCHER FOR US, the telex concluded, IS THAT HE WAS SIGNED ON TO THE LAVANDOU AS ENGINEER AT THE PORT OF CAYENNE IN FRENCH GUIANA IN PLACE OF HENRI ALEXANDRE CHOFFEL, WHO FELL INTO HARBOR AND DROWNED AFTER A NIGHT ON THE TOWN. COMPANY OWNING LAVANDOU REGISTERED IN CAYENNE. A DAVID MORGAN PRICE SERVED H.M.S. FORMIDABLE, 1952. THANK YOU. PRITCHARD.

That settled it. No good his daughter, or anybody else, trying to tell me he was innocent. Not now. Price, Choffel, Speridion—I wondered what he was calling himself now. None of the names, not even Price, was on the hotel guest list. I asked Gault about the dhow that had met up with the *Corsaire* in the Straits of Hormuz, but he knew nothing about it and wasn't really interested. "Dhows gravitate to Dubai like wasps to a honey pot. If you think he was brought in here, then you'd better try the carpet dealers, they know all the gossip. As far as I'm concerned, the *Petros Jupiter* is a U.K. problem. Choffel's no concern of mine . . ." He sat staring down at his coffee. "Who do you think would employ a man like Baldwick to recruit ships' officers?" Another pause. "And why?" he added, looking straight at me.

"I hoped you could tell me that," I said.

"Well, I can't." He hesitated, then leaned toward me and said, "What are you going to do when you meet up with this man Price, or Choffel, or whatever he's calling himself now?"

I shook my head. "I've got to find him first," I muttered.

"So you're letting Baldwick recruit you."

"Yes."

"A ship you know nothing about. God, man! You don't know where she is, who owns her, what the purpose of the voyage is. You're going into it absolutely blind. But you could be right." He nodded to himself. "About Choffel, I mean. A man like that—it makes sense. There has to be something wrong about the setup or they wouldn't be offering double rates and a bonus, and Baldwick wouldn't be mixed up in it. When's he get in to Dubai, do you know?"

"Mustafa said tomorrow."

"Have you got his address here?"

I remembered then. "A telephone number, that's all."

He went to his desk and made a note of it. "I'll have somebody keep an eye on him, then. And on this Libyan travel agent. Also, I'll make inquiries about the tanker you're joining. But that may not be easy, particularly if she's over the other side of the Gulf in an Iranian port. Well, that's it." He held out his hand. "Nothing much else I can do, except tell you to be careful. There's a lot of money washing around this port, a lot of peculiar people. It's much worse than it was when you were last here. So watch it." He walked with me to the stairs. "That boy who brought the tea. His name is Khalid. If my people pick up anything useful, I'll send him to you."

"You don't want me to come here?"

"No. From what you told me it could be dangerous. And if it's politics, not money, you've got yourself mixed up in, then my advice is take the next flight home. Your background makes you very vulnerable." He smiled and patted my shoulder. "*Salaam alykoum.*"

I walked back to the hotel, changed into a pair of swimming trunks, and had a light meal at a table by the pool. The courtyard, airless in the shadow of piled-up balconies, echoed to the murmur of voices, the occasional splash of a body diving. Afterward I lay in a chair sipping an ice-cold sherbet and thinking about the *Aurora B,* what it would have been like on the bridge, on watch, when spontaneous combustion, or whatever it was, sent her to the bottom. The people I had contacted in the insurance world—underwriters, Lloyd's agents, marine solicitors, everyone—they had all emphasized that marine fraud was on the increase. Like ordinary crime, it was tax-free, and as the stakes got bigger . . . I was thinking of Sadeq then, suddenly remembering the name the Shah's police had given him, a name he had confirmed to us as he lay in the *Dragonera's* sick bay. It had been Qasim. So what was Qasim, a man they had claimed was a terrorist, doing on board the *Aurora B* under another name? Terrorists were trained in the handling of explosives, and instantly I was seeing the fireball holocaust that was so indelibly printed on my mind, knowing that if a bomb had been cleverly placed there was no way the radio operator would be able to put out a call for help.

Was the tanker we were joining intended to go the same way, delayed-action explosives attached to the hull? And us promised a bonus at the end of the voyage! But at least Baldwick was predictable. There was nothing political about him, or about Choffel, and fraud was almost certainly less dangerous. At least, that's what I tried to tell myself, but Adrian

Gault's warning stayed in my mind. Here in Dubai anything seemed possible.

In the cool of the evening I took a stroll through the *Suk*, looking in on several stall-holders I had known. Two of them were Pakistani. One, an Afridi, dealt in old silver jewelry—bangles, Bedu blanket pins, headpieces, anklets. The other, Azad Hussain, was a carpet merchant. It was he who told me about the dhow. It wasn't just a rumor, either. He had heard it from a *naukhada* who had recently bought him a consignment of Persian carpets. They had been smuggled across the border into the little Baluchistan port of Jiwani. There had been two other dhows there, one waiting to embark cattle fodder from an oasis inland, the other under charter to Baldwick and waiting to pick up a group of Pakistani seamen being flown from Karachi.

He couldn't tell me their destination. It's a question *naukhadas* are wary of asking each other in the Gulf and he had only mentioned the matter to Azad because he was wondering why an Englishman like Baldwick should be shipping Pakistanis out of a little border port like Jiwani. If it had been hashish now, trucked down from the tribal areas close under the Hindu Kush or the Karakoram ranges of the Himalayas . . . He didn't know the *naukhada's* name or the name of the dhow, only that the seamen embarked numbered a dozen or so and the dhow had left immediately, heading west along the coast toward the Straits of Hormuz.

That night I went to bed early and for the first time, it seemed, since Karen's death I slept like a log, waking to bright sunlight and the call of the muezzin. Varsac was waiting for me when I went down, his eyes shifty, the pupils dilated, and his long face wrestling with an ingratiating smile. He wanted a loan. "Ees *très chèr*, Dubai," he murmured, his breath stale, his hand clutching at me. God knows what he wanted it for, but I had seen the ragged-turbaned little boy hovering in the entrance and I brushed Varsac off, telling him to stay in the hotel where everything was provided. The boy came running as he saw me. "What is it, Khalid?"

"The sahib send you this." He held a folded sheet of paper out to me. "You read it inside please, then nobody see."

It was very brief: "Dhow chartered by B. came in last night. Loading ship's stores. Khalid will take you to see it. Take care. You were followed yesterday. A.G." I stuffed the note into my pocket and went out into the street again, Khalid clutching hold of my arm and telling me to go down the alley opposite the hotel and at the Creek I would find his uncle waiting for me with a small boat. I should hire it, but behave as though it were a sudden thought and argue about the money. He would cross by one of the ferry launches and meet me somewhere by the wharves. Having given me my instructions, he ran off in the direction of the mosque. I stood there for a moment as though savoring the warmth of the sunlight that slanted a narrow beam between two of the older dwellings. A casual glance at the Arabs hanging around the hotel narrowed it to two, and there was another inside the entrance who seemed to be watching me, a small man in spotless robes with a little pointed beard and a *khanjar* knife at his belt. I went back into the hotel, bought an English paper, and then sauntered across to the alley that led to the Creek.

I walked slowly, reading the paper as I went. An attack on the Government by the conservationist and fishing lobbies for failing to do anything about oil pollution in the North Sea had ousted the Iranian bombers as the lead story. At the waterfront I paused, standing with the paper held up to my face, but half turning so that I could see back up the alley. There was nobody there except a big fair-bearded man strolling with his hands in his pockets. His face was shaded by the pale khaki peak of his kepi-type cap.

Khalid's uncle proved to be a hook-nosed piratical-looking rascal with a headcloth pushed well back to reveal a thin untidy fringe of black hair that straggled down each cheek to join a neat little wisp of a beard. The boat was from a *boom* loading at one of the wharves. It was little more than a cockleshell and crossing the Creek it bobbed and bounced to the wash of power boats, launches, ferries, runabouts, and load carriers. I lost sight of the man with the kepi cap and on the far side of the Creek, where we were out of the shadow of the high bank buildings and in the sun, it was hot and the smells stronger as we threaded our way through the dhows, through narrow guts between wooden walls that sun and salt had bleached to the color of light amber. He rowed me to what I think he said was a *baghla*. "Khalid say is this one."

It was a big dhow, one of the few that hadn't had its mast sawn off and was still capable of carrying sail. It had its up-curved bow thrust in against the wharf. Two men were unloading cardboard cartons of tinned goods from a trolley, carrying them across a narrow gangplank and passing them down into the hold. Khalid was there already, beckoning me to join him on the wharf. I clambered up and he grabbed hold of my hand and drew me back into the shadowed entrance to the warehouse. "Sahib say you look, then you know what ship is and who is on her."

It was a two-masted vessel with an exhaust pipe sticking up for'ard of the poop and a little group squatting in a tight huddle round a *huqqah*, or water pipe, whose stem they passed from one to the other. Khalid pointed the *naukhada* out to me, a big man with a bushy beard and wild eyes peering out of an untidy mass of black hair. "Mohammed bin Suleiman," he whispered. "Is not Dubai. Is from Ras al Khaimah."

I stood there a while, taking in the details of the dhow, memorizing the faces squatting round the bubbling water pipe. Then Khalid was tugging at my arm, pulling me farther back into the warehouse. The man in the kepi cap was coming along the wharf. I could see him clearly now, the sunlight providing his burly figure with a black shadow and glinting on the fair skin and the blond sun-bleached beard. He came abreast of the little group on the dhow's poop and stopped. I couldn't hear what he said, but it was in English with a strong accent and he indicated the warehouse. Then he was coming toward us and we shrank back into the dim interior, slipping behind a pile of mealie bags.

He stopped in the entrance, pushing his cap back and mopping his brow as he shouted for a man called Salima Aznat who was apparently in charge of the warehouse. He wore locally made sandals with curved-up toe guards, blue trousers, and a white short-sleeved shirt with sweat stains under the arms. "*Waar is het?*" he muttered to himself. "*Waar hebben zy het verstopt?*" It sounded like Swedish, or Dutch maybe. He turned, beckoning to the Arabs loading the dhow, then began moving slowly into the warehouse, peering at the labels on the larger wooden crates, checking the stenciling on the sides.

"Who is he?" I whispered as he was joined by the warehouseman and the two of them disappeared into the cavernous recesses of the building. But Khalid didn't know. "Is at your hotel," he said.

"One of Baldwick's people?"

He nodded. The sound of voices echoed from the far end and a moment later there was the slam of a crate and the rumble of a trolley being dragged toward us. The little group was coming back now with two or three cases on the trolley. They reached the entrance and paused, so that I saw the man very clearly—the bleached hair, the pale eyes, his bare arms like freckled gold in the sunlight. He was talking quickly, radiating a ponderous sense of nervous energy. A round, Dutch-looking face. Hals! I was remembering what Baldwick had said at Balkaer when he'd talked about pollution. It had to be Pieter Hals. And as the little group stood there for a moment in the sun I could see the letters stenciled on the wooden sides of the nearest case: RADIO EQUIPMENT—FRAGILE—HANDLE WITH CARE. The word FRAGILE was stenciled in red.

Back at the hotel I found that Pieter Hals had checked in

that morning. I also inquired about Price, but nobody of that name had stayed in the hotel for the past month, at any rate. I was convinced then that the dhow had taken him straight to the ship and that he was there on board. I didn't see Hals again that day, and though I met up with several people I had known before and had a word with Perrin on the phone, none of them could tell me anything about Baldwick's tanker people or where the vessel lay. I even took a taxi at considerable expense to Port Rashid, but every ship in the harbor was owned by old, established companies.

That evening, strolling along the waterfront just as dusk was falling, I saw bin Suleiman's dhow haul out into the crowded waterway and watched her crew hoist the lateen mainsail as she motored with a soft *tonk-tonk* round the downtown bend toward the open sea. From this I concluded that Baldwick's employers must have their tanker loading at Mina Zayed in the neighboring sheikhdom of Abu Dhabi, a supposition that was to prove hopelessly wrong.

That night I had dinner at the hotel, in the roof garden restaurant where Varsac and our two other ships' officers had got themselves a corner table with the sort of view over the dog-legged waterway that a sheikh's peregrine would have, poised high in the air before a stoop. The Creek was an ink-black smudge curving between dimly lit buildings. The only brilliance seemed to be the floodlit tracery of some sort of palace and Port Rashid with its cranes and ships and an oil rig lying to, its reflection all brightly illuminated in the loading lights. Varsac hailed me as soon as I entered the room and when I paused at their table I found myself confronted by a ferrety little Glaswegian engineer with ginger hair and a grating accent. A cigarette burned unheeded on the plate beside him and in the middle of the table was an ashtray full of stubs. "Ah'm Colin Fraser," he said, holding out his hand. "What's yur nem?"

"Trevor Rodin."

"And yur job on boord?"

"Second mate."

"Aye, weel, ah'm an engineer mesel', so we'll not be seeing very much of each other now. Sit down, man, and have a drink."

The other man, a big Canadian, pulled out a chair for me, smiling, but not saying anything. I sat down. There wasn't anything else I could do. Fraser turned out to be a casualty of the Iraqi-Iranian war. He had been in one of the cargo vessels stranded in the Shatt al Arab. It was Greek-owned and had been badly shelled. The end of it was her owners had abandoned her and he had been thrown onto the beach, an engineer with shrapnel wounds in the shoulder, no ship, no money, not even a fare-paid passage home. "Bankrupt, the bastards were." The world was still in recession, the beach a cold place to be. "Och, the stories ah could tell yer. Ah bin on rigs, ferry boats, aye, on dhows, too, an' if it hadna bin for our mootual friend Len B. . . ."

He was drinking whiskey and was half cut already, his voice rambling on about the despicable nature of employers and how it was they who had kept him out of a job, a black mark against his name and the word passed from owner to owner, even out to this godforsaken end-of-the-earth dump. "Ah couldna get a job oot here if I was to promise the effing agent a whole year's salary. It's me politics, see." As far as I could gather, he was well to the left of the Militant Tendency and back home in Glasgow had been a Union troublemaker. "Colin Fraser. Ye remember, surely? It was all in the papers. I took three cargo ships doon the Clyde and anchored them roond the Polaris base so the nuclear subs couldna move in or oot."

He also claimed to have been a member of the IRA for a short time. Stranded in Belfast when his ship couldn't unload because of a dock strike, he had been given a Kalashnikov and had gone gunning for the RUC in the Falls Road district with a bunch of teenagers. "Made bombs for them, too, in a hoose

doon in Crossmaglen. But they didna pay me. Risking me life
ah was . . ." It was an aggrieved voice that went on and on,
the Glasgow accent getting harder, the ferrety face more vicious. In the end I ignored him and talked to the Canadian
who had been recruited by Hals as first mate. His name was
Rod Selkirk. He had been a trapper and a sealer, had then met
Farley Mowat, whose book *Never Cry Wolf* had affected him
deeply, and after that meeting he had stopped killing animals
for a living and had switched to coasters, trading into the
ports of the Maritimes and the Gulf of St. Lawrence. "Guess
I'm okay on navigation, but when it comes to figures . . ." He
shrugged, his body as massive and solid as you would expect
of a man who had spent most of his life in the hard North of
Canada. His round, moonlike face broke into a smile, causing
the puffed lids of the mongoloid eyes to crease into fat-
crinkled almond slits. "I'm an inshore navigator really, so
reck'n I'll never make it any higher. I'd never pass the exams,
not for my master's ticket."

"Where did you meet Pieter Hals?" I asked him.

"Shatt al Arab, same as Colin here. I was tramping, and they
just about blew us out of the water. The Iranians. They
couldn't reach the Iraqi shore, not to hit anything worthwhile,
so they took it out on us. Just for the hell of it, I guess—a bit of
target practice. Infidels don't count anyway, know what I
mean?" The smile spread into a grin. He was a likable giant
and he hardly drank at all, his voice very soft, very restful.

"What's Hals's job?" I asked.

"Captain."

Hals had only been first mate when he'd hit the headlines
and been sacked for the bomb threats he had made in the
Niger. "Is that why he's joined this Baldwick outfit?" I thought
he might see it as his only chance for promotion after what
he'd done, but the Canadian said, "No, it was pollution. He's
got something in mind," he murmured hesitantly. But when I
questioned him about it, he said he didn't know. "You ask

Pieter. Mebbe he'll tell you, once we get aboard. Right now, he doesn't talk about it." He was watching me uncertainly out of those slit eyes. "Marine pollution mean anything to you?"

He hadn't read the papers, didn't know about Karen, and when I told him she'd blown up a stranded tanker to save the coast from pollution, he smiled and said, "Then you and Pieter should get on. He blames it all on the industrial nations, says they'll pollute the world to keep their bloody machines going. You feel like that?"

"The transport of oil presents problems," I said cautiously.

"That's for sure." He nodded, expressing surprise that it was Baldwick who had recruited me, not Pieter Hals. "I never met Baldwick," he said, "but from what I hear . . ." He gave an expressive shrug and left it at that.

"*Qu'est-ce que c'est?*" Varsac was suddenly leaning forward. "What ees it you 'ear?"

"Ah'll tell yu," Fraser cut in, laughing maliciously. "Ah'll tell yu what he hears aboot Len Baldwick, that he's a fat eunuch who's made a pile pimping for oil-rich Arabs. That's the worrd from the lads ah was talking to last night. They say his fat fingers are poked up the arse of anybody who's got dirty business going in the Gulf, an' if yu think this little caper's got anything to do with saving the worrld from pollution yu're nuts. There's fraud in it somewhere, and I wouldna be surprised to find meself fixing bombs to the hull of this tanker somewhere off the coast of Africa."

Varsac stared at him, his face longer and paler than ever. "*Monsieur Baldwick, dites moi—*"

"Och, the hell wi' it." Fraser was laughing again, prodding Varsac with a nicotine-stained finger. "Yu'd hardly expect him to 'dites' yu wha' it's all aboot. He gets his cut, tha's all he cares. An' he's no sailing wi' the ship."

The Frenchman's Adam's apple jerked convulsively. "Not sailing? You know this? Ees true—certain?" He shook his head doubtfully. "I don't believe. I don't believe you know anything about it. Or about him."

"Not know aboot him!" Fraser was almost bouncing up and down in his seat. "Sure ah know aboot 'im. Ah worked for the man, didn't ah? Ran a dhow for him. That's how ah know aboot Len. Cold-hearted bastard! The Baluchi lassies, now. We'd pick 'em off a beach near Pasni. Virgins by the look of them. All bleedin' virgins. We'd take 'em across the Gulf and land them in the sand doons northeast of Sharjah. A Pakistani was behind it, some woman who gave their families a wee bit o' money and said they would be trained as nurses. Nurses, my arse! They were being sold as whoores, and it was the Pak woman and Len Baldwick made a killing in the trade. Not me. Ah just ran the bleedin' dhow for them." He called for a waiter, but nobody took any notice. "Yu got any cigarettes?" He cocked his head at me, fiddling with an empty packet. "It's clean oot, ah am."

Rumors of Baldwick's involvement in the trade had been circulating when I was last in the Gulf, but I had never before met anybody directly implicated. I sat there, staring at him, disgusted and appalled. This vicious little Glaswegian, and right beside him, the big friendly Canadian, looking as though he'd seen a devil peeping out from under a stone . . . They were like oil and water. They didn't mix. They didn't fit. And yet they'd been recruited for the same purpose. They'd be together, on the same ship, and so would I—some of us recruited by Baldwick, some by Hals.

I got to my feet. Fraser had found a waiter now and was ordering cigarettes and more drinks. I excused myself, took the elevator down to the street, and walked quickly through the alleyway to the Creek. The air was pleasantly cool, the stars bright overhead, and I sat there by the water for a long time watching the traffic and wondering what it was going to be like isolated from the rest of the world and cooped up on

board a ship with a man like Fraser. And Choffel. I wished to
God I knew about Choffel, whether he was on the ship or not.

Next morning Baldwick had arrived. He was in the lobby
when I went down, looking large and rumpled in a pale blue
tropical suit. He had another Frenchman with him, an engineer he had picked up in Marseilles, and Mustafa was flapping
around with the drivers of two Land Rovers drawn up outside
the hotel. "You get ready, please," he said to me. "We leave in
twenty minutes."

"Where for?"

But he turned away.

"Where's the ship?" I demanded, grabbing hold of him.

He hesitated. "Ask L.B. He knows. Not me."

I turned to Baldwick then, but he had heard my question
and was staring at me, his eyes red-rimmed and angry. "Just
get your things."

I hesitated. But the man was tired after the flight. He'd
been drinking and I'd know soon enough. "No, wait," he said
as I was moving away. And he asked me what the hell I'd
been up to at the GODCO offices. "And you went to see Gault.
Why?"

"How do you know?" I asked.

"Think I wouldn't have somebody keep an eye on you?" He
came lumbering toward me. "You been talking?" His tone was
menacing.

"I like to know what ship I'm sailing on, where it's berthed."

"You been asking questions?"

"Look," I said. "Adrian Gault I've known on and off for
years. Perrin, too. With time to kill I looked them up. Why
not? And of course I asked them."

"I told you to keep yer mouth shut." He was glaring at me,
and suddenly I couldn't help it, I had to know.

"Choffel," I said. "Will he be on the same ship as me?"

"Choffel?" He seemed surprised, repeating the name slowly,
his voice reluctant, his eyes sharp. "No." He was frowning

angrily, groping for the right reply. "The only engineer on board at the moment is the chief." And to settle the matter he added quickly, "His name's Price, if you want to know."

So I was right. That picture with Baldwick on the edge of it, at Sennen, when the crew came ashore. He had recruited him then, made all the arrangements for getting him to the Gulf. And now he was on board. He was there, waiting for me. I suppose I must have been staring, open-mouthed. "You don't concern yourself with Price. Understand?" He was glaring at me, conscious that the name had meant something to me, but not certain what. "You're not an engineer. You've never met him before." He was still glaring at me doubtfully and it was Varsac who came to my rescue. He had been talking very fast in French to the new arrival. Now they were both of them looking at Baldwick—the same question.

"Le tankair. *Où ça?*"

Baldwick turned his head slowly, like a bull wearily finding himself baited from another direction. "We're keeping it as a surprise for you," he growled. "Where the hell d'you think it is? In the bloody water, of course." His small eyes shifted to me, a quick glance, then he went off to get a shower.

We all had breakfast together—coffee and boiled eggs, with Baldwick's beady little eyes watching me as though I was some dangerous beast he had to keep an eye on. Afterward, when I had packed and was coming away from the reception desk after handing in my room key, Khalid suddenly appeared at my side. "For you, Said." He slipped me a blue envelope. "Sahib say it arrive last night." He was gone in a flash, scuttling out into the street, and I was left with an English air-mail letter in my hand. The writing was unfamiliar, a round, flowing hand, and the sender's name and address on the back came as a surprise. It was from Pamela Stewart.

I was thinking back to that lunch at Lloyd's, the Nelson Exhibition Room. It was all so remote. And to have reached me now she must have sent the letter off the instant Gault had reported my arrival in Dubai. The Land Rovers had started up, Baldwick shouting to me, and I slipped it into my pocket, wondering why she should have written, why the urgency.

It was just after ten as we pulled away from the hotel, Baldwick with the engineer officers in the first Land Rover, Mustafa with myself and the other deck officers in the second. There was no sign of Pieter Hals. I slit open the airmail letter and began reading it as we threaded our way through Dubai's crowded streets. It appeared to have been written in a hurry, the writing very difficult to read in places. "Dear Trevor Rodin," it began. "Daddy doesn't know I'm writing, but I thought somebody should tell you how much we appreciate what you are doing and that our thoughts are with you." It went on like that for almost half a page, then suddenly she abandoned the rather formal language, her mood changing. "I was a fool, leaving you like that. We should have gone on to a club and got drunk, or gone for a walk together, done whatever people do when the heart's too full for sensible words. Instead, I made a silly excuse and left you standing there under the Nelson picture. Please forgive me. I was upset. And my mind's been in a turmoil ever since."

I stopped there, staring down at the round, orderly writing on the blue paper, aware suddenly that this wasn't an ordinary letter. "God Almighty!" I breathed.

The Canadian was saying something. His hand gripped my arm. "It's not Mina Zayed. Abu Dhabi is west of Dubai. We've turned east."

I slipped the letter back into my pocket and looked out at the chaos of construction work through which we were driving. This was the outskirts of Dubai and he was right. We were on the coast road headed east toward Sharjah, and the *shamal* was starting to blow little streamers of sand across the Tarmac road.

"Is it Mina Khalid, you reck'n?" I shook my head. I didn't think it was deep enough. "Mebbe an SMB." He turned to

Mustafa. "They got one of the big single mooring buoys for tanker loading along the coast here?" he asked.

The Libyan stared at him blankly.

"Well, where the hell are we going?"

But all Mustafa said was, "You see. Very good accommodation. Sea view very fine."

I was staring out of the sand-blown side window, memories of childhood flooding back. Nothing had changed, only the road and a few modern buildings. The country on either side was just the same—a vast vista of sky and sand. We passed the remains of the little tin-roofed hospital where my mother had been a nurse. I could remember playing in the dunes there, pretending to be Sayid bin Maktun, the old sheikh of Dubai who had surprised a big raiding force from Abu Dhabi and slaughtered sixty of them at their camp in the desert. We played at pirates, too, using an old dugout canoe we had found washed up on a sandspit in the silted Sharjah estuary and the little Baluch boy was our slave.

I sat there, staring out as the low dunescape dropped away to the gleaming mud flats of the *subqat* that stretched out to a distant glint of the sea. The wind was stronger here, blowing out of the northwest, and I could have cried for the memory of that little Baluch boy—so thin, so scared, so dead these many years. We skirted Sharjah, the *subqat* giving way to low coastal dunes, sand blowing again in long streamers from the wheels of the leading Land Rover. Occasionally we caught glimpses of the sea, a dark blue-green shot through with the white of breaking wavetops, and the cloudless sky pearl-colored with the glare of the sun. A glimpse of the fort that had been a radio communications center in the early days and we were driving fast along the coast toward Ras al Khaimah, the interior of the Land Rover hot and full of sand, the dunes shimmering.

We stopped only once, just beyond Umm al Qaiwain, for sandwiches and coffee served on the tailgate of the leading

Land Rover. We didn't stay long, for though we were under the lee of a small dune sparsely covered with brittle dried-up furze, the wind blowing straight off the sea filled the air with a gritty dusting of fine sand. Less than an hour later we pulled into Ras al Khaimah, where the Jebel cliffs begin to form a red background. Here we were given quarters in a little fly-screened motel with cracked walls and temperamental plumbing. The skeletal ribs of a half-constructed dhow thrust pale wooden frame-ends against the blue sky.

What the hell were we doing at Ras al Khaimah? Mustafa and the Land Rovers had left as soon as our luggage had been off-loaded. And since Baldwick wouldn't talk about it, speculation was rife, particularly among the deck officers. Accustomed to think in terms of navigation, our guess was that the ship was across the other side of the Gulf in Iranian waters, or perhaps loading at one of the island tanker terminals, Abu Masa or Tumbs. The engineers didn't care so much. Fraser had got hold of a bottle of scotch and the man from Marseilles, Jean Lebois, had brought some cognac with him. Baldwick and Varsac joined them and the four settled down to drink and play poker. I went for a walk.

The motel was set in what looked like a piece of waste ground left over from the construction boom, bits of plastic, broken bottles, rusting iron scattered everywhere, half buried in the sand, and all that was left of the attempt to improve the surroundings were the remains of bushes dead of heat and neglect. But where the sand was untouched, stretching in a long yellow vista into the sun, there was solitude and a strange beauty. The wind had dropped, the sea making little flopping sounds and long white lines as the wavelets fell upon the dark glint of wet sand. And inland, beyond the radio tower, red-brown slopes rose endlessly to the distant heights of the Jebel al Harim. I sat in the sand, watching the sun go down and reading Pamela Stewart's letter again.

The round, rather careful writing, the conventional phrasing

—I could picture her face, the simple straightforward plainness of the features, the directness of the gaze from those quiet eyes, the mobility of the over-large mouth. It was the only sexy thing about her, that large mouth. So why did I remember her so clearly? "I don't know where, or in what circumstances, you will read this, or even if it will reach you, but I wish I were able to do what you are doing. We should be able to find out the truth for ourselves, not ask somebody else to do it for us. There is that, which is a natural feeling I think, but there is also something else, something I'm not sure I understand, which is perhaps why I left you so abruptly with such a silly excuse."

The sun was low now, the sky paling overhead, and the sails of a dhow stood black in silhouette against the pink of cloud shapes hanging over the Iranian shore. The energy packed into that strongly shaped body, the sense of vitality, quiet and controlled—that, too, I remembered. "I've never faced this problem before . . ." That was how the letter ended—"I've never faced this problem before, so bear with me. I will be thinking of you, and praying that all goes well." Nothing else, except her signature—"Pamela."

I sat there for a long time with the letter in my hand, thinking about it as the sun's rim touched the sea and the whole desert shore blazed with fire, wondering if she had any idea what her words meant to me—that somebody, somewhere in the world, was thinking of me and believed, however temporarily, that she cared.

And then the sun was down, the cliffs behind me darkening and the dhow was feeling its way into the Creek. I walked quickly back along the sands, hearing the *tonk-tonk* of its diesel in the fast-gathering dusk, and when I was back, at the point where the Creek widened out into a large flat sheet of water, I found it lying at anchor right off the motel. I knew then that it was bin Suleiman's dhow, but nobody came ashore from it, so that I wasn't sure Pieter Hals was on board until we embarked the following morning,

The *shamal* was blowing again then and even in the shelter of the Creek it took time to embark the six of us, the dhow's only tender being a small wooden boat. Baldwick came with us and there was a quantity of locally grown produce to load. It took altogether six trips, so that it was almost eleven before the anchor was up and we were motoring seaward. The sky was a clear, bright blue and the sun shone warm on the red cliffs, the waters of the Gulf foaming white at their base. It was a wonderful day for a sail, but where would we end up? Rod Selkirk and I were standing together on the leeward side of the high poop, both of us watching the bearded figure of bin Suleiman motionless beside the helmsman, a loose end of his turban flying in the wind. The low sandspit slid away to port and the dhow thrust its curved beak into deeper water. Would he hold his course and head for Iran, or turn along the coast?

"I don't get it," Selkirk said. "Why all the secrecy?" He had spoken to Hals when he came forward, but had got nothing out of him.

We were plugging almost dead to windward, no sails set, the dhow beginning to slam as the bows thrust into the steepening waves. "Sure looks like Iran," he said, and at that moment bin Suleiman nodded to the helmsman. The long wooden arm of the tiller was thrust over and the dhow came slowly round onto a northeasterly heading. Shouts and the deck erupting into violent activity as the big lateen sail was hoisted up the mainmast. Soon both sails were set, the engine stopped, and we were creaming along, rolling heavily with the spray flying silver in the sun and a long vista of ochre-red cliffs opening up to starboard, the Straits of Hormuz not fifty miles away.

Pieter Hals came up from below. I think he had been check-

ing the stores loaded at Dubai. He stood for a moment in the
waist of the dhow staring out at the coast, toward the little
port of Mina Saqr nestled right against the mountains. I had
been there once, in the dhow that had taken me to Baluchistan. I moved across the deck to join Hals. "Where are we
going?" I asked him.

"One of the *khawrs*." His voice sounded vague, his mind on
something else.

The *khawrs* were rocky inlets. There were a lot of them cutting deep into the Musandam Peninsula on the south side of
the Straits, none on the Iranian side. "So our ship is not in
Iran?"

"No."

"Why is it anchored in one of the *khawrs?*"

He didn't answer, still staring at the coast. And when I
repeated the question, he turned his head slowly, staring down
at me vacantly, his mind still far away. His eyes were a light
blue, crease lines in the skin at the corners, and there were
freckles under the sun-bleached beard. "You're Rodin, are
you?"

I nodded.

"Your wife," he said. "I read about that." He held out his
hand. "*Ja.* She is an example to us all." He stared at me. "Tell
me, did you know?"

"Know what?" But something in his eyes gave me the answer.

He waited.

"I was at a meeting," I said. "She did it on the spur of the
moment. When she heard the result."

"When she heard they weren't going to do anything to prevent the next oil spill."

I nodded, wishing I hadn't spoken to him now, wanting to
get away. "She didn't realize the whole ship would be blown
up," I muttered quickly. "She was not a very practical person."

"No?" He smiled. "Eminently practical, I should say. *Ja*. But not political. A pity, that. Her death achieved nothing. She should have threatened, made terms, forced them to do something. A law of the sea to control pollution. Powers of arrest, and the death penalty, if necessary—with naval vessels and aircraft constantly on patrol in restricted waters with power to take immediate action, against any ship, of any nationality. Only that way will we stop the destruction of our marine environment. You agree?"

I nodded. It was what we had so often talked about.

"Is that why you're here?" He was frowning. "You're not one of my boys. You're Len Baldwick's lot."

"Does that make a difference?"

The blue eyes seemed to look right through me. "You don't know, do you? So, why are you here?"

"Is Choffel one of your boys?" I asked him.

"Choffel?"

"The man who calls himself Price. David Price."

"The chief engineer."

"Somebody sent a dhow to pick him up from a French ship in the Straits."

"Baldwick sent it." He stood there, frowning. "Choffel? Ah!" His hand slammed down on the wooden capping of the bulwarks. "So that's it. That's who he is." He seized hold of my arm, staring at me. "Choffel! The *Petros Jupiter*. He was the engineer, *ja?*" He nodded, his lips under the pale beard spreading to the ghost of a smile. "*Goed! Zeer goed!*" And suddenly he was laughing. "Different nationalities, different motives—it will become an interesting voyage, I think." He was still laughing, a wild look in those pale blue eyes as he moved away from me, crossing the deck and climbing slowly up the steps to the poop that looked high enough and old enough to have Bligh himself pacing its deck. He seemed lost in his thoughts again, and I stood rooted to the spot, wondering just how mad or unpredictable he would prove to be. The captain of a tanker, whose whereabouts I still didn't know, officered by men of different nationalities, different motivations. "An interesting voyage," he had said.

It was a long day, sailing on a close reach, the *shamal* virtually a westerly, deflected by the red volcanic mountains. A great dish of rice and goat meat was cooked in the waist over a charcoal fire and we ate it squatting on the poop with the wooden pulpitlike thunderbox on the windward side, the mountains falling away and deep indents appearing in the coastline, so that the heat-hazed outline of its jagged cliffs had the fluted look of a red-hot organ. I had never been this close to the upthrust finger of the peninsula that was the southern side of the Straits of Hormuz. It looked hellish country, which doubtless explained the nature of the people who inhabited it. The Shihuh had a bad reputation.

Just as the sun was slanting so low that the whole dragon's-toothed line of jagged cliffs turned a bright blood-red, we turned and headed in toward them. The great sail was dipped for'ard of the mast and brought round onto the port side, the wind on the starboard quarter and the dhow piling through a sea that looked like molten lava. It was a fantastic sight, the sun going down and the world catching fire, lurid rocks toppling in pinnacles above us and all of us staring unbelievingly as we ran suddenly into black shadow, the narrow gut opening out into a great basin ringed with sheer cliffs, the whole wild, impossible place as fiery as the gates of hell and sculpted into incredible, fluted shapes.

At the far end, clamped against the cliffs, red itself like a huge rock slab, a shape emerged that took on the appearance of a ship, a long flat tank of a ship with the superstructure at the far end of it painted the same color as the cliffs, so that the one blended into the other, an optical illusion that gradually became a reality as we furled our sails and motored toward it in the fading light, the sound of our diesel echoing back from the darkening cliffs. It was hot as hell and a red flag with a hammer and sickle fluttered above the dim reddish outline of the tanker's funnel.

CHAPTER TWO

WE HAD KNOWN, of course, the instant we turned into the *khawr* that this was where the ship lay; what came as a surprise was to find her jammed hard against the side of the inlet instead of anchored out in the open. The light was going fast, the shape of her merging into the towering background of rock, no color now, the red darkening to black, and the gloom of the heat-stored cliffs hanging over us. She was a VLCC, about 100,000 tons by the look of her, the side windows and portholes of her superstructure painted out so that she looked blind and derelict, like a ship that had been stranded there a long time. I think all of us felt a sense of eeriness as we bumped alongside, the hot reek of metal, the stink of oil and effluent that scummed the water round her, the silence disintegrating into a jabber of voices as we gave vocal expression to our feelings at this strange embarkation.

But it wasn't just the circumstances of the vessel. There was something else. At least there was as far as I was concerned. I was conscious of it as soon as I had climbed aboard, so that I stood there, shocked into immobility till the heat of the deck coming up through the soles of my shoes forced me to move.

I have always been sensitive to atmosphere. I remember, when I was about ten, I went with a camel train to Buraimi and burst into tears at the sight of an abandoned village with the well full of stones. I had no idea at the time why it upset me so, but long afterward I discovered that Wahabi raiders had thrown all the males of that village down the well before blocking it up. And it didn't have to be the destruction of a village, or of whole armies, as in the Khyber, where that dreadful little triangle of flat land in the depths of the pass shrieks aloud of the thousands trapped and slaughtered. Standing on the deck of that tanker, with the cliffs leaning over me and the stars brightening, I could accept the fact of her extraordinary position, tucked in against the rock face, the mooring lines looped over natural pinnacles. The flag, too. Given that this was some sort of fraud, then the painting of the hull to match the ochre-red of the rock, the blanking out of all the windows, these became sensible, practical precautions, and the flag no more than a justification for the ship's concealment should the crew of an overflying aircraft be sharp enough to spot her. Everything, in fact, however strange, had a perfectly rational explanation—except the atmosphere.

An Arab was coming toward us along the flat steel promenade of the deck. He had a gaunt, pockmarked face and a nose like the beak of a ship. There was a suggestion of effeminacy in his voice as he greeted bin Suleiman, but beneath the old sports jacket I glimpsed the brass-bound leather of crossed braces and belt, the gleam of cartridge cases against the white of his flowing robes. This was a Bedu and equipped for fighting. "Gom," he said, in soft guttural English, and he took us back along the deck to the steel ladder that reared up on the port side of the superstructure. I could hear the faint hum of a generator deep in the bowels of the ship as we climbed to the level of B deck, where he opened the door for us, standing back and motioning us to enter.

One moment I was standing on the grating, darkness closing in from the east, and to the west, behind the first outcrops of the Jebel al Harim, the last of the sunset glow still lingering in the sky, the next I had stepped inside, into the blacked-out accommodation area, everything darkened and the lights glowing dimly. Rod Selkirk's quarters were, as usual in this type of tanker, on the starboard side, mine the next cabin inboard, so that both mates were immediately below the captain's quarters on C deck. I had a wash and was stowing my gear when Rod poked his head round the door. "Officers' saloon is just down the alley from me, and they got beer in the cooler—coming?"

"Pour one for me," I said. "I'll be right with you."

"Sure. Be seeing you, then."

He closed the door and I stood there for a moment, looking vaguely round for the best place to stow my empty bags, conscious that his sudden need of company reflected my own mood, the sense of being alone and on the brink of a voyage whose end I didn't want to think about. The cabin was hot and airless, the two windows looking for'ard obscured by an ochre-colored wash, the lights dim. I scratched at the window glass with my thumbnail, but the wash was on the outside. It annoyed me that I couldn't see out, the place seeming claustrophobic—like a prison cell. I changed into my clean white shirt, combed my hair back, my face pale and ghostly in the damp-spotted mirror, and turned to the door, thinking of that beer.

It was then, when I was already out of the cabin and had switched off the light, that the windows were momentarily illuminated from the outside, a baleful glow that revealed a tiny diamond-gleam of white where a brushstroke had lifted clear of the glass. It was in the bottom right-hand corner of the farther window, but it was gone before I could reach it, and when I crouched down, searching with my eye close to the glass, I had difficulty in locating it. Then suddenly there was light again and I was looking down onto the deck of the tanker, every detail of it picked out in the beam of a powerful torch directed for'ard at two figures standing in the bows. I saw them for an instant, then they were gone, the torch switched off, and it took a moment for my eye to adjust to the shadowy outline of the deck barely visible in the starlight. A man, carrying something that looked like a short-barreled gun, came into my line of vision, walking quickly with a limp toward the fo'c'sle, and when he reached it the torch shone out again, directed downward now, three figures, dark in silhouette, leaning forward, their heads bent as they peered into what was presumably a storage space or else the chain locker.

They were there for a moment, then there was again no light but the stars and I couldn't see them anymore, only the dim shape of the fo'c'sle with the two anchor windlasses and the mooring line winch. Several minutes passed, my eye glued to the little peephole of clear glass, but the figures did not reappear, the steel of the deck an empty platform with the black silhouette of the cliffs hanging over it. Once I thought I saw the glow of a light from a hatchway, but my vision was becoming blurred and I couldn't be sure.

I straightened up, blinking my eyes in the dark of the cabin. It was an odd feeling to be an officer on a ship and not know who was on board or what they were up to. Those shadowy figures, and the man with the gun limping toward them— probably they were just checking the mooring lines, or inspecting the lie of the anchor chain, making certain that the ship was ready to haul off and get under way, but the sense of something sinister was very strong.

I went out and shut the cabin door, standing uncertain in the dim-lit passage. There was a small baggage room opposite my door, an oilskin store next to it, then the officers' washroom and the alleyway leading down the starboard side to the mess room. I could hear the sound of voices. But still I hesitated, thinking about the men Baldwick had shipped in by dhow from Baluchistan. Had they brought the ship into the *khawr* and moored it against the cliffs, or had there been a different crew then? The crew's quarters would be on the deck below. I had only to go down there to learn if they were Pakistanis. I glanced at my watch. It was just after six-thirty. They'd probably be having their evening meal, in which case this was the moment to take a look round the ship. There'd be nobody in the wheelhouse now, or in the chart room, the radio shack too —somewhere up there on the navigating bridge there would be some indication of the ship's background, where she was from. And on the deck below, on the port side of C deck—the opposite side to the captain's quarters—would be the chief engineer's accommodation . . .

Perhaps it would all have been different if I'd gone directly to the bridge. But I thought it could wait, that just for a moment a beer was more important. And so I turned right, past the washroom, down the alleyway to the mess room door, and there, sitting talking to Rod Selkirk and the others, was Choffel.

Behind him a single long table with its white cloth stood out in sharp contrast against the soft, almost dove-grey pastel shade of the walls. The chairs, upholstered in bright orange, gave the room an appearance of brightness, even though the lights were almost as dim as in my cabin. Nevertheless, I recognized him instantly, despite the dim lighting and the fact that his chin was now thickly stubbled, the beginnings of a beard. He was wearing navy blue trousers and a white short-sleeved shirt with chief engineer's tabs on the shoulders. He looked older, the face more drawn than in the photographs I had seen, and he was talking with a sort of nervous intensity, his voice quick and lilting, no trace of a French accent.

He stopped at the sight of me and got to his feet, asking me if I would like a beer. They were all of them drinking beer, except Fraser, who had got hold of a bottle of whiskey. For a moment I just stood there, staring at him. He looked so ordinary and I didn't know what to say. In the end I simply told him my name, watching his face to see the reaction, thinking that would be enough. But all he said was, "David Price, Chief Engineer." And he held out his hand so that I had to take it. "Welcome aboard." He turned and emptied the remains of a can of beer into a glass, handing it to me and pulling up a chair, his dark eyes giving me no more than a casual glance.

My name meant nothing to him. Either he hadn't taken it in, or else he didn't realize what had happened to the *Petros Jupiter*. "You're Welsh, are you?" I asked. "Somebody told me the chief was a Greek."

He looked at me sharply. "Who? Who told you that, man?" And when I shrugged and said I couldn't remember, he gave a quick little laugh. "With a name like Price, of course I'm Welsh."

I nodded. "My wife was Welsh," I said and sat down, knocking back half the beer he had given me, very conscious of his proximity, the dark eyes and the black wavy hair streaked with grey, the stubble thick on jaw and throat.

"Your wife—where was she from, then?" His voice displayed no more than polite interest and I knew he hadn't a clue who I was or why I was here, didn't even know how she had died.

"From Swansea," I said. And I told him her maiden name had been Davies. "Karen Davies." I remembered the way she had looked, leaning against her bicycle and speaking her name to me for the first time. "Karen," I said again and his only comment was that it didn't sound very Welsh.

"Well, what about your own name?" I said. "Price doesn't sound exactly Welsh."

"No?" He laughed. "Well, let me tell you, then. Price is a bastardized form of ap-Rhys or Rees. Ap meant son of, you see. Like ap-Richard—Pritchard."

I asked him if he'd been born in Wales and he said, "Yes."

"Where?"

"I was born near Caio," he said, "in an old stone cottage about a mile from Ogofau, where my father worked." And he added, "That's hill-farming country, the real heart of Plaid Cymru where the old shires of Cardigan and Carmarthen met before they renamed them Dyfed. After me, you know." And he smiled, a humorous little smile that creased the corners of his mouth and tucked a small hollow into each cheek. "My father was a miner, you see. Started in the anthracite pits down in the valleys beyond Merthyr. It was there he got the silicosis that finally killed him."

He got up and went over to the cooler, coming back with a fresh beer for each of us. And then he was talking about the Ogofau gold mine, how it was an open cast mine in the days of the Romans, who had built a guard post at Pumpsaint and seven miles of sluices. He said there were historians who believed it was because of Ogofau that the Romans invaded Britain. "All through the occupation they were exporting something like four hundred tons of gold a year to Rome. That's what my father said."

Sitting there, staring at that Welsh face, listening to that Welsh voice telling about his childhood and about going down into the mine with his father after it had closed in the thirties —it wasn't a bit as I had expected, this meeting between myself and the *Petros Jupiter*'s engineer. He was describing what his father had told him about working underground in a mine that had been producing gold for more than two thousand years—the rock face caving in as they struck one of the old shafts, the roar of the dammed-up water engulfing them, rising chest-high as they fled and stinking of two millennia of stagnation. And then one of the crew came in, a Pakistani who said something to him about the tiller flat, and he nodded. "All right, then," he said, gulping down the rest of his beer and excusing himself. "You mates, you come off watch and that's that, but a chief engineer now . . ." And he smiled at us as he hurried out.

I stared after him unbelievingly. God knows how many ships he'd sent to the bottom, how many men he'd drowned, and he was so ordinary, so very Welsh, so pleasant even. I could see his daughter, standing there in that extraordinary house built into the cliffs above the Loire, her voice rising in

anger as she defended him—such a kindly, generous, loving father. God Almighty!

Behind me I heard Varsac saying, "I don't think he know
anyzing. If he do, why don't he tell us?" And Lebois insisting
that an officer who had been on board over a week must have
learned something. "But all he talks about is the Pays de
Galle."

The French, with their customary realism, had already accepted that it was either a scuttling job or a cargo fraud, Varsac insisting that we weren't loaded with oil at all, but
ballasted down with seawater. "You check, eh?" he told Rod.
"You're the mate. You examine the tanks, then we know." He
wiped his lips with the back of his hand, leaning forward and
smiling crookedly. "If it is seawater, not oil, then we demand
more pay, eh?"

Fraser suddenly erupted into the discussion: "Don't be
bloody stupid, man. Yu du that an' yu'll find yursel' left behind
to fry on the rocks here." He reached for the whiskey bottle.
"Yu seen the guard they got patrolling the deck. Start pokin'
yur nose into those tanks an' yu'll get a bullet in yur guts."
And he added as he refilled his glass, "Yu ask me, we're sitting
on a tanker-load of high explosives—bombs, shells, guns." He
stared at Varsac morosely. "There's enough wars, fur God's
sake."

I left them arguing over the nature of the voyage and went
back to my cabin to peer through the tiny chink of clear glass
at the deck below. I could see no movement at all, though the
stars were brighter than ever and the deck clearly visible with
the masts of the dhow like two slender sticks lifted above the
port rail. I thought I could make out a figure standing in the
shadow of the nearby derrick, but I couldn't be sure. Then a
match flared, the glow of a cigarette, and shortly afterward
two Arabs came over the rail at the point where the dhow was
moored alongside. The guard stepped out of the derrick's
shadow, the three of them in a huddle for a moment, and then

they were moving down the deck toward the bridge housing all dressed in white robes and talking together so that I knew the guard was also an Arab.

I watched until they passed out of sight below, then I straightened up, wondering who set the guards, who was really in charge? Not Baldwick, he'd only just arrived. Not Hals either.

But Hals was the most likely source of information and I went along the alleyway to the elevator. It wasn't working and when I tried to reach the exterior bridge ladder I found the door to it locked. It took a little searching to find the interior stairs. They were in a central well entered by a sliding fire door that was almost opposite my cabin.

The upper deck was very quiet. There was nobody about, the alleyway empty, the doors to the offices and day rooms of both captain and chief engineer closed. I tried the elevator, but it wasn't working on this deck either. I don't think it was out of order. I think the current had been switched off. At any rate, the door leading to the deck and the external ladder was locked, the intention clearly to restrict the movement of officers and crew.

The elevator, being on the port side, was right next to the radio officer's quarters. I knocked, but there was no answer and the door was locked. He would be the key man if it were fraud and I wondered who he was. A door opposite opened onto stairs leading up to the navigating bridge. I hesitated, the companionway dark and no sound from the deck above. At the back of the wheelhouse there'd be the chart table, all the pilot books, the log, too, if I could find it. And there was the radio shack. Somewhere among the books, papers, and charts I should be able to discover the identity of the ship and where she had come from.

I listened for a moment, then started up the stairs, treading cautiously. But nobody challenged me, and when I reached the top, I felt a breath of air on my face. I turned left into the wheelhouse. The sliding door to the port bridge wing was open and the windows were unobscured so that I could see the stars.

There was no other light, the chart table and the control console only dimly visible. But just to be there, in the wheelhouse, the night sky brilliant through the clear windows and the ship stretched out below me in the shadow of the cliffs—I stood there for a moment, feeling a wonderful sense of relief.

It was only then that I realized how tensed up I had become in the last few days. Now I felt suddenly at home, here with the ship's controls all about me. The two years at Balkaer slipped away. This was where I belonged, on the bridge of a ship, and even though she looked as if she'd been stranded against towering rocks, I was seeing her in my mind as she'd be when we were under way, the wide blunt bows plowing through the waves, the deck moving underfoot, all the world at my command.

There was no light here and it took a moment for my eyes to become accustomed to the starlit gloom. The long chart table unit formed the back of the wheelhouse, just behind the steering wheel and the gyro compass. There was a chart on it, but even in that dim light I could see that it was the plans of the Persian Gulf, which included large-scale details of the Musandam Peninsula, and no indication of where the ship had come from. This was the only chart on the table, and the one ready to hand in the top drawer, the big Bay of Bengal chart, was no help either. It was the logbook I needed, but when I went to switch on the chart table light to search the shelves, I found the bulb had been removed. I think all the bulbs in the wheelhouse had been removed.

However, the books were the usual collection to be found on the bridge of any oceangoing ship, most of them immediately recognizable by their shape—the Admiralty sailing directions, light lists, tidal and ocean current charts, nautical almanacs, and the lists of radio signals and navigational aid stations and beacons.

I turned my attention to the radio room then. This was on the starboard side, and groping my way to it I stumbled against a large crate. It was one of three, all of them stencil-marked RADIO EQUIPMENT. They had been dumped outside the entrance to the radio room which, even in the darkness, showed as a ragged gap boarded up with a plywood panel. Jagged strips of metal curling outward indicated an explosion, and the walls and deck were blackened by fire.

The sight of it came as a shock, my mind suddenly racing. Radio shacks didn't explode of their own accord. Somebody had caused it, somebody who had been determined to stop the ship from communicating with the outside world. The crates were obviously the ones Hals had loaded onto the dhow from the warehouse at Dubai. The larger one would be the single sideband radio and the other two would contain the other replacements for instruments damaged in the explosion. Was that why I hadn't seen any sign of a radio officer? Had he been killed in the blast? I was remembering Gault's warning then, feeling suddenly exposed, the others all in the mess room drinking and only myself up here on the bridge trying to find out where the ship had come from, what had happened to her.

The need to be out of the wheelhouse and in the open air, away from those grim marks of violence, made me turn away toward the door on the starboard side, sliding it open and stepping out into the night. The starboard bridge wing was so close to the cliffs I could almost touch them with my hand, the air stifling with the day's heat trapped in the rocks. The masts of the dhow lying just ahead of the port side gangway were two black sticks against the dull gleam of the *khawr*, which stretched away, a broad curve like the blade of a *khanjar* knife in the starlight. Deep down below I could just hear the muffled hum of the generator. It was the only sound in the stillness of that starlit night, the ship like a ghostly sea monster stranded in the shadow of the cliffs, and that atmosphere—so strong now that it almost shrieked aloud to me.

Standing there on the extreme edge of the bridge wing, I suddenly realized I was exposed to the view of any hawk-eyed Arab standing guard on the deck below. I turned back to the shelter of the wheelhouse. No point in searching for that logbook now. With the radio room blasted by some sort of explosive device, the log would either be destroyed or in safekeeping. Hals might have it, but more likely it was in the hands of the people who had hired him. In any case, it didn't really matter now. The destruction of the ship's means of communication could only mean one thing—piracy. She had been seized from her owners, either while on passage or else in some Middle Eastern port where the harbor authorities were in such a state of chaos that they were in no position to prevent the seizure of a 100,000-ton ship.

I had another look at the blackened fabric of the radio room. There was absolutely no doubt, it had been blasted by an explosion and that had been followed by fire. I wondered what had happened to the poor wretched Sparks. Had he been there when the explosion occurred? I didn't attempt to break into the room, but at least there was no odor of putrefaction, only the faint smell of burnt rubber and paint. I checked the crates again, wondering why they needed to replace the radio equipment. For purposes of entering a port to sell cargo or for delivering the ship a small VHF set would be quite adequate.

Other questions flooded my mind. Why hadn't they organized the replacement crew in advance, instead of harboring the ship against the cliffs here? Why the delay, running the risk of her being sighted by an Omani reconnaissance plane monitoring movements through the Straits or picked out from some routine surveillance satellite photograph? Surely speed in an operation like this was essential. I moved across to the port side to see if the radar room had also been damaged.

A shadow moved by the door to the port bridge wing. I saw it out of the corner of my eye, heard the click of metal slotting home as I spun round, and a voice, with a strong accent, said, "Who are you?"

He was standing in silhouette against the stars—the deck guard presumably, for I could see the robes and the gun. "Second mate," I said. "Just checking the bridge. No need for you to worry." My voice sounded a little hoarse, the gun pointed at my stomach. It was some sort of machine pistol.

"Below, plis. Nobody come here."

"Whose orders?" I asked.

"Below. Below. You go below—quick!" His voice was high and nervous, the gun in his hand jerking, the whites of his eyes staring.

"What's your name?"

He shook his head angrily. "Go—quick."

"Who gave you orders to keep the ship's officers off the bridge?"

"You go—quick," he repeated, and he jabbed the muzzle of his machine pistol hard into my ribs.

I couldn't see the man's face, it was in shadow, but I could sense his nervousness. "Is Captain Hals allowed on the bridge?" I asked. I don't know whether he understood the question, but he didn't answer, jabbing the gun into me again, indicating that I should get moving.

I never saw what he looked like, for he didn't come down with me into the low part of the ship, simply standing at the top of the bridge companion and motioning me below with the barrel of his pistol.

Back on C deck I went straight to the captain's office. The door was just past the central well of the stairs. There was no answer to my knock so I tried the handle. To my surprise it opened and the light was on inside. There was a desk with a typewriter on it, some papers, steel filing cabinets against the inboard bulkhead, two or three chairs. The papers proved to be invoices, and there was a radio instruction manual. The inner door leading to the day cabin was ajar and though the light was on there was nobody there. The decor was the same as in the officers' mess room, the walls grey, the furnishings and curtains orange. It looked bright and cheerful, no indication at all of any violence.

The bedroom door, outboard on the far side, was not only shut but bolted from the inside. I called out and after a moment a sleepy voice answered. "*Ja.* Who is it?" And when I told him, he asked, "Is it already time for the night food?"

I glanced at my watch. "It's almost twenty past seven," I told him.

"*Ja.* It is almost time."

I heard movement, then the door was unbolted and he emerged completely naked, his eyes barely open and his blond hair standing up in a tousled mop, so that if he'd had a straw in his mouth, he would have made a very good caricature of a stage yokel. "What is it you want?" he asked, standing there with his mouth open in a yawn and scratching himself.

"The name of the ship," I said. "I want to know what's happened to her and why."

He stopped scratching then, his mouth suddenly a tight line, his eyes watching me. "So. You want to ask questions—now—before the voyage is begun. Why?" And when I told him I'd just come from the wheelhouse he smiled, nodding his head. "Sit down." He waved me to the settle and dived back into the bedroom. "So you have seen our bombed-out radio room and come to the obvious conclusion, that there is an attempt at piracy and they make a balls of it, eh? But take my advice, Mr. Rodin, do not leap to the conclusion that they are stupid people and incompetent. They learn their lesson very well."

"What happened to the radio officer?" I asked.

"Dead, I think."

"And the other officers, the crew?"

"One, per'aps two, killed, also several wounded." There was

the sound of water running and then he said, "Better you don't ask about that." And after a moment he emerged in white shorts and shirt, running a comb through his damp hair. "You want to stay alive, you keep your mouth shut. These people are very tough."

"Who?"

"You will see in good time, my friend. There are five of them and they mean business. So, if you don't like it, better you don't do anything quick, without proper thought. Understand?"

I nodded, conscious that his choice of words distanced himself from them. "Where do you come into it?" I asked him.

He didn't even answer that, slipping the comb into the breast pocket of his shirt, watching me all the time out of those very blue eyes. Finally he said, "Per'aps when we know each other better, then maybe we could talk freely. For the present, you are the second officer and I am your captain. That is all between us. Right?"

I got to my feet then. I couldn't force him to talk. But at least I knew he wasn't part of what had already happened. "On the dhow," I said, "when we were coming up from Ras al Khaimah—" I hesitated, wondering how to put it. Since I didn't know what the operation was I couldn't be sure he was opposed to it. But I wanted him to know that, if there was any question of pollution, and he was opposing it, he could count on me. "When you knew who I was, you talked about my wife. You said Karen should have been more political, that she should have threatened the authorities, demanded a law of the sea to control pollution. Those were your words. You meant them, didn't you?"

"*Ja.* Of course. But the *Petros Jupiter,* that was only a ten-thousand-ton spillage."

"But is that the reason you're here, on this ship?"

"What reason?"

"Pollution," I said. "The same reason you risked your life in that tanker on the Niger."

"Ah, you know about that." He sat down and waved me back to my seat. "I risked my job, too. After that nobody want to employ me, not even as an ordinary seaman." He laughed. "Then I got this job."

"Through Baldwick?"

He shook his head. "I was in Dubai and I hear some talk . . ." He reached into a locker beside the table. "You like a whiskey?" He poured it neat, not waiting for me to answer. "You know, the first bad slick I ever see, the first real pollution? It was in South Africa. I had just taken my mate's certificate and was on leave . . ." His mother was apparently from Cape Town and he had been staying with relatives, some people called Waterman, who were English South African, not Afrikaaner, and very involved in the environment. "Victor was a marine biologist. Connie, too, but she had a baby to look after. You remember the *Wafra?*"

I shook my head.

"And before that, the *Kazimah?*"

He drank some of his whiskey and sat, looking down at the glass in his hand, his mind back in the past. It was the *Wafra* he talked about first. That was in 1969, he said, and he had been between ships, enjoying himself, wanting to see as much as he could of the country. He had arrived there in November, just two days before the *Kazimah* got herself impaled on the Robben rocks. "Robben is an island out in Table Bay, about seven miles from Cape Town." He paused, still looking down at his glass, and when I asked him the cause of the stranding, he shrugged and said, "The engine. *Ja*, it is always the engine. Almost every tanker gets into difficulties—" And then he was talking about the organization for the conservation of coastal birds that had been formed the previous year and how he had spent the best part of a month helping his cousin, Connie, who was a member of the organization, collect oil-soaked penguins and take them to the cleansing center. There had been a lot of people working desperately hard at penguin recovery, but even so her husband reckoned around ten thousand died.

And, earlier that same year, the whole penguin population of Dyer Island, over to the west near Cape Agulhas, had been wiped out by another oil slick. "Everything, every bloody tanker, all the oil for Europe and the West goes round the Cape. And I come back from two months wandering through the Kalahari, and over to the Skeleton Coast and Namibia, to find Connie Waterman exhausted with the effort of dealing with the *Wafra* disaster. It was the breeding season and they were literally evacuating the birds from Dyer Island to prevent them being hit again." He paused then, lifting his head and looking directly at me. "That is how I have become involved in environment." And he added, a little smile moving the hairs of his beard, "Per'aps it is true what my mother says, that I am half in love with Connie."

She had been only a few years older and he'd been tramping, no fixed abode, no attachment, seeing the world, taking life as it came. It was working with her, he said, handling the poor pitiful wrecks of birds, and all the time the terrible sense of inadequacy felt by Connie and the other men and women working so hard to save what they could, knowing that whatever they did, nothing would alter the fact that tomorrow or the next day, or the next, there would be another tanker in trouble, another oil slick, more pollution, more birds to treat— on and on and on till "the bloody bastards who own and run the sheeps are made to realize what it means when oil is vented, either intentionally or accidentally. And—" He was very tense now, very worked up, the words spilling out of him with great force—"it is not only the Cape. It is the coasts of Europe. My own country—the Nederlands—that is very vulnerable, also the U.K., France, the whole of the English Channel . . ."

He stopped there, wiping his face with his handkerchief.

"But the politicians, the bureaucrats, they don't care. Nothing will be done, nothing at all until the industrial nations that demand all this oil are themselves threatened with pollution on a massive scale." He was looking straight at me, his eyes wide and staring, his whole body radiating an extraordinary intensity. "Then maybe they get tough, so the bastards can be arrested on the high seas. And if," he went on, his teeth showing white through his beard, "when the captain is arrested, he is thrown into the sea to float in his own filthy oil until he is half dead—like the birds, eh?—like the keel-haul updated—then, I tell you, man—then there will be no more oil slicks, no more venting at sea. But not till then. You understand?" He leaned forward, tapping my knee. "You worry about the *Petros Jupiter*. What about the *Amoco Cadiz?* And the *Metula* down in the Magellan Straits—fifty thousand tons in an area where the cold makes biological breakdown of the tarry mousse much slower. Tanker after tanker. And the venting and the leaks—they go on all the time. How much oil do you think is spilled into the sea from bilges, engine rooms and illicit tank-cleaning operations? You will not believe me, but I tell you, it is one and a half million tons of oil. *Ja.*" He nodded, cracking his knuckles, an angry brightness in his eyes. "There must be a stop put to it." His mouth opened to emit a harsh barking laugh. "Drown them in it. That is good justice. Do you agree?" He was deadly serious, his eyes very wide, almost staring, and fixed on mine as though conveying some unspoken message. "So. We have another talk sometime. But when we are at sea," he added, glancing at his watch. "Now we will go to eat."

He got to his feet, padding barefoot back into the bedroom to put on some shoes, while I sat finishing my whiskey and thinking about it. Almost everybody involved in the cleaning of oiled birds had probably wished at some time it was the men responsible for the slick they were trying to clean. Rough justice, but if those responsible for a spillage were forced to swim for it in their own filth . . . it was politically impossible, of course. Karen had talked about it. So had others at the Cornish cleansing station, the women mainly. But how many nations would agree to pass and enforce such a Draconian law?

It started me thinking about the ship again and Hals saying that nothing would be done until the industrial nations were faced with the threat of massive oil pollution. Was that his plan? "An interesting voyage," he had said—"different nationalities, different motives." "What's our destination?" I asked him.

"You will be told soon."

"Do you know it?" He didn't answer that, his foot on the chair, bending to tie the laces of a new pair of canvas deck shoes. "What about the name of the ship?" I asked.

"They don't have a name for it yet."

"But the original name?"

"It has been painted out."

"Yes, but what was it?"

"You ask too many questions." He came back into the day cabin, and at that moment the door of the office was swung open and a voice behind me said, "Captain, I told you, no one is to go on the bridge." It was a soft, sibilant voice, the English quite fluent. "Is this the man?"

I swung round to see a slight, dark figure standing in the doorway. He was bearded, with thick, curly black hair, dressed in very pale khaki trousers and tunic, a checkered scarf at his throat and a pistol holstered in his leather belt. But it was the face, the dark eyes, the birthmark just visible beneath the beard . . . I jumped to my feet. "Qasim!" The name was out before I could stop myself, before I had time to think what his presence meant.

I saw the sudden wariness in his eyes, the hesitation as he considered his reply. "We have met before?" He sounded uncertain, his hand going, almost automatically it seemed, to the pistol in its holster.

"The Shatt al Arab," I said, recovering myself. "Remember? You were brought on board by the Shah's police and we took you to Kuwait."

He thought back, frowning. "Ah yes, of course." He nodded, his hand coming slowly away from the gun. "I remember now." He was smiling then, some of the tension going out of him. "You were very good to me, all of you, on board that ship. And I had had a bad time of it, you know."

"You made a good recovery I see."

"Yes, I am fully recovered, thank you. But my name is Sadeq now. Abol Sadeq." He came forward into the day cabin holding out his hand. "I am sorry. I remember your face, of course. You were the second mate, I think. But I forgot your name. Excuse me." I told him my name and he nodded and shook my hand. "Of course." He was looking at me curiously. "You have lost your wife. Mr. Baldwick told me. I am sorry." The dark eyes stared at me a moment. "Are you the man who is in the wheelhouse just now?"

"Yes."

"Why?"

"Why not, if I'm second mate?"

He laughed then. "Of course. Why not? But why don't you stay with the others? You don't like to drink? Or is it that you're curious?" He seemed to be trying to make up his mind about something. "You don't answer."

I shrugged. "I've never been on a ship where the bridge was barred to the mates."

"Well, now you are on such a ship. Until we sail." He turned to Hals. "Didn't you warn them?"

Hals shook his head. "I left that to Baldwick."

"But you are the captain and I told you . . ." He stopped there and gave a little shrug. "It does not matter now. I have just been in the mess and I told them myself." He turned back to me. "There is a guard on the deck. He is an Arab, one of the Shihuh who inhabit this part. You could have been shot." He nodded curtly, a gesture that seemed to dismiss the subject, for he was suddenly smiling, his expression transformed into one of friendliness. "I did not expect somebody on board to whom . . ." He hesitated. "I think perhaps I owe you my life."

"You don't owe me anything," I said.

He shook his head, still with that friendly smile. "If not my life, then my good health. I remember you sat by my bed. You gave me courage to stand the pain and now I must consider how to repay you." He was frowning again as though faced with a sudden intractable problem, and he turned abruptly, walking quickly out through the office.

I waited till he was gone, then shut the door and faced Hals. "You know who he is?" I asked.

"*Ja.* He is the boss. He directs this expedition."

"But you don't know his background?"

"No. Only that he gives the orders. He has the money and the others do what he tells them."

"Are they Iranians, too?"

"*Ja,* I think so."

"Terrorists?"

"Per'aps."

"Do you know what his politics are?"

"No. But when you meet him before, you talk with him then. You must know what he is."

"I'm not sure," I said. And I told him the circumstances in which we had met. "All I know is what the Shah's police said, that he was a terrorist. That means he was either a Communist or a supporter of the Ayatollah Khomeini."

"Don't he tell you which, when you are sitting beside his bed in the sick bay on board your ship?"

"I didn't ask him. The man was in desperate pain. I wasn't even sure he'd live till we reached Kuwait and got him to a doctor. You don't cross-examine a man when he is close to death and slipping in and out of a coma."

"Okay, so you don't know any more about him than I do."

He gave a shrug, turning toward the door. "We go and feed now."

"There's something else," I said.

"What?"

"This ship. You really mean you don't know its name?"

"Is that important?"

"It's the *Aurora B*," I said.

CHAPTER THREE

By the time Hals and I entered the officers' mess room the big table at the after end had been laid and there was a steward in attendance dressed in white trousers and tunic. The chief engineer was back, sitting beside Rod Selkirk with a beer in front of him, but not talking now. Sadeq wasn't there, nor was Baldwick. The steward began sounding a gong as the captain went straight to his place at the head of the table. The others followed, and when we were all seated, the steward brought in plates piled with vegetables in a dark sauce. It was a Pakistani dish—the vegetables cold, the sauce curry-powder hot. "Jesus! We got ter put oop wi' this rubbish!" Fraser's voice expressed the instinctive disgust of those unaccustomed to Eastern food.

I ate almost automatically, not talking, my mind still stunned by the knowledge that this was the *Aurora B.* Saltley wouldn't believe it. Not that I had any means of contacting him, but if I had, I knew I'd find it difficult to convince him— not only that the tanker was still afloat, but that within a few days of our meeting I was actually dining on board the *Aurora B.* It didn't seem possible. And opposite me, only one place farther down the table, was the little Welshman who had sunk the *Petros Jupiter* and was now being employed—I glanced across at him, wondering—employed to do what?

A terrorist in charge of the voyage and an engineer who was an expert in sabotage! And what was I to do about it? Knowing what I did . . . I was still looking at the chief engineer as he turned his head. Our eyes met for an instant and it was as though some spark of telepathy passed between us. Then he had turned away, to the man on his left. It was Lebois and he was speaking to him in French.

He was like a chameleon—French one moment, Welsh the next—and his name was Price. Even Baldwick called him that, though he knew damn well his name had been Choffel for years now. "Price!" he called as he came in with some letters in his hand. Presumably they had come up with us from Dubai in the dhow. "A letter for you," he said and handed it to him.

The curried vegetables were followed by a steak and some ugly-looking potatoes. The steak was deep frozen and tough, and for those who refused to face up to the potatoes there was sliced white bread that was already staling in the heat. The only thing that seemed to have maintained its freshness was the array of bottled sauces in the center of the table. I hoped the dhow had loaded some provisions in Dubai, something more interesting than those shipped at Ras al Khaimah, otherwise I could see tempers getting very frayed. Varsac pushed his plate away, Lebois too. Clearly the French were not going to take to Pakistani cooking.

Somebody—Hals, I think—wondered jokingly how long scurvy took to develop. We were discussing this, and the length of time hunger-strikers had taken to die of starvation, when I was suddenly conscious of the Welshman staring at me, his steak untouched, the letter open in front of him and a small white square of pasteboard in his hand. It was a photograph. He glanced down at it quickly, then looked across at me again, his eyes wide, the shock of recognition dawning. I knew then that the letter must be from his daughter and the photograph in his hand one of those she had taken in Nantes as I was leaving for the airport. His mouth opened as though to say something, and in that moment he seemed to disintegrate, a nerve twitching at his face, his hand trembling so violently the photograph fell into his plate.

With a visible effort, he pulled himself together, but his face looked very white as he grabbed up the photo, still staring at me with an expression almost of horror, his hands fluttering as he tried to fold the letter and put it in his pocket. He got suddenly to his feet, muttering "Excuse me" as he hurried out of the room.

"*Malade?*" Lebois asked. Varsac muttered something in reply, reaching across and scooping up the meat from the abandoned plate. A hand fell on my shoulder. I looked up to find Baldwick standing over me. "Come outside a moment." I followed him to the door. "What did you say to him?" he demanded, his little eyes popping with anger.

"Nothing. It was the letter."

"Well, leave him alone. Understand? He's chief engineer and they need him." He leaned down, his heavy-jowled face close to mine. "You can't blame him for wot your wife done to herself. That wot you had in mind?" And when I didn't say anything, he went on, speaking slowly as though to a child, "Well, if it is, cut it out, d'you understand—or you'll get hurt." And he added, still leaning over me, his face so close I could smell the whiskey on his breath, "This isn't any sort of a kindergarten outfit. You just remember that. Price is nothing to do with you."

"His name's Choffel," I said.

"Not on board here it isn't. He's David Price. That's wot you call him. Got it? And another thing—" He straightened up, jabbing his forefinger at my chest. "Don't go letting on to the others wot he done to the *Petros Jupiter*. They got enough to think about without they start chewing that over in the long night watches."

"And what's he going to do to this ship?" I asked him.

He tried to turn it into a joke. "Think you're going to have to swim for it?" He laughed and patted my shoulder. "You'll be all right."

"How do you know? You're going back in the dhow, aren't you?" And I added, "What happened to the first crew?"

The question took him by surprise. "The first crew?"

"The *Aurora B* was last heard of in the Arabian Sea, just a few hours after she cleared the Hormuz Straits."

I thought he was going to hit me then. "How do you know what ship this is?"

"Sadeq," I said.

"Yes, he told me you had met before. Asked me why the hell I'd recruited you. But what's that got to do with the *Aurora B?*"

"He was on the *Aurora B*." And I told him about the crew pictures Perrin had showed me. "So what happened to the crew?"

"I should've dumped you," he muttered. "Soon as I knew you'd been talking to Perrin and Gault, I should have got rid of you."

"Hals thinks there's probably one dead and two or three injured. What about the others?"

"None of my business," he growled. "And none of yours, see? You ask questions like that—" He shrugged his shoulders. "Go on. Get back to your meal and forget about it." And he pushed me away from him, turning quickly and going through the fire doors into the alleyway beyond. I was alone then, very conscious of the fact that Baldwick himself was beginning to get scared. He didn't want to know about the crew of the *Aurora B*. He didn't dare think about it, because if somebody had been killed, it wasn't just piracy he was mixed up in; it was murder, too.

I went back to my place at the table, but by then the others had almost finished their meal and I wasn't hungry. The questions they asked me made it clear they were under tension—all except Hals, who seemed relaxed and not in the least concerned about the nature of the voyage or where we were bound. I remember afterward, when I was sitting with a whiskey in my hand and a growing feeling of exhaustion, Rod Selkirk asked him how long the ship had been in the *khawr* and what sort of crew she had, and he said he didn't know, that, like ourselves, this was the first time he had been on board. And he added, glancing quickly at me, "The crew is mainly Pakistani, but there are others also on board." And he took the opportunity to warn us not to leave the area of our quarters. "Which means, of course, we are confined to this deck and the one above—decks B and C. That is, until we sail." And he added, "There are guards to see that this order is obeyed, and they are armed. So you stay in your quarters, please—all of you."

They wanted to know the reason, of course, but all he said was, "I don't know the reason no more than you. I don't know anything about this voyage, except that we are all being well paid for it. I will try and do something about the food, but it is not important. We are signed on for a single voyage, that is all."

"Weel, here's to the end o' it, then." Fraser raised his glass, then saw mine was empty, sloshed some more whiskey into it and went round the others, moving carefully as he topped up their glasses, whistling softly through his teeth. "If we had a piano noo—" The tune he was whistling was "Loch Lomond," and when he'd finished the round, he stood swaying in front of us and began to sing:

> "Aboot a lassie ah'll sing a song,
> Sing rickety-tickety-tin;
> Aboot a lassie ah'll sing a song
> Who didna have her family long—
> Not only did she du them wrong
> She did every one o' them in—them in,
> She did every one o' them in . . ."

By the time she'd set her sister's hair on fire and danced around the funeral pyre—"Playing a violin—olin," we were all of us laughing. "The Ball of Kirriemuir" followed and then he had switched to "Eskimo Nell," verse after verse—"Roond and roond went th' bluidy great wheel, In and oot . . ." The sweat was shining on his face, dark patches under his arms, and when I got up to go to my cabin he was suddenly between me and the door. "Where yu think yu're goin'? Is it tha' yu don't like ma singin', or is it the song?" He was almost dancing with sudden rage. "Yu a prude or somethin'?"

"I'm just tired," I said, pushing past him. I must have done it clumsily, for he lost his balance and came bouncing back at me, his arms flailing, mouthing obscenities. Somebody hauled him back, but I barely noticed. I wanted to be on my own and think things out. The fire doors closed behind me, their voices fading as I went along the alleyway to my cabin. Inside it was desperately hot, the air conditioner not working and no fans. I stripped off and had a cold shower. There was no fresh water, only seawater, which was tepid and left me feeling hotter than ever and sticky with salt. I lay on my bunk, just a towel over my stomach, listening to the sounds of the ship—the deep-buried hum of the generator, the occasional footstep in the alleyway as somebody went to the heads opposite.

It must have been about half an hour later and I was still there on the bed, when there was a knock on the door. "Mind if I come in?"

I sat up, suddenly very wide awake, for the door was opening and I could see his head in silhouette against the light outside, the stubble growth on his cheek shading the line of the jaw. "What is it? What do you want?"

"A word with you. That's all." He stood there, hesitating. "You've got it all wrong, you see. I have to talk to you."

I switched on the light and Choffel's face leaped into view. He came in and shut the door. "I didn't know, you see . . . about your wife, I mean." His face was pale, his hands clasping and unclasping. "Only just now—my daughter wrote to me . . ." He shrugged. "What can I say? I'm sorry, yes, but it's nothing to do with me. Nothing at all." He moved closer, coming into the cabin, his voice urgent. "You must understand that."

I stared at him, wondering at the nerve of the man. I didn't say anything. What the hell did one say? Here he was, the man who had put the *Petros Jupiter* on the rocks—and by doing so he had been as much the cause of Karen's death as if he'd taken her out there and killed her with a blowtorch. But what could I do—leap from my bed and throttle him with my bare hands?

"May I sit down, please? It's a long story." He pulled up a chair and a moment later he was sitting there, leaning forward, his dark eyes fixed on mine, and I thought, My God, this isn't at all how it should be, the little bastard sitting there and me still on my bunk. "Get out!" I said hoarsely. "Get out, d'you hear?"

But he shook his head. "I have to tell you—" He held his hand up as though to restrain me. "Gwyn has got it into her head you're planning to kill me, you see. She is being overdramatic, of course. But it is what she says in her letter, so I thought it best to have a word with you. If it is true, and you think I had something to do with what happened to the *Petros Jupiter*, then I understand how you must feel." His hands finally clasped themselves together, locked so tight the knuckles showed white. "First, I must explain that the *Petros Jupiter* was not at all a good ship. Not my choice, you understand. The skipper was all right, but a man who did everything by the book, no imagination at all. The deck officers were much the same, but I only saw them at meals. It was the chief engineer—he was the real trouble. He was an alcoholic. Whiskey mostly, about a bottle and a half a day—never drunk, you understand, but always slightly fuddled, so that nothing ever got done and I was expected to cover for him all the time.

I didn't know about that until we were the better part of a week out from Kuwait. He was a Greek and a cousin by marriage of the skipper. I knew then why I had got the job. Nobody who knew the ship would touch it, and I'd been on the beach, you know, for a long time . . ."

He looked at me as though seeking sympathy, then gave a shrug. "But even when I knew about him, it never occurred to me there would have been a whole voyage, more than one probably, when the oil filters hadn't been properly cleaned, almost no maintenance at all. You leave the oil filters dirty, you get lack of lubrication, you see—on the gears, both the primary and the secondary. The primary are double helical gears and the debris from them settles to the bottom and finishes up under the secondary reduction gear. In a seaway, rolling like we were that night, broadside-on to the waves, pieces of metal must have got sloshed up into the gears. We were all working flat-out, you see, on the evaporator pipes. It had been like that all the voyage, the tubes just about worn out and always having to be patched up, so I didn't think about the gears. I didn't have time, the chief mostly in his cabin, drinking, you know, and then, when we got steaming again . . ." He gave a shrug. "I didn't do anything. I didn't put anything in the gears. It was the debris did it, the debris of bad maintenance. You understand? We were only a few miles off Land's End when the noise started. It was the secondary reduction gear, the one that drives the shaft. A hell of a noise. The teeth were being ripped off and they were going through the mesh of the gears. Nothing I could do. Nothing anybody could do. And it wasn't deliberate. Just negligence."

He had been talking very fast, but he paused there, watching to see how I would react. "That was how it happened." He passed his tongue round his lips. "My only fault was that I didn't check. I should have gone over everything in that engine room. But I never had time. There was never any time, man—always something more urgent."

He was lying, of course. It was all part of the game. "What did they pay you?" I asked him.

"Pay me?" He was frowning, his eyes wide.

"For doing the job, then slipping away like that so that no one else could be blamed, only Speridion." A professional scuttler, he would only have done it for a straight fee. A big one, too, for there was the skipper of the Breton fishing boat to pay and then the cost of flying out to Bahrain and fixing passage on the *Corsaire*.

He shook his head, his dark eyes staring at me and his hands clasping and unclasping. "How can I convince you? I know how it must appear, but my only fault was I didn't check. I thought we'd make it. After we got through Biscay I thought that junk yard of machinery would see me through to the end of the voyage." Again the little helpless shrug. "I did think of going to the captain and insisting we put in for complete refit, but he was a Greek and anyway you know how it is—shipowners don't like it when you suggest anything that cuts into their profits, and after the Cape . . . Well, there was nowhere after that, so I let it go." And he added, his hands clasped very tight, "Only once in my life—" But then he checked himself, shaking his head slowly from side to side, his eyes staring at me as though hypnotized. "Can't you understand? When you've been without a job for a long time—" He paused, licking his lips again, then went on in a rush of words: "You'll take anything then, any job that comes along. You don't ask questions. You just take it."

"Under an assumed name."

His mouth opened, then closed abruptly, and I could see him trying to think of an answer. "There were reasons," he murmured. "Personal reasons."

"So you called yourself Speridion. Aristides Speridion."

"Yes."

"And you had a passport—Speridion's passport."

He knew what I was driving at. I could see it in his face. He didn't answer, his mouth tight shut.

"What happened to the real Speridion?"

He half shook his head, sitting there unable to say a word.

"My God!" I said, swinging my legs off the bunk. "You come here, telling me I don't understand, but it's not only my wife you've killed—"

"No!" He had leaped to his feet. "I took his papers, yes. But the ship was sinking and he was dead already, floating face-down in the oily water that was flooding the engine room." And he said again, urgently. "He was already dead, I tell you. He'd no use for the papers anymore."

"And Choffel?" I asked. "Henri Choffel, who fell into the harbor at Cayenne just when you needed a job." I, too, was on my feet then, tucking the towel round my waist. I pushed him back into the chair, standing over him as I said, "That was 1958, wasn't it? Just after you'd sunk the French ship *Lavandou.*"

He was staring up at me, his mouth fallen open, a stunned look on his face. "How do you know?" He seemed on the verge of tears, his voice almost pathetic as he said hoarsely, "I was going to tell you—everything. About the *Lavandou,* as well. I was just twenty-two, a very junior engineer, and I needed money. My mother . . ." His voice seemed to break at the rec-ollection. "It all started from that. I said it was a long story, you remember. I didn't think you knew. It was so long ago, and ever since—" He unclasped his hands, reaching out and clutching hold of me. "You're like all the rest. You're trying to damn me without a hearing. But I will be heard. I must be." He was tugging at my arm. "I've done nothing, nothing to be ashamed of—nothing to cause you any hurt. It's all in your imagination."

Imagination! I was suddenly shaking with anger. How dare the murderous little swine try and pretend he was misun-derstood and all he had ever done was the fault of other people. "Get out of here!" My voice was trembling, anger taking hold, uncontrollable. "Get out before I kill you."

I shall always remember the look on his face at that moment. So sad, so pained, and the way he hung his head like a whipped cur as he pushed the chair away, stepping back and moving slowly away from me. And all the time his eyes on mine, a pleading look that seemed desperately trying to bridge the gap between us. As the door closed behind him I had the distinct impression that he was like a drowning man calling for help.

Mad, I thought. A psychiatric case. He must be. How else could he try and plead his innocence when the facts stared him in the face? It was a Jekyll and Hyde situation. Only a schizophrenic—temporarily throwing off the evil side of his nature and assuming the mantle of his innocent self—could so blatantly ignore the truth when confronted by it.

God, what a mess! I lay back on the bunk again, anger draining away, the sweat cold on my body. I switched off the light, feeling exhausted and rubbing myself with the towel. Time stood still; the darkness closed round me. It had the impenetrable blackness of a tomb. Maybe I dozed. I was very tired, a mental numbness. So much had happened. So much to think about, and my nerves taut. I remember a murmur of voices, the sound of drunken laughter outside the door, and Rod Selkirk's voice, a little slurred, singing an old voyageur song I had heard a long time ago when I shared a cabin with an ex-Hudson's Bay apprentice. A door slammed, cutting the sound abruptly off, and after that there was silence again, a stillness that seemed to stretch the nerves, holding sleep at bay.

Thinking about the *Aurora B* and what would happen to us all on board during the next few weeks, I had a dream and woke from it with the impression that Choffel had uttered a fearful muffled scream as he fell to his death down the shaft of an old mine. Had he been pushed—by me? I was drenched in sweat, the stagnant water closing over his head only dimly seen, a fading memory. The time was 0125 and the faint murmur of the generator had grown to the steady hum of something more powerful—the auxiliary perhaps. I could feel it vibrating under me and some loose change I had put with my wallet on the dressing table was rattling spasmodically. I got up and put my eye to the little pinpoint of clear glass. There were men in the bows, dark shadows in the starlight, and there were others coming up through a hatchway to join them with their hands on top of their heads.

The crew! It was the crew, of course—the crew of the *Aurora B.* That's why nobody had been allowed on the bridge, why there was a guard on the deck. They had been imprisoned in the chain locker, and now they were bringing them up and hustling them across to the starb'd rail at gunpoint. But why? For exercise? For air? They were at the rail now, a dozen or more, still with their hands on their heads, and above them the cliffs towered black against the stars.

I stood back from the peephole, resting my eyes and thinking about that chain locker—what it would be like down there in daytime with the sun blazing on the deck above, the stifling heat of it, and nowhere to lie but on the coiled, salt-damp rusty links of the anchor chain. A hell hole, and nothing I could do about it, not for the moment at any rate.

The ship shuddered slightly, the beat of an auxiliary growing, a faint clanking sound. I put my eye to the peephole again. Everything was the same, the prisoners against the rail, their guards, three of them, standing watchful with automatics in their hands, the bows, lit by the flicker of torches, like a stage set with the cliffs a towering backdrop. There were two men by the anchor winch now, bending over it, and another with a hose playing a jet of water on the open vent of the hawse hole. The beat of the auxiliary slowed—it was laboring—and I saw the cliffs moving.

And then it happened and the sweat froze on my body as

one of the crew turned suddenly, another with him, their hands coming away from their heads, both of them reaching for the rail. Another instant and they would have been over, for the attention of the guards had been momentarily distracted by the winch and its turning and the anchor chain coming in. The first was half over the rail when a guard fired from the hip. The clatter of the automatic rifle came to me faint as a toy, a distant sound like the ripping of calico, and in the same instant the man straddling the rail became an animated doll, his body jerking this way and that until suddenly it toppled over, falling into the widening gap between the ship and the cliff.

A thin cry reached me, like the scream of a far-off seabird, and the other man had gone, too. Out of the corner of my eye I had seen him leap. He must have been a young man, for he had been quicker, just the one hand on the rail and vaulting over, and all three guards rushing to the ship's side, searching and pointing. More firing, and one of them running to the point of the bows, clambering up and standing there, braced against the flag post.

There was silence then, except for the clank of the anchor chain, the rest of the prisoners standing as though petrified, their hands still on their heads. For a moment nobody moved. Then the man in the bows raised his automatic to his shoulder, pointing it down at the water and firing single shots. He fired half a dozen, then stopped.

I stood back, resting my eye again. Had the second prisoner got away? I wondered who he was, whether he had found anyplace to land. When I looked again the bows were well clear of the cliffs and I could see the dark shape of the heights above us climbing in jagged pinnacles toward the Jebel al Harim. I could imagine what it would be like climbing those bare rock hills in the heat of the day, no water and the sun burning the skin off his back, the oven heat of the rocks blistering his feet. I didn't think he had a hope in hell, and the only people he would meet up there would be the Shihuh who were supposed to be distinctly hostile to Christians trespassing in their barren fortress.

The time was now 0134 and low down by the entrance to the *khawr* the stars were being blotted out one by one. It took them just on twenty minutes to inch the ship away from the cliffs so that she was lying to her anchor bows-on to the entrance. By then the whole sky was clouded over and it was almost impossible for me to see anything except when the figures in the bows were illuminated by the flickering light of hand torches as they secured the anchor chain.

I had another shower, toweled myself down, and put on my clothes. By then the ship had fallen silent again, the engine noise reduced once more to the faint murmur of the generator, and no sign of anybody on the deck below, the guards having returned the remainder of the crew to the chain locker. I couldn't see the bows now and no torches flickered there. A wind had risen, a line of white beginning to show where waves were breaking against the base of the cliffs. The *shamal* —that was why they had decided to haul off in the middle of the night. The holding here was probably not all that good. The anchor might well drag if they tried to haul off in the teeth of a gale, and if they had stayed put, they might be held pinned against the cliffs for several days. Now we could leave at first light.

It was past two. Four hours to go before the first glimpse of dawn. I opened the door of my cabin and peered out into the alleyway. There was nobody there, the lights glimmering dully, the ship still and silent except for the faint background sound of the generator. I had no idea what I was going to do. I hadn't even thought about it. I just felt I had to do something. I couldn't just lie there, knowing what ship it was and that the crew were held in the chain locker.

My first thought was to contact one of the Pakistani seamen. It was information I needed. How many guards on duty, for

instance; where were they posted; above all, how long before
we left and what was our destination? I closed the door of my
cabin and stood listening for a moment, alert for those tiny
sounds that occur on a ship at anchor so that I could identify
them and isolate them from any other sounds I might hear as I
moved about the ship. Somewhere a slight hissing was just audible beneath the low-toned persistent generator hum. It came
from the heads where the urinal flush seemed to be constantly
running, and now that I was outside Rod Selkirk's cabin, I
could hear his snoring, a regular snort followed by a whistle.
Occasionally a pipe hammered softly. An airlock, probably.
And sometimes I thought I could hear the soft thud of the
waves slapping against the ship's sides.

Those were the only sounds I could identify. A torch; I'd
need my torch. The quick flash of it in a man's face could save
me if I suddenly ran into one of the guards. I went back into
my cabin, and after getting the torch from the locker beside
my bunk, I had a last quick look through the peephole. The
line of white marking the base of the cliffs was farther off
now. The wind must be coming straight into the *khawr*, the
tanker lying wind-rode, stern-on to the cliffs. The deck below
was a long dark blur, only discernible as a blank in the sea of
broken water that glimmered white round it. I could see no
movement.

Back in the alleyway outside my cabin, I pushed through
the fire doors and started down the stairs to A deck. It was a
double flight and I paused on the landing. The deck below
was lit by the same low-wattage emergency lighting as the
officers' deck. Nothing stirred. And there were no unusual
sounds—the hum of the generator a little louder, that was all. I
continued on down, through the sliding fire doors to the alley
that ran transversely across the ship. I hesitated then, seeing
the closed doors and trying to remember visits I had made in
various ports to tankers of a similar size. This would be the

boat deck and usually there were offices facing for'ard at this
level.

I tried one of the doors. It was locked. They were all locked,
except one, which, as soon as I opened it, I knew was occupied. I cupped my hand over my torch, moving softly past a
desk littered with papers to an annex where the body of a man
lay huddled in a blanket, breathing softly, a regular sighing
sound.

He didn't look like a Pakistani and the papers on the desk,
accounts for food mainly, indicated that this was the chief
steward's office. As on the upper deck, the elevator was
switched off. Bolder now, I walked quickly down the port and
starb'd alleyways. Most of the doors were shut, but the few
that had been left latched open showed them as cabins occupied by sleeping bodies.

I went back to the stairs then, down the final flight to the
crew's sleeping quarters. There was a smell about this deck, a
mixture of stale food and human bodies overlaid with the pun-
gent scent of spices and the background stink of hot engine
oil. It was a strange feeling, wandering those empty alleyways,
knowing that all round me men were sleeping. Here and there
I could hear the sound of their snores, muted behind closed
doors, louder where the doors were open. There was one man
with an extraordinary repertoire, the tone of his snores bass on
the intake, almost treble when breathing out. I was at the
for'ard end of the starb'd alleyway then and I could hear him
quite clearly the whole length of the passage. I shone my torch
on him, but he didn't stir, and though I was certain he was one
of the Pakistani seamen, I didn't wake him. The ship was so
quiet, everything so peaceful at this level, that I thought it
worth trying to have a look outside the superstructure before
taking the irrevocable step of making contact with one of the
crew.

There were doors to the deck at each end of the transverse
alleyway, but they were locked. I went back up the stairs,

moving quickly now. At A deck again I paused. I had already tried the doors leading direct onto the external ladders at the after end of the port and starb'd alleyways, also those by the elevator. All had been locked and it was only on the off chance that I tried the starb'd doors leading out onto the boat deck. To my surprise these were not locked. Presumably the cox'n—or whoever had been in charge of the foredeck anchor party—had left them open for the convenience of the crew if the wind increased and there was a sudden emergency. I stepped out into the night, the air suddenly fresh and smelling of salt. Straight in front of me was the starb'd lifeboat, the wind thrumming at its canvas covers.

After the sleeping stillness of the crew's quarters, the noise on the boat deck seemed shattering, the night full of the sound of breaking waves, the scream of the wind in the super-structure, and astern the continual uproar of seas foaming against the base of the cliff. It was very dark and not a light anywhere. I felt my way to the rail, standing there between the after davit and a life raft in the full force of the wind, waiting for my eyes to adjust themselves. The time was 0219.

Gradually the vague outline of the ship emerged. With my head thrown back I could just make out the dark shadowy shape of the funnel, and a little for'ard of it the mast poking its top above the side of the bridge housing. Looking aft everything was black, the cliffs and the mountains above blotting out any vestige of light filtering through the cloud. For'ard I could just see the gangway hoist and beyond it the shadowy outline of the hull stretched dark against the broken white of water far below. I thought for a moment I could see the outline of one of the jib crane masts and the manifold, but beyond that the ship disappeared into a void of darkness.

I waited there for a good five minutes, but I could see no movement. Finally, I faced into the wind, feeling my way along the side of the lifeboat to the rail at the for'ard end of the boat deck, following it as it turned across the ship until I found the gap where the midships ladder led down to the central catwalk. I went down it, and down another, shorter ladder to the vast open stretch of the upper deck, not daring to expose myself on the catwalk.

I had never been alone on the deck of a tanker before, always in company, and always either in daylight or in the blaze of the ship's deck lights. Now, in the wind and in complete darkness, with the sound of broken water all round me, it was like advancing into a primeval void, and even though the tanker was quite a modest one by modern standards, the night made it seem huge.

I was pulled up almost immediately by the sudden emergence of a crouched shape. It turned out to be one of the mooring winches and the figure beyond it one of the "dead men," its head the wheel that guided the hawser from fairlead to winch.

I stood for a moment looking about me, checking for some movement, but I couldn't see a thing. The shadow of the superstructure had disappeared, nothing visible anywhere except the nebulous outline of pipes running ahead of me and disappearing into the blackness. I felt very alone then, very naked and unarmed, the steel deck under my feet, and the knowledge that it went on and on until it reached the raised fo'c'sle where the captive crew had been brought up out of the chain locker and those two poor devils had gone over the side.

I moved on, walking slowly, feeling my way with each step. Even so, I found myself tripping over the small tank washing pipes called lavomatics that were stretched across the deck at regular intervals. There were inspection hatches for each tank and purge pipes to clear the gases, and at one point I barged into a slender, screw-capped sounding pipe that was about knee-high. The deck, in fact, was littered with obstacles for a man moving warily in complete darkness, and now there was a new sound. I thought for a moment it was somebody whistling and stopped abruptly, my heart in my mouth, but it was only the wind. A little farther on, it changed. It was like somebody moaning. All about me the wind sighed and moaned and the sea made rushing, slapping noises, and at each new sound I paused until I had identified it, convinced that somewhere along this endless dark expanse of steel plating an armed guard lurked, my eyes searching ahead along the line of the raised catwalk for the telltale glow of a cigarette.

A shape emerged, grew suddenly tall, and I stopped again. I was in the center of the ship, following the line of the pipes. The shape was away to the right, very straight and tall, motionless by the starb'd rail. I crouched down, moving slowly forward in the shadow of the pipes. There was another shape to my left now. I hesitated, my heart pounding, feeling suddenly boxed in.

I stayed like that for maybe a minute, the figures on either side of me frozen motionless like myself. Gradually it dawned on me that they were farther away than I had imagined and much taller than any man could possibly be. The derricks—the jib cranes for handling pipe! I got slowly to my feet, trembling slightly and feeling a fool as I ducked under the manifold with its mass of pipes running transversely across the ship, big valves showing like crouched figures in the gloom as I negotiated the breaker that stops waves from running the length of the deck. After that there were no more pipes, only the catwalk running fore and aft.

I must have veered left, for I was suddenly confronted with a new sound, an intermittent thumping noise, as though somebody were regularly striking at the steel hull with a heavy wooden maul. The noise of the sea was louder here. I was almost at the port rail and my eyes, following the line of it aft, fastened on the outline of a thin shaft standing straight up like a spear against the blur of waves breaking in the *khawr* beyond. For a moment I stood there, not moving and wondering what it was. Then I remembered the dhow moored amidships with its two masts just showing above deck level. I went to the rail then and looked down, the dark shape of the Arab vessel just visible as it rose and fell, its wooden hull banging regularly against the tanker's side.

A man coughed and I spun round. Nothing there, but then the cough was repeated, strident now and more like a squawk. A sudden flurry and I ducked as a vague shape took wing and disappeared into the night. I went on, moving quickly, my hand on the rail, determined not to be scared of any more shadows. More roosting seabirds rose into the air and I jabbed my toe against a set of fairleads. There were inspection hatches at intervals—each hatch, and particularly the vents, appearing first as some lurking watcher. Then at last I was at the rise of the fo'c'sle deck with the foremast a slender shaft spearing the darkness above me.

A faint glimmer of light filtered through the cloud layer. I found the ladder to the fo'c'sle deck and felt my way through the litter of anchor and mooring machinery to the bows. Here for the first time I felt safe. I had traversed the whole length of the tanker from the bridge housing to the fo'c'sle unchallenged, and now, standing with my back to the bows, all the details of the ship stretching aft to the superstructure invisible in the darkness, I felt relaxed and secure.

This was nearly my undoing, for I started back along the catwalk. There were shelters at regular intervals, two between the fo'c'sle and the manifold, and four foam monitor platforms like gunhousings with ladders down to the deck. I was using my torch to peer inside the second of these firefighting platforms when a figure emerged, coming toward me along the catwalk. I just had time to reach the deck and was crouched under the platform when he passed, hurrying to the fo'c'sle with something that looked like a toolbox in his hand.

He didn't re-emerge, though I stayed there several minutes watching the point where his figure had disappeared. Cautiously I moved to the ship's rail, not daring to go back onto the catwalk. I could see the derrick now and by keeping close to the rail I was able to bypass both the breaker and the manifold. I was moving quite quickly, all the sounds of the ship, even the quite different sounds of the dhow scraping against its side, identified and familiar. A seabird squawked and flapped past me like an owl. I could see the dhow's mainmast, and had just passed the port side derrick winch, when I heard the clink of metal against metal. It came from farther aft, somewhere near the deeper darkness that must be the superstructure emerging out of the gloom.

I hesitated, but the sound was not repeated.

I moved away from the rail then, making my way diagonally across the deck toward the line of pipes running fore and aft down the center of the ship. Moving carefully, my eyes searching ahead in the darkness, I stubbed my toe against what seemed to be some sort of a gauge. There was a sounding pipe near it and another of those access hatches to the tanks below. I could see the pipes now, and at that moment a figure seemed to rise up, a looming shadow barring my way. I dropped instantly to the deck, lying sprawled against the steel edge of the access hatch, my eyes wide, probing the darkness.

There was something there. The shape of one of the foam monitor platforms perhaps, or was it a small derrick? Something vertical. But nothing moved, no sound I didn't know. I rose slowly to my feet, and at that same moment the shape moved, growing larger.

No good dropping to the deck again. He must have seen me. I backed away, moving carefully, step by step, hoping to God I wouldn't stumble over another hatch. If I could back away far enough to merge into the darkness behind me . . . The clink of metal on metal again, very close now, very clear, and the figure still seeming to move toward me.

I felt the sweat breaking out on my body, the wind cooling it instantly so that I was suddenly shivering with cold. That metallic sound—it could only be some weapon, a machine pistol like the guard in the wheelhouse had jabbed in my stom-

ach. I wanted to run then, take the chance of bullets spraying
in the hope of escaping into the darkness. But if I did that I'd
be cornered, pinned up for'ard with no hope of making it back
to my cabin.

My heel touched an obstruction. I felt behind me with my
hand, not turning my head for fear of losing sight of the shape
edging toward me. The winch—I was back at the derrick. I
dropped slowly to the deck, crawling behind one of the winch
drums and holding my breath.

Nothing moved, the figure motionless now, merging into the
darkness. Had I been mistaken? Crouched there, I felt completely trapped. He had only to shine his torch . . .

"Who's there?"

The voice was barely audible, lost in the wind. The dhow
thumped the side of the ship. A seabird flew screaming across
the deck. Silence now, only the noise of the wind howling
through pipes and derricks, making weird groans and whines
against the background rushing of waves in the *khawr*, and
the dhow going *thump—thump*.

Surely I must have imagined it?

I lifted my head above the big steel drum, staring toward
the central line of pipes, seeing nothing but the vague shadow
of the bridgelike outline of the firefighting platform, the foam
gun like a giant's pistol. Above my head the derrick pointed a
long thick finger at the clouds.

"Is there anybody there now?"

That voice again, in a lull and much clearer this time. So
clear I thought I recognized it. But why would he be out here
on the deck? And if it were Choffel, he'd have a torch with
him. He wouldn't go standing stock-still on the deck asking
plaintively if anyone was there.

I thought I saw him, not coming toward me, but moving
away to the right, toward the rail. He must have been standing exactly between me and the fire monitor platform, other-

wise I would have seen him, for he wasn't more than ten paces away.

Then why hadn't he shone a torch? If he were armed . . . But perhaps I'd been mistaken. Perhaps he wasn't armed. Perhaps he thought I was one of the guards, and, when he'd got no reply and had seen no further sign of movement, he'd put it down to his own imagination. And the fact that he hadn't used his torch could be explained by a standing order not to show a light at night except in extreme emergency.

What was he doing here anyway?

Without thinking I moved forward, certain now that it must be Choffel. Curiosity, hate, determination to see what he was up to—God knows what it was that drew me after him, but I moved as though drawn by a magnet. The outline of the rail showed clear, and suddenly beyond it the dhow's mast. The figure had drifted away, lost from sight. I blinked my eyes, quickening my step, half cursed as my foot caught against another of the tank inspection hatches. A gap in the rail, and a few yards farther aft the outline of a davit. I had reached the head of the gangway.

No sign of Choffel. I stepped onto the grating at the top. I couldn't see him, but I could feel the movement of somebody descending. The dark shape of the dhow was for'ard of the gangway so that it was obvious there must be a boat for communication between dhow and tanker.

What a moment to take him! A push, a quick push—nothing else. I could dimly see the water rushing past, small whitecaps hissing and breaking as the wind hit the sheer side of the tanker, flurries gusting down into the sea. Quickly, my hand on the rail, I began to descend. The gangway swayed, clinking against the side. I heard his voice hailing the dhow. An Arab answered and a figure appeared on the dhow's high poop, a hurricane lamp lighting his face as he held it high, and below, in the water, I saw a small wooden boat bobbing on a rope at the dhow's stern. "O-ai, O-ai!" The sound of a human voice hurled on the wind, the words unidentifiable. More voices, the cries louder, then the light of another lamp swaying up from below.

I squatted down, sure he must see me now, crouching low and pressing my body against one of the gangway stanchions, desperately willing myself to be unseen, my guts involuntarily contracting. When he had shone that torch, screening it beneath his jacket, I had seen the thin jutting pencil line of what I was certain had been the barrel of a gun.

There was a lot of activity on the dhow now, men gathered in the waist and the boat being slowly hauled along the ship's side in the teeth of the wind and the breaking waves. Crouched there I had a crane's-eye view as one of the Arabs tucked his robes up round his waist and jumped into the boat. Then they floated it down, paying out rope steadily, till it reached the staging where Choffel stood at the bottom of the gangway.

Spray flew over him as he reached down to steady the boat. Now! Now, I thought, while his mind was on the boat, and I rose to my feet, and in that instant a beam stabbed the darkness from above, groping along the side of the ship till its light fell on the boat with the Arab kneeling in it, gripping tight to the last stanchion, and Choffel just about to step into it. They remained like that for an instant, frozen into immobility, as though caught by the flash of a camera, while from aft, from the wing of the bridge came a distant cry lost in the wind.

The men on the dhow began shouting—something, I don't know what. It was unintelligible. But they were beckoning and heaving on the rope. The man in the boat let go of the stanchion. Suddenly there was a gap opening up between the boat and the gangway and I saw Choffel's face in the light of the torch, very pale and twisted in the expression of some strong emotion, his mouth open.

Then he had turned and was pounding up the gangway toward me.

I had no time to get out of his way. He came straight at me, and when he saw me he didn't stop, merely flashed his torch on my face. "You!" He clawed past me, and a moment later I saw him standing precariously balanced on the rail capping, watching for the sway of the dhow as it thumped the side. And then he jumped, a shadowy outline flying in the darkness, to finish up clasping his arms round the swaying mast and sliding down into the folds of the great furled sail.

No shouts from the bridge now, and everything dark again, the only light a hurricane lamp in the waist of the dhow. I felt rooted to the spot, standing there on the gangway peering down at the figures gathered on the dhow's deck, their big-nosed, Semitic faces staring upward. Then suddenly he was among them, standing with his gun in his hand, his cap cocked rakishly on the side of his head—I remember that distinctly, the fact that he was wearing a cap, and at an angle—and his torch stabbing here and there as he issued orders to the dim-seen, long-robed figures gathered round him.

One of them disappeared below. The engineer, I guessed, and Choffel followed him. I started down the gangway, my mind in a whirl, descending it quickly, wondering whether he would make it out to sea, what he would do with the crew, where he would head for?

I was halfway down when the dhow's engine coughed behind me, then spluttered into life. And at that instant a torch flashed out from the deck above. Somebody shouted. I waved acknowledgment, pretending I understood and was try-ing to prevent the dhow's escape. I was at the bottom of the gangway now, standing helpless, wondering whether I could swim for it, knowing I'd be swept away, and remembering the look of panic on the man's face, the way his mouth had opened—"You!" he had exclaimed, hurling himself past me. Only a man driven by fear and desperation would have made that incredible jump for the mast.

And now—now there was no way I could stop him. I should

have reacted quicker. I should have taken him on the gang-way, the moment he recognized me, when he was off-balance, held there for a second by the shock of seeing me.

A shot sounded, but not from above. It came from the dhow, the stern of it growing bigger. I couldn't believe my eyes. Instead of swinging out from the side of the tanker, it was falling back toward me. It cleared the gangway by inches, then the big hull closed in, grinding along the grating, slowly crushing it. Arab faces, pallid and jabbering with anger, peered down at me. Somewhere for'ard along the dhow's deck a voice screamed—"Go! Go now!" There was the sound of a shot, very loud, the crack of a bullet, and the beam of a torch stabbing the gloom.

The waist was abreast of me, and without thinking I seized hold of a rope, pulled myself up and over the bulwarks, and as I dropped to the deck, the Arab crew were clawing their way over the side, tumbling down onto the gangway grating to lie there in a heap, bin Suleiman among them, his eyes rolling in the light of a powerful spotlight directed from high up on the bridge wing as bullets sang through the rigging, plowing into the woodwork, sending splinters flying.

"Insh' Allah!" I think it was the naukhada's voice, but whether it was his ship or his own life he was committing into the hands of God I don't know, for Choffel was coming aft, running through the spatter of bullets. He had let go the for'ard mooring line and the dhow was sliding back, its hull grating against the gangway and along the ship's side. Then it was brought up short, still held on the stern mooring line so that it hung there for a moment, illumined by the spotlight, while the Arabs went scrambling up the gangway onto the tanker's deck. There was no sign of Choffel. Crouched there by the bulwarks, I had a vague impression of his having leaped for the steps leading up to the poop.

Slowly we began to swing away from the ship's side. The dhow was turning in the wind, swinging on the stern warp, and then in a rush we closed the tanker again, the wooden timbers on the far side crashing against the steel plates with a jar that went right through me. The deck lights were switched on, everything sharp-etched, the shattered remains of the dhow's boat drifting past and faces peering down from the rail high above. Sadeq was there. He had brushed the Arabs aside and was standing at the head of the gangway, his bearded face clear in the lights as he seized hold of a guard's machine pistol, rammed in another clip, and then, holding the gun close at his waist, swung it toward me, his movements deliberate, his expression coldly professional. There was nothing I could do, nowhere I could go, the muzzle pointing straight down at me, his hand on the trigger. Then he seemed to freeze into immobility, his eyes narrowing as he saw who it was he was about to kill. It must have been that, for after a moment's hesitation, he lifted the barrel of the gun, lifted it deliberately away from me, aiming at the dhow's poop, his finger contracting, the muzzle jerking to the spit of bullets, and the staccato chatter of it echoed by the sound of them slamming into wood, splinters flying and a man screaming.

I thought Choffel fired back, but it was just a single shot followed by a sharp twanging sound as the stern line parted. Then we were bumping along the tanker's side, the hull moving past us faster and faster, and the high wooden bulk of the poop between me and the shots being fired. I heard the engine note change, suddenly deepening, felt the throb of the screw as it gripped the water, and I got to my feet.

We were clear of the tanker's stern now and turning into the wind, no longer falling back toward the cliffs, but slowly turning into the seas, and the whole vast bulk of the brightly lit tanker stretched out high above us on the starb'd quarter. We turned till the superstructure was astern of us, and it was only then that I heard a voice calling my name. It came like a gull crying in the night, a voice of pain and fear and exasperation—"Ro-o-d-in! Ro-o-d-in!" Then—"Quick—hu-rry!"

I felt my way in the blackness over piles of rope to the outline of the high poop deck, found the wooden steps leading up
to it, and came out onto the top of the dhow's great after castle to see the dim outline of a figure sprawled across the helm.
"Take her, man! The entrance. There's a launch, you see—
inflatable—take time to launch it though." His voice came
slowly, full of coughs and gurgles, so that I knew there was
blood in his throat.

"You're hit," I said. It was a bloody stupid remark.

"Take the helm," he gurgled, slipping away from me in the
dark and sliding to the deck.

The dhow yawed, the swept-up curve of the bows swinging
away to port, the wind lifting the furled sail so that it flapped
with a loud cracking noise. I looked up from the dark shape
sprawled at my feet to see the lit tanker with the frowning
cliffs behind it swinging across our stern. The movement
quickened, the wind catching the bows, and I dived for the
helm, throwing my weight against the long timber arm of it,
forcing it over to port. I felt the pressure of the water on the
rudder and slowly the bows steadied and began to swing back
into the wind.

I waited until the tanker was directly astern of us, then I
centered the helm, holding the dhow into the wind, hoping I
was steering for the entrance. There was no chance of doing
anything for Choffel or even finding out how badly he was injured. The dhow wasn't easy to steer. Like most straight-
keeled vessels I had to anticipate her movements, countering
each attempt of the head to pay off with a slight correction to
the helm. She waddled and yawed like an old woman and
once the wind got hold of her she was hard to control, very
slow to respond, and the engine laboring.

Ahead, I couldn't seem to see anything beyond the ship's
stem, the lights of the tanker producing just enough of a glow
to illumine the waist with its muddle of ropes, pulleys, sleeping mats, and cooking gear, and the mast with the great roll of

sail strapped to the curved wing of the spar. These were all very clearly picked out, the upswing of the prow, too. But beyond that there was nothing, just stygian blackness.

I could hear Choffel groaning. Once I thought he cried out. But the dhow required all my concentration and when I did glance down at him I couldn't see him. That was when I remembered he was armed, but the dhow was paying off, the wind catching hold of the rolled-up sail, and the bows falling off. Part of the sail had come loose, a fold of it billowing out in a dark bubble of canvas so that I thought I'd never get the bows back into the wind.

Away to port I could hear the sound of breaking waves, could just make out a line of white. Dark cliffs loomed, the line of white nearer, the sound of the waves louder. We were being set down onto the south shore of the *khawr*—or was it the land closing in as we neared the entrance? With the helm hard over, the bows slowly swung through the wind. I could feel it on my left side now, my eyes searching the darkness to starb'd, ears strained for the sound of breakers. I should have looked at that chart more closely, up there on the tanker's bridge when I had the chance. There was a box fixed to the poop deck just for'ard of the helm, a big wooden box with an old-fashioned brass-knobbed binnacle in it. But I didn't want to use my torch, and anyway I'd no idea where exactly the tanker had been moored in relation to the entrance, what the bearing would be. All I could remember was that the entrance was narrow and dog-legged, the bend being leftward going out.

The line of white was very close now, the cliffs barely visible in the night. I put the helm over and the bows swung easily to starb'd. I glanced astern at the lights of the tanker. They were swinging across our starb'd quarter and already she looked quite small, the reddish glow of the cliffs behind her fading. I was being forced off course, but the line of broken water to port was still closing in and nothing visible to starb'd.

I heard a cry and saw a figure standing clutching at the orna-
mental rail near the thunderbox on the port side, his arm
pointing for'ard. I checked the helm, peering beyond the
vague flapping bundle of the sail. A dark line showed high
above the bows, the shape of low hills, and in that instant I
heard waves breaking and dragged the helm across to starb'd.

There was no response.

The wind had strengthened. It was blowing half a gale and
I knew we were nearing the entrance. But there was nothing I
could do, the long arm of the helm right over and the dhow
not responding, her head held in the grip of the wind and the
engine laboring. I watched appalled as the looming outline of
the land ahead grew clearer, the sound of the surf louder.

And then the engine note changed, a sudden surge of power
and the bows were coming round. I caught a glimpse of a
figure crouched—or more likely collapsed—over some sort of a
control rod set into the deck. But it was only a glimpse, for we
were turning to port and in the entrance now, the blackness of
land on either side, the wind howling and waves breaking all
round us.

It was like that for five, perhaps ten, minutes. It seemed an
age. Then suddenly the wind died away, the sea took on a regular pattern with only the occasional break of a wave. We
were out of the *khawr*. We were out into the Persian Gulf and
the dhow was bashing her way through the waves, rolling
wildly, the engine racing and everything rattling and shaking
as we steamed into the night with no land visible anymore,
just an empty void of darkness all round us.

PART V

Virgins Unlimited

CHAPTER ONE

DAWN BROKE with ragged clouds streaming low overhead and a lumpy sea. It was a grey world, visibility growing reluctantly, but as the light increased gaps appeared in the overcast, glimpses of clear sky showing a greenish tinge. The dhow wallowed sedately, rolling as her bows plowed into the waves, and the beat of the engine was unhurried and regular. We were at least ten miles from the shore. I could see it on the starb'd quarter, low down to the south and west of the familiar Group Flash Two of the Didamar light, the dark line of it turning an arid brown as the sun rose.

We were out into the Hormuz Straits, into the main shipping lanes. There was a tanker quite close with its steaming lights still showing white, another hull-down, and a third coming up astern. I had the binnacle box open and was steering a full point east of north. Choffel, when I had hauled him off the engine speed-control linkage, had muttered about the tanker's launch being very fast, powered by a single big outboard. But I thought it more likely they would be searching the inshore traffic zone, between the Didamar and Tawakkul lights, not right out here between the west- and eastbound tanker lanes.

There was blood on the deck where Choffel had lain after collapsing at the helm, blood on the carved end of the helm itself. But he hadn't bled where he had lain clutching the speed-control lever, or in the vicinity of the thunderbox where he had hauled himself up by the rail to warn me we were driving onto the north side of the entrance. And when I had got him down to bin Suleiman's hovel of a cabin and laid him out on a sleeping mat with a stinking salt-stiffened blanket to cover him, I didn't think he had been bleeding then.

A pity Sadeq hadn't killed him. Now it was up to me. I yawned, my eyes heavy-lidded, my body sagging with fatigue. I had had no sleep and I always found the first twenty-four hours at sea a little trying.

I couldn't just pitch the man over the side. Or could I? Fate had delivered him into my hands as though of intent, so why didn't I do it—now, while I was too tired to care whether he was a corpse or not? If I didn't do it now, if I let him stay there, then I'd be responsible for him. I'd have to feed him. I'd have to do something about his wound. It was in his stomach, he'd said. And I'd have to clean him up. My God! Acting as nurse and sick-bay attendant to the man who had sent Karen to her death! If that was what I'd have to do, then Fate had played a dirty trick.

In the east the clouds were turning a flaming red, the sea catching fire as it had done that evening at Ras al Khaimah. It seemed a long time ago. A gap in the clouds took on the appearance of an open furnace, the ragged edges gleaming like red-hot clinkers. I saw a heraldic lion crouched in the cloud gap. I blinked my eyes and it was a dragon breathing fire, its scales all crimson, and then the sun appeared, a bright red orb that slowly turned through vermilion and orange-yellow to a searing glare that changed the sea to a brilliant purple and the waves to glittering gold. Suddenly it was hot, the sun burning up the clouds, the fire-brown streak of the Musandam Peninsula lost in haze.

How far to Qisham, the big island on the north side of the Straits? I couldn't remember. And there was Larak, and inside of that Hormuz itself, both of them much smaller islands. I stood leaning on the helm, swaying with it as I tried to remember the chart, my eyes drooping, half-closed against the glare. Surely I was far enough out? Why not turn now, head eastward into the sun? The Straits were like a horseshoe facing north. As long as I kept to the middle, steering clear of all the ships, and of the islands and reefs of Ras Musandam, following the curve of the Iranian coast, there was no reason why the dhow should attract the attention of sea or air patrols from either side, and at an estimated six to eight knots we should reach the border between Iran and Pakistan sometime tomorrow night. Gwadar. If I could anchor off Gwadar. Must check the fuel. I didn't know whether we had enough to reach Gwadar. But that was the nearest place that had an air service to Karachi. Two days to Gwadar. And if we were short of fuel, then I'd have to sail the brute. Through slitted eyes I stared up at the great curved spar with the sun-bleached, heavily patched sail bagged up round it. My head nodded and I caught myself, wondering whether one man could possibly set it alone. But my mind drifted away, abandoning any thought of how it could be done, unable to concentrate. I was thinking of Hals, and Sadeq—Baldwick, too. A kaleidoscope of faces and that little ginger-haired Glaswegian. Sadeq spraying bullets. Standing at the head of the gangway, very much the professional, a killer. I couldn't recall the expression on his face, only the fact that he was about to cut me down and didn't. "I owe you my life," he had said, and now I couldn't recall his expression. Not even when he'd lifted the barrel and fired at Choffel. Hate, pleasure, anger—what the hell had he felt as the bullets slammed into the poop?

There comes a moment when exhaustion so takes hold of the body that the only alternative to sleep is some form of physical activity. When I opened my eyes and found the sun's glare behind me and the dhow rolling along almost broadside to the waves, I knew that point had arrived. The sun was higher now, the time 0823 and a big fully loaded tanker was pushing its bow wave barely a mile away. I wondered how long I had been dreaming at the helm with the dhow headed west into the Persian Gulf. Not that it made much difference, with no chart and only the vaguest idea where we were. I hauled the tiller over, bringing the bows corkscrewing through the waves until the compass showed us headed east of north. There was a rusty iron gear lever set in the deck close by the engine control arm and after throttling right down, I put the lever into neutral. Lengths of frayed rope, looped through holes cut in the bulwarks either side of the tiller arm, enabled me to make the helm fast so that we were lying wind-rode with our bows headed east into the Hormuz Straits.

I went for'ard then, into the waist of the vessel, running my eye over the bundled sail as I relieved myself to leeward. Then I went round the ship, checking the gear. It was something I would have had to do sooner or later, but doing it then I knew it was a displacement activity, putting off the moment when I would have to go into the dark hold of the shelter under the poop and deal with Choffel.

The dhow was rolling heavily. With no cargo to steady her, she was riding high out of the water, heeled slightly to starb'd by the wind and wallowing with an unpredictable motion, so that I had to hold on all the time or be thrown across the deck. I was feeling slightly nauseous, dreading the thought of that dark hole as I made my way aft. The entrance to it was right by the steps leading to the poop, the door closed with a large wooden latch. I couldn't remember closing it, but perhaps it had banged to on a roll. I pulled it open and went in.

It was the smell that hit me. Predominantly it was the hot stink of diesel oil, but behind that was the smell of stale sweat, vomit, and excrement. At the stern of the cabin two shuttered windows either side of the rudder post showed chinks of light. I had settled Choffel on a mat on the starb'd side. We had been heeled to starb'd then, as we were now, but sometime during the night, or perhaps in the dawn when I was off course, he must have been rolled right across the ship, for I found his body precariously huddled on the port side. I could only just see it in the dim light from the doorway, the blanket I had wrapped him in flung into a heap at his feet and his hands pressed against the timbers of the deck in an effort to hold himself steady.

He looked so lifeless I thought for a moment he was dead. I was not so much glad as relieved, his stubble-dark features white against the bare boards, his eyes wide and staring, and his body moving helplessly to the sudden shifts of the ship wallowing in the seaway. I started to back away, the smell and the diesel fumes too much for me. The engine noise was much louder here, and though it was only idling, the sound of it almost drowned the groans of the ship's timbers. They were very human groans, and seeing the man's head roll as the deck lifted to a wave, I had a sense of horror, as though this were a ghost come to haunt me.

Suddenly I felt very sick.

I turned, ducking my head for the doorway and some fresh air, and at that moment a voice behind me murmured, "Is that you, Gwyn?" I hesitated, looking back. The dhow lifted to the surge of a wave, rolled to starb'd, and as it rolled his body rolled with it, his groan echoing the groan of the timbers. "Water!" He suddenly sat up with a shrill gasp that was like a scream suppressed. One hand was pressed against the boards to support him, the other clutched at his stomach. He was groaning as he called for water again. "Where are you now? I can't see you." His voice was a clotted whisper, his eyes staring. "Water, please."

"I'll get you some." It was the salt in the air. I was thirsty myself. The salt and the stench, and the movement of the boat.

There was a door I hadn't noticed before on the port side. It opened onto a store cupboard—oil cans and paint side by side with sacks of millet, some dried meat that was probably goat, dates and dried banana in plastic bags, a swab and buckets, bags of charcoal and several large plastic containers. These last were the dhow's water supply, but before I could do anything about it, my body broke out into a cold sweat and I had to make a dash for the starb'd bulwarks.

It was very seldom I was sick at sea. The wind carried the sickly smell of the injured man to my nostrils as I leaned out over the side retching dryly. It would have been better if I had had more to bring up. I dredged up some seawater in one of the buckets. We were on the edge of a slick and it smelled of oil, but I washed my face in it, then went back to that messy cubbyhole of a store. There were tin mugs, plates, and big earthenware cooking pots on a shelf that sagged where the supports had come away from the ship's side. I had a drink myself, then refilled the mug and took it in to Choffel.

He drank eagerly, water running down his dark-stubbled chin, his eyes staring at me with a vacant look. It was only when he had drunk nearly the whole of a mugful that it occurred to me the water was probably contaminated and should have been boiled. In Karachi everybody boiled their water and I wondered where the containers had last been filled. "Where am I? What's happened?" He was suddenly conscious, his eyes searching my face. His voice was stronger, too. "It's dark in here. Would you pull the curtains, please?"

"You're on a dhow," I said.

The ship lurched and he nodded. "The shots—Sadeq." He nodded, again feeling at his stomach. "I remember now." He was quite lucid in this moment, his eyes, wide in the gloom, looking me straight in the face. "You were going to kill me, is that right?"

"Do you want some more water?" I asked him, taking the empty mug.

He shook his head. "You think Sadeq saved you the trouble." He smiled, but it was more a grimace. "I've shat my pants, haven't I? Fouled myself up." And he added, "This place stinks. If I had something to eat now . . ." The ship rolled and I had to steady him. "I'm hungry, but I can't contain myself." He gripped hold of my arm. "It's my guts, is it?"

My fingers where I had held him were a sticky mess. I reached for the blanket, wiping my hand on the coarse cloth. I could clean him up, but if I got water anywhere near the wound it would probably bleed again. I started to get to my feet, but the clutch of his hand on my arm tightened convulsively. "Don't go. I want to talk to you. There are things . . . Now, while I have the strength . . . I was going to escape, you see. I was going to Iran, then maybe cross the Afghan frontier and get myself to Russia. But you can't escape, can you—not from yourself, not from the past."

His voice was low, the tone urgent. "No," he said, clutching hold of me tighter still as I made to rise. "The *Lavandou*. You mentioned the *Lavandou*. My third ship. A boy. I was just a boy and my mother dying, you see. Cancer and overwork and too much worry. She'd had a hard life and there was no money. My father had just died, you know. His lungs. Working in the mines he was when just a boy. The anthracite mines down in the Valleys. He was underground. Years underground. A great chest he had, and muscles, huge muscles. But when we laid him to rest he was quite a puny little chap—not more than a hundred pounds." His voice had thickened and he spat into the mug, dark gobs of blood.

"Better not talk," I said.

He shook his head urgently, still clutching me. "I was saying —about the *Lavandou*. I was twenty-two years old . . . and desperate." His fingers tightened. "D'you know what it is to be desperate? I was an only child. And we'd no relatives, you see. We were alone in the world, nobody to care a bugger what happened to her. Just me. God! I can still see her lying there, the whiteness of her face, the thinness of it, and all drawn with pain." His voice faltered as though overcome. "They knew, of course. They knew all about how desperate I was.

'She needs to go into a clinic.' Private, you see—not waiting for the National Health. And me at sea, unable to make sure she got proper attention. 'It's your duty,' they said. And it was, too —my duty. Also, I loved her. So I agreed."

He stared up at me, his eyes wide, his fingers digging into my arm. "What would you have done?" His breath was coming in quick gasps. "Tell me—just tell me. What would you have done, man?"

I shook my head, not wanting to listen, thinking of Karen as he said, "The ship was insured, wasn't she? And nobody got hurt, did they?" His eyes had dimmed, his strength fading. I loosened his fingers and they gripped my hand, the cold feel of them communicating some deep Celtic emotion. "Just that once, and it went wrong, didn't it—the Lloyd's people twigged what I'd done, and myself on the run, taking another man's name. God knows, I've paid. I've paid and paid. And Mother . . . I never saw her again. Not after that. She died and I never heard, not for a year. Not for over a year." He spat blood again and I could see his eyes looking at me, seeking sympathy.

What do you do—what the hell do you do when a creature like that is dying and seeking sympathy? At any moment he'd start talking about the *Petros Jupiter*, making excuses, asking my forgiveness, and I didn't know what I could say to him. I thought he was dying, you see—his eyes grown dim and his voice very faint.

"We're wasting fuel," I said, unhooking his fingers from my hand. I think he understood that for he didn't try and stop me, but as I got to my feet he said something—something about oil. I didn't get what it was, his voice faint and myself anxious to get out into the open again, relieved at no longer being held by the clutch of his hand.

Clouds had come up and the wind had freshened. Back on the poop I put the engine in gear and headed east into the Straits. We were broadside to the waves, the dhow rolling and corkscrewing, spray wetting the parched timbers of her waist as the breaking seas thumped her high wooden side. I was hungry now, wondering how long the *shamal* would blow. No chance of a hot meal until I could get the dhow to steer herself and for that I'd need almost a flat calm. But at least there were dates in the store.

I secured the helm with the tiller ropes and made a dash for it, coming up with a handful just as the bows swung with a jarring explosion of spray into the breaking top of a wave. I got her back on course, chewing at a date. It was dry and fibrous, without much sweetness, and so impregnated with fine sand that it gritted my teeth. They were about the worst dates I had ever eaten, but being a hard chew they helped pass the time and keep me awake.

Toward noon the wind began to slacken. It was dead aft now, for all through the forenoon hours I had been gradually altering course, following the tankers as they turned south through the last part of the Straits. Soon our speed was almost the same as the breeze, so that it was hot and humid, almost airless, the smell of diesel very strong. The clouds were all gone now, eaten up by the sun, the sky a hard blue and the sea sparkling in every direction, very clear, with the horizon so sharp it might have been inked in with a ruler. There were a lot of ships about and I knew I had to keep awake, but at times I dozed, my mind wandering and only brought back to the job on hand by the changed movement as the dhow shifted course.

I could still see the Omani shore, the mountains a brown smudge to the southwest. The wind died and haze gradually reduced visibility, the sun blazing down and the dhow rolling wildly. The sea became an oily swell, the silken rainbow surface of it ripped periodically by the silver flash of panicked fish. The heat ripened the stench from the lazarette beneath my feet. Twice I forced myself to go down there, but each time he was unconscious. I wanted to know what it was he had said about oil, for the exhaust was black and diesel fumes hung over the poop in a cloud. I began listening to the engine, hearing strange knocking sounds, but its beat never faltered.

Water and dates, that was all I had, and standing there, hour after hour, changing my course slowly from south to sou'-sou'east and staring through slitted eyes at the bows rising and falling in the glare, the mast swinging against the blue of the sky, everything in movement, ceaselessly and without pause, I seemed to have no substance, existing in a daze that quite transported me, so that nothing was real. In this state I might easily have thrown him overboard. God knows there were fish enough to pick him clean in a flash, and skeletons make featureless ghosts to haunt a man. I can't think why I didn't. I was in such a state of weary unreality that I could have had no qualms. I did go down there later, toward the end of the afternoon watch—I think with the conviction he was dead and I could rid myself of the source of the stench.

But he wasn't dead. And he wasn't unconscious either. He was sitting up, his back braced against the stern timbers and his eyes wide open. It just wasn't possible then. I couldn't pick him up and toss him overboard, not with his eyes staring at me like that. And as soon as he saw me he began to talk. But not sensibly. About things that had happened long, long ago—battles and the seeking after God, beautiful women and the terrible destruction of ancient castles.

He was delirious, of course, his mind in a trance. And yet he seemed to know me, to be talking to me. That's what made it impossible. I got some seawater and began cleaning him up. He was trembling. I don't know whether it was from cold or fever. Maybe it was fear. Maybe he'd known and that's why he was talking—you can't throw a man to the fishes when he's talking to you about things that are personal and take your mind back, for he was talking then about his home in Wales, how they had moved up into the old tin hills above a place called Farmers, a tumbledown longhouse where the livestock were bedded on the ground floor to keep the humans warm in the bedroom above. It was odd to hear him talking about Wales, here in the Straits with Arabia on one side of us, Persia on the other. "But you wouldn't know about the *Mabinogion* now, would you?" he breathed.

I told him I did, that I had read it, but either he didn't hear me or he didn't take it in. His mind was far away on the hills of his youth. "*Carreg-y-Bwci*," he murmured. "The Hobgoblin Stone. I've danced on it as a kid in the moonlight, a great *cromlech* on its side—and the Black Mountain visible thirty miles away. It never did me any harm," he added in a whisper. His hand reached out toward me. "Or am I wrong, then? Was I cursed from that moment?" The dhow rolled, rolling him with it, and he clutched at his guts, screaming.

I steadied him and he stopped screaming, gulping air and holding on to me very tightly. I got his trousers open at the fly and in the light of my torch could see the neat hole the bullet had punched in his white belly. He wasn't bleeding now and it looked quite clean, only the skin round it bruised and bluish; but I didn't dare turn him over to see the other side, in the back where it must have come out.

I cleaned his trousers as best I could and all the time I was doing it he was rambling on about the *Mabinogion,* and I thought how strange; the only other person ever to talk to me about it was Karen. She'd got it from the traveling library, asking for it specially. And when she had read it she had insisted that I read it, too, the four branches of it containing some of the oldest stories of the Welsh bards. A strange book full of fighting men who were always away from home and wives that gave themselves to any valiant passerby, and everything, it seemed, happening three times over—all the trickery, the treachery, the blazing hopes that led to death. Some of its eleven stories had borne a strange resemblance to the tribal life in the hills where my mother's people had come from—the feuds, the hates, the courage, and the cruelty. And this man talking of the country above Lampeter where Karen and I had stayed one night in a wretched little inn with hardly a word of English spoken to us.

It was just after we were married. I had been on leave from the Gulf and had borrowed her father's car to drive up to the Snowdonia National Park. Just short of Llanwrtyd Wells I had turned north to look at the Rhandirmwyn dam and we had come out of the wild forested country beyond by way of an old Roman road called the Sarn Helen. I could even remember that huge *cromlech* lying on its side, the sun shining as we stopped the car and got out to stand on the top of the earth circle in which it lay, and the late spring snow was like a mantle across the rolling slopes of distant mountains to the south. And as I was zipping up his trousers, hoping he wouldn't mess them up again, I saw him in my mind's eye, a wild Welsh kid dancing on that stone in the full light of the moon. A demonstration of natural wickedness, or had he really been cursed? I was too tired to care, too tired to listen any longer to his ramblings. And the stench remained. I left him with some water and dates and got out, back into the hot sun and the brilliance of sea and sky.

By sundown the sea was oily calm, the dhow waddling over the shallow swells with only a slight roll. She would now hold her course for several minutes at a time, so that I was able to examine the rusty old diesel engine in its compartment below the lazarette. I found the fuel tank and a length of steel rod hung on a nail to act as a dipstick. The tank was barely a quarter full. It was quite a big tank, but I had no idea what the consumption was so no means of calculating how far a quarter of a tank would take us.

The sunset was all purples and greens with clouds hanging on the sea's eastern rim. Those clouds would be over Pakistan and I wondered whether we'd make it as I stood there munching a date and watching the sun sink behind the jagged outline of the Omani mountains and the color fade from the sky.

To port night had already fallen over Iran. The stars came out.
I picked a planet and steered on that. Lighthouse flashes and
the moving lights of passing ships, the confusion of the waves
—soon I was so sleepy I was incapable of holding a course for
more than a few minutes at a time.

Toward midnight a tanker overhauled us, outward-bound
from the Gulf. I was steering southeast then, clear of the
Straits now and heading into the Gulf of Oman. The tanker
passed us quite close and there were others moving toward the
Straits. Once a plane flew low overhead. Sometime round
0200 I fell into a deep sleep.

I was jerked awake by a hand on my face. It was cold and
clammy and I knew instantly that he'd come back to me out of
the sea into which I'd thrown him. "No. I didn't do it. You
must have fallen." I could hear my voice, high-pitched and
scared. And then he was saying, "You've got to keep awake. I
can't steer, you see. I've tried, but I can't—it hurts so."

I could smell him then and I knew he was real, that I wasn't
dreaming. I was sprawled on the deck and he was crouched
over me. "And the engine," he breathed. "It's old. It eats oil. I
can hear the big ends knocking themselves to pieces. It needs
oil, man."

There were cans of oil held by a loop of wire to one of the
frames of the engine compartment. The filler cap was missing
and there was no dipstick. I poured in half a can and hoped
for the best. The engine certainly sounded quieter. Back on
the poop I found him collapsed again against the binnacle box
and the dhow with its bows turned toward the North Star. A
tanker passed us quite close, her deck lights blazing, figures
moving by the midship derricks which were hoisting lengths
of pipe. How I envied the bastards—cabins to go to, freshwater
showers, clean clothes and drinks, everything immaculate, and
no smell. I couldn't make up my mind whether it was food I
wanted most or some ice-cold beer. The cold beer probably.
My mouth was parched with the salt, my eyes gritty with lack

of sleep. Choffel lay motionless, a dark heap on the deck, and the minutes passed like hours.

Strange how proximity alters one's view of a person, familiarity fostering acceptance. I didn't hate him now. He was there, a dark bundle curled up like a fetus on the deck, and I accepted him—a silent companion, part of the ship. The idea of killing him had become quite remote. It was my state of mind, of course. I was no longer rational, my body going through the motions of steering quite automatically, while my mind hovered in a trance, ranging back over my life, reality and fantasy all mixed up and Karen merging into Pamela. And that black-eyed girl with a cold cursing me in French and spitting in my face. Guinevere. How odd to name a girl Guinevere.

"That's my daughter," he said.

I blinked my eyes. He was sitting up, staring at me. "My daughter," he said again. "You were talking about my daughter." There was a long silence. I could see her very clearly, the pale clear skin, the square strong features, the dark eyes and the dark hair. "She tried to stop me. She didn't want me to go to sea again—ever." He was suddenly talking about her, his voice quick and urgent. "We have some caves behind our house. '*Champignons! Parfait pour les champignons,*' she said. So we grew mushrooms, and it worked, except we couldn't market them. Not profitably. She would keep us. That was her next idea. She was a typist. She did a course, you see—secretarial—after she left school. 'I can earn good money,' she said. But a man can't be kept like that, not by his daughter. He's not a man if he can't stand on his own feet . . ." His voice faded, a despairing whisper that was thick with something he had to bring up. "The *Petros Jupiter*," he breathed. A fish rose, a circle of phosphorus on the dark water behind him. "She was in tears she was so angry. 'They'll get at you,' she said. 'They'll get at you, I know they will.' And I laughed at her. I didn't believe it. I thought the *Petros Jupiter* was all right." He choked, spitting something out onto the deck. "And now I've got a bullet in my guts and I'll probably die. That's right, isn't it? You'll see to that and she'll say you murdered me. She'll kill you if you let me die. She's like that. She's so emotional, so possessive. The maternal instinct. It's very strong in some women. I remember when she was about seven—she was the only one, you see—and I was back from a year's tramping, a rusty old bucket of a wartime Liberty called *St. Albans*, that was when she first began to take charge of me. There were things to mend—she'd just learned to sew, and cooking . . . living in France girls get interested in the cuisine very young. She'd mother anything that came her way—injured birds, stray puppies, hedgehogs, even reptiles. Then it was people and nursing. She's a born nurse, that's why she works in a clinic, and beautiful—like her mother, so beautiful. Her nature. You know what I mean—so very, very beautiful, so . . ." His voice choked, a sobbing sound.

He was crying. I couldn't believe it, here on this stinking dhow, lying there with a bullet in his guts, and he was crying over his daughter. A beautiful nature—hell! A little spitfire.

"It was after the *Stella Rosa*. You know about the *Stella Rosa*, don't you?"

"Speridion."

"Of course, you mentioned him." He nodded, a slight movement of the head in the dark. "Speridion had been paid to do it, only the thing went off prematurely, blew half his chest away. There was an inquiry and when that was over I went home. She was still at school then, but she'd read the papers. She knew what it was all about, and she'd no illusions. 'You're a marked man, Papa.' She never called me Dad or Daddy, always Papa. That was when she began to take charge, trying to mother me. Jenny wasn't a bit like that. Jenny was my wife's name. She was a very passive, quiet sort of person, so I don't know where my daughter got it from."

He stopped there, his voice grown weak; but his eyes were

open, he was still conscious, and I asked him about the *Aurora B.* "Did you know it was the *Aurora B?*"

He didn't answer, but I knew he'd heard the question, for I could see the consciousness of it in his eyes, guessed in the wideness of their stare his knowledge of what my next question would be. Yes, he knew about the crew. He nodded slowly. He knew they were kept imprisoned in the chain locker. "You couldn't help but know, not living on board as I was for over a week." And when they'd called for power to the main anchor winch, he'd known they'd have to bring the prisoners up out of the chain locker and he had come on deck to see what happened to them. "You saw it, too, did you?" His voice shook. And when I nodded, he said, "That's when I decided I'd have to get away. I could see the dhow and I knew it was my last chance. In the morning it would be gone. That was when I made up my mind." His voice dropped away. "Always before I've stayed. I never believed it could happen—not again. And when it did—" He shook his head, murmuring—"But not this time. Not with a cold-blooded bastard like Sadeq. And there was you. Your coming on board—" His voice died away completely.

"There are two ships," I said. "Did you know that?"

I thought he nodded.

"What happened to the other?"

He didn't answer.

"The seizing of *Aurora B*," I said, catching hold of him and almost shaking him. "That went wrong, didn't it? That was the first one, and it went wrong."

He stared up at me, his eyes wide, not saying anything. "And then they grabbed the second ship, the *Howdo Stranger*. Did you see her?"

"No." He said it fiercely, an urgent whisper. "I don't know anything about it. Nothing at all."

"Are they going to meet up? Is that why they're getting the *Aurora B* officered and ready for sea?" His eyes had closed, his body limp. "Where are they going to meet up? Where are they going to spill their oil? They're going to spill it on the coast of Europe. Isn't that the plan?" I was shaking him violently now, so violently that he screamed out in pain like a shot rabbit.

"Please, for God's sake!" His voice was thick with blood and hardly audible.

"Where?" I shouted at him.

But he had fainted away, mumbling something about the salvage, which I didn't understand, his body collapsing in the grip of my hand. I cursed myself for having been too rough, the man in a coma now, his body shifting limply to the movement of the ship. I went back to the helm then, and though I called him several times, repeating my questions over and over again, he never answered.

I passed the time watching the fish rise, pools of brightness in the night, and our wake a fading lane of sparkling brilliance. We were well into the Gulf of Oman now, the fish more numerous than ever and the sea's phosphorescence quite spectacular. Sharks went under us leaving torpedolike wakes, and shoals of fish broke up like galaxies exploding. It was a fantastic pyrotechnic show of brilliant white lights forming below the surface of the sea and then bursting, constantly vanishing only to reappear, another patch of dark water suddenly illuminated.

Dawn came at last—a greying in the east, on the port bow. My second dawn at the dhow's helm and still nothing hot to eat, only dates and unboiled water. It came quickly, a magic burst of violent color thrusting in flame over the horizon and then the sun like a great curved crimson wheel showing its hot iron rim and lifting fast, a visible movement.

I had parted company with the tanker traffic at the beginning of the dawn watch, steering a course just south of east that I hoped would close the coast in the region of the Pakistan-Iran frontier. There were moments when I thought I could see it, a vague smudge like a brown crayon line away to port just for'ard of the thunderbox. But I couldn't be sure, my eyes playing me tricks and the sun's rapidly growing heat drawing moisture from the sea, the atmosphere thickening into a milky haze. Another eighteen hours! I went below and dipped the fuel tank. It was almost empty. Smears of dried blood marked the poop deck.

Choffel's eyes were closed, his head lolling. His features, his whole body seemed to have shrunk in the night, so that he was like a wax doll curled up there by the binnacle.

I secured the helm and went up into the thunderbox to squat there with my bottom hung out over a slat and bare to the waves, my head poked out above the wood surround, looking at the dhow and the injured man and the water creaming past. Afterward I stripped off and sluiced myself down with buckets of seawater. And then I carried him back to the lazarette.

It was too hot for an injured man on the deck. That's what I told myself anyway, but the truth was I couldn't stand him there. He had begun mumbling to himself. *"Jenny!"* He kept on saying Jenny, so I knew he was talking to his wife. I didn't want to know the intimate details of their life together. I didn't want to be drawn closer to him through a knowledge of his own private hell. *"Jenny, oh my darling—I can't help."* He choked over the words. *"I've nothing left to give you."* And then he whispered, *"The stomach again, is it? He said he'd bring more pills."* He nodded, playing the part. *"Yes, the doctor's coming, darling. He'll be here any minute."* His eyes were closed, his voice quite clear, trembling with the intensity of recollection. *"Doctor!"* His eyes were suddenly open, staring at me, but without sight. *"Have you brought them? For the pain. It's in the belly . . ."* I put him down quickly and fled, back into the sunlight and the sanity of steering.

A few minutes later the engine gave its first tentative cough. I thought perhaps I was mistaken, for it went on as before, giving out full power. But it coughed again, checking, then picking up. It picked up on the dip of the bows, so I knew it was now dependent on the last vestige of fuel being slopped back and forth in the bottom of the tank. I suppose we covered another two or three miles under increasingly uneven power, then suddenly all was quiet, only the splash and gurgle of water along the ship's side. The engine had finally died, the tiller going slack as we lost way.

The air was heavy and very still, only occasional cat's-paws ruffling the oily calm that stretched away on all sides until lost in the white glare of the heat haze. A sudden whisper of spray to starb'd and the whole surface of the sea took off, a thousand little skittering slivers of silver breaking the surface, and behind the shoal a dozen king mackerel arched their leaping bodies in pursuit, scattering prisms of rainbow colors in the splash of a myriad droplets. Again and again they leaped, the shoals skittering ahead of them in a panic of sparkling silver; then suddenly it was over, the oily surface of the sea undisturbed again, so undisturbed that the voracious demonstration of the hard piscatorial world below might never have been.

It was very humid, unseasonally so, since it was still the period of the northeast monsoon, and now that we were into the Arabian Sea we should have had the benefit of at least a breeze from that direction. The current, which was counterclockwise for another month, would have a westerly set and would thus be against us. I spent over an hour and all my energy unfurling and setting the heavy lateen sail. To do this I had to shin up the spar with a butcher's knife from the store and cut the rope tie-ers. The rest was relatively simple, just a matter of hard work, using the block and tackle already attached to the spar and another that acted as a sheet for the sail. With so little wind, it hung over me in folds, flapping to the slow motion of the ship. But it did provide some shade on deck and in an instant I was wedged into the scuppers fast asleep.

I woke to the sound of water rushing past, opening my eyes

to see the great curved sail bellied out and full of wind. Even as I watched, it began to shiver. I leaped to my feet, wide awake and diving up the steps to the tiller, hauling it over just in time to avoid being taken aback. The wind was northwest about force 3, still in the *shamal* quarter, so that I could only just lay my course. The coast was clearly visible now. The haze had gone, the day bright and clear, the sea sparkling, and tht sun was almost overhead. I glanced at my watch. It was 1305. I couldn't believe it. I had been asleep for something like four hours.

We were making, I suppose, about three knots and as the afternoon wore on the Iranian coast vanished from my sight. And since visibility was still good, I thought it probable I was opposite Gwatar Bay, which is on the frontier between Pakistan and Iran. It is a deep bay with salt flats and the bed of a river coming in from Baluchistan. Visualizing the chart I had so often had spread out before me on the chart table, I reckoned we were less than forty miles from Gwadar. No shipping now to point the way, the sea empty to the horizon, except once when a sperm whale blew about half a mile away and shortly afterward shot vertically out of the water like some huge submarine missile, leaping so high I could just see the flukes of its tail before it toppled with a gigantic splash back into the sea. At sunset I thought I could make out a line of cliffs low on the port bow. They were of a brilliant whiteness, wind-carved into fantastic towers and minarets so that it was like a mirage-distorted view of some incredible crystal city. Was that the Makran coast of Baluchistan?

Night came and I was still at the helm, the wind backing and getting stronger, the dhow thundering along at six knots or more. Suddenly it was dark. I had to start thinking then, about what I was going to do, how I was going to make it from dhow to shore. I had only a rough idea how far I had come, but at this rate, with the wind still backing and freshening, and the dhow empty of cargo, it looked as though I could be off Gwadar about one or two in the morning—presuming, of course, that the disappearance of the coast in the late afternoon really had been the bay and river flats that marked the frontier. I wondered how far off I would be able to see Gwadar at night. In daylight it was visible for miles, a great five-hundred-foot-high mass of hard rock sticking up out of the sea like an island. It was, in fact, a peninsula, shaped like a hammerheaded shark with its nose pointing south, the body of it a narrow sandspit with the port of Gwadar facing both ways, east and west, so that there was safe anchorage in either monsoon—always provided a vessel could weather the rock and cliffs of the peninsula's broad head.

My years at sea told me that the prudent thing to do would be to lower the great lateen sail and let the dhow drift through the night, hoisting again at dawn when I could see where I was. But what if the wind went on increasing? What if I couldn't hoist the bloody thing? Seeing it there, bellied against the stars, I knew it needed several men on the tackle to be sure of taming the power of that sail. And I was tired. God! I was tired.

Prudence can't compete with the lethargic urge to leave things as they are, and so I went plunging on into the night, relying on being able to pick up the automatic light on top of the headland, ignoring the nagging doubt in my mind that said it was probably out of order. If I hadn't been so tired; if I hadn't had the urgent need to contact the authorities and get a message out to the world about the *Aurora B;* if the wind had only died—at least, not backed so much into the south where it shouldn't have been at this time of the year; if the light had been working or I had taken into consideration that with the wind south of west there might be an onshore set to the current . . . if—if—if! Disasters are full of ifs, and I was a trained deck officer with a master's certificate—I should have known, even if I wasn't a sailing man. The sea never forgives an error of judgment, and this was an error due to tiredness. I was so god damn weary, and that brute of a sail, bellied out to port like a black bat's wing against the stars.

It came at me when I was half asleep—the roar of breaking waves and a darkness looming over the bows, blotting out the stars. In an instant I was wide awake, my heart in my mouth and the adrenaline flowing as I hauled on the tiller rope, dragging the heavy steering bar over to port. Slowly, very slowly the dhow turned its high bow into the wind. I thought she'd never make it, that she'd fall off and go plunging away downwind and into the cliffs, but she came up into the wind at last, and there she hung. She wouldn't go through it on to the other tack. And if she had, then I realized the lateen rig required the whole spar to be tipped up vertically and manhandled round the mast. An impossible task for one man with the wind blowing 5 or 6.

I didn't move fast enough. I can see that now. I should have secured the helm and hauled in on the sheet until the sail was set flat and as tight in as it would go. But even then I don't know that she'd have completed the tack. Not with just the one sail, and anyway I couldn't be in two places at once. The wind, close inshore, was so strong it was all I could do to manage the tiller, and when she wouldn't go through the wind, I just stayed there, my mind a blank, the sail flogging in giant whipcracks, the sea and the waves all contributing to the confusion of noise, and the dhow taken virtually aback, driving astern toward the surf breaking in a phosphorescent lather of light.

And while I crouched there, hauling on the tiller which was already hard over, I watched appalled as the bows fell away to port, the lateen filling with a clap like thunder and the dhow lying over, driving virtually sideways into a maelstrom of broken water, and the cliffs above me looming taller and taller, half the stars in the sky blotted out and the movement of the deck under me suddenly very wild.

We struck at 0227. I know that because I checked my

watch, an action that was entirely automatic, as though I were in the wheelhouse of a proper ship with instruments to check and the log to fill in. We had hit a rock, not the cliffs. The cliffs I could vaguely see, a black mass looming above white waters. There was a thud and the rending sound of timbers breaking, and we hung there in a welter of broken waves with spray blowing over us and the dhow pounding and tearing itself to bits.

I had no idea where I was, whether it was the Gwadar Peninsula we had hit, or some other part of the coast. And there was nothing I could do. I was completely helpless, watching, dazed, as the prow swung away to port, everything happening in slow motion and with a terrible inevitability, timbers splintering amidships, a gap in the deck opening up and steadily widening as the vessel was literally torn apart. Years of neglect and blazing heat had rendered the planks and frames of her hull too brittle to stand the pounding and she gave up without any pretense of a struggle, the mainmast crashing down, the great sail like a winged banner streaming away to drown in the boiling seas. Then the for'ard half of the dhow broke entirely away. One moment it was there, a part of the ship, the next it was being swept into oblivion like a piece of driftwood. For a moment I could see it still, a dark shape against the white of broken water, and then suddenly it was gone.

I heard a cry and looking down from the poop I saw Choffel's body, flushed out from the lazarette by the wash of a wave and floundering in what little of the waist remained. I had my torch on and in the beam of it I saw his face white with his mouth open in some inarticulate cry, his hair plastered over his forehead, and his arm raised as a wave engulfed him. I remember thinking that the sea was doing my work for me, the next wave breaking over him and sweeping him away, and the same wave lifting the broken stern, tilting it forward and myself with it. There was a crash as we hit the rock, and a scraping sound, the mizzen falling close beside me and the remains of the dhow, with myself clinging to the wooden balustrade at the for'ard end of the poop, swept clear and into the backwash of broken water close under the cliff.

There was no sign of Choffel then. He was gone. And I was waist-deep in water, the deck gyrating wildly as it sank under me, weighed down by the engine, and then a wave broke over me, right over my head and my mouth was suddenly full of water, darkness closing in. For a moment I didn't struggle. A sort of fatalism took charge, an *"Insh' Allah!"* mood that it was the will of God. Choffel had gone and that was that. I had done what I was intended to do and I didn't struggle. But then suddenly it came to me that that wasn't the end of it at all, and as I sank into the surge of the waves and quiet suffocation, Karen seemed to be calling to me. Not a siren song, but crying for all the life that would be destroyed by Sadeq or the twisted mind of Hals when those two tankers released their oil on the shores of Europe. I struggled then. I started fighting, threshing at the engulfing sea, forcing myself back to the buffeting, seething white of the surface, gulping air and trying desperately to swim.

CHAPTER TWO

THE SUN WAS BURNING HOLES IN MY HEAD, my eyelids colored blood, and I was retching dribbles of saltwater. I could hear the soft thump and suck of waves. I rolled over, my mouth open and drooling water, my throat aching with the salt of it, my fingers digging into sand. A small voice was calling, a high piping voice calling to me in Urdu—"Wake up, sahib. You wake up, plees." And there were hands on my shoulders, shaking me gently.

I opened my eyes. There were two of them, two small boys, half naked and dripping water, clutching at their sodden loincloths, their eyes round with the shock of finding me, their bodies burnt brown by the sun and the salt. Behind them was a boat drawn up on the sand, a small open boat, the wood bleached by the sun to a faded grey, the hull black with bitumen. Slowly I pushed myself up, my eyes slitted against the sand glare. The wind had gone, the sea calm and blue with sparkling wavelets falling lazily on the sloping shore. Away to the left, beyond the boat, a very white building sprawled hull-down among some dunes. Behind the dunes I could see the brown tops of mud-brick houses and in the far distance the vague outline of a headland. Two mules were grazing on the sparse grass of the dunes behind me. "What's the name of that village?" I asked.

The dark little faces stared at me uncomprehendingly. I pointed toward the white building and the roofs beyond.

"Name? You tell me name of village." They laughed, embarrassed. I switched to Urdu then, speaking slowly since these were Baluchi and I knew my accent would be strange to them.

"Coastguards," they said, speaking almost in unison. "Gwadar Coastguards."

Gwadar! I sat with my head in my hands, feeling drained. So I had made it. And now there was a new battle to fight. I had to explain myself—on the telephone to Karachi—talk to officials, to the Lloyd's agent, to all the people who had to be alerted. And I was tired, so deadly tired. It wasn't just my body that was exhausted—it was my brain, my mind, my will. Vaguely I remembered swimming clear of the wreck, hanging onto a piece of the dhow's broken timbering and the seas breaking over me, rocking me into the oblivion of total exhaustion. A piece of timber, part of a mast by the look of it, lay half-submerged a little way along the shore, rolling gently back and forth in the wash of the small waves breaking.

A man appeared, a bearded, wrinkled face under a rag of a turban peering down at me. He was talking to the boys, a quick high voice, but words I could not follow, and they were answering him, excitedly gesturing at the sea. Finally they ran off and the old man said, "I send them for the Havildar."

He knew there had been a dhow wrecked during the night because bits of it had come ashore. He asked me whose it was, where it had come from, how many others had been on board —all the questions I knew would be repeated again and again. I shook my head, pretending I didn't understand. If I said I was alone they wouldn't believe me. And if I told them about Choffel . . . I thought of how it would be trying to explain to a village headman, or even some dumb soldier of a coastguard, about the *Aurora B*, how we had taken the dhow, cutting it free in a hail of bullets . . . How could they possibly accept a story like that? They'd think I was mad.

I must have passed out then, or else gone to sleep, for the next thing I knew the wheel of a Land Rover was close beside my head and there were voices. The sun was hot and my clothes, dry now, were stiff with salt. They lifted me up and put me in the back, a soldier sitting with his arm round me so that I didn't fall off the seat as we jolted along the foreshore to the headquarters building, which was a square white tower overlooking the sea. I was given a cup of sweet black coffee in the adjutant's office, surrounded by three or four officers, all staring at me curiously. It was the adjutant who did most of the questioning, and when I had explained the circumstances to the increasingly skeptical huddle of dark-skinned faces, I was taken in to see the colonel, a big, impressive man with a neat little mustache and an explosive voice. Through the open square of the window I found myself looking out on the brown cliffs of the Gwadar Peninsula. I was given another cup of coffee and had to repeat the whole story for his benefit.

I don't know whether he believed me or not. In spite of the coffee I was half asleep, not caring very much either way. I was telling them the truth. It would have been too much trouble to tell them anything else. But I didn't say much about Choffel, only that he'd been shot while we were trying to get away in the dhow. Nobody seemed to be concerned about him. His body hadn't been found and without a body they weren't interested.

The colonel asked me a number of questions, mostly about the nationality of the men on the tanker and where I thought they were taking it. Finally he picked up his hat and his swagger stick and called for his car. "Follow me, please," he said and led me out into the neatly whitewashed forecourt. "I now have to take you to the Assistant Commissioner, who will find it a difficult problem since you are landed on his lap, you see, with no passport, no identification, and the most unusual story. It is the lack of identity he will find most difficult. You say you have been ship's officer in Karachi. Do you know somebody in Karachi? Somebody to say who you are?"

I told him there were a lot of people who knew me—port

officials, shipping agents, some of those who worked at the
Sind Club and at the reception desk of the Metropole Hotel.
Also personal friends. He nodded, beating a tattoo on his knee
with his stick as he waited for his car. "That will help, perhaps."

The car arrived, the coastguard flag flying on the hood,
and as we drove out of the compound, he pointed to a long
verandaed bungalow of a building just beyond an area of
sand laid out with mud bricks baking in the sun—"Afterward,
you want the hospital, it is there."

"I'll be all right," I said.

He looked at me doubtfully. "We get the doctor to have a
look at you. I don't like you to die with me when you have
such an interesting story to tell."

We passed one of those brilliantly colorful trucks, all tinsel
and florid paintings, like an elaborately decorated chocolate
box; conclusive proof to the wandering haziness of my mind
that I really was in Pakistan. From fine-ground sand and a
cloud of dust we moved onto Tarmac. Glimpses of the sea,
long black fishing boats anchored off, their raked masts dancing in the sun—this was the eastern side of the Gwadar Peninsula, the sea still a little wild, the shore white with surf. There
was sand everywhere, the sun glaring down.

"We have a desalination plant, good water from the sea, all
by solar." The colonel's voice was far away, the driver's forage
cap perched on his round black head becoming blurred and indistinct against the moving backcloth of open bazaar booths
and mud-brick buildings. "We see Ahmad Ali Rizivi now."
The car had stopped; the colonel was getting out. "This is
what you call the town hall. It is the house of the Assistant
District Commissioner."

We were in a dusty little open space, a sort of square. A jan-
itor in long robes sat in the doorway. I was vaguely conscious
of people as I followed the colonel up the steps and into the
dark interior. A clerk sat on a high stool at an old-fashioned

desk; another ushered us in to an inner office where a man rose from behind a plain wooden desk that might have been a table. He waved us to chairs hastily placed. It was cooler and there were framed maps and texts on the wall—texts from the Koran I presumed. And the inevitable picture of Jinnah—Quaid-i-Azam, the man who had led Pakistan out of the Empire, out of India, to independence and partition. The pictures came and went, the voices a dark murmur as a hot wave of weariness broke over me, my head nodding.

Coffee came, the inevitable coffee, the colonel's hand shaking me, the Assistant District Commissioner gesturing to the cup, a bleak smile of hospitality. He wanted me to tell it again, the whole story. "From the beginning, please." His eyes had no warmth. He didn't care that I was exhausted. He was thinking of me only as a problem washed up by the sea onto his territory, the survivor of a wreck with an improbable story that was going to cause him a lot of trouble. There was a clerk there to take notes.

"He is Lord of the Day," the colonel said, nodding at Rizivi and smiling. "He is the Master here. If he says, 'Off with his head,' then off with his head it is." He said it jokingly, but the smile did not extend to his eyes. It was a warning. Who was the Lord of the Night, I wondered, as I drank the hot sweet coffee, trying to marshal my thoughts so there would be some sort of coherence in what I had to tell him.

I have only the vaguest memory of what I said, or of the questions he asked. Afterward there was a long pause while he and the colonel talked it over. They didn't seem to realize I understood Urdu, though it hardly made any difference since I was beyond caring whether they believed me or what they decided to do about me, my eyes closing, my mind drifting into sleep. But not before I had the impression that they were both agreed on one thing at least—to pass the problem to higher authority just as soon as they could. People came and went. The colonel was alone with me for a time. "Mr. Rizivi arrange air passage for you on the next flight." The Assistant District Commissioner came back. He had spoken to Quetta on the R/T. "You go to Karachi this afternoon. Already we are consulting with Oman to see if your story is true."

I should have made the point then that the *Aurora B* would probably have sailed by the time arrangements had been made for a reconnaissance flight over the *khawr*, but my mind was concentrated entirely on the fact that I was being flown to Karachi. Nothing else mattered. We were in the car again and a few minutes later the colonel and his driver were thrusting me along a veranda crowded with the sick and their relatives to an office where an overworked doctor in a white coat was examining a man whose chest was covered with skin sores. He pushed him away as we entered, peering at me through thick-lensed glasses. "You the survivor of the wrecked dhow?"

I nodded.

"They talk of nothing else." He jerked his head at the crowded veranda. "Everybody I see today. They all have a theory, you see, as to how it happened. How did it happen? You tell me." He lifted my eyelids with a dark thumb, brown eyes peering at me closely. "They say there is no *naukhada*, only a solitary English. Is you, eh?"

I nodded, feeling his hands running over my body. "No fractures. Some bruising, nothing else." He pulled open my shirt, a stethoscope to his ears, his voice running on. Finally he stood back, told me there was nothing wrong with me except lack of sleep and nervous exhaustion. He gave me some pills and made me take one of them with a glass of water right there in the stuffy confines of his little consulting room. After that I don't remember anything at all until I was in a Land Rover being driven out to the airfield, the wind and dust blowing, the land flat, a desert scene with passengers and officials standing in the glare of the sun, baggage lying round them on the ground.

The plane came in, a Fokker Friendship bright as a dragonfly against the hard blue of the sky, the gravel airfield spouting long streamers of dust as its wheels touched down. The adjutant himself saw me onto the plane and remained beside it until the door of the fuselage was finally closed. We took off and from my window I had a good view of Gwadar as we climbed and banked, the hammerheaded peninsula with an area of water and green trees like an oasis on one corner of its barren top, and below it, in the sand, the glass-glinting square of the desalination plant, then the town, neat acres of brown, the white of the Coastguard buildings, and the sea on either side with the fishing boats lying off or drawn up on the sand.

And against it all I suddenly saw Choffel's face, his mouth wide open, the black hair plastered to his white forehead and his arm raised as he sank from sight in the wash of a wave. Somewhere down there his body floated in the blue sea, pale skeleton bones beginning to show as the fish picked him clean.

I remember thinking about the eyes and that I should have done something to help him. His features were so appallingly vivid as I stared through the window at the line of the coast stretching away far below.

And then the wheels touched down and I opened my eyes to find we had landed in Karachi. One of the pilots came aft from the flight deck insisting that nobody move until I had got off the plane. There was a car waiting for me and some men, including Peter Brown, the Lloyd's agent. No Customs, no Immigration. We drove straight out through the loose-shirted untidy mob that hung around the airport entrance, out onto the crowded Hyderabad-Karachi road, the questions beginning immediately. Sadeq—I had referred to a man called Sadeq. Who was he? What did he look like? But they knew already. They had had his description from the oil company's Marine Superintendent in Dubai. They nodded, both of them, checking papers taken from a colored leather briefcase with a cheap metal clasp.

Peter Brown was sitting in front with the driver, neatly

dressed as always in a tropical suit, his greying hair and some-
what patrician features giving him an air of distinction. He
was a reserved man with an almost judicial manner. It was the
other two, sitting on either side of me in the back, who asked
the questions. The smaller of them was a Sindhi, his features
softer, his dark eyes sparkling with intelligence. The other was
a more stolid type with a squarish face heavily pockmarked
and horn-rimmed glasses slightly tinted. Police, or perhaps
Army—I wasn't sure. "He had another name."

"Who?" I was thinking of Choffel.

"This Sadeq. A terrorist, you said." The small man was
riffling through the clipful of papers resting on his briefcase.
"Here—look now, this telex. It is from Mr. Perrin at the
GODCO offices in Dubai." He waved it at me, holding it in
thin dark fingers, his wrist as slender as a girl's. "He said—
that's you, I'm quoting from his telex you see . . . He said
Sadeq was an Iranian terrorist, that he had another name, but
that he did not know it, which may be true as it is several
years back during the Shah's regime." He looked up. "Now
you have met him again perhaps you recall his other name."
He was peering at me sideways, waiting for an answer, and
there was something in his eyes—it is difficult for eyes that are
dark brown to appear cold, but his were very cold as they
stared at me unblinkingly. "Think very carefully, please." The
voice so soft, the English so perfect, and in those eyes I read
the threat of nameless things that were rumored of the security section of Martial Law prisons.

"Qasim," I said, and he asked me to spell it, writing it down
with a gaudy-colored pen. Then both of them were asking
questions, most of which I couldn't answer because I didn't
know what offenses Qasim had committed against the Shah's
regime before the Khomeini revolution or what he was doing
on board the *Aurora B* under the name Sadeq, why he had
hijacked the ship, what the plan was. I didn't know anything
about him, only his name and the fact that the dead Shah's

police had said he was a terrorist. But they didn't accept that and the questioning went on and on. I was being grilled and once when I nodded off the little man slapped my face. I heard Brown protest, but it didn't make any difference, the questions continuing and becoming more and more searching.

And then, suddenly, when we were into the outskirts of Karachi on the double track of the Shahrah-e-Faisal, they stopped. "We will take you to the Metropole now so you can sleep. Meanwhile, we will try to discover some more about this man Choffel." He leaned over to Peter Brown. "Let us know, please, if you have any information about these ships from London."

The Lloyd's agent nodded. "Of course. And you will let me know the result of the Omani Air Force reconnaissance."

The little man pursed his lips, a smile that was almost feminine. "You're finding this story difficult to swallow, are you?" Brown didn't answer and the man leaned forward. "Do you believe him?" he asked.

Brown turned and looked at me. I could see the uncertainty in his eyes. "If he isn't telling the truth, then he's lying. And I don't at the moment see any reason for him to lie."

"A man has disappeared." The cold dark eyes gave me a sideways glance. He took a newspaper cutting from the clip of papers. "This is from the Karachi paper *Dawn*, a brief news item about a tanker being blown up on the English coast. It is dated ninth January. Karen Rodin. Was that your wife?"

I nodded.

"It also says that a French engineer, Henri Choffel, accused of sabotaging the tanker and causing it to run aground, is being hunted by Interpol." Again the sly sideways glance. "The man who is with you on this dhow—the man you say is shot when you were escaping from the *Aurora B*—his name also is Choffel . . . What is his first name? Is it Henri?"

"Yes." I was staring at him, fascinated, knowing what he

was thinking and feeling myself suddenly on the edge of an abyss.

"And that is the same man—the man Interpol is looking for?"

I nodded.

"Alone on that dhow with you, and your wife blown up with the tanker he wrecked." He smiled and after that he didn't say anything more, letting the silence produce its own impact. The abyss had become a void, my mind hovering on the edge of it, appalled at the inference he was drawing. The fact that I hadn't done it was irrelevant. It was what I had planned to do, the reason I was on the *Aurora B*. And this little man in Karachi had seen it immediately. If it was such an obvious conclusion . . . I was thinking how it would be when I was returned to the U.K., how I could avoid people leaping to the same conclusion.

The car slowed. We were in Club Road now, drawing into the curb where broad steps led up to the wide portico of the Metropole. We got out and the heat and the dust and noise of Karachi hit me. Through the stream of traffic, beyond the line of beat-up old taxi cars parked against the iron palings opposite, I glimpsed the tall trees of the shaded gardens of the Sind Club. A bath and a deck chair in the cool of the terrace, a long, ice-cold drink . . . "Come, please." The big man took hold of my arm, shattering the memories of my *Dragonera* days as he almost frog-marched me up the steps into the hotel. The little man spoke to the receptionist. The name Ahmad Khan was mentioned and a key produced. "You rest now, Mr. Rodin." He handed the key to his companion and shook my hand. "We will talk again when I have more information. Also we have to decide what we do with you." He gave me a cold little smile and the Metropole seemed suddenly a great deal more luxurious. "Meanwhile, Majeed will look after you." He nodded in the direction of his companion who was talking now to an unshaven, loosely dressed little man who had been hovering in the background. "Can I give you a lift?" he asked the Lloyd's agent.

Peter Brown shook his head. "I'll see Rodin settled in first."

"As you wish." He left then and I watched him go with a sense of relief, his slim silhouette changing to powder blue as the glare of the street spotlighted his pale neat suit. "What is he—Intelligence?" I asked.

Brown shrugged. "Calls himself a Government Information officer."

"And the other?"

"Security, I presume."

We took the elevator to the second floor, tramping endless cement-floored corridors where bearers, sweepers and other hangers-on lounged in overemployed idleness. The Metropole occupies a whole block, a large square of buildings constructed round a central courtyard. The first floor is given over to offices—almost every room with a sign over it, the names of countless small businesses and agencies. I glanced at my watch. It was still going, the time 1736. We stopped at a door and the policeman handed the key to the unshaven little man who had accompanied us. He in turn handed it to the bearer who was now in close attendance. The room was big and airy, with a ceiling fan turning slowly and the windows open and looking out onto the huge courtyard. Kites were coming in to roost on the trees and window ledges, big vulturelike birds, drab in the shadows cast by the setting sun. "You will be very comfortable here." The policeman waved his hands in a gesture that included the spartan beds and furniture, the big wardrobes and tatty square of carpet, a note of envy in his voice. The Metropole to him was probably the height of glamour.

He searched the drawers and the wardrobes, checked the bathroom. Finally he left, indicating the unshaven one and saying, "Hussain will keep watch over you. And if there is something more you have to tell us, he knows where to find me."

"Is there?" Brown asked as the door closed behind him.

"Is there what?"

"Anything more you have to tell them."

"No."

"And it's true, is it—about the *Aurora B?*"

I nodded, wondering how I could get rid of him, wanting nothing except to get my head down now and sleep while I had the chance. It was even more important to me than food. He moved to the phone, which was on a table between the two beds. "Mind if I ring the office?" He gave the switchboard a number and I went into the bathroom, where the plumbing was uncertain and the dark cement floor wet with water from a leaking pipe. When I had finished I found the unshaven Hussain established on a chair in the little entrance hall and Brown was standing by the window. "I think I should warn you—a lot of people are going to find this story of yours a pretty tall one. You realize we've no record of a tanker ever having been hijacked. Certainly no VLCC has been hijacked before. That's straight, old-fashioned piracy. And you're saying it's not one, but two—two tankers boarded and taken without even a peep of any sort on the radio. It's almost inconceivable."

"So you don't believe me?"

He shook his head, pacing up and down the tattered piece of carpeting. "I didn't say that. I just think it's something people will find difficult to accept. One, perhaps, but two—"

"The first one went wrong."

"So you said. And you think a bomb was thrown into the radio room—a grenade, something like that?"

"I don't know what happened," I said, sitting on the bed, wishing he would go away as I pulled off my shoes. "I've told you what I saw—the radio shack blackened by fire and a hole ripped in the wall. I presume they met with resistance on the bridge, discovered the radio operator was going to send a Mayday, and dealt with the situation the only way they knew."

"And this happened, not in the Indian Ocean, but when the *Aurora B* was still in the Gulf?"

"Yes. When she was in the Straits, probably."

"So the radio contact with the owners, made when the ship was supposed to be somewhere off the coast of Kutch, was entirely spurious. That's what you're saying, isn't it?—that it never happened, or rather it was made from a quite different locality and was not the captain reporting to the owners, but the hijackers conning them." He nodded to himself. "Ingenious, and it's been done before. But usually with nonexistent ships or cargoes, and not on this scale, not with oil involved and big tankers. Fraudulent insurance claims, we know a lot about those now—I've had instances myself. But always general cargo ships. Small ones, usually old and in poor condition. Four at least I can remember, all single-vessel owners, two of them had only just changed hands. They were all cargo frauds based on forged documents." He began describing the intricacies of the frauds—bills of lading, packing lists, manufacturers' certificates in two cases, even an EEC certificate of origin in one case, all forged.

"I'm tired," I said irritably.

He didn't seem to hear me, going on to tell me a complicated story of transshipment of car engines from a small freighter at the height of the port's congestion when there were as many as eighty ships anchored off Karachi awaiting quay space. But then he stopped quite suddenly. "Of course, yes, I was forgetting—you're tired." He said it a little huffily. "I was simply trying to show you that what you've been telling us is really very difficult to believe. These are not small ships, and GODCO is certainly not a single-vessel owner. They are, both of them, VLCCs, well-maintained and part of a very efficiently operated fleet." He was gazing out of the window at the darkening shadows. "Maybe they picked on them for that reason." He was talking to himself, not me. "Being GODCO vessels, maybe they thought their disappearance would be accepted—something similar to the disappearance of those two big Scandinavians. They were in ballast and cleaning tanks with welders on board or something. An explosive situation. That's what I heard, anyway."

"It's got nothing to do with it," I said. "This is quite different."

"Yes indeed. Quite different. And it doesn't sound like fraud." He had turned from the window and was staring at me. "What do you reckon the purpose is?"

"How the hell do I know? I was only on board the ship a few hours."

"And the cost of it," he muttered. "They'd need to have very substantial backers, particularly to escalate the operation to a second tanker at short notice." He glanced at his watch. "You want to rest and it's time I was getting back to the office. There'll be people at Lloyd's who'll be greatly cheered to know the *Aurora B* at any rate is still afloat. I'll telex them right away."

"You'll be contacting Forthright's, will you?"

He nodded. "They'll have a full account of it waiting for them in their office tomorrow morning. Mr. Saltley can then take what action he thinks fit." He lifted his head, looking at me down his long nose. "If they locate this ship, the one you say is the *Aurora B*, then there'll be all sorts of problems. Maritime law isn't exactly designed to cope with this sort of thing. And you'll be in the thick of it, so much depending on your statement. On the other hand, if she's sailed and the subsequent search fails to locate her . . ." He paused, watching me curiously. "That's why I stayed on, to warn you. What happens if they don't believe you? If they think you're lying, then they'll want to know the reason and that may lead them to jump to conclusions." He smiled. "Could be awkward, that.

But let's take things as they come, eh?" He clapped me on the shoulder. "Have a good rest. I'll see you in the morning."

Sleep came in a flash and I awoke sweating to a surge of sound, red lights flickering, and a wild voice. My body, naked under the coarse sheets, felt battered and painful, my limbs aching. I had no idea where I was, staring wide-eyed at the big fan blades above my bed, revolving slowly to reflect a kaleidoscope of colors. And that voice. I sat up. A woman was singing, a high Muslim chanting, and the surging sound was an Eastern band, the shriek of pipes and tam-tams beating.

I pulled back the sheet and stumbled to the window, conscious of the stiffness of my muscles, the ache of a deep bruise in my pelvis, and stared down into the courtyard, which was a blaze of light, girls in richly colored saris, tables piled with food and drink. A wedding? So much tinsel decoration, balloons and lanterns, and the men loutish and ill-at-ease in their bright suits. The singing stopped. The music changed to Western jazz played fast and the crowd mingled, men and women clinging uncertainly, dancing double time. A bird swirled up like a great bat, the lights red, yellow, and green, and somebody pointing so that I drew back quickly, conscious that I was standing there stark naked. But it was the bird they were pointing at.

A shadow moved beside me. "You all right, sahib?" It was my watchdog.

I couldn't sleep for a long time after that, listening to the band and the high chatter of voices, the lights flickering on my closed eyes, and thinking about what was going to happen when they found the ship. Would they arrest her on the high seas? Who would do it—the British, the Americans, who? And what about me? Nobody was going to thank me for handing them such a problem. I wondered what Sadeq would do when the Navy came on board, what explanation he would give. Would he still be flying the hammer and sickle? And Baldwick —I suddenly remembered Baldwick. Baldwick wouldn't be able to leave without the dhow. He'd still be on board. What would his explanation be, or would Sadeq dispose of him before he had a chance to talk? I could see Sadeq, as I had glimpsed him when I was crouched below the poop, the gun at his waist, the bearded face fixed in what was almost a grin as he sprayed bullets with cold professional accuracy—and Baldwick thrown backward, his big barrel of a stomach opened up and flayed red. Choffel—my mind was confused. It was Choffel whose stomach had been hit. And I was in Pakistan with information nobody was happy to hear . . . except Pamela and those two sailing men, her father and Saltley. If I was in England now, not lying here in Karachi with a wedding thumping out jazz and Eastern music . . .

I suppose I was in that limbo of half coma that is the result of shock and exhaustion, my mind in confusion, a kaleidoscope of thoughts and imaginings all as strange as the lights and the music. Darkness came eventually, and sleep—a sleep so dead that when I finally opened my eyes the sun was high above the hotel roof and Hussain was shaking me. He was even more unshaven now and he kept repeating, *"Tiffin. Tiffin,* sahib." It was almost ten o'clock and there was a tray on the small central table with boiled eggs, sliced white bread, butter, marmalade and a big pot of coffee.

My clothes had gone, but the notes and traveler's checks that had been in my hip pocket were on the table beside me. Kites wheeled in a cloudless sky. I had a quick shower and breakfasted with a towel wrapped round my middle. A copy of *Dawn* lay on the table. "Founded by Quaid-i-Azam Mohammed Ali Jinnah," it said—"Karachi, 21 Safar, 1400." The lead story was about Iran, the conflict between the IRP and the left-wing Mujaheddin. I could find no mention of a dhow being wrecked off Gwadar or of anybody being washed ashore there.

The bearer came with my clothes—laundered, ironed, and reasonably dry. As soon as I was dressed I rang the office of

Lloyd's agents down near the Customs House, but Peter Brown was out and the only other person I knew there, a Parsi, had no information to give me. So I sat by the window, reading the paper from cover to cover and watching the kites. Hussain refused absolutely to allow me out of the room and though I had a telephone call from Brown's office it was only to say he would contact me as soon as he had any information. I could have done with a drink, but the hotel was under strict Islamic laws and drier than the sands of Baluchistan.

Just after midday Ahmad Khan arrived, the jacket of his blue suit slung over his shoulder, his tie loosened. "There is no ship," he said in his rather high lilting voice. He was standing in the middle of the room, his dark eyes watching me closely. "Muscat report their aircraft have overflown all the *khawrs* of the Musandam Peninsula. There is no tanker there." He paused to let that sink in. "Also, Gwadar report no body being washed into the coast."

"Was there any sign of the man who jumped overboard?" I asked.

"No, nothing. And no sign of the ship."

"I told you they would have sailed the morning after we escaped. Have they made a search along the tanker routes?"

"Oman say they are doing it now. I have told my office to let me know here as soon as we receive a report." He threw his jacket onto the nearest bed, picked up the phone, and ordered coffee. "You want any coffee?"

I shook my head. Just over two days at full speed, the ship could be nine hundred, a thousand miles from the Straits, clear of the Oman Gulf, and well out into the Indian Ocean—a hell of a lot of sea to search. "What about other ships? Have they been alerted?"

"You ask Mr. Brown that. I have no information."

His coffee came, and when the waiter had gone he said, "You don't wish to amend your statement at all?"

I shook my head. "No, not at all."

"Okay." And after that he sat there drinking his coffee in silence. Time passed as I thought about the route the tanker would have taken, and wondered why he was here. It was just twelve-thirty when the phone rang. It was Brown and after a moment he handed it to me. All shipping had been alerted the previous night. So far nothing had been reported. "I've just been talking to the Consul. I'm afraid they're a bit skeptical."

"Do you mean they don't believe me?"

"No, why should they? I don't think anyone's going to believe you unless the tanker actually materializes."

"Do you?"

There was a moment's hesitation. "I might if it wasn't for your story about Choffel. Let's wait, shall we? If the body turns up, or we get a sighting of that tanker . . ." His voice drifted away apologetically. "Anyway, how are you feeling now—rested?"

"Yes, I'm all right."

"Good, good." There was a pause while he searched round for something else to say. "Glad you're all right. Well, if I hear anything I'll give you a ring." There was a click and he was gone.

The conversation left me feeling lonely and disconsolate. If he didn't believe me, the little Sindhi Intelligence man sipping noisily at his coffee certainly would not. Hussain arranged for lunch to be brought up from the café below, a spiced rissole, hot chili, with slices of white bread and some tinned fruit. Ahmad Khan hardly spoke and I was speculating what was going to happen to me when it was realized the tanker had vanished. Obviously, once outside the Gulf of Oman, it would be steering well clear of the shipping lanes. Clouds were building in the white glare above the rooftops and the kites were wheeling lower.

Suddenly the phone rang. It was Ahmad Khan's office. Muscat had reported both reconnaissance planes back at base. They had been in the air over three and a half hours and had

covered virtually the whole of the Gulf from the Straits right
down to Ras al Had, southeast of Muscat, and had also flown
three hundred miles into the Arabian Sea. Of all the tankers
they had sighted only five or six had approximated to the size
of the *Aurora B*, and none of those had answered to the description I had given. Also, most of the ships sighted had been
contacted by radio and none had reported seeing anything
resembling the *Aurora B*. All the ships sighted had been in the
normal shipping lanes. They had seen nothing outside these
lanes and the search had now been called off. The same
negative report had been made by seaborne helicopters searching the Musandam Peninsula and the foothills of the Jebel al
Harim. That search had also been called off.

He put the phone down and picked up his jacket. "I am instructed to escort you to the airport and see that you leave on
the next flight to the U.K. Please, you will now get ready."

"Any reason?"

He hesitated, then gave a little shrug. "I don't think it mat-
ters that you know. Your allegations have been discussed in
the highest quarters. They are regarded as very sensitive. Accordingly your Consul has been informed that you are persona
non grata in this country. You understand?"

I nodded. I felt suddenly as though I had some contagious
disease, everybody distancing themselves from me. But at
least I was being allowed to leave.

"You come now, please." Ahmad Khan had his jacket slung
over his shoulder and was standing waiting for me. I had nothing, only the shirt and trousers in which I had arrived. "I'll
need a sweater, something warm. It's winter in London."

But all he said was, "That is for your Consul. Come, please."
Hussain was standing with the door open. We went back
down the cement corridors, the room bearer following us a little forlornly. We left him at the elevator, muttering to himself.
A driver was waiting for us at the reception desk, a big,
serious-looking man with a black mustache and a sort of tur-

ban, who led us out to an official car. We went first to the Ab-
dullah Haroon Road Bazaar, where I had passport photos
taken, and after that we drove out on the Khayaban-i-Iobal
road to the British Consulate, which was close to the Clifton
seaside resort. I had been there once before. It was up a long
drive through a well-tended estate and gardens.

I asked to see the Consul himself, but he, too, was distancing himself from the whole affair. He wasn't available and I
had to be content with a grey-haired, harassed-looking Pakistani, who issued me with temporary papers, and then, by raiding some emergency stores, produced a pair of patched grey
flannel trousers and a blue seaman's jersey, socks, and a pair of
boots.

It was in this peculiar rig that thirteen hours later I arrived
at Heathrow. Ahmad Khan had stayed with me until I was actually on the plane. In fact, he saw me to my seat, accompanied by the senior steward. It was a PIA aircraft full of emi-
grants going to join relatives in Britain, a bedlam of a journey
with the toilets awash and one or two children who had never
seen a flush toilet before in their lives. I don't know what the
chief steward was told, but he and the stewardess kept a very
careful watch over me, with the result that I had excellent service, my every want attended to immediately.

Brown had not seen fit to see me off and I had been refused
permission to telephone. However, I was told he had been informed of my time of departure and flight number, and I presumed he would have passed this on to Saltley so that he
would know my ETA at Heathrow. But there was nobody
there to meet me and no message. I was delayed only a few
moments at Immigration and then I was through and just one
of the great flood of humanity that washes through London
Airport. There is nothing more depressing than to be on your
own in one of the terminals, all of London before you and nobody expecting you, no plans. The time was 0827 and it was
Sunday. Also it was blowing hard from the northwest and rain-

ing, the temperature only a little above freezing—a typical late-January day. I changed my salt-stiffened franc notes and Emirate currency, got myself a coffee and sat over it, smoking a duty-free cigarette and thinking over all that had happened since I had left for Nantes ten days ago. No good ringing Forthright's—the office would be closed and I hadn't Saltley's home number.

In the end I took the tube to Stepney Green and just over an hour later I was back in the same basement room, lying on the bed, smoking a cigarette with the legs of passersby parading across the top of the grime-streaked window. I was looking at the typescript of my book again. "You left it here," Mrs. Steinway had said to me when she brought it down from her room on the ground floor back. "The girl found it lying on the floor beneath the bed after you'd gone." From flipping idly through the pages I began to read, then I became engrossed, all our life together and Balkaer, Cornwall, the birds—it all flooded back, the bare little basement room filled with the surge of the Atlantic breaking against the cliffs, the cry of seabirds, and Karen's voice. There was a strange peacefulness in the words I had written, a sense of being close to the basics of life. In this moment, in retrospect, it seemed like a dream existence and I was near to tears as the simplicity and richness of our lives was unfolded, so vividly that I could hardly believe the words were my own. And at times I found myself thinking of Choffel, those bare hills and the simplicity of his boyhood, Cornish cliffs and Welsh hills, the same thread and at the end the two of us coming together on that dhow.

Next day I phoned Forthright's, but Saltley's secretary said he would be at the Law Courts all morning. He was expecting me, however, and she said I could see him in the late afternoon, around four if that was convenient. I was back in the world of marine solicitors, insurance, and missing tankers.

CHAPTER THREE

"YES, BUT WHAT'S THE MOTIVE?" I was sitting facing Saltley across his desk and when I told him I didn't know, he said it was a pity I hadn't stayed on board instead of jumping onto the dhow just because I was determined to destroy Choffel. "If you'd stayed, then you'd have discovered their destination, and sooner or later you would have had an opportunity to get a message out by radio."

"Unlikely," I said.

He shrugged. "There are always opportunities." And when I pointed out that at least he now knew the tanker was still afloat, which was more than he could have expected when he employed me, he said, "I appreciate that, Rodin, but I've only got your word for it."

"You don't believe me?" My voice trembled on the verge of anger.

"Oh, I believe you. You couldn't have made it up, not all the people and the astonishing sight of a tanker against cliffs at the head of that inlet. But the ship isn't there any longer. To get a claim for millions of dollars set aside we've got to be able to prove the *Aurora B* is still afloat."

"And my word isn't good enough?"

"Not in law. Now if Choffel were still alive . . ." He was leaning on his desk, his hands locked together on top of the thick file his secretary had left with him. "Is there anything else he told you that's relevant? Anything at all? You were on that dhow together for two days."

"He was wounded and a lot of the time he was unconscious, or nearly so."

"Yes, of course." But then he began to take me through every exchange of words I had had with the man. I found it very difficult to recall his exact words, particularly when he had been rambling on about his boyhood and his life up there in the bare Welsh hills, and all the time those blue eyes staring at me unblinking. Finally Saltley asked me why I thought he had seized the dhow. "Surely it wasn't just to get away from you?"

"I don't know."

"Were you really going to kill him?"

"Possibly. I can't be sure, can I?"

"You said his daughter had told him, in that letter of hers, that you were going to kill him. Is that right?"

"Yes, that's what he said."

He was silent for a long time, thinking. "If I put you in court, as a witness, they'd dig that out of you right away. They'd say you were mentally unhinged at the time, that you weren't responsible for your actions, and that you now don't know what is true and what is the product of your imagination."

"They'll know soon enough," I told him angrily. "In a few weeks from now the *Aurora B* will appear in some port or other and Sadeq will carry out his mission. They'll know then, all right."

He nodded. "And Choffel gave no hint to you at any time what that mission might be?"

"No."

"Or the destination?"

"I tell you, no."

"Did you ask him?"

"About the destination?"

"Yes. Did you specifically ask him what it was?"

"I think so," I murmured, staring at him and trying to remember, feeling as though I were already in the witness box and he was cross-examining me. "I think it was during that first night at sea. We were through the Straits then and into the Oman Gulf and he'd somehow dragged himself up to the poop to tell me the engine needed oil. He started talking about the ships he'd been in, the *Stella Rosa* and the engineer whose name he'd taken. I asked him about the *Aurora B* and the other ship, and what they were going to do with the oil, where they were going to spill it. It had to be something like that and I thought it was probably a European port, so I asked him where. I remember I kept on asking him where and shaking him, trying to get it out of him."

"And did you?"

"No, I was too rough with him. He was screaming with pain, his mind confused. He said something about salvage, at least that's what I thought he said. It didn't make sense unless he was harking back to the first ship he destroyed, the *Lavandou*, which was supposed to have sunk in deep water but drifted onto a reef instead."

"Salvage." Saltley repeated the word, staring past me into space. "No, I agree. It doesn't make sense. Do you think he knew what the destination was?"

But I couldn't answer that, and though he kept on at me, probing in that soft voice, the blue eyes fixed on mine in that disconcerting stare, it wasn't any good. "Oh well," he said finally, "we'll just have to accept that he hadn't been told the ship's destination." He relaxed then, that crooked mouth of his breaking into a smile that made him suddenly human. "Sorry. I've been pressing you rather hard." He took his hands from the file and opened it, but without looking down, his mind elsewhere. Finally he said almost briskly, "If we accept your story as correct, then there are certain assumptions that can be made. First, the *Aurora B* is afloat with a full cargo of oil. Second, since the Omani air search has failed to sight her, she has sailed from the inlet where she has been hiding and is at sea somewhere in the Indian Ocean. The Pakistan Air Force also flew a search. Did you know that?"

I shook my head and he tapped the file. "A report came in yesterday. Search abandoned, no sighting. Now we come to the main assumption." He hesitated. "Not so much an assumption as a pure guess, I'm afraid. The *Aurora B*, you think, is headed for a European port, which means she will pass south of the Cape and head up the Atlantic coast of Africa. We will say, for the purpose of our assumptions, that the *Howdo Stranger* is well ahead of her—has, in fact, passed the Cape into the Atlantic. Is that your reading of the situation?"

"It could be anywhere," I said guardedly. The man was a lawyer and I wasn't going to commit myself.

He smiled. "The first hijack was bungled. That's your theory, isn't it? The evidence being the damaged radio room and the crew imprisoned in the chain locker. Incidentally, there's no report of that man who jumped overboard being found, so we'll have to presume that he's dead. They then hijacked a second tanker and the operation is successful. They now have two tankers. One is dispatched on its mission. The other is to follow when it is crewed-up with what one might call Baldwick's mercenaries. And since the second one has now sailed it seems obvious that the plan is for a joint operation. That means a rendezvous. You agree?"

I nodded. "That's what I was trying to get out of Choffel."

"You said it was the destination you were trying to get out of him—the target, in other words."

"That and where the two ships were going to meet."

"And he said something about salvage."

"I think that's what he said. But he was confused and in pain. I can't be certain. I was very tired."

"Of course." There was a moment's silence, then he said, "That's it. They'll meet up somewhere and then they'll act in concert, the two of them together." He leaned back and stretched his arms, yawning to relieve the tension of the half hour he had spent taking me step by step through my story. "We don't know where they'll meet. We don't know the target or what the motive is. And unless the ships are sighted, or alternatively, that man is found alive on the Musandam Peninsula, there's absolutely nothing to substantiate your quite extraordinary story—and I use the word there in its original and exact meaning." He took a slip of paper from the open file and handed it to me. "That was posted in the Room at Lloyd's yesterday. *The Times* and the *Telegraph* both carried it this morning on their foreign news pages."

The slip was a copy of a Reuters report from Muscat referring to rumors emanating from Pakistan that a Russian tanker was concealed on the Omani coast south of the Hormuz Straits. It stated that the Air Force, having carried out a thorough search of the coast and of the Arabian Sea adjacent to Oman, had proved the rumors to be quite unfounded.

"And this came in this morning." He handed me another Reuters message datelined Karachi. It referred to my by name as the source of the rumor—"A shipwrecked Englishman, Trevor Rodin, has been repatriated, his story of a tanker concealed in an inlet on the Omani side of the Gulf having been proved incorrect. It is considered possible that Rodin may have had political motives and that his story was intended to damage the friendly relations existing between Pakistan and Oman, and also other countries."

"I think you may find yourself the focus of a certain amount of official attention," he added as I handed it back to him. "The whole area is very sensitive."

Saltley's warning proved only too accurate. The following day, when I returned from buying some clothes after opening an account at the local bank and depositing the check he had given me, Mrs. Steinway informed me the police had been asking for me. "Haven't done anything wrong, have you, luv?"

She was a real East Ender, and though she said it jokingly, her eyes watched me suspiciously. "'Cos if you have, you don't stay here, you understand?"

They had asked when I would be back, so I was not surprised to have a visit from a plainclothes officer. I think he was Special Branch. He was quite young, one of those shut-faced men who seem to rise quickly in certain branches of the Establishment. He wasn't interested in what I could tell him about the hidden tanker or about Choffel, it was the political implications that concerned him, his questions based on the assumption that the whole story was a concoction of lies invented to cause trouble. He asked me what my political affiliations were, whether I was a Communist. He had checked with the Passport Office that I was the holder of a British passport, but was I a British resident? Was there anybody who knew me well enough to vouch for me? He was a little more relaxed after I told him I owned a cottage on the cliffs near Land's End and that my wife had died in the *Petros Jupiter* explosion. He remembered that and he treated me more like a human being. But he was still suspicious, taking notes of names and addresses and finally leaving with the words, "We'll check it all out and I've no doubt we'll want to have another talk with you when we've completed our inquiries. Meanwhile, you will please notify the police if you change your address or plan to leave the country, and that includes shipping as an officer on board a U.K. ship. Is that understood?" And he gave me the address of the local police station and the number to ring. "Just so we know where to find you."

It was dark by the time he left—a cold, frosty night. I put on the anorak I had bought that morning and walked as far as the river. I was feeling isolated and very alone, quite distant from all the people hurrying by. Lights on the far bank were reflected on a flood tide and the sky overhead was clear and full of stars. I tried to tell myself that an individual is always alone, that the companionship of others is only an illusion,

making loneliness more bearable. But it's difficult to convince
yourself of that when loneliness really bites. And what about
my relationship with Karen? I leaned on the frosted stonework
of an old wharf, staring at the dark flowing water and wishing
to God there was somebody I could talk to, somebody who
knew what it was like to be alone, totally alone.

I was very depressed that evening, staring at the river,
shivering with cold and watching the tide make. When I went
back to pick up the typescript so that I would have something
to read over a meal, Mrs. Steinway came out of her back room
with the evening paper in her hand. "I just been reading about
you. It is you, isn't it?" she asked, pointing to a paragraph
headed: "MISSING TANKER MAN RETURNED TO U.K." It was the
Reuters story, datelined Karachi. "No wonder you've got the
law keeping tabs on you. Is it true about the tanker?"

I laughed and told her I seemed to be about the only one
who thought so.

"They don't believe you, eh?" The bold eyes were watching
me avidly. "Well, can't say I blame them. It's a funny sort of
story." She smiled, the eyes twinkling, the heavy jowls wob-
bling with delight as she said, "Never mind, luv. Maybe
there's one as will. There's a young woman asked to see you."

"Me?" I stared at her, thinking she was having a bit of fun.
"Who? When?"

"Didn't give her name. I didn't ask her, see. You'd been
gone about ten minutes and she said it was urgent, so I told
her she could wait in your room. Course, she may be a newspaper girl. But she didn't look it. I've had them before, see,
when there was that Eddie Stock here and they mistook him
for the fellow that did the Barking shotgun holdup . . ."

But by then I had turned and was hurrying down the basement stairs. It had to be her. There was nobody else, no girl at
any rate, who could have found out where I was. Unless
Saltley had sent his secretary with a message. I don't know
whether the eagerness I felt stemmed from my desperate need

of company or from a sexual urge I could hardly control as I jumped down the last few stairs and flung open the door of my room.

She looked up at my entrance, the jut of her jaw just as determined, but the squarish, almost plain face lit by a smile. There were other parts of her that jutted, for she was wearing slacks and a very close-fitting jersey-knit sweater. A fleece-lined suede coat lay across the bed and she had the typescript of my book in her hands. She got up and stood facing me a little awkwardly. "I hope you don't mind." She held up the dog-eared typescript. "I couldn't resist." She was unsure of herself. "Salty was very stuffy about it at first—the address, I mean. But I got it out of him in the end. Such an incredible, marvelous story. I just had to see you." She had a sort of glow, her eyes alight with excitement.

"You believe it, then?"

"Of course." She said it without the slightest hesitation. "Salty said nobody could possibly have invented it. But then, of course," she added, "we want to believe it, anyway—Daddy, Mother, me, Virgins Unlimited . . . I told you about the syndicate, didn't I?—the rude name they call it. The other syndicates, too." She was nervous, talking very fast. "You don't mind, do you?" She put the typescript carefully down beside her coat. "I read a couple of chapters, that's all, but I've learned so much—about you and what you want out of life. I'd like to take it with me. It's so moving."

"You like it?" I didn't know what else to say, standing there, gazing at her and remembering that letter I'd received at Ras al Khaimah.

"Oh yes. What I've read so far. If I could borrow it . . . There's a publisher, a friend of ours, lives at Thorpe-le-Soken . . ." Her voice trailed away. "I'm sorry. I'm being bossy. Daddy says I'm always trying to run other people's lives for them. It's not true, of course, but I'm afraid I sometimes give that impression. Do sit down, please." She looked quickly round the room and I could almost see her nose wrinkling at the bare bleakness of it. "Did you get a letter from me?" She said it in an offhand way, busying herself with picking up her coat and hanging it on the hook of the door. "Perhaps the bed will be more comfortable. That chair's an arse-breaker, I can tell you." She plumped herself down on the far side of the bed. "Well, did you?" She was watching me intently, her eyes bright. "Yes, I see you did. But you never replied."

I hesitated, my blood beginning to throb at the invitation I thought I could see in her eyes. "Yes, the dhow brought it to me." I sat down on the bed beside her and touched her hand. "And I did reply to it. But if you believe my account of what happened you'll realize the reply is still on board that tanker."

Her fingers moved against mine. "I only know what Salty told me. Daddy and I were at his office late this afternoon. He gave us an outline, but very brief. Daddy was there to decide what action should be taken as a result of your report." She gripped my hand. "When I insisted Salty give me your address, and Daddy knew I intended seeing you, he said to give you his warmest thanks for risking your neck and achieving—well, achieving the impossible. Those were his words. And Salty thought the same, though of course he didn't say so. What he said was that he'd only given you what had been agreed, but that if your information resulted in any of the GODCO claims being set aside, then there would be a proper recompense."

"I had my own motives," I muttered.

"Yes, I know that. But it's just incredible what you did, and all in less than two weeks."

"Luck," I said. "I was following Choffel."

She nodded. "Tell me what you said. Would you, please?"

"To Saltley?" I half shook my head, remembering that long cross-examination and not wanting to go over it all again. But then I thought it might help for her to know, so I started to tell her about Baldwick coming to see me at Balkaer. But that wasn't what she wanted. It was the letter. "What did you say—in that letter I never received. Please tell me what you said."

I shook my head. It was one thing to write it in a letter, another to say the same words to her face. I took my hand away and got up. "I don't really remember," I muttered. "I was touched. Deeply touched. I said that. Also, that I was lonely—a little afraid, too—and your letter was a great comfort . . . to know that somebody, somewhere, is concerned about whether you live or die, that makes a great difference."

She reached out and touched my hand. "Thank you. I didn't know how you'd feel. It was so—" She hesitated, blushing slightly and half smiling to herself. "After I posted it—I felt a bit of a fool, getting carried away like that. But I couldn't help it. That was the way I felt."

"It was nice of you," I said. "It meant a great deal to me at that moment." And I bent down and kissed her—on the forehead, a very chaste kiss.

"Go on," she said, and giggled because she hadn't intended it as an invitation. "You started telling me about the man who came to your cottage. I interrupted, but please . . . I want to know everything that happened after I left you that day at Lloyd's." She patted the bedspread beside her. "You went off the following day by air for Nantes . . ."

I took it up from there, and now she listened intently, almost hanging on my words, so that halfway through, when I was telling her about my eerie night walk the length of the tanker's deck, I suddenly couldn't help myself—I said, "I warn you, if you stay and listen to the whole thing I may find it very difficult to let you go."

"I could always scream the house down." She was suddenly laughing and her eyes looked quite beautiful. But then she said quickly, "Go on, do—how did you and Choffel end up alone on that dhow together?"

But at that moment footsteps sounded on the stairs. There was a knock at the door. "Can I come in?" It was Saltley. He checked in the doorway, smiling at the two of us sitting on the bed, his quick gaze taking in the details of the room. "So this is where you've holed up."

"Why have you come?" I was on my feet now, resenting the intrusion.

He unbuttoned his overcoat and seated himself on the chair. "Have the police been to see you?" And when I told him about the Special Branch visit, he said, "That was inevitable, and I warned you." He was staring at me, the smile gone now and his eyes cold. "Are you sure you didn't shoot Choffel?"

"Why do you ask? I told you how it was."

And Pamela, suddenly very tense, asked, "What's happened?"

He turned to her and said, "It was just after you left. A girl came to see me, a dark-haired, determined, very emotional sort of person. A secretary at some clinic in France, she said. She had flown in from Nantes this morning and had been given my name and the address of the office by the Lloyd's agent."

I sat down on the bed again, conscious of his eyes on my face. "Choffel's daughter."

He nodded, and my heart sank, remembering her words as I had left for the airport. "She claims you killed him. Says she'll go to the police and accuse you of murder. Did you kill him?"

"No. I told you—"

He waved aside my protest. "But you intended to kill him, didn't you? That's why you went to Colchester to check what other names he used, why you went to Nantes, why you got the Lloyd's agent to take you to see his daughter. You were tracking him down with the intention of killing him. Isn't that true?"

I didn't say anything. There was no point in denying it.

"So the girl's right."

"But I didn't kill him."

He shrugged. "What does that matter? He's dead. You had

the opportunity and the intention." He leaned forward and gripped my arm. "Just so that you see it from her point of view. I'd like you to get yourself lost for a time. Sooner or later the man's body will turn up. They'll find a bullet in his guts and you'll be arrested." And he added, "I don't want you charged with murder before those tankers materialize."

"And when they do?" I asked.

"We'll see. If they do, then part of your story will be corroborated and they'll probably believe the rest of it, too. At least, it's what I would expect." He asked me to continue then with the account I had been giving Pamela. "There're one or two things toward the end I'd like to hear again." His reason was fairly obvious; if I was lying, then it was almost inevitable I'd slip up somewhere, small variations creeping in with each telling.

The first thing he picked me up on was Choffel's reference to the *Lavandou* and what had followed. "His mother was ill. That's what you said in my office. She was dying, and it was to get her the necessary treatment that he agreed to scuttle the ship. Did he tell you he was only a youngster at the time, twenty-two or twenty-three?"

"Yes," I said. "Twenty-two, he told me."

"That's what his daughter said. Twenty-two, and the only ship he ever sank. Did he say that to you?"

"No, not in those words."

"But he implied it?"

I nodded, the scene coming back to me, the sound of the sea and the stinking lazarette, and the dhow wallowing. "Only once, he said, or something like that. He was talking about the *Lavandou*—how the operation had gone wrong and Lloyd's had twigged it. I remember that because it was an odd way of putting it."

"You didn't tell me that. Why not?"

"Well, it's what you'd expect him to say, isn't it?"

"You said that before, when you were trying to shake the destination out of him."

"Not the destination," I corrected him. "I'd been asking him that, yes. But when I was shaking him, and shouting 'Where' at him, it was where the two tankers were going to meet I was asking him."

"And he didn't know."

"I'm not sure he even understood. His mind was wandering —not quite delirious, but bloody near it. I think he was probably referring back to one of the ships he'd wrecked. It might even have been the *Petros Jupiter*. There was a Dutch salvage outfit trying to get her off the Kettle's Bottom before he'd even come ashore."

"And where do you think those tankers are going to meet up?"

"You asked me that before. I don't know."

"Have you thought about it?"

"Not really. I've had other things—"

"Well, I have. So's Michael." He turned to Pamela. "We discussed it for quite a while after you'd left. We even got the charts sent up. If the destination is Europe—" He turned back to me. "That's what you think, isn't it—that the target is somewhere in Europe? If it is, then it's over twelve thousand miles from the Hormuz Straits to the western approaches of the English Channel. That's about forty days slow steaming or just over twenty-eight at full speed; and they could meet up at countless points along the west coast of Africa." And he added, "The only alternative would be the Cape, but I am not aware the Iranians have ever shown any interest in Black Africa. So I agree with you, if there is a target, then it's somewhere in Europe, where several countries hold Iranian prisoners—the Germans and ourselves certainly."

We discussed it for a while, then he left, taking Pamela with him. He had his car outside, and when he said he had arranged to meet her father for a drink at their club, she immediately got up. "Can I take this?" She had picked up the type-script and was holding it gripped under her arm.

I nodded dumbly, standing there, watching, as the lawyer helped her on with her coat. "I'm glad you didn't kill the man," he said, looking at me over his shoulder and smiling. "His daughter was quite positive the *Lavandou* was the only ship he wrecked."

"She was bound to say that," I told him angrily.

He nodded. "Nevertheless, I found her very convincing. She said he had paid dearly for that one criminal action."

That phrase of his struck a chord, and after they had left, when I was standing at the window, staring up at the street and thinking about the way she had accepted his offer of a ride, as though coming to see me had been just an interlude and her own world so much more congenial than this bare lit-tle room and the company of a man who might at any moment be charged with murder, it came back to me. Choffel had used almost identical words: "God knows, I've paid," he had said, and he'd repeated the word "paid," spitting blood. Had he re-ally become so desperate he'd taken jobs he knew were dubi-ous and then, when a ship was sunk, had found himself picked on, a scapegoat though he'd had no part in the actual scut-tling? Could any man be that stupid, or desperate, or plain un-lucky? The *Olympic Ore*, the *Stella Rosa*, the *Petros Jupiter*—that was three I knew about, as well as the *Lavandou*, and he'd used three different names. It seemed incredible, and yet . . . why lie to me so urgently when he must have known he was dying?

I thought about that a lot as I sat alone over my evening meal in a crowded Chinese restaurant. Also about his daughter —how angry she had been, calling him an innocent man and spitting in my face because I didn't believe her. If she could more or less convince a cold-blooded solicitor like Saltley . . .

But my mind shied away from that, remembering the *Petros Jupiter* and that night in the fog when my whole world had

gone up in flames. Suddenly I knew where I would lie up
while waiting for those tankers to re-emerge. If they wanted to
arrest me, that's where they'd have to do it, with the evidence
of what he'd done there before their eyes.

I didn't tell the police. I didn't tell anyone. I left just as
dawn was breaking, having paid my bill the night before, and
was at Paddington in time to catch the intercity express to
Penzance. And when I arrived at Balkaer, there it was just as I
had left it, the furniture and everything still in place, and no
board up to say it was for sale. It was dark then and cold,
hardly any wind and the sea in the cove below—only a gentle
murmur. I got the fire going, and after hanging the bedclothes
round it to air, I walked back up to the Kerrisons' and had a
meal with them. They had met me at Penzance and Jean had
seemed so pleased to see me I could have wept.

That night I slept on the sofa in front of the fire, unwilling
to face the damp cold of the empty bedroom upstairs. The
glow of the peat was warm and friendly, and though memories
crowded in—even the sofa on which I lay conjured a picture of
Karen, her dark eyes bright with excitement as it was knocked
down to us for next to nothing at the tail end of a farmhouse
sale—they no longer depressed me. Balkaer still felt like home
and I was glad I had come, glad I hadn't put it up for sale immediately, the key still with the Kerrisons.

There was no wind that night, the air very still and the
wash of the sea in the cove below muted to a whisper. The
place was snug and warm and homely, my mind at peace now.
Choffel was dead. That chapter of my life was closed; it was
the future that mattered now.

But in the morning, when I walked up to the headland and
stood staring out across the quiet sea at the Longships light
and the creaming wash of the Atlantic swell breaking on the
inshore rocks, the wretched man's words came back to me:
"You can't escape, can you, from either yourself or the past." I
knew then that the chapter of my life that had started out

there in the fog that night was not closed, would never be
closed.

This was the thought that stayed with me as I tramped the
clifftop paths alone or went fishing off Sennen in Andy's boat.
The weather was good for late January, cold with little wind
and clear pale skies. It was on the fourth day, when I was
fishing out beyond The Tribbens, that I felt Choffel's presence
most. The swell was heavier then and the boat rocking; I suppose it was that which conjured up the memory of that dhow
and what had happened. And his words . . . I found myself
going over and over those rambling outbursts of his, the face
pale under the stubble, the black curly hair, and the stench,
the dark eyes staring. It all came back to me, everything he
had said, and I began to wonder. And wondering, I began to
think of his daughter—in England now and hating my guts for
something I hadn't done.

The line tugged at my hand, but I didn't move, for I was
suddenly facing the fact that if I were innocent of what she
firmly believed I had done, then perhaps he was innocent, too.
And I sat there, the boat rocking gently and the fish tugging at
the line, as I stared out across the half-tide rocks south of The
Tribbens to the surf swirling round the Kettle's Bottom and
the single mast that was all that was left above water of the
Petros Jupiter. "I've paid and paid." And now the girl was accusing me of a murder I hadn't committed.

I pulled in the line, quickly, hand-over-hand. It was a crab,
of all things—a spider crab. I shook it loose and started the engine, threading my way back through the rocks to the jetty. It
was lunchtime, the village deserted. I parked the boat and
took the cliff path to Land's End, walking fast, hoping exertion
would kill my doubts and calm my mind.

But it didn't. The doubts remained. In the late afternoon a
bank of fog moved in from seaward. I just made it back to
Sennen before it engulfed the coast. Everything was then so
like that night Karen had blown herself up that I stood for a

while staring seaward, the Seven Stones' diaphone bleating faintly and the double bang from the Longships loud enough to wake the dead. The wind was sou'westerly. I was suddenly imagining those two tankers thundering up the Atlantic to burst through the rolling bank of mist, and only myself to stop them—myself alone, just as Karen had been alone.

"Think about it," Saltley had said. "If we knew where they were meeting up . . ." And he had left it at that, taking the girl's arm and walking her down the street to where he had parked his low-slung Porsche.

Standing there, down by the lifeboat station, thinking about it, it was as though Karen were whispering to me out of the fog: "Find them. Find them. You must find them." It was a distant foghorn, and there was another answering it. I needed an atlas, charts, the run of the pilot books for the coasts of Africa, dividers to work out distances and dates. Slow-steaming at eleven knots, that was two hundred and sixty-four nautical miles a day. Forty days, Saltley had said, to Ushant and the English Channel. But the *Aurora B* would be steaming at full speed—say, four hundred a day—that would be thirty days, and she had left her hidey-hole by the Hormuz Straits nine days ago. Another twenty-one to go . . . I had turned automatically toward Andy's cottage above the lifeboat station, something nagging at my mind, but what I didn't know, conscious only that I had lost the better part of a week, and the distant foghorn drumming at my ears with its mournful sense of urgency.

It was Rose who answered the door. Andy wasn't there and they didn't have a world atlas. But she gave me a cup of tea and after leaving me for a while returned with the *Digest World Atlas*, borrowed from a retired lighthouse keeper a few doors away, a man, she said, who had never been outside of British waters but liked to visualize where all the ships passing him had come from. I opened it first at the geophysical maps of Africa. There were two of them right at the end of section

one, and on both coasts there were vast blanks between the
names of ports and coastal towns. The east coast I knew. The
seas were big in the monsoons, the currents tricky, and there
was a lot of shipping. The Seychelles and Mauritius were too
populated, too full of package tours, and the islands closer to
Madagascar, like Aldabra and the Comores Archipelago, too
likely to be overflown, the whole area liable to naval surveillance.

In any case, I thought the rendezvous would have been
planned much nearer to the target, and if that were Europe
then it must be somewhere on the west coast. I turned to the
main maps, which were on a larger scale of one hundred and
ninety-seven miles to the inch, staring idly at the offshore coloring, where the green of the open Atlantic shaded to white as
the continental shelf tilted upward to the coastal shallows. I
was beginning to feel sleepy, for we were in the kitchen with
the top of the old-fashioned range red-hot, the atmosphere
overwhelming after the cold and the fog outside. Rose poured
me another cup of tea from the pot brewing on the hob. Tris-
tan da Cunha, St. Helena, Ascension—those were all too far
away. But on the next page, the one for North and West
Africa, there was Hierro, Gomera, Palma, all out-islands of the
Canaries and on the direct route. The Selvagens, too, and the
Desertas, and Porto Santo off Madeira. Of these, only the Selvagens, perhaps the Desertas, could be regarded as possibles,
the others being too well populated.

The tea was strong and very sweet, and I sat there wrapped
in the cozy warmth of that hot little kitchen, my head nodding
as my mind groped for something I knew was there but could
not find. Andy came back and I stayed on and had a meal
with them. By the time I left the fog had cleared and it was
very close to freezing, the stars bright as diamonds overhead
and the flash of the Longships and other lights farther away,
the glimmer of ships rounding Land's End, all seemingly
magnified in the startling clarity.

Next morning I went up to the main road at first light and
hitched a ride in a builder's van going to Penzance. From there
I got the train to Falmouth. I needed charts now and a look at
the Admiralty pilots for Africa, my mind still groping for that
elusive thought that lurked somewhere in my subconscious,
logic suggesting that it was more probably a rendezvous well
offshore, some fixed position clear of all shipping lanes.

The first vessel I tried when I got to the harbor was a general
cargo ship, but she was on a regular run to the Maritimes,
Halifax mainly, and had no use for African charts. The mate
indicated a yacht berthed alongside one of the tugs at the
inner end of the breakwater. "Round-the-worlder," he said.
"Came in last night from the Cape Verdes. He'll have charts
for that part of the African coast." And he went back to the
job I used to do, checking the cargo coming out of the hold.

The yacht was the *Ocean Brigand*. She flew a burgee with a
black Maltese cross with a yellow crown on a white background and a red fly. Her ensign was blue and she had the letters RCC below her name on the stern. She was wood, her
brightwork worn by salt and sun so that in places bare wood
showed through the varnish, and her decks were a litter of
ropes and sails and oilskins drying in the cold wind. The skipper, who was also the owner, was small and grey-haired with a
smile that crinkled the wind lines at the corners of his eyes.
He had charts for most of the world, the pilots, too. "A bit out
of date, some of them," he said. "But they cost a fortune now."

He sat me down at the chart table with a Bacardi and lime
and left me to find what I wanted. "Still some clearing up to
do." He smiled wearily. "We had it a bit rugged off Finisterre
and the Bay was mostly between seven and nine. Silly time of
year really to return to England, but my wife hasn't been too
good. Packed her off to hospital this morning."

I had never been on a real oceangoing yacht before, the
chart table so small, tucked in on the starb'd side opposite the
galley, yet everything I'd ever needed in the way of navigation

was there—except radar. He hadn't got radar, or Decca nav. And there was no gyro compass. But everything else, including VHF and single-sideband radio.

I went through all his charts that showed any part of Africa and in the end I was no better off than I had been with the lighthouse keeper's atlas. It had to be the last stretch, even as far north as the Bay of Biscay, but more likely somewhere in the neighborhood of those Spanish and Portuguese islands off the coast of Spanish Sahara and Morocco. And of these the Desertas and the Selvagens, being without water and therefore more or less deserted, seemed most likely. But even then, with the pilot book open in front of me, I didn't see it. Like the chart, it referred to both groups of islands by their Portuguese names. There was no indication that there might be an anglicized version of the name Selvagen.

A pair of seaboots appeared in the companionway to my right and the owner leaned his head down, peering over my shoulder. "Ah, I see you're reading up on the Madeira-Canaries passage, but I doubt whether your friends would have put into either the Desertas or the Selvagens. No water, no safe anchorage, and both of them bloody inhospitable groups of islands by all accounts. Never been there myself, but our vice-commodore now, he went to the Selvagens I seem to remember—1980, I think . . ." He went past me into the saloon, putting on a pair of half spectacles and peering along a battened-in shelf of books. "Here we are." He handed me a carefully plastic-wrapped copy of the *Royal Cruising Club Journal*. "There's a glimpse of what he calls the Salvage Islands. A little more descriptive than the pilot."

It was a short piece, barely two pages, but it was the title that caught and held my attention—"A Look at the Salvage Islands." "We sailed two days ago from Funchal . . ." Averaging probably no more than a hundred miles a day, that was in line with the pilot, which gave the distance from the southernmost of the Desertas to Selvagem Grande as one hundred and thirty-five miles. The names were the same, too, except for the "m" where it was singular—Selvagem Grande and Selvagem Pequena—and so that there should be no doubt whatsoever he had written, "I had always hoped to visit the Salvage (Salvagen) Islands." He must have got the English name from somewhere and my guess was the Navy—at some time in the distant past British sailors had anglicized it and called them the Salvage Islands, just as they had called Ile d'Ouessant off the Brittany coast of France Ushant. And looking at the Atlantic Ocean Chart 2127 I saw that here the group were named the Salvagen Is.—an "a" instead of an "e."

Was that what Choffel had meant when he talked of salvage? Was it the Salvagen Islands he had been referring to?

There was Selvagem Grande and Selvagem Pequena, and an even smaller one called Fora. And I remembered that a mate I had served under had once described them to me as we were steaming between Gibraltar and Freetown—"Spooky," he had said of the smaller Selvagem. "The most godforsaken spooky bit of a volcanic island I ever saw." And reading the *Journal*, here was this yachtsman's daughter using almost the same words—"Spooksville," she had called it, and there had been the wrecked hulk of a supertanker hung on the rocks, her father claiming he had never seen a more dreadful place.

"They were on their way to the Caribbean," the owner said. "Just two of them on the leg south from Madeira to the Canaries." He gave me another drink, chatting to me for a while. Then a doctor arrived and I left him to the sad business of finding out what was wrong with his wife. There had been just the two of them and it was the finish of their second circumnavigation.

I phoned Forthright's from the station, making it a personal call on reverse charges. Fortunately Saltley was in, but when I told him about the Salvage Islands, he said he and Stewart had already considered that possibility and had read the piece in the *RCC Journal*. In fact, they had chartered a small plane

out of Madeira to make a recce of the islands and he had received the pilot's report that morning. The only tanker anywhere near the islands was the wreck stranded on the rocks of
Selvagem Pequena. "Pity you've no date for the rendezvous. It
means somebody keeping watch out there." He checked that I
was at Balkaer and said he'd be in touch when he'd spoken to
Michael Stewart again.

It was almost dark when I got back to the cottage and there
was a note pinned to the door. It was in Jean's handwriting.
Saltley had phoned and it was urgent. I trudged back up the
hill and she handed me the message without a word. I was to
take the next ferry out of Plymouth for Roscoff in Brittany and
then make my way to Gibraltar via Tangier. "At Gibraltar he
says you can hide out on a yacht called *Prospero* which you'll
find berthed in the Marina." And Jean added, "It's important,
Trevor." Her hand was on my arm, her face staring up at me,
very serious. "Jimmy will drive you there tonight."

"What's happened?" I asked. "What else did he say?"

"He didn't want you to take any chances. That's what he
said. It's just possible there'll be a warrant issued for your arrest. And it was on the radio at lunchtime."

"On the radio?" I stared at her.

"Yes, an interview with Guinevere Choffel. She gave the
whole story, all the ships her father had sailed in, including
the *Petros Jupiter*—but differently from what you told us. She
made him out a poor, unfortunate man trying to earn a living
at sea and always being taken advantage of. Then, right at the
end, she accused you of murdering him. She gave your name
and said she'd be going to the police right after the program.
It was an extraordinary statement to come over the radio.
They cut her off, of course. But the interview was live, so
nothing they could do about it."

I was in their sitting-room, leaning against the door, and I
reached into my pocket for a cigarette. I felt suddenly as
though the world of black and white had been turned upside

down—Choffel declared innocent and myself the villain now. I offered her the packet and she shook her head. "Vengeance," she said, a look of sadness that made her gypsy features suddenly older. "That's Old Testament stuff."

"I didn't kill him." The match flared, the flame trembling slightly as I lit my cigarette.

"It was in your mind."

She didn't need to remind me. I half closed my eyes, inhaling the stale duty-free nicotine, thinking of Choffel. She didn't have to start lecturing me, not now when I was being hounded out of the country. I wondered how he had felt, making up stories nobody believed. And then to seize that dhow just because I was on board the tanker, confronting him with his guilt. Did that make me responsible for the bullet in his guts?

"Would you like me to try and see her?"

"What the hell good would that do?"

She shrugged, shaking her head. "I don't know." There were tears in her eyes. "I just thought it might be worth a try. If I could get her to come down here. If she saw where the *Petros Jupiter* had been wrecked, what a threat it had been to all our lives—if I told her, woman to woman, the sort of person Karen was, what she had done and why . . . Perhaps she'd understand then. Don't you think she would?" Her voice faltered and she turned away. "I'll go and see what Jimmy's up to," she said. "You phone Plymouth and find out when the ferry leaves."

In fact, there wasn't one until noon next day so I had a last night at Balkaer and took the early train from Penzance. I felt very lost after saying good-bye to the Kerrisons, feeling I would never see them again, or Balkaer, and that I was now a sort of pariah condemned like Choffel to roam the world under any name but my own, always looking over my shoulder, half afraid of my own shadow. Even when I had boarded the ferry, my temporary papers given no more than a cursory glance, I positioned myself at the rail so that I could see everyone who

boarded the ship, until at last the gangway was pulled clear
and we sailed.

It was the same when I got to France. There was no trouble
on landing, yet I still glanced nervously over my shoulder at
the sound of footsteps, watchful and suspicious of anybody
going in the same direction as myself. It was all in my imagination, of course, and a psychiatrist would probably have said
I was developing a persecution mania, but it was real enough
to me at the time, that sense of being watched. And so was the
stupidity of it, the sheer craziness of it all. It was like a night-
mare what was happening. A man wrecks a ship, your wife
kills herself trying to burn up the oil spill he's caused, and you
go after him—and from that simple, natural act, the whole
thing blows up in your face, the man dead and his daughter
accusing you of killing him. And nobody to prove you innocent.

Just as there had been nobody to prove him innocent. That
thought was in my mind, too.

How quickly you can be brainwashed, by changing circumstances or by the behavior of other human beings. How
strangely vulnerable is the human mind when locked in on itself, alone with nobody to act as a sounding box, nobody to
say you're right—right in thinking he'd sunk those ships, right
to believe he was the cause of Karen's death, right to believe
in retribution.

Alone, the nagging doubt remained. An eye for an eye?
"The Old Testament," Jean had said, and even she hadn't
thought I was right, insisting that I do what Saltley said. The
best friends a man could hope for and they had not only
helped me run away, but had insisted I had no alternative. A
lawyer, the media, two such good friends—and I hadn't killed
him. The stupid little bitch had got it wrong, leaping to conclusions. I could have thrown her father overboard. I could
have taken him back to the tanker. Instead, I had cleaned him
up, given him water . . . I was going over and over it in my

mind all the way to Tangier, and still that sense of unreality. I couldn't believe it, and at the same time that feeling of being watched, expecting some anonymous individual representing Interpol or some other Establishment organization to pick me up at any moment.

I reached Tangier and nobody stopped me. There was a levanter blowing through the Strait and it was rough crossing over to the Rock, Arabs and Gibraltarians all being sick among a heaped-up mass of baggage. Nobody bothered about me. There was no policeman waiting for me on the jetty at Gibraltar. I got a water taxi and went round to the marina, the top of the Rock shrouded in mist and a drizzle of rain starting to fall.

Prospero, when I found her, was about fifty feet long, broad-beamed, with a broad stern and a sharp bow. She looked like a huge plastic and chrome dart with a metal mast against which the halyards flapped unceasingly in the wind, adding to the jingling metallic symphony of sound that rattled across the marina. Terylene ropes lay in tangled confusion, the cockpit floorboards up, the wheel linkage in pieces. A man in blue shorts and a blue sweater was working on what looked like a self-steering gear. He turned at my hail and came aft. "You're Trevor Rodin, are you?" He had broad, open features with a wide smile. "I had a telex this morning to expect you. I'm Mark Stewart, Pamela's brother."

He didn't need to tell me that. They were very alike. He took me below into the wood-trimmed saloon and poured me a drink. "Boat's a bit of a mess at the moment, but with luck we'll get away by the end of the week." They had originally been planning to make Malta in time for the Middle Sea Race, but his father hadn't been able to get away and Saltley, who usually navigated for them, was tied up on a case he felt he couldn't leave. "So we're still here," he said. "Lucky, really." And he added, "Pamela and the Old Salt will be here tomorrow. There's Toni Bartello, a Gibraltarian pal of mine, you, and me. That's the lot. Anyway, going south we shouldn't get anything much above seven or eight, so it should be all right. Pam's not so good on the foredeck—not so good as a man, I mean—but she's bloody good on the helm, and she'll stay there just about forever, no matter what's coming aboard."

"Where are we going?" I asked.

"Didn't Salt brief you?"

I shook my head. No point in telling him I'd been offered the boat as a hideout for a couple of weeks until somebody somewhere sighted those tankers.

He took me over to the chart table and from the top drawer produced Chart No. 4104, Lisbon to Freetown. He spread it out. "There. That's where we're going." He reached over, putting the tip of his forefinger on the Selvagen Islands.

PART VI

The Black Tide

CHAPTER ONE

GIBRALTAR WAS A STRANGE INTERLUDE, quite unreal in a sense, the Rock towering above us and most of those in the marina in holiday clothes and a holiday mood. The sun shone and it was quite warm by day, except in the wind which blew hard from the east. There was a lot to do, for the boat had been stripped of everything to get at the hydraulics, which ran the length of the hull and had sprung a leak, and there were stores to get, water and fuel to load. Each day I listened to the BBC news on the radio above the chart table, half expecting to hear my name and hoping to God I wouldn't.

I had asked Saltley, of course, as soon as he'd arrived on board. But as far as he knew no warrant had been issued for my arrest. "I'm not at all sure the Choffel business comes within their jurisdiction." We were down in the bare saloon then, his bags opened on the table as he changed into work clothes—jeans and T-shirt. Pamela was changing up for'ard and Mark had taken the taxi back into town. "It's probably a question of where the killing took place."

"He was shot on the dhow."

"Yes yes." I think he was a little tired after his flight, his voice impatient. "That's Arab territory. But the dhow was tied up alongside the tanker, and if it could be proved that the *Aurora B* was still a British ship, then they would have jurisdiction, the killing having occurred on British territory." He zipped up his trousers and reached for the drink I had poured him. "Personally I don't think she has a hope in hell of getting you arrested. So just relax and concentrate on the job in hand, which is finding that bloody tanker."

"But if you thought that, why did you tell Jean Kerrison to get me on the next ferry to France?"

He looked at me over his drink, the lopsided face and the china blue eyes suddenly looking a little crafty. "I wasn't taking any chances, that's all. I wanted you here." He raised his glass, smiling. "Here's luck—to us both." And he added, "I'm not a criminal lawyer, but I do know something about the law as it applies internationally. For that girl to have you arrested, she's either got to prove you killed her father on British territory or get whatever country it happened in—the Oman, say—to order your arrest, and since this yacht is British territory it then depends on whether we have an extradition treaty with the Oman."

"But when she went to the police . . . Jean Kerrison heard a program on the radio, an interview with her, which ended with her saying she was going straight to the police and a warrant would be issued for my arrest on a charge of murder. Did she go to the police?"

He shrugged. "I've no idea."

"But presuming she did, what would happen next? What action would the police take?"

"I think it would depend on the evidence she produced. I imagine it's pretty thin, but if she did convince them then her statement would be sent on to the office of the Director of Public Prosecutions with whatever comments the police felt were warranted, together with the results of any inquiries they may have instituted. It would be up to the Public Prosecutor then."

"And what happens when they discover I've fled the country?" I was remembering the Special Branch man's instructions to notify the nearest police station of any change of address. They would almost certainly trace me to Balkaer and question the Kerrisons. I was angry with him then, feeling he was using me. Fleeing the country was the most damning thing I could have done.

"They may notify Interpol," he said. "But by the time they've traced you to Gibraltar, we'll almost certainly be at sea. Forget about it," he added. "If we find that tanker waiting for us out there by the Selvagens, then that part of your story will be confirmed. Once they believe that, they'll believe the rest."

I had to accept that, since it was my only hope, but I should have stayed. I should have faced her accusations, reiterating the truth of what had happened. Instead, I had run away at the instigation of this ruthless bastard who was only interested in finding the missing tankers and saving his friend's skin. If I'd had any guts I'd have walked off the boat then and there and taken the next plane back to London. But I didn't. I stayed on board and each day I listened to the BBC news, waiting, always waiting to hear my name mentioned.

We sailed for the Selvagens on Saturday, February 6. It was just six days since the Kerrisons had driven me into Penzance to catch the Brittany ferry, seventeen days since the *Aurora B* had left her bolt-hole in the Musandam Peninsula. "She'll be about halfway," Saltley said. "Just rounding the Cape, probably." We were standing at the chart table, the boat heeled over as we plowed our way through the Strait, thrashing to windward with the bows slamming and sheets of spray hitting the mains'l with a noise like gunshot. "That is, if she's steaming at full speed. Pity we've lost that levanter." He smiled at me, looking more like a gnome than ever in his bulky oilskins. "Hope you're a good sailor. It could be a hard beat."

Only the previous day the wind had gone round to the southwest and now it was blowing force 5 to 6, a dead-noser, for it was southwest we needed to go. "I had reckoned on reaching the islands in less than six days, which would make it day twenty-two of the *Aurora B*'s voyage. But if it's going to go on blowing from the southwest we'll be increasing our miles through the water considerably. It could make a difference of two or three days."

We had the Rock and the African shore in sight all through the daylight hours. It was wind against current most of the time, with steep breaking waves and a movement more violent than I had ever previously experienced. It was impossible to stand without holding onto one of the hand grips all the time, and in the cockpit we were all of us wearing our safety harnesses clipped to securing wires.

It was toward dusk, when the wind had eased slightly, that I took my first trick at the helm under Pamela's supervision, the others having got their heads down in preparation for the long hours of darkness when they would be standing lone watches. It was then, with my hands gripping the wheel, that I began to appreciate the extraordinary power of an ocean racer. Until then I had only seen them at a distance, but now, feeling that wind-driven power under my hands and vibrant throughout the ship, I experienced a feeling of intense excitement, a sense of overwhelming exhilaration as though I were a god riding the sea on a white-winged Pegasus. And when Pamela clapped me on the shoulder and said, "You'll do, mate," I felt a wave of pleasure as though I were a kid and had passed some sort of a test. She got up, bracing herself with a hand on the bar-taut mainsheet. "You're on your own now. I need a pee and there's the evening meal to get."

She left me to my own devices then, so that for almost two hours the ship was mine, and as we powered to windward I found myself reveling in the extra thrust that came from slight adjustments of the wheel, the way I could slide her over the worst of the waves, and once in a while Pamela, keeping an eye on me from the galley, gave me a little smile of approval. With no makeup on, a dirty old woolen cap pulled down over her head, and yellow oilskins, she looked more like a ship's boy than the owner's daughter, and how she could cook with the boat pitching and slamming I couldn't imagine. When Toni Bartello finally relieved me and I went below, I found I had no interest in food and had to get my head down or be sick.

The seasickness didn't last, but the sou'wester did. The wind seemed fixed in that quarter, staying there for almost a week, sometimes light, sometimes blowing a near-gale, and always we were beating.

It was a strange life, the five of us cooped up together, at such close quarters, and in some respects in such rugged conditions, that it was almost the equivalent of serving as a seaman in the Navy two centuries ago. Most of my working life had been spent at sea, so that it was difficult for me to understand at first why anyone would do it for pleasure, particularly a girl. So little space and no privacy, the violence of the movement—and yet it worked, our lives ruled by the sea and the wind, and little time or energy to think who it was had left the bunk warm for me when I came below tired after a sail change or a long spell at the wheel with the salt of the wind-driven spray crusted on my face.

The sun shone most of the daylight hours and when the wind dropped and we had the engine on, all of us up in the cockpit with a drink in our hands, then it was different. We were relaxed, talking uninhibitedly about our lives, or speculating what we would find when the Selvagens appeared over the horizon. Would we find the *Howdo Stranger* sitting there, waiting? And if so, what would she be called now, what false name would they have painted on her bows and stern? We had a lot of fun inventing names for her, and for the *Aurora B*, laughing uproariously at simple jokes, like twinning them and calling them *Castor* and *Bollocks*. We laughed a lot at silly ordinary things, ate enormously, and drank well. It was, in fact, a singularly happy ship, made more so I think by the presence of a girl who was a good cook, a good sailor, and good company. There were times when I found it difficult to take my eyes off her, for it was getting warmer all the time and ghosting along in light airs after Saltley had decided we needed to save our fuel, she was wearing very little at the midday pour-out.

We were drinking wine, not spirits, but it was strong Spanish stuff and I suppose my interest in her showed. It was on the eighth day, when the wind had at last gone round to the northwest, where it should have been all the time. I had the middle watch and when I took over from Mark he brewed us mugs of cocoa and joined me in the cockpit. "Lovely night," he said, staring up at the stars. He was silent for a long time after that, so I knew he had something on his mind. At last he came out with it. "Look, Trevor—hope you don't mind, but I think I'd better tell you." He paused there, not looking at me, his face in silhouette against the light of the compass. "About Pam," he went on awkwardly, burying his face in his mug and speaking very quietly. "I know she admires you, thinks you're quite a guy, in fact. And you're not exactly—well, disinterested. I don't mind myself, your eyeing her, I mean. But if I've noticed it, then Salt will have, too, and he is . . . well, in love with her, I suppose. It's generally recognized—in the family, I mean—that she'll marry him in the end. You see, he's been after her ever since she left finishing school—oh, before that . . . since ever almost—hanging round her like a bee round a honey pot." He finished his cocoa and got up very abruptly. "You don't mind my mentioning it, I hope, but if you could just keep your mind concentrated on the job in hand . . ."

He dived down the companionway then, leaving me alone at the wheel. The boy was embarrassed and I knew why. Saltley might be an older man with a lopsided face, but he'd been to the right schools, belonged to the right clubs. He had the right background, and above all, he was the man their father turned to when there was underwriting trouble. Also—and perhaps this rankled more than anything—they knew my own family background.

I didn't sleep much that night and in the morning Saltley asked me to take a noon sight myself and work out our position. It made me think he had put Mark up to it. But we were under spinnaker now, sailing on a broad reach at just over six knots, and with only another day to go before we raised the Selvagens it was obviously sensible to make use of my professional capabilities and get a check on his last fix.

I took the sights, and when I had finally got a position, there was only a mile or two in it, Selvagem Grande bearing 234°, distant eighty-three miles. It was now twenty-six days since the *Aurora B* had sailed. Only two or three more days to go. It depended how much of a lift the strong Agulhas current had given her, what speed she was making. She could be a little faster than we reckoned, or slower. It was just conceivable the rendezvous had already taken place. But Saltley didn't think so. "Things always take a little longer than people reckon." But he was convinced the first tanker would be in position at least two days ahead of schedule, just in case. "That means we could find the tanker already there. I don't think it will be, but it's just possible." He gave me that lopsided smile. "We'll know tomorrow." And he added, "Wind's falling light. We may have to run the engine later."

It was only now, as we neared our objective, that we began to face up to the fact that if we were right, then we were the only people who could alert the countries bordering the English Channel and the southern North Sea to the possibility of a major marine disaster. In putting it like that I am being a little unfair to Saltley. The thought would have been constantly in his mind, as it was in mine. But we hadn't talked about it. We hadn't brought it out into the open as something that could make the difference between life and death to a lot of people, perhaps destroy whole areas of vital marine habitat.

And that evening, sitting in the cockpit drinking our wine with the last of the sun's warmth slipping down to the horizon, I began to realize how far from the reality of this voyage the three younger members of the crew were. Pam and Mark, they both knew it could affect them financially, but at their age that was something they took in their stride. Sailing off like this to some unknown islands had been fun, a sort of treasure hunt, a game of hide-and-seek, something you did for kicks, an adventure. I had to spell it out to them. Even then I think they saw it in terms of something remote, like death and destruction on the television screen. Only when I described the scene in the *khawr* as the dhow slid away from the tanker, with Sadeq standing at the top of the gangway, a machine pistol at his hip spraying bullets down onto us, only then, when I told them about Choffel and the stinking wound in his guts, and how bloody vulnerable we could be out there alone by the Selvagens facing two big tankers that were in the hands of a bunch of terrorists, did they begin to think of it as a dangerous exercise that could end all our lives.

That night it was very quiet. We had changed from spinnaker to a lightweight genoa at dusk and the boat was ghosting along at about four knots in a flat calm sea. I handed over to Mark at midnight and my bunk was like a cradle rocking gently to the long Atlantic swell. I woke sometime in the small hours, a sliver of a moon appearing and disappearing in the doghouse windows, the murmur of voices from the cockpit.

I was in the starb'd pilot berth, everything very quiet and something about the acoustics of the hull made their voices carry into the saloon. I didn't mean to listen, but then I heard my name mentioned and Mark saying, "I hope to God he's right." And Pam's voice answered him. "What are you suggesting?"

"He could be lying," the boy said.

"Trevor isn't a liar."

"Look, suppose he did kill that French engineer . . ."

"He didn't. I know he didn't."

"You don't know anything of the sort. And keep your voice down."

"He can't hear us, not in the saloon. And even if he did kill the man, that doesn't mean he's wrong about the tankers."

Her brother made an angry snorting sound. "You've had the flags out for him ever since the Old Salt sent him off in search of the *Aurora B.*"

"I think he's got a lot of guts, that's all. Getting himself on board that tanker, then getting away on the dhow with the man he was looking for. It's quite incredible."

"Exactly. Salt thinks it's so incredible it must be true. He says nobody could have made it all up. The next thing is every word he's uttered is gospel, so that here we are, out in the Atlantic, everything hung on that one word 'salvage.' And I'm not just thinking of the money. I'm thinking of Mum and Dad, and what's going to happen to them."

"We've all of us got stop-loss reinsurance," she said. "Mine is for fifty thousand excess of thirty. Daddy's is a lot more I know. It probably won't save us, but it'll help."

"I told you, I'm not thinking of the money."

"What then?"

"If Trevor's lying . . . All right, Pam, let's say he's told us the truth, say it's all gospel truth, but we've got it wrong about where they're going to meet up and there's no tanker waiting at the Selvagens, how do we ever prove that the vessels we insured aren't lying at the bottom of the sea? We've got to show that they're afloat and in the hands of Gulf terrorists, otherwise that cleverly worded war zone exemption clause doesn't operate."

"The tanker will be there. I'm sure it will." There was a long pause, then she said, "It's Daddy you're worried about, isn't it?" He didn't answer and after a while she said, "You're thinking of suicide, is that it? D'you think he might—do you think he really might?"

"My God!" His voice sounded shocked. "The way you put it into words. 'You're thinking of suicide'—just like that, and your voice so bloody matter-of-fact."

"You've been skating round it." Her tone was sharp and pitched high. "You know you have, ever since you brought up the question of what we'll find when we get to the island. If Trevor's wrong and our tanker doesn't turn up, if nothing happens to prove that the two of them are still afloat, then the money we lose—that's everything, the house, this boat, all Mother's jewelry, her clothes even—it will be nothing to the damage Daddy will suffer . . . all his friends, his whole world. At his age he can't start again. He'd never be able to at Lloyd's anyway. You can't make a comeback when everybody knows you cost your Names just about every penny they possess. Do you think I don't know this? I've been living with it for the last month or more, knowing that for him it'd be the end of the world. I don't think he'd want to go on living after that. But whether he'd go as far as to take his own life . . ."

"I'm sorry, Pam. I didn't realize."

She seemed to ignore that, for she went on almost as though he hadn't spoken: "And don't start hitting out at Trevor without stopping to think what it's like to see your wife burn herself up in an attempt to save some seagulls. Or at me either. I may have hung out some flags as you put it, but what have you done, or Salty, any of us? He found the tanker and though he wasn't doing it for us—" There was a crash and I heard her say, "Bugger! That's my hat gone overboard." There was a stamp of feet on deck, the sound of sails flapping. A few minutes later the girl's figure slipped past me as she went to her quarters up for'ard.

I awoke to the smell of bacon frying, the sun already burning up the dawn clouds. A haze developed as the morning wore on, the sun very hot and Pamela dressed in shorts with a loose-tailed shirt reading a book on the foredeck in the shadow of the spinnaker. It wasn't until after lunch that we began to detect a smudge like a tiny cloud growing on the horizon. It was straight over the bows and couldn't be anything else but Selvagem Grande. It grew steadily in size, and though our eyes were constantly searching, there was no satellite smudge that could represent the tanker.

By 1500 we could see the island quite clearly and had altered course to pass to the north of it. It was a sort of Table Mountain in miniature, the highest point five hundred and ninety-seven feet according to the Admiralty pilot, and cliffs rising sheer to four hundred feet. These cliffs formed an unbroken line, heavily undercut and edged white by the breaking swell, their flat tops arid and desolate with a cap of black basalt sitting on the red sandstone like chocolate on a layer cake. No trees anywhere, no sign of vegetation, just the two layers of rock with a new light structure perched like a white pimple on the summit of one of the basalt *picos*.

The wind was backing into the north and for a time we were busy handling the spinnaker and setting a working genoa. It was blowing force 3 or 4 by the time we got everything stowed and by then we were close off the northern end of the island with no sign of any other vessel. There was still a chance that the tanker was hidden from us by the southern part of the island, but our hopes faded as we rounded Punto do Risco and began to run down the western side. There were plenty of shearwaters, which is the main reason the Portuguese government declared the island a nature reserve, but otherwise the place looked totally lifeless. There were some shacks by the landing place on the southwestern side and a roped pathway climbed steeply to the lighthouse, but apart from that, the only sign of any human presence was the mass of Communist slogans painted on the rocks. This ugly display of giant graffiti had presumably been put there by fishermen who had been ardent supporters of the revolution.

Off the landing place we turned back onto our original course, heading for Selvagem Pequena ten miles away. This is quite a different sort of island, being little more than an above-water reef, but with the wind increasing we could soon make out the white of waves breaking on the horizon. By sunset the remains of the wrecked tanker were visible and we could see right across the island to where waves were breaking on the smaller reef island of Fora, a mile or so to the west. From Fora a chain of above-water rocks six to twelve feet high extended several miles to the north. This was the Restinga do Ilheu de Fora, but there was no tanker waiting there, and with visibility now vastly improved, we could see there wasn't even a fishing vessel anywhere within a radius of a dozen miles of us. We were the only vessel afloat in the neighborhood of the Selvagen Archipelago.

Once this had sunk in we felt suddenly very lonely. The islands had an atmosphere of their own. If there was any place at sea that could be described as unfriendly I felt this was it and I found myself remembering that word "spooky." It was a strange word to use about a group of islands, but now that I was among them I knew it described their atmosphere exactly. They were spooky and I wondered how long Saltley would be willing to hang round them waiting for a tanker that might never turn up.

I voiced my misgivings that evening, not in front of the others, but to Saltley alone. We had had an excellent meal hove-to on the starb'd tack four miles to the east of Selvagem Pequena, the light on the main island just visible over the bows. I took him up on deck on some pretext or other and told him bluntly that I'd no real confidence in the conclusion we had reached. "I'm not even sure Choffel used the word 'salvage.' It sounded like it, that's all. If you remember, I made that quite clear."

He nodded. "Understood. But Mike and I didn't come to the same conclusion solely on the basis of what you had told me. We worked it out for ourselves. Unless they were going to operate independently, they'd want to rendezvous as near the target as possible."

"It doesn't have to be an island," I said. "There's all the mainland coast, or better still a fixed position out at sea."

He shook his head. "The mainland would be too risky, but we did give a lot of thought to a sight-fixed rendezvous. It's what you or I would choose. But we're navigators. Terrorists tend to be urban creatures. They wouldn't trust a rendezvous that was arrived at by using a sextant and tables stuffed with figures. They'd want a fixed point they could see." We were in the bows then and he had his hands in his pockets, balancing himself easily to the plunging movement of the ship. "You picked the Selvagens, so did we, and the more we thought about it, the more ideal they appeared. And now I've seen them—" He turned his head to port, staring westward to where the sound of the seas pounding Selvagem Pequena came to us as a continuous deep murmur. "No ship's captain wants to tangle with that lot. They give this group a wide berth, and the silly idiot who ran his vessel onto the rocks there only goes to make the point that it's a bloody dangerous place." He turned then, walking slowly back toward the empty cockpit lit by the faint glow of the lights below. "Don't worry about it," he said. "Our friend will turn up. I'm sure of it."

"Maybe," I said. "But probably not tomorrow or the next day or the next—just how long are you prepared to hang around here?"

"For three weeks if necessary," he said. And when I asked him if we'd got enough food on board, he answered curtly, "If we have to stay that long, it's water, not food, that will be the problem."

I thought it might be the humans, too, for the prospect of hanging round these godforsaken islands for three weeks appalled me. But, as his words indicated, we were committed now and no point in leaving until we were absolutely sure this wasn't the meeting place.

That night it came on to blow. Even though we were hove-to there was a lot of movement and the noise of the wind in the rigging and waves breaking made it difficult to sleep. Saltley seemed to be up and about most of the night, checking

our position against the light on Selvagem Grande and sometime in the early hours, at the change of the watch I think, the
ship was put about with a great crashing of gear and slatting of
sails, feet pounding on the deck and somebody shouting to run
her off as the jib sheet was caught up on the winch. All this I
heard as in a dream, clinging to my bunk, not wishing to be
roused from the half sleep in which I lay. A cold wind came
down through the open hatch and when, after running for
some minutes, they turned about again, bows into the wind
and hove-to, I distinctly heard Mark call out, "The light's
gone." And a moment later—"It's raining. I can't see a bloody
thing." As I fell back into slumber again, I was thinking of the
red-painted slogans on the rocks and the waves breaking over
the Pequena and Fora reefs, hoping to God Saltley knew his
stuff as an inshore navigator.

The next thing I knew the first grey light of a dismal dawn
was filtering into the saloon. Toni Bartello was shaking me
violently. "We're reefing. Get up, please." And as I stirred he
yelled in my ear—"Oilskins and seaboots. There's a lot of water
in the cockpit and it's raining like hell."

It was a foul morning, the wind near gale force and poor
visibility. I have seen plenty of rough seas, but it's one thing to
observe them from high up in the closed-in comfort of a big
ship's wheelhouse, quite another to face steep breaking waves
virtually from sea level. Saltley told me to take the wheel
while the rest of them, all except Pamela who was still fast
asleep, reefed the main and changed down to storm jib, and
all the time the crash of seas bursting against the hull, spray
flying across the deck, and everything banging and slatting as
the boat bucked and rolled and the wind came in blustering
gusts.

"Where are the islands?" I yelled to Saltley as he half fell
into the cockpit. We were hove-to again and nothing visible
except a bleak circle of storm-tossed water and grey scudding
clouds.

"Over there," he yelled, putting on his harness and making a vague gesture toward the porthand shrouds.

All that day we only saw them once, but that once was enough to scare us badly, for we suddenly saw heavy breaking seas quite close on the starb'd bow and as we put about, I caught a glimpse of that wrecked tanker's superstructure, a dim ghost of a shape seen through a blur of rain and spray. After that Saltley took no chances and we ran south for a good hour before turning and heaving-to again.

Later the rain eased and the wind dropped, but we had been badly frightened and even when there were no more clouds and the stars paling to the brightness of the young moon, we still kept to two-man watches. Dawn broke with high peaks aflame in the east as the sun rose firing the edges of old storm clouds. No sign of the islands, no ship of any sort in sight, the sea gently heaving and empty to the horizon in every direction.

Fortunately, we were able to get sun sights and fix our position. We were some twenty miles east-southeast of Selvagem Pequena. We had already shaken out the reefs and now we set the lightweight genoa. The contrast was unbelievable, the ship slipping fast through the water, the sea almost flat calm and the decks dry, not a drop of spray coming aboard.

Saltley took the opportunity to check his camera. It was a good one with several lenses, including a 300 mm. telephoto lens. He also took from his briefcase some official GODCO pictures of both the *Howdo Stranger* and the *Aurora B*. He asked us to study them carefully so that if our tankers turned up, however brief the sighting, we'd still be able to identify them. Later he put them in the top drawer of the chart table, so that if we needed to check any detail they'd be ready to hand.

It was the middle of the afternoon before we raised Selvagem Grande. We sailed all round it and then down to Pequena and Fora. No tanker, nothing, the wind falling very light, the sea almost a flat calm with ripples that caught the slanting sun in reflected dazzles of blinding light. It was quite hot and toward dusk a haze developed. This thickened during the evening till it was more a sea fog, so that we had another worrying night with no sign of the light on Selvagem Grande, and no stars, and the moon no more than a ghostly glimmer of opaque light.

In the end we turned eastward, sailing for three hours on a course of 090°, going about and sailing a reciprocal three hours on 270°. We did that twice during the course of the night and when dawn came there was still the same thick clammy mist and nothing visible.

We were making toward Selvagem Grande then and by the time breakfast was over and everything washed up and stowed, the sun was beginning to burn up the mist, and just visible as a golden disk hung in a golden glow. Water dripped in rainbow drops from the gold-painted metal of the main boom and the only sound on deck was the tinkling gurgle of water slipping past the hull.

Shortly after 1000 I handed the wheel over to Pamela. Saltley was dozing in his bunk, which was the starb'd quarter berth aft of the chart table, and Toni and Mark were up in the bows servicing the snap-shackle end of the masthead spinnaker hoist which was showing signs of chafe. I paid a visit to the heads, had a shave, and then began checking Saltley's DR position. I was just measuring off the distance run on each course during the night when Pamela called down to ask me how far off the island was supposed to be?

"According to the dead reckoning at ten o'clock approximately nine miles," I said. "Why—can you see it?"

"I think so."

"Speed through the water?" I asked.

She checked the electric log and reported 4.7 knots. We had covered perhaps two and a half miles since the last log entry. "I've lost it now," she called down. "The mist comes and goes."

I dived up into the cockpit then, for if she really had seen the island it must be a lot closer than Saltley's dead reckoning indicated. The sun's pale disk was barely visible, the mist iridescent and so full of light it hurt the eyes. Visibility was little more than a mile. She pointed away to port. "The bearing was about two-thirty."

"The island should be on the starb'd bow," I told her.

"I know." She nodded, staring into the mist, her eyes narrowed, all her hair, including her eyebrows, sparkling with moisture. "I just caught a glimpse of it, very pale and quite sheer." But in a mist it is so easy to imagine you can see what you are expecting to see. "I'm sure it was those sandstone cliffs."

I stayed with her, conscious of her proximity, the female scent of her, finding the bluntness of her hands on the wheel, the intentness of her square determined face somehow attractive. She was such a very capable girl, so unemotional, quite the opposite of Karen. There had been an early-morning watch when everybody was still asleep and she had joined me in the cockpit, sitting so close that every time the boat rolled I could feel the pressure of her body against mine. I had touched her then and she had let me, till without saying a word, but smiling quietly to herself, she had gone below to get breakfast. But that was two days ago, when we were hove-to in the gale.

"There!" She pointed and I saw the mist had thinned. Something glimmered on the edge of visibility. The boat lifted on a swell and I lost it behind the port shrouds. "Gone again," she breathed. It was as though we were sailing along the edge of a cloud, a lost world, all blinding white, sea and air merged together and fleeting glimpses of blue overhead. Then I saw it myself, like a pale cliff rising out of the opaque miasma which was the horizon.

Her brown hands shifted on the wheel, the boat turning to put that pale glimmer of a cliff close on the port bow, our sight of it unobstructed by the sails. I was standing now, my eyes narrowed against the sun glare, the mist coming and going, and nothing visible any longer but a glimmering void. "What do you think?" she asked. "I'm steering two-forty. Shall I hold on that or get back to two-seventy?"

I hesitated. Had we really seen the cliffs of Selvagem Grande, or had it been a trick of the mist in the confusing glow of the sun's hidden light? I brushed the moisture from my eyelashes, watching for the horizon to appear again. "I'll hold on, then," she said. "I'm certain it was the cliffs."

I nodded, imagining I saw something again. But when I shifted my gaze I could see the same vague shape on the edge of visibility wherever I looked. A trick of the light. I closed my eyes, resting them against the glare, and when I opened them I could see a horizon emerging and there, over the bows, was that cliff, shining palely in that opaque world of mist and sun. "Something there," I murmured, reaching for the binoculars, and she nodded, standing herself now and steering with her bare foot on the wheel, her hair hanging loose and all bright with moisture like an autumn web. Swirls of mist and a little breeze cat's-pawing the surface of the sea. The binoculars were useless, making the mist worse. Then the veil was drawn back, drifting astern of us, and suddenly we were in hazy sunshine, with the horizon hardening to a line and those cliffs emerging again and sprouting a funnel.

No doubt about it now, it was a ship hull-down ahead of us. I shouted to Saltley, my voice echoing Pamela's, and the others came tumbling up on deck. The breeze was picking up and we were moving through the water at a good five knots. Nobody spoke, all of us staring intently, willing it to be the ship we were looking for. The minutes passed slowly, the hull gradually lifting above the horizon until at last we knew it was a tanker. What is more, she was hove-to; either that or she was anchored, for the bearing didn't change.

The time was 1117. The date February 19. Day thirty since the *Aurora B* had sailed. Saltley turned to Pamela. "I think I'd like you sunbathing on the foredeck. A bikini if you would,

Pam, and a towel so that you can wave as we go close under their stern. I'll be down below taking pictures through the hatch."

Mark took the helm and Saltley briefed him very precisely. What he wanted was clear photographic evidence of the name and port of registry painted on the tanker's stern. We would then sail up the vessel's port side and he would take shots of the name on the bows.

By the time Pamela came on deck again, stripped almost to the bare flesh and bronzed like a young Amazon, the mist was a dirty smudge astern of us, the sun shining out of a clear blue sky. There was more wind now, the boat close-hauled and slipping fast through the water, the air getting warmer. The tanker was lying with her bows pointing north. She was about three miles away, and beyond her, to the northwest, we could just see the black basalt tops of Selvagem Grande lifting above the horizon.

Through the glasses it was already possible to see that the superstructure, which had looked almost white glimmering at us through the mist, was in fact painted emerald green, the funnel white with a bright red band and two golden stars. The hull was black and as soon as all the details of the vessel were clearly visible Saltley was checking them against the photographs laid out on the cockpit seats. It was difficult to be sure about her tonnage, but everything else matched, except the color. The *Howdo Stranger* had been painted in the GODCO colors of blue hull with a blue funnel above a sand-yellow superstructure.

There was little doubt in my mind, or in Saltley's. Every little detail of the deck layout matched, and as we closed with her, making to pass close under her stern, I knew she was about the same tonnage. "Don't forget," Saltley said to Mark as he dived below. "Get right under her stern, then gybe."

We came down on her very fast, the black hull growing, until it towered above us, massive as an iron breakwater. High up on the bridge wing there was a little knot of men watching us. I counted seven—a motley group, with only one of them in any sort of uniform. Pamela was lying stretched out on the foredeck. Two men in overalls appeared on the upper deck just below the lifeboat, one of them pointing as Pamela sat up and turned her head. Then she got languidly to her feet. They waved and we waved back, the group on the bridge watching us. I saw the flash of binoculars and then we lost them as we passed under the massive steel wall of her stern. And there close above us was the name SHAH MOHAMMED—BASRA picked out in white and startlingly clear against the black of the hull.

A man leaning over the stern rail was joined by others, all of them waving. The yacht yawed, swinging round. "Duck!" Saltley shouted. The boom came over with a crash, the sail slatting, everything in a tangle, and down below Saltley crouching out of sight, the camera with its telescopic lens directed at the ship's name, the shutter clicking. Even with the naked eye we could see the second "o" of the original name just showing as a faint raised shadow in the gap between SHAH and MOHAMMED.

Everything was very quiet, no sound of engines as we sorted out the deck, coming round onto the port tack and sailing up the side of the tanker. In repainting the hull they appeared to have used only one coat, for here and there glimpses of the old blue showed through the black, and when we reached the bows, there it was again, the shadow of the "o" just visible in the middle of SHAH MOHAMMED, which was again painted white so that it stood out with great clarity.

Saltley passed up an aerosol foghorn and Mark gave three blasts as we sheered away, back onto our original course. The tanker remained silent, the same little knot of watchers now transferred to the port bridge wing. Through the glasses I could see one of them gesticulating. Then, when we were almost a mile away, the *Shah Mohammed* suddenly emitted two

deep long-drawn-out belches from its siren as though expressing relief at our departure.

The question now was, did we head for the nearest port
with the evidence we had or wait for the *Aurora B* to show
up? I wanted to get away now. I hadn't liked the look of the
little group on the bridge wing. All the original crew must be
locked up in her somewhere and the sooner she was arrested
the more chance there was that they'd be got out alive. But
Saltley was adamant that we must wait. "Who do you suppose
is going to arrest her?"

"Surely the Navy—"

"In international waters? Didn't you see the flag she was
flying, the colors they'd painted her in? Black, white, and
green, with red and two stars on the hoist—those are the Iraqi
colors. I think *Lloyd's List* will show the *Shah Mohammed* to
be properly registered as an Iraqi vessel. They're sure to have
made it legal, to that extent, and if they have, then the Navy
couldn't possibly act without government authority, and you
can just imagine the British Government authorizing the seizure of a ship belonging to Iraq. It could upset the Arab
world, spark off a major international row."

I thought his twisted legal mind was splitting straws. "And
if we wait," I said, "until we have evidence of the two ships
meeting—what difference will that make?"

He shrugged. "Not a lot, I admit. But two ships meeting at a
lonely group of islands does suggest a purpose. At least it's
something I can argue."

"But you've got the proof already," Mark insisted. "That's
the *Howdo Stranger* out there. No doubt of it. Repainted.
Renamed. But it's still the same ship, the one Dad insured and
the owners claim has disappeared. It's there. And you've got
photographs to prove it."

"Given time and a court of law." Saltley nodded. "Yes, I
think we probably could prove it. But I've got to persuade top-
level civil servants at the Foreign Office to advise the Secre-

tary of State he's justified in authorizing what amounts to a
flagrant breach of international law. I've got to convince them
there's no risk to them or to the country, that what they find
on board will prove absolutely the hostile and deadly nature
of the operation." He was standing in the hatch and he leaned
forward, his hands on the teak decking. "If you can tell me
what that operation is . . ." He paused, his eyes staring at me,
very blue under the dark peaked cap. "But you don't know, do
you? You don't know what it's all about and you never
thought to question Choffel about it." His eyes shifted to the
stationary tanker. "So we wait for the *Aurora B*. Agreed?" He
stared at us for a moment, then, when nobody answered him,
he turned abruptly and went down into the saloon.

A moment later he was back with glasses and a bottle of
gin, a conciliatory gesture, for I don't think he liked it any
more than I did. We drank in moody silence, none of us
doubting now that the *Aurora B* would appear in due course,
but all wondering how long it would be before we were
released from our lonely vigil.

The rest of the day proved fine and bright. We lay hove-to
off the western coast of Selvagem Grande till nightfall, then
shifted our station two miles to the north with the light bearing 145°. There was no sign of the tanker. I was certain she
was still there, lying hove-to without lights. Saltley was certain, too, but when the moon rose and still no sign of her, he
had sail hoisted and we backtracked toward the position
where we had originally found her.

I didn't like it and I said so. I was certain our metal mast
would show up as a clear blip on their radar screen. After a
while we turned southwest toward Selvagem Pequena, reduc-
ing sail until we were moving a little more than three knots.
We heard the swell breaking on the rocks before we could see
the island, and then suddenly there was our tanker lying just
to the south of Fora.

We turned then, heading north, back toward Selvagem

Grande. "I think she's seen us." Mark was watching through the glasses. "She's under way and heading toward us."

We hoisted the genoa again and seemed to hold our own for a while, then she came up on us very fast, steaming at full ahead and pushing a mountain of water ahead of her broad deep-laden bows. We altered course to starb'd as though making for the landing place on Selvagem Grande. The tanker also altered course, so that the bows were less than a cable's length away as she steamed up abreast of us. A searchlight stabbed the night from high up on her superstructure, flooding the water round us until it picked up the white of our sails and fixed on us, blindingly, as the long black hull went thumping past. The stink of diesel fumes enveloped us seconds before we were picked up by the massive bow wave and flung sideways into the suck and break of such a massive bulk being driven through the water at about fifteen knots.

For a moment all hell seemed to break loose. Toni Bartello was flung against me so that I ended up half-bent over one of the sheet winches with a sharp pain in the lower part of my rib cage. Pamela was on her knees clinging to the guardrail and down below the crash of crockery and other loose objects flying about the saloon was almost as loud as the slatting of sails and boom. And all the time the searchlight remained fixed on us.

Then suddenly we were out of the wash, everything preternaturally quiet. Blackness closed over us as the searchlight went out. It took a little while for my eyes to become accustomed to the darkness. Somebody said, "She had her nav lights on." I could see the broad back of her now, the stern light showing white and the Iraqi flag picked out by the steaming light on her after-mast. Moonlight gradually revealed the surface of the sea. Was this her final departure? Had the *Aurora B* arrived in the darkness? We searched the horizon, but saw no sign of another tanker, and shortly after 0300 we lost sight of the *Shah Mohammed* behind the dark outline of Selvagem Grande.

When dawn broke the sea was empty, no vessel in sight.

We were north of the island ourselves then, all of us very tired and arguing wearily about what we should do. In the end, we turned downwind with the intention of checking that the tanker hadn't returned to her old position south of Fora. Shortly after noon I heard Toni Bartello wake Saltley to tell him he had sighted the smaller islands and a tanker lying to the south of them.

We were all up then, putting about and changing sail so that we lay hove-to with the tanker just in sight like a sheer rock on the edge of visibility. We kept it in sight all afternoon, lying drowsily on deck, stripped to the waist and warm in the sun.

Toward evening the wind began to back, the air thickening till we could no longer see the tanker. A small boat came out from under the lee of Pequena, its bows lifted and moving fast. It was an inflatable with three men in it. We could hear the sound of its outboard clear and strident above the growing rumble of the reef surf as it made straight toward us. Only when it was a few yards off did the man at the wheel cut the engine and swing it broadside to us. One of the three stood up, clasping the top of the windshield to steady himself. "Who is captain here?" His face was narrow with a high-bridged nose and a little black mustache, and his accent was similar to Sadeq's.

Saltley stepped into the cockpit, leaning forward and gripping hold of the guardrail. "I'm the captain," he said. "Who are you?"

"What you do here, please?" the man inquired.

"Are you Portuguese?"

The man hesitated, then shook his head.

"You're from that tanker?"

"Yes."

"The *Shah Mohammed?*"

Again the hesitation. "I ask you what you do here?" he repeated. "Why you wait in these islands?"

"We're waiting for another yacht to join us. And you—why are you waiting here?"

"How long before the yacht arrive?"

"A day, two days—I don't know."

"And when it arrive, where you go then?"

"The Cape Verde Islands, then across the Atlantic to the Caribbean. Are you the captain of the *Shah Mohammed?*"

"No."

"Well, tell your captain he came too close last night. I shall, of course, make a report. You tell him."

"Please? I don't understand." But obviously he did, for he said something to the man at the wheel and the engine burst into raucous life.

"What are you waiting here for?" Saltley yelled to him.

The man waved a hand to the driver and the engine quietened to a murmur. "We wait here for instructions. We have new owners. They have resold our cargo so we wait to know where we go." He leaned his weight on the inflated side of the boat. "You in Selvagen Islands before this?" And when Saltley shook his head, the man added, "Very bad place for small ships, Portoogese fishermen no good. Understand? They come aboard in the night, kill people, and throw them to the sharks. Okay?"

"Do you mean they're pirates?" Saltley smiled at him. "You understand the word piracy?"

The man nodded. "Yes, pirates. That is right. These very perilous islands. You go now. Meet friends at Cape Verde. Okay?" Without waiting for a reply he tapped the driver on the shoulder. The motor roared, the bows lifted, and they did a skid turn, heading back toward Pequena.

"What did he mean by pirates?"

Saltley looked round at Mark. "A warning, probably. Depends whether I satisfied him we were going transatlantic."

That night, just in case, we had two of us on watch all the time. The wind continued to back until it was sou'westerly with a thin cloud layer. Toward dawn the clouds thickened and it began to drizzle. Visibility was down to little more than a mile and no sign of the tanker. After feeling our way cautiously south and west for nearly two hours we suddenly saw broken water creaming round the base of a single rock. This proved to be Ilheus do Norte, the northernmost of the chain of rocks running up from Fora. We turned due south, picked up Selvagem Pequena, skirting the island to the east in thickening visibility.

We wasted more than two hours searching to the south'ard before turning northeast and heading for Selvagem Grande. We were running then in heavy rain and we were tired, so that when we did sight the vague outline of a ship on our starb'd quarter it took us a little time to realize it wasn't the *Shah Mohammed*. It was coming up on us quite slowly and at an oblique angle, its shape lost for a moment in a downpour, then reappearing, closer and much clearer. Its hull was black, the superstructure a pale green, and the white funnel had a red band and two stars; the same colors as the *Shah Mohammed*, but there was a difference in the layout, the stern deck longer, the davits farther aft, and the derricks were a different shape. I recognized her then. "It's the *Aurora B*," I said, and Saltley nodded, standing in the hatch with the GODCO photographs in his hand.

She was called the *Ghazan Khan* now, the name painted white on the bow and standing out very clearly against the black of the hull. She passed us quite close, steaming at about eight knots, the grating platform at the top of the lifted gangway plainly visible, the memory of Sadeq standing there firing down at us suddenly vivid in my mind. We altered course to

cross her wake and again the name GHAZAN KHAN was painted
on her stern and the port of registry was Basra.

Day thirty-two and the time 1447. "Well, that's that," Saltley said. "All we need now is a picture of the two of them together."

We got this just over an hour later, the two tankers lying
within a cable's length of each other a mile or so to the east of
Selvagem Grande. We went in close enough for Saltley's telescopic lens to record the white-painted names on the two fat
sterns, then veered off to take shots of the two of them in
profile. We didn't go in close, for the *Ghazan Khan* had her
gangway down and the *Shah Mohammed*'s high-speed inflatable was alongside. They could, of course, be going over the
plans for their operation, but it did occur to me they might
also be considering what to do about us. We went about and
headed southeast for Tenerife, sailing close-hauled into a confused and lumpy sea.

The wind was still backing and as darkness fell Saltley made
a near-fatal decision, ordering Pam to take the wheel and put
her about, while the rest of us eased the sheets and got her
going at her maximum speed downwind. It was certainly
much more comfortable, and though the island of Madeira
was farther than the Canaries, if the wind continued to back
and held in the south all next day it would be a lot quicker,
and he needed to get to a telephone as soon as possible.

The course took us to the west of Selvagem Grande and as
we picked up the faint glimmer of the light through a mist of
rain, I wished Stewart had fitted his yacht with radar. Presuming the tankers had now left for their final destination, I would
like to have known what course they were steering. Saltley
joined me at the chart table and we discussed it for a while—
all the various possibilities—while the aroma of onions assailed
us from the galley as Pamela fried up a corned beef hash.

I had the first watch, taking over from Mark as soon as I
had finished my evening meal. The course was just west of

north, the rain dying away to intermittent showers and the
wind almost dead aft so that we were running goose-winged
with the main to port and the genoa boomed out to starb'd.
Alone at the wheel I was suddenly very conscious of the fact
that I was the odd man out. The other four were all part of the
yacht, part of the owner's life, moving in a world entirely
different from mine. Through the hatch I could see them sitting over their coffee and glasses of Spanish brandy, talking
excitedly. And well they might, for they had the proof they
needed.

But what about me? What had I got out of the voyage? I
was back to the uncertainty of that wild accusation, to fear of
arrest, perhaps trial and conviction. All very well for Saltley to
say that once the tankers had reappeared, the nature of their
operation known, then confirmation of the statements I had
made would include acceptance of my version of what had
happened to Choffel. But there was no certainty of it and already I was feeling that sense of withdrawal from the others
that is inevitable when an individual knows he is destined to
take a different path. Brooding over it, sitting at the helm of
that swaying, rolling yacht with the wind at my back and the
waves hissing past, everything black, except for the lit saloon
and Pamela, with her arms bare to the elbows and the polo-
necked sweater tight across her breasts, talking animatedly—I
felt like an outcast. I felt as though I were already consigned
to oblivion, a nonperson whom the others couldn't see.

Ridiculous, of course! Just a part of that accident of birth
that had plagued me all my life, drawn to the Middle East yet
not a part of it, neither a Christian nor a Moslem, just a lone,
lost individual with no real roots. I was thinking of Karen then,
my one real lifeline—apart from my poor mother. If only Karen
were alive still. If only none of it had happened and we were
still together, at Balkaer. In the darkness I could see the fire
and her sitting in that old chair, the picture superimposed on
and obliterating the lit saloon below. But her face . . . I

couldn't see her face, the features blurred and indistinct, memory fading.

It was then, with my mind far away, that I heard a sound above the hiss of the waves and the surge of the bows, a low murmur like an approaching squall.

The sound came from astern and I looked over my shoulder. There was a lot of wind in the sails and it was raining again, but the sound coming to me on a sudden gust was a deep pulsing murmur. A ship's engines. I yelled to Saltley and the others. "On deck!" I yelled, for in a sudden panic of intuition I knew what it meant. "For your lives!" And as they came tumbling up I saw it in the darkness, a shadow coming up astern of us, and I reached forward, pressing the self-starter and slamming the engine into gear. As I yelled to them to get the boom off the genoa, I felt the first lift of the mass of water being driven toward us.

Everything happened in a rush. Saltley seized the wheel, and as the boom came off the genoa, he did something I would never have done—he put the yacht about, screaming at me to tag on the genoa sheet. Mark and Toni were back in the cockpit, the winch squealing as the big foresail was sheeted home, the yacht heeling right over and gathering speed as she powered to windward, riding on the tanker's bow wave, spray flying in solid sheets as the black hull thundered past our stern, smothering us with the surge of her passage. We were driving down the side of the tanker's hull, back-winded and trying to claw our way clear, the tip of our mast almost touching the black plates as we yawed. Then we were into the wake, everything in sudden appalling turmoil, the boat swamped with water. It swept clean across us. Somebody slammed the hatch, trying to close the doghouse doors as he was flung into the guardrails with a cry of pain. I grabbed him, then lost him as I was swept aft, my feet half over the stern before I could seize hold of anything.

I was like that for a moment and then we were clear, Saltley still gripping the wheel like a drowned limpet, the rest of us distributed all over the cockpit area. "Did you see a light?" Mark shouted in my ears. "Somebody flashing a light—up by the stern. I swear it was." His hair was plastered to his skull, his face dripping water. "Looked like Morse. A lot of flashes, then daa-daa . . . That's 'm' isn't it?" Pamela's voice called up from below that there was a foot of water in the saloon. "Or 't.' It could be a 't' repeated." I lost the rest, listening to something else.

Saltley heard it, too, the deep rumble of an engine borne on the wind and dead ahead of us. "Ease sheets!" he screamed and spun the wheel as the bows of the second tanker emerged like a half-tide rock out of the darkness ahead. The yacht turned away to starb'd, but too slowly, the wall of water taking us on the port bow, slamming us over, then lifting us and sweeping us from end to end. We took it green, a sea breaking over my chest and flinging me against Saltley. Somebody was gripping hold of my ankles as I was swept to starb'd, and then the rumbling giant was sliding past our starb'd quarter and the sails were drawing, pulling us away from that sliding wall of steel. The wake hit us as the tanker passed, but not as badly as before. Suddenly all was quiet and we were free to pick ourselves up, the boat slipping smoothly through the water and the sound of those engines fading into the night like a bad dream.

We were lucky. None of us had been wearing a safety harness, and though we were all suffering from bruises and cuts and were in a state of shock, nobody had been washed overboard and no bones had been broken.

It was only after we were back on course, everything sorted out on deck and beginning to clear up below, that I remembered the light Mark had seen flashing from the stern of that first tanker. But he couldn't tell whether it had been the flash of a torch or a cabin light being switched on and off, the flashes seen through the circle of a porthole. It could even have been somebody accidentally triggering off the safety light on a lifebuoy.

One thing we were in no doubt about, the two ships coming up on us like that had been deliberate, an attempt to run us down. It couldn't be anything else, for they had been steaming west of north and on that course there was nothing after Madeira anywhere in the North Atlantic until they reached Greenland.

We finished the bottle of brandy, deadening the shock of such a near disaster, then went into two-man watches for the rest of the night. In the morning, with the wind beginning to veer into the west and the sky clearing to light cirrus, we could see the Desertas lifting above the horizon and clouds hanging over the high mountains of Madeira.

All day the islands became clearer and by nightfall Funchal was just visible as a sparkling of lights climbing the steep slopes behind the port. The wind was in the west then and falling light, a quiet sea with a long swell that glinted in the moonlight. I had the dawn watch and it was beautiful, the colors changing from blue-green to pink to orange-flame, the bare cliffs of the Desertas standing brick-red on our starb'd quarter as the sun lifted its great scarlet rim over the eastern horizon.

This I knew would be the last day on board. Ahead of me Madeira lifted its mountainous bulk into an azure sky and Funchal was clearly visible, its hotels and houses speckled white against the green slopes behind. I could just see the grey top of the breakwater with its fort and a line of naval ships steaming toward it. Just a few hours now and I would be back to reality, to the world as it really was for a man without a ship. It was such a lovely morning, everything sparkling and the scent of flowers borne on the wind, which was now north of west so that we were close-hauled.

I began thinking about the book then. Perhaps if I wrote it all down, just as it had happened . . . But I didn't know the end, of course, my mind switching to Balkaer, to that morning when it all started with the first of the oiled-up bodies coming ashore, and I began to play with words, planning the way it would open. Twelfth Night and the black rags of razorbacks washing back and forth down there in the cove in the slop of the waves . . .

"Morning, Trevor." It was Pamela, smiling brightly as she came up into the cockpit. She stood there for a moment, breathing deeply as she took in the scene, her hair almost gold as it blew in the wind, catching the sunlight. She looked very statuesque, very young and fresh. "Isn't it lovely!" She sat down on the lee side, leaning back and staring into space, not saying anything, her hands clasped tight together. I sensed a tension building up and wondered what it was, resenting the intrusion, words still building in my mind.

Ripples stirred the surface of the sea, a flash of silver as a fish jumped. "Something I've got to tell you." She blurted the words out in a tight little voice. "I admire you—what you've done this last month, the sort of man you are, your love of birds, all the things you wrote. I think you are a quite exceptional . . ."

"Forget it," I said. I knew what she was trying to say.

"No. It's not as easy as that." She leaned forward on the lift of the boat and put her hand over mine on the wheel. "I don't regret that letter, you see. It's just that I don't know." She shook her head. "I don't understand myself really, but I think what it was—I was reaching out for a new dimension. That's what you represented to me, something different, something I'd never really come across before. Are you a vegetarian?"

"I've eaten everything I've been given, haven't I?" I said it lightly, trying to laugh her out of the tense seriousness of her mood.

"But in Cornwall, you were vegetarian, weren't you?"

"Karen was. I conformed. I had to. We'd no money to buy meat, and we grew our own vegetables."

"Yes, of course. I've still got the typescript, by the way. But what I was trying to say—I was like somebody who's been carnivorous all her life and is suddenly faced with the idea of becoming a vegetarian. It's so totally different. That's what I meant by new dimension. Do you understand?"

I nodded, not sure whether I did or not. No man likes to be faced with an attractive girl making a statement of rejection, and certainly not in the dawn with the sun coming up and the sea and the sky and the land ahead all bright with the hopes of a new day. "Forget it," I said again. "You've no cause to reproach yourself. I'll keep the letter under my pillow."

"Don't be silly."

"And when I'm feeling particularly low . . ." Saltley's head appeared in the hatch and she took her hand away.

"Thank you," she breathed. "I knew you'd understand." And she jumped to her feet. "Two eggs for the helm?" she asked brightly. "Our last breakfast and everything so lovely. Two eggs and four rashers." She nodded and disappeared below to the galley. Saltley stared at me a moment, then his head disappeared and I was alone again, my thoughts no longer on the book, but on Karen and what I had lost. The future looked somehow bleaker, the feeling of separation from the others more intense.

CHAPTER TWO

IT WAS SHORTLY AFTER NOON when we turned the end of Funchal breakwater, lowering sail as we motored to a berth alongside a Portuguese tug. I had been to Madeira only once before, tramping in an old Liberty ship, and then the long dusty breakwater had been almost empty. Now it was crowded, for there was some sort of NATO exercise on with warships of half a dozen nations lying alongside and U.S. off-duty sailors already at baseball practice among the cranes and stacked containers.

Saltley didn't wait for Customs and Immigration. At the end of the jetty, beyond a complex huddle of masts and radar, with Canadian and Dutch flags fluttering in the breeze, there was a missile destroyer flying the white ensign. Neatly dressed in his shoregoing rig of reefer, blue trousers, and peaked cap, he crossed the tug and was lost immediately among the stevedores working two Panamanian-registered cargo ships. He had a long walk, for the tug to which we had moored was only about a third of the way along the jetty, just astern of a Portuguese submarine and only a few yards beyond the fort, its stone wall rising sheer out of the rock on which it was built.

Nobody seemed interested in our arrival and we sat on deck in the sunshine, drinking beer and watching the kaleidoscope of tourist color across the harbor, where crowded streets climbed steeply up from the waterfront with slender ribbons of roads disappearing in hairpin bends a thousand feet above houses smothered in bougainvillea. I could see the twin towers of Monte and the Crater's cobbled way dropping sheer into the town, and to the west the massed array of big hotels culminated in a promontory with Reid's red roofs and hanging gardens dropping to the sea.

It was the medical officer who arrived first, just after we had finished a very late lunch. He was still in the saloon improving his English over a scotch when Saltley returned. He had contacted Lloyd's and reported the two GODCO tankers still afloat, but under different names. Fortified by Navy hospitality, he had then waited for Lloyd's to contact the authorities and check with their Intelligence Services for any listing of the *Shah Mohammed* and the *Ghazan Khan*. It had been almost an hour before he had the information he wanted. Both tankers had recently been acquired by an Iraqi company with offices in Tripoli and both had been registered in Iraq on January 16, port of registry Basra. As far as could be ascertained from a quick check, Lloyd's had no information as to their present whereabouts, possible destination, or nature of cargo, if any. "And the authorities show no inclination to get Britain involved," Saltley added as Pamela sat him down to a plate of tinned ham and egg mayonnaise.

It was late afternoon before we were cleared and by then the destroyer's captain was on board with a Rear Admiral Blaize, who was in charge of the NATO exercise, a small man with rimless glasses, his face egg-shaped and very smooth so that he had a cold hostile look until he laughed, which he did quite often. Saltley's suggestion that the tankers be stopped and searched if they entered the English Channel had been rejected. "The Navy is not empowered," the admiral said, "to take that sort of action on the high seas in peacetime. I can tell you this, however. In view of the fact that Mr. Rodin is on board here with you and the public interest that was aroused by certain statements he made before leaving the country, MoD are passing the information you've given on to the For-

eign Secretary, copy to the Department of Trade. I imagine
the Marine Division of the DoT will be keeping watch on the
situation through H.M. Coastguards. Oh, and a personal request from the Second Sea Lord. I think you said he's a sailing
friend of yours."

"I've met him several times," Saltley said.

"He asked me to say he thinks it important you return to
London as soon as possible and bring Rodin with you. I'm having one of my officers check now and make provisional reser-
vations on the first flight out, whether it's to Gatwick,
Heathrow, or Manchester. That all right with you?"

Saltley nodded and the admiral relaxed, leaning back against
the pilot berth. "Now perhaps I can have the whole story firsthand." His eyes fastened on me. "I think perhaps if you would
run over very briefly your side of it, the events that led to all
of you setting off for a doubtful rendezvous in the Selvagen
Islands." He laughed. "Wish they'd given me authority to
mount a search. It would have been good practice for the motley crowd I'm commanding at the moment." He laughed again,
then stopped abruptly, sipping his pink gin and waiting for me
to begin.

It was the first of a number of times I would be called upon
to repeat my story in the next few days. And when Saltley had
finished describing the meeting of the tankers and how they
had nearly run us down in the dark, the admiral said, "I think
what I would do in the circumstances is keep a very close
watch on them after they enter the Channel and alert other
nations of our suspicions. As soon as they enter territorial
waters, then it's up to the nation concerned to take whatever
action is considered appropriate."

"Will you be advising the MoD to that effect?" Saltley
asked.

"I'll be making a report, certainly."

"That wasn't what I asked, Admiral." Saltley was leaning
across the table, his voice urgent. "At twenty knots the West-

ern Approaches are only three days' steaming from where we last saw them, just west of Selvagem Grande. This time tomorrow they could be into the Channel. They could be into Le Havre, Southampton, Portsmouth even, by first light the following morning. That's how urgent it is." And he added, "If it were Brest now . . ."

There was a tap on the doghouse roof and a naval lieutenant peered down through the hatch to say there was only one seat vacant on the first plane out in the morning, which was a TAP scheduled flight via Lisbon. He had booked that and also a seat on a tourist charter plane to Gatwick later in the day.

"No flights tonight?" Saltley asked.

"None, sir. The next flight out is the one to Lisbon." And he went on to tell us that the captain of the Portuguese tug had to meet a freighter coming in and required us to shift our berth immediately.

We did this as soon as the admiral had left, moving our warps to the submarine, which now had a queue of Portuguese sightseers entering by the for'ard hatch and coming out at the stern, some of the bulkier ladies severely testing the serious demeanor of the sailors detailed to assist them. As soon as we were tied up, Saltley and I packed our bags and we all went ashore to the Casino Park, the big circular concrete and glass hotel built on the high ground overlooking the old town and the harbor. Our first priority was hot baths, and having booked two rooms and checked that there was no way we could reach London any quicker, Saltley got on the phone to Michael Stewart while Pamela bathed in his room and the rest of us shared my bathroom and shower.

I came down to find the night outside the glassed-in reception area very still and studded with stars. I ordered a glass of Sercial and stood at the window sipping the fortified wine and looking up to the floodlit castle and all the myriad lights twinkling on the slopes high above. Pamela joined me and we took our drinks outside, strolling through the lawned gardens to the stone parapet overlooking the harbor. The water below us was oily calm, the lights of the ships along the jetty reflected in the flat black surface.

We stood there for a time, talking quietly, both of us strangely relaxed and at ease. But then, as we finished our drinks and began to walk slowly back, Pamela suddenly said, "I think I should warn you, about Salt. He's quite ruthless, you know. He'll use you. He's good at his job, you see." She looked up at me, smiling a little hesitantly. "Someday I'll probably marry him, so I do know the sort of man he is, how single-minded he can be. Right now he has only one interest, and it's not the same as yours. He's not really concerned with the damage those tankers could do, except incidentally as a potential insurance claim. He just wants to prove their true identity. That lets my father's syndicates out and chalks up another success for him. Do you understand?" She had stopped by a rose bed, her blunt fingers toying with a dark red bloom as she leaned down to smell it. "Where there's fraud involved, he's like a bloodhound. He'll follow the scent quite regardless of anybody else."

"Yes, but anything I say can only support his case."

She nodded, her eyes large and luminous in the dim light. "I expect you're right, but we won't be alone again after this and I felt I should warn you. On board you've seen perhaps his nicest side. But on the job, remember he's a real professional and determined to be accepted as the best there is. Anyway, good luck when you reach London." She smiled abruptly, then went on into the hotel to join the others who were now standing at the bar.

Later we took a taxi to Gavinas, a fish restaurant built out over the sea beyond the old whaling station to the west of Funchal. We had fish soup, I remember, *espada*, which is the black scabbard fish peculiar to Madeira, the light *vinho verde* to drink, and fresh strawberries to finish with. It was a strange meal, for it was part celebration, part farewell, and sitting over

our coffee and Malmsey we were all of us a little subdued,
Saltley and myself faced now with the problem of convincing
the authorities, the other three with a voyage of some eight
hundred miles ahead of them. And all the time the flop and
suck of the waves around the concrete piers below us.

We left shortly after ten and the last we saw of the depleted
crew was three faces calling farewell from the dark interior of
the taxi as it drove them on from the Casino Park to the harbor. "Think they'll be all right?" Saltley murmured. "Mark's
taken the boat from Plymouth to the Hamble and once across
the Channel, but Madeira to Gib . . ." He stared dubiously at
the taxi's rear lights as it swung into the Avenida do Infante.
"And Pamela, too," he muttered. "Mike would never forgive
me if anything happened to them."

"They'll be all right," I said.

"He's only nineteen, you know." The taxi disappeared down
the hill and he turned abruptly into the hotel. "Well, let's have
a drink. I expect you're right."

It was over that drink that he suddenly said to me, "You
may find there's some delay when you get to Gatwick. If there
is, don't worry. These next few days could be very hectic, so
any little problem you encounter may take a while to resolve."

His words could only mean one thing. "You heard something—when you were on the destroyer."

He didn't answer and I was remembering what Pamela had
said about him. "They'll arrest me, is that what you mean?"

"No, I don't think so. But since we won't be together on the
flight home I thought it only fair to warn you." Which meant,
of course, he wouldn't lift a finger to help me unless it suited
him and he thought I could be useful. "The deadline is very
tight," he murmured half to himself. "If they are in the Western Approaches tomorrow evening, then I've got to get planes
up and the ships located by the following morning."

"They may not be bound for the Channel."

"Where do you think they're headed for—the States?" He

gave me a lopsided smile and shrugged. "The Americans would have them boxed in and boarded before they were within miles of the eastern seaboard, and they know it. They'll be in the Channel tomorrow night, I'm certain they will."

We went to our rooms shortly afterward and in the morning he was gone. The moment of reality had arrived. I was on my own again, and though I was prepared for it, it still came as a shock after living for several weeks in the close company of others. But then the coach arrived and for a while my thoughts were diverted by the long coastal drive to Santa Cruz and the airport with its views of the Desertas and the lighthouse standing white and lonely on the eastern tip of Madeira.

We were flying against the sun so that it was dark by the time we were over the Channel. The man next to me was sleeping peacefully to the background hum of the engines, everybody in the plane very quiet, even the stewardesses no longer rushing about. All during the flight I had been thinking over what Saltley had said the previous night, and now, over the English Channel, with a strange feeling in my guts that those tankers were somewhere down below me, I found my mind made up. If they were going to detain me at the airport —and I was certain Saltley knew something that he hadn't passed on to me—then I had nothing to lose. I tore a page out of the inflight magazine *Highlife* and scribbled on a blank space: "Please request press or other media representatives Gatwick to meet Trevor Rodin on arrival—2 Iraqi tankers, *Shah Mohammed* and *Ghazan Khan*, expected English Channel imminent. Terrorists on board. Target not yet known. URGENT URGENT URGENT. Rodin." I reached up and rang for the stewardess.

She was tall and slightly flushed, her hair beginning to come adrift and a faint smell of perspiration as she leaned over the recumbent figure next to me and asked whether she could get me anything. I handed her the slip of paper and when she had read it, she continued to stare at it, her hands trembling slightly. "It's all right," I said. "I'm quite sane."

Her eyes darted me a quick look, then she hurried away and I saw her conferring with the senior stewardess beside the pantry, both of them staring in my direction. After a moment the older girl nodded and slipped through the door to the flight deck. I sat back then, feeling suddenly relaxed. It was done now. I had committed myself, and even if the captain didn't radio ahead, the girls would almost certainly talk.

After a few minutes the head stewardess came down the aisle to me. "Mr. Rodin?" I nodded. "Would you come with me, sir. The captain would like a word with you."

He met me in the pantry area, a tall, thin, worried-looking man with stress lines running down from the nose and greying hair. The door to the flight deck was firmly closed. "I read something about you, some weeks back. Right?" He didn't wait for a reply. "I cannot, I'm afraid, communicate with the media. That's a matter for the airport authority. If they see fit, they'll contact them."

"But you'll tell them about the tankers, won't you?" I asked.

"I'll tell them, yes. But it will be for you to convince them after we've landed. Okay?" He half turned toward the door to the flight deck, then checked. "You mean what you've written here, do you?" He held the torn scrap from *Highlife* under my nose. "Terrorists. Are you sure?"

"Quite sure," I said.

"You escaped in a dhow. I remember now." Grey, worried eyes stared at me for a moment. "But that was in the Gulf. How do you know these tankers will be in the Channel now?"

I told him how we had sailed out to the Selvagen Islands, had seen them rendezvous there, and then been nearly run down in a deliberate attempt to obliterate us. "The way you say it—" He was watching me very closely. "I don't know." He shook his head. "Why are you on your own? What happened

to the marine solicitor?" When I told him Saltley had taken
the early flight via Lisbon, there was a sudden wariness in his
eyes and I was conscious of a tenseness building in him. He
glanced at the stewardess. "Get Dick, will you? He's my navigator," he said and began talking about airspeed, winds, and
our ETA at Gatwick, his voice suddenly matter-of-fact.

The navigator was a big man and as soon as he had shut the
flight deck door, the captain turned to me and in a quiet,
slightly strained voice said, "Mind if we check you over?"

"For weapons, do you mean?"

"Just in case." He nodded to the navigator and the two of
them pressed forward, forcing me to the back of the pantry,
where the captain ran his hands under my arms and between
my legs, the muscles of his neck corded into tense knots and
the navigator standing off, his fists clenched ready.

"Is that necessary?" I asked as he straightened up, letting out
his breath, his body relaxing.

"We have to be careful." His eyes still had that wary look.
"You know about the controllers' strike at Lisbon, I suppose?"

I stared at him, a feeling of shock running through me.
"Strike? I don't know anything about a strike." I was thinking
of Saltley marooned in Lisbon and myself alone with nobody
to confirm my story.

"You could have heard about it at the airport. The staff was
full of it."

"I heard nothing. I didn't ask."

His mouth was shut in a tight line, the jaw muscles visible
as he watched me. "No—well, probably you didn't know then.
They walked out during the morning, a manning schedule we
were told. But we'll be landing soon. I've no time to check
with Lisbon. They could take an hour or more to make sure
your man is stranded there or not."

"So you'll do nothing?" I suppose my own fears, the strain in
my voice, something communicated itself to him, for the wary
look was back in his eyes.

"I'll report to Gatwick, of course. I've said that already."

"And the media?"

He hesitated. "I'll have a word with the PR man, if he's still there. He likes to know when there's a—" He checked himself. I thought perhaps he had been going to say "when there's a nut on board." "When anything unusual is happening. That satisfy you?"

I didn't know whether he believed me or not, but I knew it was the best I could hope for from him. I nodded and he let me out of the pantry, requesting me in a neutral, official voice to return to my seat. I was conscious of the two of them and the chief stewardess watching me as I pushed past the line for the toilets and went back down the aisle. By the time I was in my seat again the officers had disappeared, the door to the flight deck was closed, and the stewardesses were seeing to last-minute requests as they had a final clear-up. The man next to me was still sleeping, the engines whispering very quietly now as we lost height. Everything was normal again.

The only thing that wasn't normal was my state of mind. I could think of nothing but the fact that Saltley wouldn't be around when we landed in England. I would be on my own, the only person available to the authorities who had seen those tankers rendezvous in the Selvagens. Would they believe me without Saltley's physical presence to confirm it? A voice on the telephone from Lisbon wasn't the same at all. Would they believe anything I said? I was thinking of the captain—the wariness, the tenseness, the way he had summoned the heaviest of his crew, the search for arms. Would Forthright's help, or Lloyd's—would their Intelligence Services have discovered anything to corroborate my story?

The seat belt sign came on, the flaps slid out from the wings, and I heard the rumble of the undercarriage going down. I felt suddenly sick, a void in my stomach and my skin breaking out in a sweat. It was nerves, the tension of waiting, wondering what was going to happen. And then we were down with the runway lights flashing by and I braced myself, breathing deeply, telling myself I had nothing to be afraid of, that the truth was the truth, something I couldn't be shaken on, so that eventually they must believe me.

The plane came to a halt and a chill wind blew in as the fuselage door was thrown back. We filed out past the chief stewardess, who said her usual piece, hoping I'd had a good flight, and I saw her eyes widen in confusion as she realized who it was. And when I boarded the bus one of the airport staff got in with me and kept his eyes on me all the way to the arrivals area.

The time was just after 1930 GMT when I joined the line at the U.K. passports desk. It moved quickly so that in a moment I was handing my temporary papers to the Immigration officer. He glanced at them and then at me, his glasses reflecting the glint of the lights, his eyes faintly curious. "What happened to your passport, sir?"

"I lost it."

"Where?"

"I left it on board a tanker in the Persian Gulf."

He looked down at some papers on the desk beside him. "And this is your correct name—Trevor McAlistair Rodin?" He turned and nodded to a man over by the wall. "This gentleman will look after you now." The man came quickly forward, positioning himself at my elbow. He took my papers and said, "This way, please."

He led me through into the Customs Hall, where he arranged for my baggage to be cleared and brought to me. "Am I under arrest?" I asked, not sure whether he was airport police or CID.

"Just a few questions, that's all, at this stage." We went upstairs and into one of the airport offices. When he had sat me down at the desk facing him, I asked to see his credentials. He was a detective-inspector of the Surrey police force. I started to tell him about the tankers then, but he stopped me almost immediately. "I'm afraid that's nothing to do with me. I'm told the information you gave the captain of your aircraft about tankers and terrorists has already been passed to the proper authority. My concern is a much earlier statement you made, about how you escaped in some native craft in the Persian Gulf with a French engineer named Choffel. I'd be glad if you'd now go through that again, so that I can prepare a statement for you to sign."

I tried to argue with him, but he was insistent, and he gave me the usual caution about the possibility of evidence being used against me. When I told him about the statement I had already made in London a month ago, he said, "That's the Metropolitan area, Special Branch by the sound of it." He was an ordinary-looking man, quite human. "I have my orders, that's all."

"Who from?"

"The chief constable."

"But not because of what I said about those tankers. It's because Choffel's daughter has accused me of killing her father, isn't it?"

"She made a statement, yes."

"But there's no warrant for my arrest."

He smiled then. "Nobody has told me to do anything more than get a statement from you, all right?"

"And it'll go to the chief constable?"

He nodded. "He'll then pass it on to the office of the Director of Public Prosecutions or not as he thinks fit. That's why I had to caution you." He pulled his chair into the desk and got his pen out. "Now, shall we get started? I don't imagine you want to be all night over it any more than I do."

There was nothing for it then but to go over the whole story from the beginning, and it took time, for he was summarizing it as we went along and writing it all out in longhand. By eight-thirty I had only got as far as my arrival on the tanker and the discovery that it was the *Aurora B.* He rang down to somebody for sandwiches and coffee to be sent up from the cafeteria. It was while we were eating them, and I was describing how Sadeq had stood at the top of the gangway firing down onto the deck of the dhow, that the door opened and I turned to find myself looking up at the shut face and hard eyes of the man who had visited me in my Stepney basement.

He handed a piece of paper to the detective. "Orders from on high."

"Whose?"

"Dunno. I'm to deliver him to the Ministry of Defense—Navy." He turned to me. "You slipped out of the country without informing us. Why?" I started to explain, but then I thought what the hell—I had been talking for an hour and a half and I had had enough. "If you haven't bothered to find out why I'm back here in England, then no point in my wasting your time or mine."

He didn't like that. But there wasn't much he could do about it, his orders being simply to escort me, and the local inspector wanting to get his statement completed. It took another half hour of concentrated work to get it into a form acceptable to me, so it was almost ten before I had signed it. By then two journalists had tracked me down, and though the Special Branch man tried to hustle me out of the terminal, I had time to give them the gist of the story. We reached the police car, the reporters still asking questions as I was bundled in and the door slammed. Shut-face got in beside me, and as we drove out of the airport, he said, "Christ! You got a fertile imagination. Last time it was a tanker hiding up in the Gulf and an Iranian revolutionary firing a machine pistol, now it's two tankers and a whole bunch of terrorists, and they're steaming into the Channel to commit mayhem somewhere in Europe."

"You don't believe me?"

He looked at me—his face deadpan, not a flicker of reaction

in his eyes. "I don't know enough about you, do I?" He was staring at me for a moment, then suddenly he smiled and I caught a glimpse of the face his wife and children knew. "Cheer up. Presumably somebody does or our branch wouldn't have been asked to pick you up." The smile vanished, his face closed up again, and I thought perhaps he didn't have a family. "Lucky the local CID were taking an interest in you or you might have gone to ground in another East End basement." And he added, his voice harder, more official, "You can rest assured we'll keep tabs on you from now on until we know whether those tankers are real or you're just a bloody little liar with an outsized capacity for invention."

There wasn't much to be said after that and I closed my eyes, my mind wandering sleepily in the warmth of the car. Somebody at the Admiralty wanted a firsthand account of our meeting with those tankers. The Second Sea Lord—a friend of yours, the admiral at Funchal had said to Saltley—and Saltley wasn't here. Was it the Second Sea Lord who wanted to see me? Whoever it was, I'd have to go over it all again, and tomorrow that statement I had signed would be on the chief constable's desk, and he'd pass it on. Any official would. It was such a very strange story. He'd leave it to the Director of Public Prosecutions. And if those tankers blew themselves up . . . There'd be nobody then to prove I hadn't killed Choffel. They'd all be dead and no eyewitness to what Sadeq had done.

That feeling of emptiness returned, sweat on my skin and the certainty that this shut-faced man's reaction would be the reaction of all officialdom—myself branded a liar and a killer. How many years would that mean? "Why the hell!" I whispered to myself. Why the hell had I ever agreed to return to England? In Tangier it would have been so easy to disappear —new papers, another name. Even from Funchal. I needn't have caught that charter flight. I could have waited and caught the next flight to Lisbon. No. The controllers were on strike there. I was thinking of Saltley again, wondering where he was now, and would he back me, could I rely on him as a witness for the defense if those tankers were totally destroyed?

It was past eleven when we reached Whitehall, turning right opposite Downing Street. "The main doors are closed after eight-thirty in the evening," my escort said as we stopped at the Richmond Terrace entrance of the Ministry of Defense building. Inside he motioned me to wait while he went to the desk to find out who wanted me. The custody guard picked up the phone immediately and after a brief conversation nodded to me and said, "Won't keep you a moment, sir. Two-SL's Naval Assistant is coming right down."

My escort insisted on waiting, but the knowledge that two such senior men had returned to their offices in order to see me gave me a sudden surge of confidence. That it was the Second Sea Lord himself who was waiting for me was confirmed when a very slim, slightly stooped man with sharp, quite penetrating grey eyes arrived, and after introducing himself as Lieutenant Commander Wright, said, "This way, sir. Admiral Fitzowen's waiting to see you." The "sir" helped a lot and I seemed to be walking on air as I followed him quickly down the echoing corridors.

The admiral was a big, round-faced man in a grey suit which seemed to match the walls of his office. He jumped up from behind his desk to greet me. "Saltley told me you could give me all the details. I was talking to him on the phone to Lisbon this morning."

"He's still there, is he?" I asked.

But he didn't think so. "Told me he'd get a train or something into Spain and fly on from there. Should be here sometime tomorrow. Now about those tankers." He waved me to a seat.

"Are they in the Channel?"

"Don't know yet, not for sure. PREMAR UN—that's the French admiral at Cherbourg—his office has informed us that two tankers were picked up on their radar surveillance at Ushant some forty miles offshore steaming north. They had altered course to the eastward just before moving out of range of the Ushant scanner. It was dark by the time we got their report and the weather's not good, but by now there should be a Nimrod over the search area and the French have one of their Navy ships out looking for them." He began asking me questions then, mostly about the shape and layout of the vessels. He had pictures of the GODCO tankers on his desk. "So Saltley's right, these are the missing tankers."

I told him about the "o" of *Howdo Stranger* still showing faintly in the gap between *Shah* and *Mohammed.* "Salt made the same point. Says his photographs will prove it." He leaned toward me. "So what's their intention?" And when I told him I didn't know, he said, "What's your supposition? You must have thought about it. Sometime in the early hours we're going to have their exact position. If they are in the Channel I must know what their most likely course of action will be. You were on the *Aurora B.* That's what it says here—" He waved a foolscap sheet at me. "When you were in England, before Saltley got you away in that yacht, you made what sounded at the time like some very wild allegations. All right . . ." He raised his hand as I started to interrupt him. "I'll accept them all for the moment as being true. But if you were on the *Aurora B,* then you must have picked up something, some indication of their intentions."

"I had a talk with the captain," I said.

"And this man Sadeq."

"Very briefly, about our previous meeting." I gave him the gist of it and I could see he was disappointed.

"And the Englishman who recruited you—Baldwick. Didn't he know anything about the objective?"

I shook my head. "I don't think so."

"Tell me about your conversation with the captain, then." He glanced at his notes. "Pieter Hals. Dutch, I take it."

It was the better part of an hour of hard talking before he was finally convinced I could tell him nothing that would indicate the purpose for which the tankers had been seized. At one point, tired of going over it all again, I said, "Why don't you board them, then? As soon as you know where they are—"

"We've no authority to board."

"Oh, for God's sake!" I didn't care whether he was a Sea Lord or what, I was too damned tired of it. "Two pirated ships and the Navy can't board them. I don't believe it. Who's responsible for what goes on in the Channel?"

"Flag Officer, Plymouth. But I'm afraid CINCHAN's powers are very limited. He certainly hasn't any powers of arrest. Unlike the French." He gave a shrug, smiling wryly as he went on. "Remember the *Amoco Cadiz* and what the spillage from that wreck did to the Brittany coast? After that they instituted traffic lanes off Ushant. Later they insisted on all tankers and ships with dangerous cargoes reporting in and staying in a third lane at least twenty-four miles off the coast until they're in their correct eastbound lane, which is on the French side as they move up-Channel. And they have ships to enforce their regulations. Very typically the British operate a voluntary system—MAREP, Marine Reporting." And he added, the wry smile breaking out again, "I'm told it works—but not, of course, for the sort of situation you and Saltley are envisaging."

I brought up the question of boarding again, right at the end of our meeting, and the admiral said, "Even the French don't claim the right of arrest beyond the twelve-mile limit. If those tankers came up the English side, there's nothing the French can do about it."

"But if they're on the English side," I said, "they'd be steaming east in the westbound lane. Surely then—"

He shook his head. "All we can do then is fly off the coastguard plane, take photographs, and in due course report their behavior to their country of registry and press for action."

I was sitting back, feeling drained and oddly appalled at the Navy's apparent helplessness. All the years when I had grown up thinking of the Navy as an all-powerful presence and now, right on Britain's own doorstep, to be told they were powerless to act. "There must be somebody," I murmured. "Some minister who can order their arrest."

"Both Saltley and yourself have confirmed they're registered at Basra and flying the Iraqi flag. Not even the Foreign Secretary could order those ships to be boarded."

"The Prime Minister, then," I said uneasily. "Surely the Prime Minister—"

"The PM would need absolute proof." He shrugged and got to his feet. "I'm afraid what you've told me, and what Saltley has said to me on the phone, isn't proof."

"So you'll just sit back and wait until they've half wrecked some European port."

"If they do come up-Channel, we'll monitor their movements and alert other countries as necessary." The door had opened behind me and he nodded. "In which case, we'll doubtless see each other again." He didn't shake hands. Just that curt, dismissive nod and he had turned away toward the window.

Back along the echoing corridors then to find Shut-face still waiting. A room had been booked for me at a hotel in the Strand and when he left me there with my bags he warned me not to try disappearing again. "We'll have our eye on you this time."

In the morning, when I went out of the hotel, I found this was literally true. A plainclothesman fell into step beside me. "Will you be going far, sir?" And when I said I thought I'd walk as far as Charing Cross and buy a paper, he said, "I'd rather you stayed in the hotel, sir. You can get a paper there."

I had never been under surveillance before. I suppose very few people have. It was an unnerving experience. Slightly eerie in a way, a man you've never met before watching your every movement—as though you've been judged guilty and condemned without trial. I bought several papers and searched right through them—nothing. No mention of anything I had told those two journalists at Gatwick, no reference anywhere to the possibility of pirated tankers steaming up the English Channel.

It could simply mean they had filed their stories too late, but these were London editions and it was barely ten o'clock when I had spoken to them. Hadn't they believed me? I had a sudden picture of them going off to one of the airport bars, laughing about it over a drink. Was that what had happened? And yet their questions had been specific, their manner interested, and they had made notes, all of which seemed to indicate they took it seriously.

I didn't know what to think. I just sat there in the foyer, feeling depressed and a little lost. There was nothing I could do now, nothing at all, except wait upon others. If they didn't believe me, then sooner or later the Director of Public Prosecutions would make up his mind and maybe a warrant would be issued for my arrest. Meanwhile . . . meanwhile it seemed as though I was some sort of nonperson, a dead soul waiting where the souls of the dead wait upon the future.

Suddenly the Special Branch man was at my elbow. There was a car at the door and I was to leave for Dover immediately. I thought for a moment I was being deported, but he said it was nothing to do with the police. "Department of Trade—the Minister himself, I believe, and you're to be rushed there as quickly as possible." He hustled me out to a police car drawn up at the curb with its blue light flashing and two uniformed officers in front. "And don't try slipping across to the other side." He smiled at me, a human touch as he tossed my bags in after me. "You'll be met at the other end." He slammed the door and the car swung quickly out into the traffic, turning right against the lights into the Waterloo Bridge approach.

It had all happened so quickly that I had had no time to question him further. I had presumed he was coming with me. Instead, I was alone in the back, looking at the short-haired necks and caps of the men in front as we shot round the Elephant & Castle and into the Old Kent Road. There was a break in the traffic and I asked why I was being taken to Dover. But they didn't know. Their instructions were to get me to Langdon Battery as quickly as possible. They didn't know why, and when I asked what Langdon Battery was, the man sitting beside the driver turned to me and held up a slip of paper. "CNIS Operations Center, Langdon Battery. That's all it says, sir. And a Dover patrol car will meet us at the last traffic circle before the docks. Okay?"

The siren was switched on and we blazed our way through the traffic by New Cross Station. In moments, it seemed, we were crossing Blackheath, heading through the Bexley area to the M2. The morning was grey and windtorn, distant glimpses of Medway towns against the wide skies of the Thames estuary and my spirits lifting, a mood almost of elation. But all the men in front could tell me was that their instructions had come from the office of the Under-Secretary, Marine Division, at the Department of Trade in High Holborn. They knew nothing about any tankers. I leaned back, watching the forestry on either side flash by, certain that the ships must have been sighted. Why else this sudden call for my presence at an operations center near Dover?

Half an hour later we were past Canterbury and at 1122 we slowed at a second traffic circle just outside Dover with the A2 dipping sharply between gorse scrub hills to the harbor. A local police car was waiting where the A258 to Deal branched off to the left and we followed it as it swung into the traffic circle, turning right onto a narrow road leading directly to the square stone bulk of Dover Castle. To the left I had fleeting glimpses of the Strait, the sea grey-green and flecked with white, ships steaming steadily westward. A shaft of sunlight picked out the coast of France, while to the east a rainstorm blackened the seascape. Just short of the Castle we swung left, doubling back and dipping sharply to a narrow bridge over the A2 and a view of the docks with a hydrofoil just leaving by the eastern entrance in a flurry of spray.

The road, signposted to St. Margaret's, climbed sharply up rough downland slopes round a hairpin bend and in a moment we were turning through a narrow gateway into MoD property with tall radio masts looming above a hilltop to our left.

Langdon Battery proved to be a decaying gun emplacement of First World War vintage, the concrete redoubt just showing above a flat gravel area where a dozen or more cars were parked. But at the eastern end the emplacement was dominated by a strange, very modernistic building, a sort of *Star Wars* version of an airport control tower. We stopped alongside a white curved concrete section and an officer from the local police car opened the door for me. "What is this place?" I asked him.

"H.M. Coastguards," he said. "CNIS—Channel Navigation Information Service. They monitor the traffic passing through the Strait."

We went in through double glass doors. There was a desk and a receptionist drinking coffee out of a Government-issue cup. My escort gave her my name and she picked up a microphone. "Captain Evans, please . . . Mr. Rodin has just arrived, sir." She nodded and smiled at me. "Captain Evans will be right down."

Opposite reception was a semicircular enclave with display boards outlining the work of the Operations Center—a map of the Strait showing the east-west traffic lanes and the limits of the radar surveillance, diagrams showing the volume of traffic and marked drop in collisions resulting from traffic separation, radar surveillance, and the reporting in by masters carrying noxious and dangerous cargoes, pictures of the Coastguards'

traffic patrol aircraft and of the Operations Room with its
radar screens and computer console. "Mr. Rodin?"

I turned to find a short, broad man with a lively face and a
mane of greying hair. "David Evans," he said. "I'm the Regional Controller." And as he led me up the stairs to the left of
the reception desk, he added, "The SoS should be here shortly
—Secretary of State for Trade, that is. He's flying down from
Scotland."

"The tankers have been sighted then?"

"Oh yes, there's a Nimrod shadowing them." The first-floor
area was constructed like a control tower. "The Operations
Room. That's the lookout facing seaward and the inner sanc-
tum, that curtained-off area in the rear, is the Radar Room.
We've three surveillance screens there, also computer input
VDUs—not only can we see what's going on, we can get almost instant course and speed, and in the case of collision situ-
ations, the expected time to impact. The last position we had
for those two tankers was bearing 205° from Beachy Head,
distance fourteen miles. The Navy has sent *Tigris*, one of the
Amazon-class frigates, to intercept and escort them up-Channel."

"They're past Spithead and the Solent then?"

He checked on the stairs leading up to the deck above. "You
were thinking of Southampton, were you?"

I nodded.

"You really thought they were going to damage one of the
Channel ports?"

I didn't say anything. He was a Welshman, with a Celtic
quickness of mind, but I could see he hadn't grasped the implications, was dubious about the whole thing.

"They're rogues, of course." He laughed. "That's our term
for ships that don't obey the COLREGS. They didn't report in
to the French when they were off Ushant, nor to us, and now
they're on our side of the Channel, steaming east in the west-

bound lane. That makes them rogues several times over, but then they're under the Iraqi flag, I gather." He said it as though it was some sort of flag-of-convenience. "Well, come on up and meet our boss, Gordon Basildon-Smith. He's responsible for the Department of Trade's Marine Division. We've got a sort of subsidiary Ops Room up here."

It was a semicircular room, almost a gallery, for on one side glass panels gave a view down into the lookout below. There were several chairs and a desk with a communications console manned by a young auxiliary coastguard woman. A group of men stood talking by a window that faced west with a view of the harbor and the solid mass of Dover Castle. One of them was the man who had addressed that meeting in Penzance the night Karen had destroyed the *Petros Jupiter*. "Good. You're just in time," he said as Captain Evans introduced me. He seemed to have no inkling he was in any way connected with her death. "I want the whole story, everything that happened, everything you saw in those islands. But make it short. My Minister will be here any minute now."

He wanted to be sure they really were the missing tankers, listening intently and not interrupting until I told him about the pictures Saltley had taken and how the old name was still just visible on the stern of the *Shah Mohammed*. "Yes, yes, it was in the report we had from Admiral Blaize. Unfortunately, we don't have the pictures yet. But Captain Evans here has flown off his coastguard patrol plane with instructions to go in close—" He turned to the Regional Controller. "That's right, isn't it, David? He has taken off?"

Evans nodded. "Yes, sir. Took off—" He glanced at his watch. "Three minutes ago."

There was a sudden flurry of movement as a voice announced the arrival of the Secretary of State for Trade. In an instant I was almost alone and when I looked down through the glass panels I saw a tall, dark man with thinning hair and prominent ears being introduced to the watch officers and the auxiliaries. He said a few words to each, moving and smiling like an actor playing a part, then he was climbing the stairs to the upper deck and I heard him say in a clear, silvery voice, "The French have been alerted, of course?" And Captain Evans replied, "We're co-operating very closely with them, sir. In fact, it was PREMAR UN who originally alerted us—that was when they passed Ushant and failed to report in." He introduced us, but the Minister's mind was on the problem he now faced. "What about other countries—the Belgians, the Dutch?" Evans said he couldn't answer that and a Navy officer present asked if he should check with Flag Officer, Plymouth. "I'm sure it's been done, sir. As C-in-C Channel he's bound to have given his opposite number in all NATO countries the information Admiral Blaize passed to us from Funchal."

"Check, would you?" the Minister said.

A woman's voice announced over the PA system that the tankers had now been picked up on the Dungeness scanner. Course 042°. Speed 18.3 knots. "And the Germans," the Minister said. "Make certain the Germans have been notified. They have at least two Kurdish groups in custody." He turned to Basildon-Smith. "What do you think, Gordon—leave it as it is or inform the PM?"

Basildon-Smith hesitated. "If we bring the PM into it, then we need to be clear as to what advice we're going to offer." And in the pause that followed Evans's Welsh voice said quietly, "What about the journalists, sir? They've been pressing me all morning for a statement."

"Yes, Gordon told me." The Minister's voice was sharper and he passed a hand over his eyes. "How many?"

"There must be twenty or more now."

He turned to me, his dark eyes hostile. "You should have kept your mouth shut. What was the idea?" He stared at me, and I suddenly remembered he had been a lawyer before going into politics. "Trying to pressure us, is that it? Or trying to divert attention from your own problems. You're accused of killing a Frenchman. That right?" And when I didn't answer, he smiled and nodded, turning to Evans. "Where are they?"

"In the Conference Room, sir."

"Ah, that nice, circular, very expensive room of yours with the pretty view of the Strait." He moved to the desk and sat down, his eyes fastening on me again as he took a slip of paper from his pocket. "We'll assume for the moment that your statement is correct insofar as those tankers are concerned. To that extent your story is confirmed by this marine solicitor—" He glanced down at his aide-mémoire. "Saltley. Any news of him?" There was silence and he nodded. "We must take it then that he's still stuck in Lisbon. Pity! A trained, logical, and unemotional"—he was looking at me again—"witness would have been very helpful to me. However . . ." He shrugged. And then, working from his single-sheet brief, he began to cross-examine me. Was I sure about the identity of the second tanker? What were conditions like when we had sighted it? "You must have been tired then. Are you sure it was the *Aurora B?*" And then he was asking me about the night when the two of them had tried to run us down. "That's what makes your story less than entirely convincing." And he added, "My difficulty, you see, is that there are three witnesses at sea and unobtainable, and this man Saltley still lost apparently somewhere between here and Lisbon."

I pointed out, of course, that Saltley had been present when Admiral Blaize had come on board the *Prospero* in Funchal, but all he said was, "Yes, but again it's secondhand. Still . . ." He fired a few more questions at me, chiefly about the men who had visited us in the inflatable off Selvagem Pequena, then got up and stood for a moment at the window staring out to the harbor and an odd-looking craft with a slab-fronted superstructure and a pile of giant fenders balanced on the stern. "All right." He turned, smiling, his manner suddenly changed. "Let's deal with the media. And you," he said to me, "you'll come too and back up what I say."

"And the PM, sir?" Basildon-Smith asked.

"We'll leave that till we've seen these buggers through the Strait."

The Conference Room was big and circular with combined desks and seats custom-built on a curve to fit its shape. Venetian blinds covered the windows. The place was full of people and there were television cameras. In the sudden silence of our entry the lash of a rainstorm was a reminder of the room's exposed position high up over the Dover Strait.

The Minister was smiling now, looking very assured as he addressed them briefly, giving a quick résumé of the situation and concluding with the words, "I would ask you all to bear in mind that these vessels are registered in Iraq, flying the Iraqi flag. We do not *know* they are planning mischief. All we know, as fact, is that they failed to report in to the French at Ushant and that they are now steaming east in the westbound traffic lane to the great danger of other vessels."

"And avoiding arrest by keeping well away from the French coast," a voice said.

"Yes, that is a perfectly valid point. As you know, we still do not have powers of arrest, not even in our own waters. Much as we should like these powers—"

"Why don't you bring in a bill then?" somebody asked him.

"Because we've not had an experience like the French. There's been no equivalent of the *Amoco Cadiz* disaster on the English coast." Inevitably he was asked whether the Prime Minister had been informed, but instead of answering the question, he turned to me and I heard him say, "Most of you will recall the name Trevor Rodin in connection with a missing tanker, the *Aurora B,* and some of you may have seen a Reuters report issued this morning containing statements made by him yesterday evening after he had flown in from Madeira. Because those statements will have to be borne in mind when we come to the point of deciding what action we take, if any, I thought it right that you should hear what he has to say from his own lips."

He nodded toward me, smiling as those near me moved aside so that I stood isolated and exposed. "May I suggest, Mr. Rodin, that you start by giving the gist of the information you gave the Second Sea Lord last night, then if there are any questions . . ." He stepped back and I was left with the whole room staring at me. "Go on." "Tell us what you said." "Do what the Minister says." Urged by their voices I cleared my throat, cursing the man for his cleverness in switching their attention to me and getting himself off the hook. Then, as I began speaking, I suddenly found confidence, the words pouring out of me. I could feel their attention becoming riveted, their notebooks out, scribbling furiously, and the faint whir of cameras turning.

I told them everything, from the moment we had reached the Selvagen Islands, and then, in answer to questions, I went back over what had happened in the Gulf, the extraordinary sight of the *Aurora B* moored against those ochre-red cliffs. It was such a wonderful opportunity to present my case and I had just started to tell them of my escape and what had happened on the dhow when somebody said there was a report in from the pilot of the coastguard patrol plane. I lost them then, everybody crowding round the DoT press officer. I had been talking for nearly twenty minutes and I think their attention had begun to wander long before the report came in that confirmed the shadow of the old name showing on the *Shah Mohammed*.

I walked out, past some officers and a spiral staircase leading down to the bowels of the old fort, to a glassed-in passageway. The rainstorm had moved off into the North Sea and a shaft of watery sunlight was beamed on the waves breaking against the harbor walls. I thought I could see the atomic power station at Dungeness and I wondered how much of what I had said would find its way into print, or would it all be submerged in the threat posed by Sadeq and his two tankers? Something was going to happen, out there beyond the wild break of the seas, but what? Down below the horizon, beyond the black louring clouds of that rainstorm, the ports of northern Europe lay exposed and vulnerable. I should have said that. I should have talked about pollution and Pieter Hals, not concentrated so much on my own troubles. If Karen had been there, she would have seen to it that I concerned myself more with the threat to life, the sheer filth and destruction of oil slicks.

I was still standing there, trying to figure out how long it would be before those tankers came into sight, when one of the BBC's TV news team asked if they could do an interview. "Nothing's going to happen for some time, so it seems a good opportunity."

It was a good opportunity for me, too. They filmed it outside with the lookout and the Strait in the background and I was able to channel it so that for part of the time I was talking about the problems of pollution and what men like Hals stood for.

"That's the first we've heard of Hals being on board. You've claimed all along they're terrorists. Why would Captain Hals join them?"

I couldn't answer that. "Perhaps he was desperate and needed a job," I said. "Or he could have been thinking that a really catastrophic disaster in one of the major European ports would force governments to legislate against irresponsible tanker owners."

"Europort, for instance. Is that what you're saying—that they'll go for Europort?"

"Perhaps." I was remembering Hals's actual words when he had said nothing would be done—nothing until the nations that demand oil are themselves threatened with pollution on a massive scale. There was almost a quarter of a million tons of

oil in those tankers. The Maas, the Noord Zee Canal, the Elbe
—they were all prime targets.

I had an audience now of several journalists and was still
talking about Hals when somebody called to us that the Flag
Officer, Plymouth, was on the phone to the Minister requesting instructions now that a Navy frigate was in close company
with one of the tankers and had identified it as the *Aurora B*.
There was a rush for the Conference Room and I was left
standing there with only a watchful policeman for company.

I was glad to be on my own for a moment, but shortly afterward the Minister came out with Basildon-Smith and they
were driven off in an official car—to the Castle, the police
officer said, adding that it was past one and sandwiches and
coffee were available from the canteen. Several journalists and
most of the TV men drove off in their cars, heading for the
hotel bars at St. Margaret's. Clearly nothing was going to happen for some time. It began to rain again.

I went back into the Operations Center and had a snack,
standing looking out of the windows of the Conference Room.
Time passed slowly. I had a second cup of coffee and lit a cigarette, rain lashing at the windows. Later I strolled along the
glassed-in passageway to the lookout. There were one or two
reporters there and the watch officer was letting them take it
in turns to look through the big binoculars. Nobody took any
notice of me until Captain Evans came in to check the latest
position of the tankers. He also checked the latest weather
position, then turned to me and said, "Care to see them on the
radar?" I think he was tired of explaining things to land-
lubbers, glad to talk to a seaman.

He took me through the heavy lightproof curtains at the
back. "Mind the step." It was dark after the day-bright lookout, the only light the faint glow from a computer console and
the three radar screens. It was the left-hand screen that was
linked to the Dungeness scanner and the circling sweep
showed two very distinct, very bright, elongated blips to the

south and east of Dungeness. "What's the course and speed now?" Evans asked.

"Just a minute, sir. They've just altered to clear the Varne." The watch officer leaned over, fed in three bearings on the central monitoring screen, and at the touch of a button the computer came up with the answer: "060° now, sir. Speed unchanged at just over eighteen."

"Looks like the Sandettié light vessel and the deepwater channel." Evans was speaking to himself rather than to me. "Outside the French twelve-mile limit all the way." He looked round at me. "Should be able to see them any minute now." And he added, "That friend of yours, Saltley—he'll be arriving at Dover airport in about an hour. Apparently he's chartered a small Spanish plane." He turned quickly and went out through the curtains. "Try calling them on Channel 16," he told the woman auxiliary manning the radio. "By name."

"Which one, sir? The *Ghazan Kahn* or the—"

"No, not the Iraqi names. Try and call up Captain Hals on the *Aurora B*. See what happens."

It was while she was trying unsuccessfully to do this that the watch officer in the lookout reported one of the tankers was visible. The Secretary of State came back from lunching with the Governor of Dover Castle and those not working in the lookout were hustled out.

Another squall swept in and for a while rain obliterated the Strait, so that all we could see was the blurred outline of the harbor. Saltley arrived in the middle of it. I was on the upper deck then, looking down through the glass panels, and I could see him standing by the state-of-readiness boards in front of the big map, talking urgently to the Minister and Basildon-Smith, his arms beginning to wave about. He was there about ten minutes, then the three of them moved out of sight into the Radar Room. Shortly afterward he came hurrying up to the gallery, gave me a quick nod of greeting, and asked the auxiliary to get him the Admiralty. "If the DoT won't do anything, maybe the Navy will." He looked tired and strained, the bulging eyes red-rimmed, his hair still wet and ruffled by the wind. He wanted the tankers arrested or at least stopped and searched to discover the identity of the people running them and whether they had prisoners on board.

The squall passed and suddenly there they were, plainly visible to the naked eye, with the frigate in close attendance. They were almost due south of us, about seven miles away, their black hulls merged with the rain clouds over the French coast, but the two superstructures showing like distant cliffs in a stormy shaft of sunlight.

Saltley failed to get Admiral Fitzowen and after a long talk with somebody else at the Admiralty, he put in a call to Stewart. "I've a damned good mind to contact the Prime Minister myself," he said as he joined me by the window. "Two pirated ships sailing under false names with a naval escort and we do nothing. It's bloody silly." I don't know whether it was anger or tiredness, but there was a slight hesitancy in his speech that I had never noticed before. In all the time I had been with him in the close confines of the *Prospero* I had never seen him so upset. "There's thirty or forty million involved in the hulls alone, more on the cargoes. I told the Minister and all he says is that underwriting is a risk business and nobody but a fool becomes a Member of Lloyd's without he's prepared to lose his shirt. But this isn't any ordinary risk. A bunch of terrorists —you can't counterclaim against them in the courts, there's no legal redress. The bloody man should act—on his own responsibility. That's what we have Ministers for. Instead, he's like a little boy on the pier watching some pretty ships go by."

The bearing of the tankers was very slowly changing. Both VHF and R/T channels were filling the air with irate comments from ships finding themselves heading straight for a bows-on collision, the CNIS watch officer continually issuing warnings for westbound traffic to keep to the inshore side of the land and maintain a sharp radar watch in the rainstorms.

They were all in the lookout now, the Minister, Basildon-Smith, and Captain Evans, with Saltley hovering in the background and everybody watching to see whether the tankers would hold on for the Sandettié light vessel and the deepwater channel or turn north. A journalist beside me muttered something to the effect that if they ran amok in Ekofisk or any of the bigger North Sea oilfields there could be catastrophic pollution.

It was at this point that I was suddenly called to the lookout and as I entered the big semicircular glassed-in room I heard the Minister ask what the state of readiness of the Pollution Control Unit was. His voice was sharp and tense, and when Evans replied that he'd spoken to Admiral Denleigh just before lunch and the whole MPCU organization was alerted, but no dispersant stockpiles had yet been moved, he said, "Yes yes, of course. You already told me. No point in starting to shift vast quantities of chemical sprays until we have a better idea of where they'll be needed."

"They may not be needed at all, sir," Evans said.

The Minister nodded, but his expression, as he turned away, indicated that he hadn't much hope of that. "I should have been speaking at a big party rally in Aberdeen this afternoon." His voice was high and petulant. "On oil and the environment." He was glaring at the head of his Marine Division as though he were to blame for bringing him south, maybe losing precious votes. But then he saw me. "Ah, Mr. Rodin—this man Hals. He's not answering. We've tried repeatedly, VHF and R/T. Somebody's got to get through to him." His eyes were fixed on mine. "You've met him. You've talked to him. I'm sending you out there. See if you can get through to him."

"But—" I was thinking of the dhow, the way I'd left the ship. "How?" I asked. "How do you mean—get through to him?"

"*Tigris* is sending a helicopter for you. It's already been flown off, so it should be here any minute. Now about this story of somebody flashing a light from one of the tankers. Saltley here says you and a young man on this yacht both thought it was some sort of signal. Morse code. Is that right?"

"I didn't see it myself," I said, and started to tell him about the circumstances. But he brushed that aside. "The letter 'm,' that's what Saltley here has just told me. Is that right?"

"Several quick flashes, then two longs," I said. "We were in the tanker's wake then—"

"Two longs, that's 'm' in Morse, isn't it?"

"Or two 't's. But we were being flung about—"

"You think it could have been part of a name." He turned to Saltley again. "One of the crew held prisoner on board signaling with a torch or a light switch, trying to give you the destination." He moved forward so that he was standing by the radar monitor, his eyes fastening on me again. "What do you say, Rodin? You stated quite categorically that in the case of the *Aurora B* members of the crew were being held prisoner. Was this an attempt, do you think, to communicate and give you the target these terrorists are aiming at?"

"It's a possibility," I said.

"No more than a possibility?" He nodded slowly. "And the only one to see it was this boy. In a panic, was he? You'd nearly been run down."

"Excited," I told him. "We all were, but nothing wrong with his ability to observe accurately."

He smiled thinly. "Then it's a pity he wasn't able to decipher more of the message—if it was a message. There's an 'm' in several of our estuary names, the Thames, the Humber—"

"And the Maas," Evans said sharply. "Ports like Amsterdam, Hamburg, Bremen, and Rotterdam, there's two 't's there." He pointed to the plot marked up on the large-scale chart laid out on the flat surrounded below the lookout windows. "If it's our coast they're headed for, they'll have to turn soon or they'll be blocked by the Fairy and North Hinder banks."

"Suppose the target were the North Sea oilfields?"

Evans shook his head. "Those tankers are already loaded. They'd have no excuse."

The *chop-chop-chop* of a helicopter came faintly through the glass windows. I turned to Saltley. "Is this your idea?" I was remembering Pamela's warning that evening in Funchal. "Did you put it into his head?" I could see myself being lowered by winch onto the deck of the *Aurora B.* "Well, I'm not going," I said, watching, appalled, as the helicopter emerged out of the rain, sidling toward us across the wind.

"Don't be a fool," he said. "All we want is for them to see you, on the bridge of the *Tigris.* A loud hailer. It's more personal than a voice on the air."

I think the Minister must have sensed my reluctance, for he came over and took me by the arm. "Nothing to be worried about. All we want is for you to talk to him, make him see reason. And if you can't do that, then try and get the destination out of him. In any terrorist situation, it's getting through, making contact—that's the important thing."

"Hals isn't a terrorist," I said.

He nodded. "So I gather. You and he—you talk the same language. You're both concerned about pollution. He won't talk to us here, but he may to you, when he sees you right alongside him. Commander Fellowes has his instructions. Make contact with him, that's all I ask. Find out what the target is." He nodded to the naval liaison officer, who took hold of my other arm, and before I could do anything about it I was being hurried down the stairs and out to the parking lot. The noise of the helicopter was very loud. It came low over the top of the lookout and I watched, feeling as though I was on the brink of another world, as it settled like a large mosquito in a gap between the gorse bushes. The pilot signaled to us and we ducked under the rotor blades. The door slid open and I was barely inside before it took off, not bothering to climb, but making straight out over the Dover cliffs, heading for the *Tigris.*

Five minutes later we landed on the pad at the frigate's stern and I was taken straight to the bridge, where the captain was waiting for me. "Fellowes," he said, shaking me by the hand. "We're going close alongside now. Hope you can get some sense out of them. They're an odd-looking crowd."

The bridge was built on a curve, not unlike the lookout, but the changed view from the windows was quite dramatic. From the shore-based Operations Center the tankers had been no more than distant silhouettes low down on the horizon. Now, suddenly, I was seeing them in close-up, huge hunks of steel plating low in the water, the *Aurora B* looming larger and larger as the relatively tiny frigate closed her at almost thirty knots. "We'll come down to their speed when we're abreast of the superstructure, then the idea is for you to go out onto the open deck and talk direct." He handed me a loud hailer. "Just press the trigger when you want to speak. Don't shout or you'll deafen yourself. It's a pretty loud one, that." He turned his head, listening as the ship's name was called on VHF. It was the Dover Coastguards wanting to know whether contact had yet been made with the *Aurora B*. He reached for a mike and answered direct: "*Tigris* to Coastguard. Helicopter and passenger have just arrived. We're all set here. Am closing now. Over."

We were coming in from the west at an oblique angle, the bulk of the *Aurora B* gradually blotting out the shape of the other tanker, which was about a mile to the east. The Dover cliffs showed as a dirty white smudge on our port side and there were several ships in the westbound lane, foam at their bows as the waves broke over them. Closer at hand, two small drifters danced on the skyline, and almost dead ahead of us, I could see the ungainly lanterned shape of a light vessel.

"The Sandettié," Commander Fellowes said. "We'll be in the deepwater channel in ten to fifteen minutes." Behind him the radio suddenly poured out a torrent of French. It was the fishery protection vessel now shadowing the tankers from the eastbound lane. We could just see it past the *Aurora B*'s stern steaming northeast ahead of a large ore carrier. "Ready?" Fellowes asked me, and I nodded, though I didn't feel at all ready. What the hell was I going to say to Hals?

I was still thinking about that, the loud hailer gripped in my hand, as he led me out onto the starb'd side deck below the tall square needle of the radar mast. The *Tigris* was turning now, her speed slowing as we ranged alongside the tanker's superstructure. I could see the length of its deck, all the pipes and inspection hatches that I had stumbled over in the night, the long line of the catwalk. And right above me now the wheelhouse with faces I recognized framed in its big windows. Sadeq was there and the Canadian, Rod Selkirk, and two men I didn't know, both of them dark and bearded. And then Hals appeared, his pale hair and beard framed in the glass of the bridge wing door. I raised the loud hailer to my lips. "Captain Hals." I had my finger locked tight round the trigger and even my breathing came out in great audible puffs. "This is Rodin. Trevor Rodin. I was with you in the Gulf, that *khawr*—remember? It's Rodin," I repeated. "Please come out onto the bridge wing. I want to talk to you."

I thought he was going to. I saw the uncertainty on his face, could almost read his intention in the expression of his eyes. We were that close, it seemed. "I must speak to you, Pieter. About pollution." He moved then. I'm certain of it, reaching out to slide open the door. But then Sadeq was beside him, and one of the others. A moment later they were gone, all three of them, the glass panel empty.

"Ask for his destination," Fellowes said. "That's what CIN-CHAN wants and he's got the SoS breathing down his neck. Try again."

But it was no use. I kept on calling over the loud hailer, but there was no response. And no faces at the window, the bridge appearing blind now as the tanker plowed on. "Well, that's that, I guess." Fellowes turned away, walking quickly back to his wheelhouse. I remained there, the wind on my face, sensing the heel of the ship as the *Tigris* pulled away from the tanker, dropping back until the light vessel became visible beyond the blunt rounded stern. It was so close now that the name SANDETTIÉ stood out very clear on its hull. We were in the deepwater channel.

It was then, just as I was turning to follow the captain back into the shelter of the frigate's bridge, that something happened, up there on the tanker's high superstructure. The door to the bridge wing was suddenly slid back, four men stumbling out in a cloud of thick billowing smoke. And the tanker was turning. I could see the bows shifting away from us, very slowly. She was turning to starb'd, toward the Sandettié bank, toward the other tanker. And her speed was increasing. She was drawing ahead, her stern turning toward us so that I could no longer see what was happening, the bridge wing empty, no sign of anybody, only the smoke hanging in a haze behind the superstructure. I dived back into the frigate's wheelhouse and as I came through the door I heard Fellowes's voice calling: "*Tigris* to Coastguard. Something odd going on. The *Aurora B* is shifting course. She's turning to starb'd. Also she's on fire. There's smoke pouring out of the wheelhouse area. Looks as though she intends to close the other tanker. Over."

"Any change of speed?" It was Evans's voice.

"Yes, she's increased at least a knot. Her bows are pointing diagonally across the channel now. And she's still turning . . ."

"*Aurora B, Aurora B.*" It was Evans again, his voice a little higher. "You're standing into danger. *Ghazan Khan.* This is Dover Coastguard. We have you on our radar. You are approaching collision course. I repeat—collision course. You are standing into danger."

Silence then. A deathly hush on the frigate's bridge and the tanker still turning. And just below the clouds, circling ponderously, was the Nimrod, the pilot quietly confirming that from where he was, right above the tankers, collision appeared inevitable. Then, suddenly, a new voice: "*Tigris*. This is the Secretary of State for Trade. I want you to stop that tanker, put a shot across the bows. Acknowledge."

"I can't, sir," Fellowes replied. "Not at the moment. She's stern-on to us and the other ship's right ahead of her in the line of fire." And almost in the same breath he was dictating a signal to CINCHAN and ordering gun crews closed up. The loudspeaker crackled into life again, a different voice calmly reporting: "On collision course now." It was the watch officer on surveillance duty in the Radar Room fourteen miles away. "Two minutes forty-seven seconds to impact."

"My God!" It was the Minister again. "*Tigris*." His voice was suddenly firm and decisive. "That rogue tanker. Open fire immediately. On the stern. Take the rudder off, the propeller too."

"Is that an order, sir?" And as the Minister said, "Yes yes, an order," a voice I recognized as Saltley's said, "If that Navy ship opens fire, I have to tell you it could be argued later that you were responsible for the subsequent collision."

There was a short silence. Fellowes was handed a signal, gun crews were reporting, and the frigate was gathering speed, turning to starb'd. I could see the bows of the *Aurora B*, now barely half a mile from the long low shape of the ship she was going to ram, and in that moment I had a clear mental picture of the wheelhouse and Hals standing there in the smoke and flame steering his ship to total destruction. It was deliberate. It had to be. Like Karen—immolation, death, it didn't matter, the object a disaster that would shake Europe into action. And in the silence the Minister's voice shouting, "Open fire, man. Hurry! There's barely a minute to go."

I heard Fellowes give the order, and in that same moment a new voice erupted on the air: "Rodin! Are you there? Can you hear me?" It was Pieter Hals. "It's fixed now. Nothing they can do." There was a crash, a spurt of flame from the for'ard gun turret, and instantaneously a matching eruption from the tanker's stern. It was low down on the waterline, a single shot, and the whole blunt end of the *Aurora B* instantly disintegrated into a tangle of steel, like a sardine can ripped open at one end. The ship staggered at the impact, smoke and flames and the debris of torn-out steering gear and bollards splashing the sea. But it made no difference. The gaping hole, and the sea rushing in—it didn't alter her course, it didn't stop her progress through the water. With her steering entrails hanging out of her stern she went plowing on, and in the sudden silence Hals screaming, "It's fixed, I tell you. Nothing you can do about it. Seconds now . . ." There was a noise like ripping calico, the sound of a great gasp of air—"Go-o-d!"

I heard it, but somehow I didn't take it in, the moment of Pieter Hals's death. My gaze, my whole consciousness was fixed on the *Aurora B*'s bows. They were turning now, turning back to her original course—but too slowly. Steadily, relentlessly they were closing the gap that separated them from the other tanker. There was no further order to fire, nothing *Tigris* could do, the oil-filled bulk of the tanker plowing on and everybody holding their breath waiting for the moment of impact.

It came, strangely, without any sound, a crumpling of the bows, a curling up and ripping open of steel plates below the *Howdo Stranger*'s superstructure, all in slow time. And it went on and on, for the collision was at an oblique angle and the *Aurora B* went slicing up the whole long side of the other tanker, ripping her open from end to end, and the sound of that disembowelment came to us as a low grinding and crunching that went on and on, endlessly.

It stopped in the end, after what seemed a great while, the two black-hulled leviathans finally coming to rest with barely two or three cables of open water between them, water that became dark and filthy, almost black, with the crude oil bubbling out of them, the waves all flattened by the weight of it. No fire. No smoke. Just the oil bubbling up from under the sea like a volcano erupting.

The Nimrod made a slow pass over the scene, the pilot reporting: "From where I'm sitting it looks as though both tankers are aground on the Sandettié. One has her port side completely shattered. She was going astern at the moment of collision so she really got herself carved up. She still has her engines at full astern. I can see the prop churning up the seabed, a lot of brown mud and sand mixing with the oil pouring out of her tanks. The other tanker—the rogue—she's got her bows stove in, of course, and it looks as though she's holed on the starb'd side right back as far as the pipe derricks. A lot of oil coming out of her, too . . ."

And Pieter Hals dead. I was quite certain he was dead. That sound had been the chatter of automatics. "Looks like the Kent coast is going to get the brunt of it," Fellowes said quietly. The forecast was for the westerly winds to back southeasterly and increase to gale force in the southern North Sea. And since oil slicks move at roughly one thirtieth of the wind speed he reckoned the first of the oil would come ashore right below the Langdon Battery Operations Center at about noon the next day.

*　　*　　*

It was two days later, after dark, that I finally arrived back at Balkaer, stumbling down the cliff path in the starlight, the squat shape of the cottage showing black against the pale glimmer of the sea. There'd be a fire to welcome me, Jean had said when I'd phoned her from London, and now I could see the smoke of it drifting lazily up. I could hear the beat of the waves in the cove, the sound of them surging along the cliffs. Suddenly I felt as though I had never been away, everything so familiar. I would lift the latch and Karen would come running . . .

The key was there in the door and it wasn't locked. I lifted

the latch and pushed it open. The bright glow of the fire lit
the interior, shadows flickering on the walls, and I was thinking of her as I closed the door, shutting out the sound of the
sea in the cove. And then I turned, and my heart stood still.

She was sitting in the chair. In her own chair. Sitting there
by the fire, her hands in her lap, her head turned toward me
and her face in shadow. She was watching me. I could feel her
eyes on me and my knees were like water.

"Karen."

I heard myself breathe her name, and the figure rose from
the chair, her firelit shadow climbing from wall to ceiling, so
big it filled the room.

She spoke then, and it wasn't Karen, it wasn't her voice.

"I'm so sorry," she said. "I'm afraid I startled you." The
voice was liquid, a soft lilt that was Welsh like Karen's, but a
different intonation. "Jean Kerrison—" She pronounced it
Jarne. "They're out this evening, at St. Ives. So she gave me
the key, said I could wait for you here."

"Why?" I had recognized her now and my voice was hostile,
thinking of the miles of beaches black with oil, all those ships,
men working round the clock—the *Petros Jupiter* all over
again, and now Choffel's daughter, here at Balkaer. Had they
found his body? Was that it? Was he still alive? "Why?" I said
again. "Why have you come here?"

She gave a shrug. "To say I am sorry, I suppose." She had
turned away so that the fire's glow was on her face and I could
see the determined line of the jaw, the broad brow beneath
the jet-black hair. "Did Jarne tell you she came to see me? In
London. Almost a month ago, it was. She came to my hotel."

"Jean—to London!" I was still staring at her.

"She want to tell me about the ship my father is in, the
Petros Jupiter, and how you were out in a boat searching for
your wife in a fog when she destroyed it. She want to tell me
also what kind of man you are, so that I would know, you see,
that you were not the man to kill my father." I had moved to-

ward the fire and the flames lit her face as she looked at me, her expression strangely serene. "She is very fond of you, I think." And she added, "You are a lucky man to have people like Jarne and Jim Kerrison who will do so much for you. She almost convince me, you see."

"So you still think I killed him?"

"It's true, then. You don't know." She half shook her head, sitting down again and smiling gently to herself. "I don't believe it when she tell me you don't know."

I stared at her, feeling suddenly very tired. "What is all this? Why are you here?"

"I tell you, to say I am sorry. I didn't believe you, but now I know." And then she blurted it out: "I have withdrawn everything—everything I say about you. I should have done that after Jarne saw me, but instead I went back to France. I do not say anything, not then. But now . . . There is a full statement from the Pakistani crew. Everything you say about how my father is shot and wounded is confirmed. It was that man Sadeq." She hesitated, and there were tears in her eyes. Then she said, her voice almost choked with emotion, "So now I am here. To apologize to you, and to ask you something . . ." Again the hesitation. "A favor." There was a long silence. At length she said, "Will you tell me what happened please, on the *Aurora B*, when you meet my father, and later, particularly later, when you are together on the dhow?"

I had slumped into my usual chair, unable to think of anything at that moment but the fact that I was cleared. Free! Free of everything now, except the past. Just as he had said, no one can escape that.

"Please," she said. "I want to know."

"It's all in my statement."

"I know it is. I have read it. But that is not the same, is it now? I would like you to tell me yourself."

Go through it all again! I shook my head.

"Please," she pleaded. And suddenly she was out of the chair, squatting on the rush matting at my feet. "Don't you understand? What I did to you, the accusations, the anger, the hate —yes, hate—was because I loved him. He was such a gentle, kindly man, and with my mother dead, he was all I had. He brought me up, and whatever he did wrong was done out of love for my mother. Try to understand, will you—and forgive." Silence then and the firelight flickering on her face, her eyes staring at me very wide. "What did you talk about, on that dhow? What did he say? He must have said much. All that time together, two days. Two whole days."

I nodded slowly, the memory of him in that stinking cubbyhole under the poop coming back. And now, looking down on her, crouched there at my own fireside, I understood her need. She was his daughter. She had a right to know. So in the end I told her everything, even admitting to her that when I'd joined him on the dhow it had been with the intention of killing him.

She didn't comment on that. She didn't interrupt me once, and as I talked, her face so intent, her dark eyes seeming to hang on my words, it was like talking to Karen again.

Hammond Innes, a Scot born in England, wrote his first published book when he was nineteen years old. *The Black Tide* is his twenty-fifth novel. He started as a financial journalist, served as an artillery officer in the Middle East and Italy during World War II, then took to full-time writing. An internationally acclaimed author, each of his novels is the result of a journey exploring a strange country. He is also a keen yachtsman and a deeply committed conservationist. In 1978, he was made a Commander of the British Empire. Hammond Innes and his wife Dorothy, an actress who is now a writer, live in a timbered Tudor house in Suffolk, England.